IN DOG WE TRUST

A GOLDEN RETRIEVER MYSTERY BY

NEIL S. PLAKCY

Neil S. Plakcy

In Dog We Trust

Three Shots

Santiago Santos sat down at my kitchen table to examine the audit trail on my laptop. One of the conditions of my computer use while on parole was the installation of keystroke software, which tells Santos, my parole officer, which keys have been pressed, and which windows they were pressed in. It captures emails, usernames, passwords and chat conversations, and only he has the password to see what's been recorded.

While I made coffee for both of us, he looked at the log. "Computer looks fine," he said, pushing it away as I brought two mugs to the table. In the Pennsylvania state parole system, officers visit parolees at their homes. I'd been to his office in Bensalem, for my first visit and to fill out paperwork, and he'd been out to my townhouse in Stewart's Crossing once a month since then.

Like many computer hackers, I had little formal training. I had a bachelor's and master's degrees in English, but I'd never taken more than a couple of introductory courses in programming.

Yet I had a talent for it. I could sit down in front of a screen, hit a couple of keys, and find my way into even the most secure website. I never sent anyone a virus, and I never caused malicious mischief; all I ever wanted to do was find hidden data, explore protected directories, read confidential memos. It was knowledge I was after, not material gain.

Try convincing a judge of that.

My skills had brought me cash, an underground reputation—and a year's sentence in a minimum-security prison. The corrections system in the state of California was operating at maximum capacity, so as a non-violent offender I was released after six months, with two years on parole.

By the age of forty, I'd lost my career, my marriage, and both my parents. So I'd left Silicon Valley and come back home, to Bucks County, PA, to regroup and start over. Just before his death, my father had moved to a townhouse in River Bend, a development on the edge of Stewart's Crossing, and I took the place over when I was paroled.

One of the conditions of my parole was that I find a career that did not involve regular computer work. I was allowed to use the internet only to send and receive emails, to look for work, and other ordinary purposes—reading the *New York Times*, playing solitaire, and so on. Every time I turned on my computer, my fingers itched toward forbidden sites, but I held back, not least because of the tracking software.

Santiago Santos opened a file folder he'd brought with him and gave it a quick glance. He's Puerto Rican, with a bachelor's degree in sociology from Drexel, and looks like an amateur boxer, about 5-8, stocky, with muscular forearms. I wasn't sure which of those characteristics helped him most in dealing with his clients.

"How's the writing going?" he asked.

When I returned to Pennsylvania, I began trying to develop a freelance technical writing business. I had ten years' experience, but I knew the felony conviction I'd have to admit to on job applications would lead to a constant stream of rejection from potential employers. As a freelancer, I could avoid the kind of paperwork that would keep me from full-time employment.

"OK. I got a new project last week, modifying a manual for a blood pressure machine. If I do a good job with this, they'll have me update all their documentation."

"You know about that?" he asked. "Blood pressure machines?"

I sat down across from him. My own blood pressure was high; I worried about saying the wrong thing in front of him, about his power to violate my parole and send me back to prison in California. "I'm just cleaning up the grammar, making sure the steps are easy to follow," I said. "If I have any technical questions about how the product works, I email the project manager."

He nodded. "And how about your teaching?"

Shortly after returning to Bucks County, I'd seen an ad for adjunct faculty at Eastern College, my undergraduate alma mater. Because the department chair had been a favorite professor of mine, he took pity on me and gave me a safe, if temporary, job as an adjunct instructor in the English department, which enabled me to pay my bills. "OK. Lots of papers to grade. A lot of these kids don't understand basic grammar."

"Big problem these days," Santos said, taking a sip of his coffee and nodding in appreciation. Ten years in Silicon Valley had made me a coffee snob; I bought the best beans, ground them myself, used filtered water. "Most of my clients can't even write a resume or a decent letter applying for a job."

"I'm not surprised. If college kids can't write..."

"More of my clients are like you these days," he said. "Professional guys, guys with careers and college." He looked up at me. "Any chance of getting a full-time job at Eastern?"

I shook my head. "Not with a felony on my record. And even if I didn't have that little problem, you need a PhD to get a full-time job at Eastern, and right now, they're only hiring minorities."

Oops. Was I supposed to say something like that in front of a Hispanic person? Santos didn't say anything, but it was probably just another black mark in my file.

"Your contract goes until when—May?"

"Yup. It doesn't look like they'll have any work for me this summer; their enrollment goes way down, and preference goes to the full-time faculty. But I'm hoping I can go back in the fall."

He made some notes in the folder, then looked up at me. "The last time we talked, you said that this teaching job was temporary, just a stopgap until you got your business going. I don't want you to put too much emphasis on it, if it can't lead to something full time. You've got to focus on developing your client base. You've got what, three actual clients?"

I nodded.

"Any one of those decides to cut back, you could end up in financial trouble. And guys in financial trouble are vulnerable to getting into legal trouble."

I swallowed hard and shifted in the stiff wooden chair.

"By the time I see you next month," he said, "I want you to have a plan together for developing your business. How you're going to exploit your contacts, build your client base. Financial projections for the next six months."

I had avoided most people I knew before my conviction out of embarrassment, but the need to pay bills—and stay out of jail—is a powerful motivator. "I can do that."

"Good. I'm not trying to be a hard-ass, Steve. I want you

to succeed. But if you don't have a plan in place, you're going to fail. And you know what failure means, right?"

I knew. If I didn't provide the means to support myself, the State of California would take over, returning me to that drafty cell at a state prison and three lousy meals a day.

Santos stood up. "Let's say four weeks from today, same time, same station," he said.

As soon as he left, I grabbed my parka and went out for a walk. The March weather had been cold, windy and damp for a week or more, and it was a struggle to motivate myself to keep up my regimen of morning and evening walks, part of my program to keep from sitting around the house brooding. That evening, though, I wanted to get outdoors and shake off the tension his visits always bring.

I often like to walk alongside the nature preserve that backs up against River Bend in the evening. There's a long stretch between River Road and the guardhouse, and when I'm there I can imagine I'm in the midst of a wilderness instead of the middle of suburbia.

I waved at the old guy manning the gate, and then side-stepped a big pile of poop, left behind by a dog belonging to one of my neighbors. Probably one of those who ostentatiously carried plastic bags but never stooped to using one.

Many of my dog-owning neighbors liked to walk along the preserve, including my next-door neighbor, Caroline Kelly, who owned a golden retriever named Rochester. I guess the smells out there are more interesting than the ones on our street, even though it's lined with maples and oaks and nearly every house has a dogwood or lilac tree or a flowerbed filled with the first daffodils and tulips of spring.

I was brooding about the ever-present possibility that I'd be sent back to prison when I heard three short bangs that sounded like someone was shooting off firecrackers, but without the whistle and the whine. The sounds stood out because the rest of the night was so silent—not even a distant siren or the roar of a motorcycle.

A fast-moving black SUV roared past me a moment later, skidding gravel. Rochester came galloping up toward me as soon as it had gone, the handle of his extension leash bouncing behind him the way a convict in a cartoon might drag his ball and chain.

In Dog We Trust

I knew it was Rochester because of the madras bandana that Caroline kept slung around his neck. "Hey, boy, hey," I said, reaching out to grab him. "Where's your mom? How'd you get away from her?"

As soon as I had hold of his leash, Rochester executed a sharp 180-degree turn and started running back the way he'd come, this time dragging me along with him. "Rochester! Stop!" I called. "Sit, boy, sit!"

I'd never cared for Rochester. I guess it was clear to him that I didn't like dogs, and he made it his personal mission to reinforce that opinion. He did a good job of it, too. He was too big, too enthusiastic, too shaggy. Whenever I stopped to talk to Caroline, Rochester tried to jump on me, and Caroline couldn't keep him in line. She took him for obedience lessons every Saturday, but his exuberance still overwhelmed his manners.

He had huge paws and a big head. His fur was fine and attached itself to me if I even passed within five feet of him, giving my lint brush lots of use. He had big jowls, too, and there was usually a line of drool hanging from them he was happy to wipe off on me. His paws were often muddy, and somehow the tip of his tail was always wet, and when he whipped it against my leg it stung like the touch of a wasp.

Galloping down the street, he ignored my commands to stop, but quickly I saw why he was in such a hurry.

A narrow, grassed-over path from the access road into River Bend led off to an old Revolutionary War cemetery at the edge of the preserve. Caroline had told me she often took Rochester up that path, and cars used it to turn around when they realized they were approaching the entry to a gated community.

As I neared where the grassy path met the roadway, I saw Caroline Kelly lying on the ground. All the activity of the past few minutes formed into a pattern in my head—the shots fired, the speeding car, the loose dog. I looked around as adrenaline raced through my veins. Was the shooter still there? No, he or she must have left in the car that passed me.

I walked up to Caroline, and leaned down next to her. Blood seeped out of her jacket, and there was a growing pool next to her leg. I remembered learning in college biology that if the femoral artery, running through the thigh, was severed, you could bleed out in a matter of minutes.

"Caroline?" I asked. "Caroline, can you hear me?" I had no idea how to do CPR and I was worried I'd do the wrong thing, somehow hurt her further.

I watched for a minute but could not see any rise and fall in her chest. I flipped open my cell phone, my hands shaking, and found my friend Rick Stemper's cell number. Rick was a police detective in Stewart's Crossing, and I knew he'd tell me what I should do.

Rick and I hadn't been great friends at Pennsbury High; I think we'd shared a couple of classes together. But when I'd been back in town for a few weeks, I was standing in line at The Chocolate Ear, a new café in the center of town, when I thought the guy behind me looked familiar. By the time I had my extra-hot tall coffee, his name had come to me.

"Rick?" I asked. I stuck my hand out. "Steve Levitan."

He'd put on a few pounds since high school—but hadn't we all. Otherwise he looked the same; unruly mop of brown hair, broad shoulders, athletic build. There were bags below his eyes and a couple of laugh lines around his mouth, but in general, he looked pretty good. "Hey, long time no see," he'd said, and we'd started to fill each other in on the intervening years.

He had joined the Stewart's Crossing police department after graduating from Penn State with a degree in criminal justice. His ex-wife liked worrying if her hubby would come home at night, and once Rick moved from beat cop to plainclothes, she couldn't muster up the enthusiasm any more. Six months after he'd made detective, she had dumped him for a fire fighter

We'd bonded over mutual bitterness. I remember him asking that day, "If a tree falls in the forest and kills your ex-wife, what do you do with the lumber?"

I laughed. "Are you still in contact with her?"

"As far as I'm concerned, she's moved to Whoragon," he said. "And I don't mean Portland."

"Somebody's shot Caroline Kelly," I said, when Rick answered his phone. "My next-door neighbor. I think she's dead." My voice was higher than normal, and I was panting for breath after that quick run with Rochester.

"Whoa, Steve, hold on!" Rick said. "Where are you?"

I described the spot, between River Road and the entrance to River Bend. "I'm on my way," he said. "Did you call 911?"

"Not yet."

"Do it." He disconnected, and I called the emergency number.

The dispatcher was calm and professional. She led me through what had happened and where I was, and promised to send police and an ambulance.

All the while, Rochester paced around me, alternating between barking and whimpering. He'd strain to go over to Caroline's body, then when I pulled him back he'd jump up on me, as if he was trying to convince me to do something more than just wait for the police to arrive.

I shivered in the cold, damp breeze, starting at every noise, worried that whoever had shot Caroline hadn't been in that car, that he was still lurking in the wooded preserve. But the one-two punch of a visit from Santiago Santos, and the discovery of Caroline's body, had knocked all the initiative out of me. All I could do was sit on the ground with the big golden dog next to me, and wait for whatever fate had in store.

Rochester

I remembered the first time I'd met Caroline, a few months before. Moving back to Pennsylvania from Silicon Valley had been more expensive than I'd anticipated, and I'd run through a lot of the money my dad had left me. The townhouse was paid off—but there were still utilities and taxes and the business of putting food on the table.

It was December 15 and I was just about ready to put on a paper hat and practice saying, "Would you like fries with that?" when I stumbled on an opening for adjunct faculty at Eastern College, my alma mater, a 'very good small college' just upriver from Stewart's Crossing. I had to get up to the college as soon as possible that morning to meet with the department chair before the college closed down for Christmas break.

I rushed through a quick shower, cut my chin while shaving, and didn't realize that I'd forgotten a belt until I'd locked the door behind me. I was opening my beat-up BMW sedan, the one I'd bought new twelve years before, when out of nowhere a huge golden beast came galloping toward me. I might have taken it for a lion if not for the long red tongue lolling out of its mouth as it ran. I heard a woman call, "Rochester! Come back here!"

The beast, which appeared to share its name with Jack Benny's valet, pinned me against the car, placing its large paws on my chest and licking my face. My CV and transcript pages went flying.

"Rochester! Down!" The woman pulled the dog's collar, and he fell to the ground, where he began sniffing my feet. "I'm so sorry," she said. She wore a maroon turtleneck, pressed jeans and expensive sneakers. "I thought he was upstairs, and when I opened the front door he shot out past me."

Rochester rolled over onto his back, and the woman reached down to rub his belly. "You're just a little too friendly, aren't you, Rochester?" she asked.

She stood and stuck her hand out. "Hi, I'm Caroline Kelly. I live next door."

Our townhouses were connected in a pod of sixteen—eight backing on eight. My kitchen wall abutted Caroline's living room, and sometimes when I was fixing dinner I heard her come home and greet her dog, and for a moment or two—but just that long—I missed having someone to come home to. Not my ex-wife, you understand. Just someone.

Then I looked down and realized Rochester had left muddy paw prints on my khaki slacks. Too late, no time to change. "Sorry, I'm in a rush," I said. "Job interview in—" I looked at my watch "twenty minutes."

She called "Good luck!" and held Rochester's collar as I backed down the driveway. After that, we'd seen each other out walking. Ours was a friendly community, lots of joggers, walkers, and dog owners, and I nodded to her as often as to any of the other neighbors.

Poor Caroline. We'd talked, and I'd entertained the idea that I might ask her out to dinner sometime, when I felt a little more comfortable mentioning my parole on first dates. I felt sad that her life had been extinguished, and that I'd never had the chance to get to know her better.

While I waited, the occasional car passed, heading in or out of River Bend, and every time I heard the crunch of gravel I thought Rick or the ambulance was arriving. The night was quiet, and a brisk wind rose up, moving the clouds across the sky. Rochester sat on his haunches and began howling, and even though I didn't like him, the mournful tone pierced my heart.

There was a coppery smell in the air that I thought might be Caroline's blood, mixed with auto exhaust and a swampy tang rising from the canal, a few hundred feet away, beyond a narrow wooded area. I felt sick, but I managed not to throw up. Between keeping watch for Rick and trying to control Rochester, I had too much to do to indulge my distress. Darkness fell, but there was a three-quarter moon shining, and I could make out the outline of Orion and his fiery sword.

Rick was there first, followed by Fire Rescue and a blue and white squad car with "Stewart's Crossing Police" emblazoned on both sides. I stood off to the side, holding Rochester's leash, as he strained and barked, wanting to know what was going on with his mom.

Two guys spilled out of the ambulance and assessed Caroline's situation. Because they didn't load her up and speed away, I could tell that my initial thought was correct—she was dead.

The two officers in the squad car set up a perimeter around the area and Rick called for crime scene investigators. For the next couple of hours there was a flurry of activity—lights being set up, people searching, evidence collected, photos taken.

I couldn't remember the last time there had been a homicide in Stewart's Crossing. It's the kind of small town that falls under the radar most of the time. We were named for a guy who ran a ferry service across the river, the eighteenth century equivalent of being called Yellow Cab, PA. Our most famous citizens are a minor soap opera actress and a professor at Princeton University who studies why chameleons change color. The VFW post runs a Memorial Day parade, where the kids from the high school drama club dress up as wounded veterans, teenagers wrapped in bloody bandages, hobbling on crutches, plastic guts spilling out of their T-shirts.

When I was in high school, our chapter of the Future Farmers of America set up a demonstration farm in the parking lot of the high school. Jeff DiSalvo's prize bull got loose when Jeff was attempting to demonstrate gelding, and it trampled the chicks, the ducklings and two lambs. That was about the extent of the violence in Stewart's Crossing.

Since we'd reconnected, Rick and I often met up for a beer at The Drunken Hessian, a place we'd always wanted to get in when we were under age. Now that we were old enough, some of the thrill had worn off, but that's the way it is with most things. When he came over to talk to me, he reminded me of the only other homicide in town during our lives, a shooting that had taken place there while I was in California. "But we do a lot of accident investigation and reconstruction," he reassured me. "We have a crime lab and access to a lot of sophisticated equipment through the county."

By then, the coroner's office had taken Caroline's body away, and Rochester had stopped straining and jumping. Instead, he sat on his haunches at my feet, alert to everything that was going on. Rick pulled out his notepad and had me walk him through everything I'd seen or heard, starting with the three shots. Then he nodded and said, "Good. Now I need you to tell me everything you know about Caroline."

"It's not much," I said. "I moved into the townhouse in November, but I didn't meet her until just before Christmas. She works for a bank in center city, but I don't know the name.

I know she has a degree in English from SUNY, and an MBA, but I don't remember from where." My voice warbled a little, and I still felt panicky.

"OK, take it easy, Steve. That's her dog?"

I nodded. "She was walking him."

"She do that same time every day?"

"Pretty much." I saw him write that down, and my brain ran off. So somebody had been watching her, waiting to kill her. Oh, my God.

"Steve?" I heard Rick say, though I was busy imagining horrible scenarios for poor Caroline. "Stay with me, here."

I came back to the present. "Sorry. You were asking?"

"She have any regular visitors? A boyfriend, maybe?"

I shook my head. "She mentioned a guy from New York," I said. "I saw his car in her driveway one weekend-- a black Porsche Cayenne."

He asked a lot more questions, and I found it sad that I knew so little about Caroline after living next to her for five months. "OK, why don't you go home now?," he said. "I know where to find you if I need anything else."

I was being dismissed, which was fine with me. "What about the dog?"

"What about him?"

"What do I do with him?"

Rick shrugged. "Can you keep him until we find out next of kin, see what plans she made?"

"I'm not a dog person. I don't know how to take care of one."

"You feed it, you walk it, you pick up after it," Rick said. "Smart guy like you, college professor, you can figure it out."

I looked at Rochester. He was a big, hairy, slobbering beast, but he'd just lost his mother, and I remembered the piercing sound of his howls. I could keep him for a day or two. "You'll call me when you know what to do with him?"

"Will do," he said.

When I tugged on Rochester's leash and said, "Come on, boy, you're coming to my house," he strained to go where Caroline's body had lain, but I reined him in. He looked up at me, in the glare of the police car's headlights, and in his face I thought I could see an understanding. His mother was not coming back. He was stuck with me, at least for a while.

As we walked home, I was lost in thought about Caroline, and Rochester kept stopping every few feet to sniff or lift his leg. As my house came in sight, and with it Caroline's right next door, I remembered that Rochester had to have food, bowls, toys—who knew what else. All of it locked up inside Caroline's townhouse.

We'd swapped house keys after we met, though I'd never had cause to use her key before. Rochester planted himself in her driveway and would not be moved onward, no matter how I tried to convince or drag him. He agreed to walk up to the townhouse's courtyard, and I let him in through the gate, then pulled it closed behind him.

"I'll be right back, boy, I promise," I said. "I have to get the key."

He lay down and rested his head on his front paws, regarding me with a baleful glance. "I promise, Rochester."

I hurried to my own door, trying to remember where I'd stored Caroline's key. I thought it was in my kitchen junk drawer, and I pawed through the take-out menus, loose screws, flashlight batteries and plastic doodads until I found it. I wasn't quick enough, though; I heard Rochester start to howl next door as I rushed out.

"I'm coming, boy!" I called. I jumped through the flowerbed between the houses and showed my head over the gate. He leaped up and launched himself at me as I walked in.

"I didn't leave you," I said, reaching down to scratch behind his ears. "I had to get the key." He rewarded me with a smear of drool across my leg.

I opened the front door and turned on the light in the living room. I shivered as I realized I was walking into a dead woman's house, but there was no getting around it. I needed Rochester's stuff.

The cushions of the black lacquer futon were covered in a fine layer of golden hair and the *Courier-Times* had been tossed atop the matching coffee table. A bookcase made of planks and black-painted blocks spanned one long wall, filled with books.

I followed Rochester into the kitchen, where I started assembling his stuff. There was a lot of it. Food and water bowls, and a half-full twenty-pound bag of dry dog food. A shelf of vitamin bottles, dog shampoo, leashes and collars and flea products. Scattered around the floor were a variety of heavy plastic dog toys and rawhide bones in various states of chewing.

Caroline's model has a small bedroom off the living room, which she had fitted out as an office, and I found a big empty box there, beneath a sign that read, "I want to be the kind of person my dog thinks I am."

I was loading the box when the front door burst open and I heard someone say, "Police! Don't move!"

I froze like a statue. Rochester, however, did not obey. He rushed toward the door, barking. Then I heard a voice say, "Hey, boy, how did you get in here?"

"Rick?" I called. "It's me, Steve."

Rick came around the corner from the entry, his gun drawn. One of the uniformed cops was behind him. When he saw it was indeed me, he holstered it. "What are you doing in here?"

"You told me to keep the dog," I said. I motioned toward the box I was packing. "I needed his stuff."

"How'd you get in?"

"We traded keys a while ago."

"You're disturbing a crime scene," the uniform said.

"I saw the crime scene, Officer," I said. "It was out beyond the guard house, and there was lots of blood."

"The dog's got to eat," Rick said. "Let him get the stuff."

Rick sent the uniform back out to his car, and picked up the box for me, when it became evident that Rochester wasn't budging unless I had his leash, and I couldn't manage both dog and box.

The street was dark and silent. After six months in prison, I loved the freedom of coming and going as I pleased, and I relished the quiet and serenity I felt under the canopy of stars. But the sense of peace I'd always found in River Bend was gone now that violent death had paid a call.

Rick left the box just inside my gate and returned next door. I hurried the dog across to my house, opened my front door, and unhooked Rochester's leash. He bounded ahead of me, his nose to the floor, sniffing every inch of my downstairs as I carried his stuff inside and piled it on my kitchen table.

The last time I'd been around dogs much was when I was in college, back when it seemed everyone wore flannel shirts and blue jeans and had little dogs named Trotsky. I wasn't quite sure what to do with such a huge creature, but I figured he had to be hungry.

"You eat yet?" I asked, when Rochester came to sit on his haunches and stare at me. "Probably not. How much of this do you get?"

I peered at the bag, which was printed in both English and French. I established that he was indeed a "*chien de grande race*," or large breed dog, and followed the instructions. I poured half a cup of the dry chunks into one metal bowl and filled the other from the tap. I put both down on the floor by the sliding glass doors that led out to my patio, and he attacked the food with gusto.

I stood and watched him for a minute. In the space of a few hours I'd seen my neighbor murdered and inherited custody of a seventy-pound dog with a voracious appetite. All in all, not a typical day. And I still had papers to grade. I didn't have much appetite for dinner myself, so I opened my backpack and spread my work out on the kitchen table. With a big sigh, Rochester sprawled out at my feet, and while I alternated grading papers with worrying about Caroline and wondering what had happened to her, he slept.

Romantic Hero

I gave up on grading around nine o'clock, and went upstairs to my bedroom. When he moved into the townhouse, my dad had sold all the furniture I grew up with and bought everything new, including a queen-sized pillow-top mattress on top of an elevated sleigh bed. It's pretty high, but like him, I'm tall and have long legs so it never bothered me. Rochester hopped his front paws up to the edge of the mattress but couldn't seem to leverage his whole body up. That was fine with me.

"Your bed is downstairs," I said. "This one's mine."

He looked at me. As I started pulling off my shirt, he went down to all fours again, and padded out of the room. "Good boy."

Then I heard him running. He came hurtling back into the bedroom, and with a flying leap ended up on the bed, where he settled down and stared at me. "Did you sleep in your mother's bed?"

He did not respond, but he kept his eyes on me. "Oh, well, it's only for a day or two." I stripped down to my shorts and got into bed, pushing him over to one side. "You can stay, but you've got to share." He seemed to agree.

Lying there, thinking of Caroline, I remembered the only time I'd been in her townhouse before that night. I'd gotten the job at Eastern, and on my way home from teaching, I often stopped at my favorite spot in town, The Chocolate Ear café, for a raspberry mocha—a reward for reading and grading my students' ungrammatical papers. The owner, a pastry chef from New York named Gail Dukowski, used the best quality beans, Guittard chocolate syrup, and home-made whipped cream, and despite my coffee snobbery I'd been seduced by the sweet drink. The fact that she was pretty and liked to flirt was a plus.

A lot had changed in Stewart's Crossing during the years I'd been away. The feed store had been replaced by a real estate office, the local bank names had been painted over with national ones, and doctors had taken over several of the old Victorians. America's three obsessions: property, money and health, all sandwiched together in a downtown area that still has one traffic light, though a steady stream of Land Rovers,

BMWs, and Volvos are always circling, competing for the few available parking spaces.

One of the best changes was the opening of The Chocolate Ear. In the 1960s, the old stone building on Main Street was a hardware store where my father bought the odd nail or high-intensity flashlight, and then when it closed it sat derelict for a long time until Gail, who had grown up in neighboring Levittown, returned to Bucks County and opened the café. She painted the interior a pale yellow, which made the room seem sunny even in winter, and decorated the walls with vintage posters advertising chocolate products, many of them in French. The white wire tables and matching chairs seemed like they'd come direct from Paris, though they'd been padded with cushions more comfortable to American bottoms.

The café always smelled of something delicious—lemon tarts, strawberry shortcake, or hot chocolate topped with cinnamon. The glass-fronted case was filled with exquisitely decorated pastries—petit fours covered in white fondant with tiny sugar flowers, individual key lime tarts scalloped with whipped cream, fudge brownies studded with walnuts and chocolate chips. The signature cookie was a chocolate version of the elephant ear, a curly pastry with a rich cocoa flavor. An industrial-quality Italian coffee machine churned out mochas, lattes and cappuccinos, filling the room with the sound of drips and foams.

Usually I stayed at the café to savor my drink, but one Friday in late January there was a water leak in the kitchen, and the sound of the plumber banging away wasn't conducive to grading. So I took my coffee back home, and as I stepped out of the Beemer, clutching the paper cup and a pile of student essays, Rochester came out of nowhere once again, this time trailing his leash behind him.

I saw him coming too late, and the coffee and the papers went flying in opposite directions. Caroline was very apologetic, helping me collect all the paper, and then she offered to make me a coffee to replace the one I'd lost. "I have a great espresso machine and I never get to use it," she said. "Please?"

I didn't want to face grading without my treat, so I agreed. "I'm so sorry he attacked you again," she said, pushing the golden retriever in the door ahead of us. "I took today off to practice handling him. I've wanted a dog for ages, but it wasn't until I moved out here that I had a place for one. He came from a rescue group—can you imagine someone wanting to give up a sweetheart like Rochester?"

I understood why someone might want to get rid of a gargantuan beast like him—what I couldn't see was getting him in the first place. "Is that where you went to college?" I asked, as we walked into the kitchen. "Rochester?"

"No, he's named after Rochester in *Jane Eyre*."

In that moment, I knew a lot about Caroline Kelly. Though full-figured, she had a pretty face, and she dressed well and knew how to use makeup and hairstyle to her advantage. The low-necked sweater she was wearing accentuated her cleavage, and I liked the way her jeans hung low on her hips. I figured she was educated, because she knew *Jane Eyre*, and successful, because townhouses in River Bend start around $300,000.

True to her word, she had a very fancy espresso machine. "I've got Kona beans in the freezer," she said, opening the door and pulling them out. "I'll just slip some in the grinder."

I started to like Caroline even more. A woman who appreciated good coffee was a real find. My ex-wife, also known as "The Jewish American Princess of Darkness, Satan's Favorite Squeeze," only drank iced tea, heavily dosed with artificial sweeteners. She used to bitch about the smell of coffee in the house, saying it made her nauseous. I'd have to give up brewing my own each time she was pregnant.

Caroline's kitchen was full of the latest and most high-end appliances, everything shiny stainless or bright primary colors. I noted her top-of-the-line Kitchen Aid stand mixer, a hanging tray of copper-bottomed pans, and a wooden block of German knives.

Caroline's coffee offerings included a half dozen unopened bottles of syrup, from vanilla to orange to raspberry, and a couple of twist-top canisters of toppings. While she bustled around making the coffee, I looked around her house from the vantage point of her kitchen table. The kitchen was at the front of the house, with a big picture window that looked out on the street. The butcher block table matched the blond wood of the cabinets.

Her decorating was minimalist with a touch of Southeast Asia—a single bamboo screen, teak and bleached linen, with the occasional statue of a grinning monkey or a reflective Buddha. When I asked, she told me that she'd lived in Korea for a couple of years as a teenager, and it had formed her sense of style.

I could even see it in the way she dressed—very simply, with just a hint of Asian influence. She'd traded her usual sneakers for black Japanese sandals with white socks, and around her wrist she wore a thick gold bracelet she told me was made of Thai gold. "They call it a baht bracelet," she said. "That's the Thai money. A friend of my dad's in the service had one, and he used to joke that if you were ever captured in the jungle you could break a link off to bribe the chief to let you go."

I wondered if she'd seen that friend of her dad's as the same kind of romantic hero as Rochester—like Michael Douglas in *Romancing the Stone*, or Harrison Ford as Indiana Jones. It would be hard for an average guy to match up to those role models—a desk job in Philadelphia or some Bucks County hamlet doesn't lend itself to larger-than-life escapades. But maybe she'd like a guy with a criminal record—even if it was only for computer hacking. I filed that thought away for the future.

I heard the buzz of the coffee grinder, and then a percolating noise as the brown liquid dripped into the glass pot. Rochester came over and rested his big golden head on my leg, leaving behind a trail of drool and a fine coating of blonde hairs on my black jeans. He settled into a heap in the doorway that led back to the living room. Yet another reason to have a dog, I thought—to create an obstacle course in your own home.

As we drank our coffee, we traded bits and pieces of background. I mentioned my divorce and relocation, but left out the part about meeting Santiago Santos at a nondescript office building in Doylestown and showing him the ways I was becoming a solid citizen. I learned she had relocated from New York to take a job in finance with a bank in Philadelphia, an easy commute from the train station in Yardley, the next town downriver.

"There's a guy I used to date who lives in New York, and I see him now and then, but it's nothing serious," she said. "But other than him, the guys I've met around here are total washouts. You know, sometimes I feel like behind my back someone has enrolled me in the Dork of the Month Club, and every few weeks, instead of books or CDs or baskets of fruit, I get some dufous standing at my door, wearing high-water pants, a pencil folder in his shirt pocket, and one of those ribbon things running around behind his head holding his glasses in place."

I laughed. Of course a guy like that couldn't match up to a man who wore a gold baht bracelet, knew how to shoot a semi-automatic weapon and how to perform first aid on a sucking chest wound. Could I? Or would I end up another on Caroline's list of losers, the computer geek who was too dumb to avoid prison?

While we talked, Rochester remained sprawled on the white tile floor in the doorway, snoring softly. At one point his body began to twitch and he made some whimpering noises. "He's probably chasing ducks in his dreams," Caroline said. "There's a dog park in Leighville, and I've taken him there a couple of times, but I spend the whole time making sure he doesn't try to hump every other dog."

The way she looked at him was so sweet and loving; I could tell she and the big golden had a strong bond, and I envied that a little. Some people like dogs, I figured, and some didn't. I was one of the ones who didn't. And I wasn't willing to accept the chaos that a dog would bring into my life. I was still enjoying my solitude, the way I didn't have to answer to anyone but Santiago Santos.

"I guess I should get home," I said then. "I've got a stack of freshman comp essays to grade on 'a food that has a personal meaning to me.' I figure I'll be reading a lot about pizza and burgers, while correcting dangling modifiers, unyoking fused sentences, and introducing my students to the concept of punctuation and its place in the grammatically correct sentence."

Remembering Caroline, I felt a few long-ignored stirrings. Just my luck; I find a smart, pretty woman who's single and maybe interested in me, and she gets killed before I can even think of making a move.

The next time I ran into Caroline it was at The Chocolate Ear, on a Saturday morning. The usual suspects were there—the people who always seemed to be hanging around the café when I stopped by. My childhood piano teacher, Edith Passis;

Gail, the café owner; and her grandmother Irene.

I stepped up in line behind Caroline, noting the Oriental simplicity of her white blouse, black jacket, and black slacks. With her hair pulled up into a knot, she looked fresh and pretty, and I wondered again if she'd go out with me, if I asked, and if the parole would be a deal-killer.

We started to chat while we waited, and then sat down across from each other at one of the white wire tables. "I'm still finding my way around," she said, breaking a biscotti and dipping it in her coffee. "The other day I got lost trying to find my way to Newtown on the back road."

Her fingers were long and delicate, with a French manicure on the nails. I've always been a sucker for a woman with beautiful hands. "If you need to know how to find anything, just ask," I offered. "I know my way around."

"But you've lived here less than I have."

"I grew up here. I was born in Trenton, but my parents relocated to Stewart's Crossing when I was two."

"And you've been here ever since?"

"College upriver in Leighville; New York for nine years; then Silicon Valley for ten. I've been back here a few months, but in many ways it seems like I never left."

"I wish I had a home town," she said. She clasped her coffee cup in both hands. "I was an Army brat, and we moved around a lot. People say it must have been romantic to live overseas, but not when all you ever saw was a military base."

"Where do your parents live now?"

"My dad was killed in the first Gulf War," she said. "And my mom died last year. So it's just me." She smiled. "And Rochester, of course."

"I'm sorry," I said. "My mom died about the time your dad did, and then my dad sold our house and bought the townhouse next to yours for his retirement. Did you know him? He didn't get to spend much time there. He only lived in the townhouse for a few months before he passed away."

"I think I said hello to him a couple of times," Caroline said. "I'm sorry I didn't get to his funeral. I know some of the other neighbors went."

How could I tell her that the State of California had prevented me from looking after him in his final illness, had even kept me from his funeral? "It was a busy time," I said, trying for vagueness.

Caroline left a few minutes later, and then Edith came over to sit with me. "Do I seem more confused to you lately, Steve?" she asked.

"Confused? No, why?"

"I feel so distracted. It's been hard for me to concentrate on reading or playing the piano. And I've been losing track of my finances, too. I'm worried someone might be stealing from me, because checks have gone missing."

I contemplated Edith's decline as I cupped the white china mug which held the remains of my raspberry mocha. She had been a friend of my parents, and I remembered her at parties at our house, her black hair teased into a beehive. She wore glasses that feathered up at the edges and thigh-high black leather boots.

Edith had become a touchstone for me in the few months since I'd been back, and it worried me that she might not be around much longer. I had lost so many people who had mattered to me – both my parents, my ex-wife, many friends who hadn't wanted to stand by me while my case made its way through the court system. I wasn't ready to lose Edith, too.

"Sometimes I think maybe it's just that I'm getting confused," she continued. "I don't know what to think. And it's all so disturbing, after Walter worked so hard to leave me well-fixed."

I'd heard about criminals who preyed on the elderly, scammers who needed help moving money into the country or who promised elaborate yet unnecessary home repairs, which evaporated once the money had been paid. But Edith Passis had always been so smart and confident. I couldn't believe someone was taking advantage of her.

I looked out through the mullioned windows at Main Street, thinking about what I could say. Edith must have been over eighty, and still lived in the same small bungalow where she'd spent a lifetime giving piano lessons to local kids. I remembered sitting at her upright piano, struggling to master the simplest of songs. For three years, my parents forced me to trudge to Mrs. Passis's house once a week, until they gave me up as a lost cause. Back then, she'd had true Black Irish looks— coal-black hair, pale white skin and bright blue eyes. When I returned to Stewart's Crossing, though, I discovered her hair had gone stark white, and a medication she took tinted her skin a salmon-pink. The blue eyes were still as fierce and blue, though. Though I'd never say it to her face, I thought she looked like a gerbil, as if she ate chopped lettuce at every meal and lived in a pile of shredded newspaper.

Her fingers were arthritic now, so she could no longer keep up with her students, and she'd given up all but the most advanced pupils, those she could help by ear. In addition, once a week she drove upriver to Eastern to tutor a couple of advanced piano students.

She had always been so strong and vibrant, but that day, she seemed to have shrunk and faded. "I'm just finding it harder and harder to remember things," she continued, shaking her head. "I saw you talking to Caroline earlier. Gail told me that she was a CPA. I was thinking of asking her to help me sort things out."

"That's a great idea, Edith. She seems like a nice person."

"I can't imagine who could do this to me," Edith said. "I don't have any children, you know, and none of my nieces or nephews live anywhere in the area. But I think Caroline could help me."

I was relieved. If anyone was cheating Edith, Caroline would be able to help her. She wasn't my responsibility, of course, but my parents were dead and she had no children, and I felt a connection to her that went back many years, to dust motes dancing in the sunlight as I struggled to master Scott Joplin and "The Caisson Song."

Lying restlessly in bed, Rochester snoring lightly next to me, I worried about Edith, and wondered if Caroline had been able to figure out what was wrong before she died. I resolved to call Edith the next morning and let her know what had happened to Caroline, and see how she stood.

Then I turned on my side and tried, once again, to fall asleep.

The House Guest

Just before I dozed off, Rochester jumped down and made himself comfortable on the tile floor in the master bathroom—choosing a spot where he could, by raising an eyebrow, keep tabs on me. In the morning, I woke around seven-thirty, stretching and rubbing the sleep from my eyes. Rochester's head bobbed up next to me, his front paws planted on the mattress.

I'd almost forgotten about the events of the night before. But seeing him there brought it all back. "I suppose you want to go for a walk," I said, yawning.

His head banged on the mattress a couple of times. I took that for a yes.

But by the time I had pulled on a pair of sweat pants, an Eastern t-shirt, socks, sneakers and a fleece-lined jacket, Rochester had crawled under my bed and didn't want to leave.

I lay down on the floor next to him. A few of his golden hairs had already lodged in my carpet, and I sneezed. "Come on, boy, let's go." I reached a hand under the bed to stroke the top of his head. "I know, you had a rough day yesterday. I did, too. But you've got to go out for your walk."

I looked up at the clock on my bedside table. "And I have to get to class soon. So that means we have to go walk now."

He just lay there looking at me. I grabbed the metal chain around his neck and pulled. He splayed his front paws out to slow the motion, but I knocked them inward with my other hand and kept pulling. By the time I had his head out from under the bed he'd given up and was moving forward under his own steam.

Before I could get up, he was climbing on top of me, trying to lick my face. "Get off of me, you big moose!" I said, laughing. "This is all some big game to you, isn't it?"

He took off down the hall while I was still getting up, one hand on his leash, and it was like a slapstick routine, me tumbling and stumbling as I struggled to get my footing while being dragged along by a big golden beast. It was no use being angry with Rochester; as soon as you got the steam going, he'd do something to make you laugh.

We got out the front door, and stopped in the courtyard

while I turned and locked up. The gate to the driveway was still closed, and Rochester and I were confined in a narrow area together. Without warning, he jumped on me, placing his front paws on my stomach and his big head just below my face. The move was enough to knock me back against the door.

For a moment I thought he was begging me not to make him go out again, where the bad people had hurt his mommy— but then I realized it was just another game. "Get down, you big moose," I said, and I pushed down on the top of his head. I'd swear he snickered at me as I opened the gate, and then he took off at Indy 500 pace for the end of the driveway.

A walk with Rochester was a lot different from the walks I took myself. He powered down the street, at the end of the retractable leash, stopping frequently to sniff or pee. Just when I caught up, he took off again. I'd only brought one plastic bag with me, but he didn't care, and left samples of his handiwork in three separate spots. After the first, I'd tossed the bag, so for the second and third drops I had to stand around looking guilty and hoping we could escape unnoticed.

The sun had just risen, and there was frost on the lawns, sparkling in the early light. All around us, I heard River Bend awakening—courtyard gates opening and closing, mothers calling kids, car doors slamming and engines starting up. It was shaping up to be a cool, cloudless day; a bluebird swooped into an oak tree ahead of us, and a squirrel chattered as he jumped from tree to tree.

I was struck with a terrible sadness. Caroline would not see this day. She would never walk Rochester again on a crisp morning like this, filled with the promise of spring. She would never drive down to the station in Yardley for her train to Philadelphia, or come home in the gathering twilight to the welcome of her dog.

It was amazing how fast a life could come apart. Within a year, I'd turned forty, then lost my father, my job, my freedom, my marriage and, as part of the divorce, my home in Silicon Valley. I'd struggled to put my life back together—but Caroline wouldn't have that chance. There were some body blows you couldn't recover from.

We saw a few neighbors, and waved, but everyone seemed to be in a hurry to leave for work. It wasn't the same as in the evening, when people stopped to say hello or share information. Rochester and I did a big circuit of the neighborhood, staying away from the area where Caroline had been shot, and returned to my driveway, where I picked up the newspaper.

Rochester sprawled on the kitchen floor, panting, and I refilled his water bowl. He jumped up, lapping the water and spilling half of it on the tile floor, then settled down again to watch me.

While I waited for the water to boil for my morning oatmeal, I scanned the pages for news of Caroline's murder. I found a tiny report in the "Crossing Connections" section that a woman had been shot and killed along the perimeter of the park. Police were investigating and were waiting to release her identity pending notification of relatives.

I poured a half cup of food into Rochester's bowl and replenished his water supply, then showered and dressed for work. It was a Wednesday, which meant that I taught technical writing from 9:30 to 10:45, and freshman comp from 11:00 – 12:15. I usually hung around for while after that, chatting with colleagues and making myself available in case one of my students had the uncharacteristic desire to discuss his or her lack of course progress with me. "You be a good boy, Rochester," I said, as I was leaving. "Take a nice long nap and I'll walk you when I get home."

Rochester had taken up a position under my dining room table, and from there he watched me leave. From the car, I used my cell phone to call Rick and see if he knew where Rochester was going, but all I could do was leave a message.

I called technical writing my alphabet class, because the students ran from Alyssa Applebaum to Layton Zee—who insisted on the first day, "Call me Lay. All my buds do."

I wasn't Layton's bud, but I refrained from saying so. He was an interesting case; he came to class every day, did the in-class work, and joined in the discussions. But he never handed in any papers. He reminded me of a kid I knew when I was at Eastern, who supplied half the campus with a variety of recreational drugs and who was his own biggest customer. He had gone on to run his own cosmetics business, so perhaps there was hope for Lay Zee.

All through class I kept thinking about Caroline Kelly and wondering what could have caused someone to kill her. I love to read mysteries, and quite often the solution is right there under the detective's nose, but the author drags out the discovery just to fill up two hundred pages. In those cases I figured out who did it long before the detective did, and often gave up on the book when it seemed like I was looking over the shoulder of an idiot.

But it wasn't so easy in real life. All morning I was distracted, lecturing from rote and answering questions with half my brain. Could it have been something as simple as an angry ex-boyfriend? I hadn't lived next door to Caroline long enough to know much about her life beyond the dog and the guy with the Porsche Cayenne who'd come to stay one weekend.

She was a creature of habit, as dog owners often are— walking Rochester every day and night at the same time— which Rick seemed to think had made it easy for someone to find the right time and place to shoot her. But why? What hidden secrets lay behind the ordinary façade she presented to the world?

Years of reading mysteries had taught me that even the blandest-seeming person can have hidden traumas, long-dormant issues that percolate to the top and cause horrific actions. I knew, for example, that Caroline was a military brat, and that she'd spent time in Korea as a teenager. Had something from her past come back to haunt her? Had her Southeast Asian connections influenced more than just her furniture and jewelry? What if a high school classmate had become a high-level drug dealer and she'd been laundering money for him through her bank?

I shook my head to clear it. I was being ridiculous. The chances that my quiet next-door-neighbor was an accountant by day and a drug smuggler by night were about as good as the chances that Mary and I would get back together and live happily ever after—which is to say so small that it could only be seen with an electron microscope.

Freshman comp passed in the same sort of fog, and after class I went up to the faculty lounge, where I saw Jackie Devere, a full-time professor I'd become friends with, making herself a cappuccino. "You're lucky you didn't get shot, too," she said, when I told her what had happened. "If you'd been a few minutes later it might have been you."

"I never thought about that. I just assumed they were shooting at her."

"But why would someone shoot her?" she asked. "You said she was quiet."

I shrugged. "You know the saying. Still waters run deep. Though if that's the case, we've got a lot of Mindanao Trenches here at Eastern."

"The poor dog," she said. "To lose her mother, and then be caged up in a strange house."

"He's not caged up," I said. "He can go anywhere in the house he wants."

"You didn't put him in a cage?"

"He's not a circus animal."

"I don't mean a cage. I mean a crate. You leave a young dog like that in a crate during the day so he doesn't tear up the house while you're gone."

I remembered seeing a big metal box in Caroline's kitchen. At the time, I'd been so concerned with getting Rochester's food, and then with the police, that I hadn't thought to wonder what it was doing there.

"I think I'd better get home," I said. I grabbed my cell phone and beat-up leather backpack and hurried to my car, giving up on the idea of meeting with any phantom students. All the way home I imagined seeing my house in shreds when I opened the door.

It wasn't too bad. Rochester had gotten hold of a stuffed bear my ex-wife had given me one Valentine's Day, its paws wrapped around a box of chocolates. That year I'd given her a book of Spanish love poems in translation. She'd taken one look at the book, then appropriated the chocolate. The bear had been with the stuff Mary had packed up and shipped to Stewart's Crossing while I was in prison, and I'd never gotten rid of it. I guess I needed to remind myself that I'd loved someone once, and been loved back.

Bear stuffing was scattered around my tile floor. The head was under the dining room table, three paws lay in the kitchen, and Rochester was still working on the torso when I came in.

"Not yours!" I said, trying to tug the poor bear out of his mouth. He wouldn't give it up. "Listen, mister, you are a guest in this house. And not for much longer, either. Now give me that bear!" I pulled and tugged, and what was left of it exploded into a pile of fluff.

As soon as I had the living room cleaned up, I called Rick. "I need to take this dog wherever he's going," I said. "Soon." I ranted for a couple of minutes about the stuffed bear, but even to my ears it sounded dumb.

"She didn't make any arrangements," Rick said, when I let him get a word in. "Her only living relative is a great-aunt in upstate New York. She's too old to take him. I'm interviewing the co-workers later. Maybe one of them will want him."

"What do I do in the meantime?"

"If you don't want to hold on to him, you can always take him to the pound."

I hung up and looked at Rochester. He lay at my feet, his head on his paws in a gesture that seemed to say he was sorry. My anger deflated. "It was time for me to get rid of that bear anyway. But you're going into that crate from now on, mister."

I dragged him out to the courtyard to wait while I went next door to Caroline's. I knew it wasn't the crime scene, and Rick hadn't told me to stay out, so I figured it was OK to go over there and get the crate. Caroline's doormat read, "Who are you? Why are you here? What do you want? Go away!" I'd never noticed it before, and I laughed as I let myself in.

Once inside, I couldn't resist a detour to check out the bookcase. As I'd expected, it was filled with a combination of English lit books and popular best-sellers, leaning towards female authors and romantic plots. *Jane Eyre* was filed alphabetically under Bronte, and I decided I'd borrow it for a few days and refresh my memory of her dog's namesake.

It was creepy snooping around a dead woman's home. And I couldn't ignore that what I was doing was snooping. I was looking for some more dog toys to keep Rochester from chewing up my stuff—but along the way I was noticing that Caroline's closet was filled with business suits and white blouses, that her library of DVDs leaned toward romantic comedies, and that all her diplomas were framed and hung on the wall of her office.

A laptop computer sat on her desk, and I was tempted to turn it on and snoop around. Maybe there was a clue lurking there on the hard drive, an electronic diary that expressed her fears, a date book with a fateful meeting. But Santiago Santos, sitting on my right shoulder, told me it was wrong. I wasn't a cop, so I had no busy trying to figure out who killed Caroline. Leave that to the police.

And don't leave your fingerprints on any unauthorized computers.

I flattened the cage and carried it back to my house, with *Jane Eyre* and the rest of Rochester's toys, along with doggie toothpaste, shampoo, and a whole plastic bucket of grooming supplies. I wasn't planning to brush his teeth, trim his nails, or use any of the other expensive products, but I figured I'd have them prepared for his next owner. I played tug-of-war with Rochester for a while, until he got bored and went back to sleep under the dining room table.

I went up to my office—in my model, it's on the upper level—and checked my email. There were a couple of messages from my tech writing clients, and I had a small project that kept me busy until it started getting dark, when I took Rochester for a walk. This time I had plenty of grocery bags with me, and I found I enjoyed having some company.

True, I didn't go as fast with Rochester as I did alone, and I didn't appreciate having my arm yanked out of its socket when he saw a dog or cat or squirrel he wanted to play with, but I was getting accustomed to him. I would be sorry to see him go—but go he would.

My ex-wife had always said I was too self-centered to be in a relationship. She was probably right; at least, I didn't go along with every decision she made and every idea she had. She always said she was the flexible one, who accommodated herself to my moodiness, and my need to spend quiet hours reading. By the time I got out of jail and moved to Stewart's Crossing, she'd already latched onto the guy who would be husband number two.

I didn't begrudge her any happiness. We both felt we had settled for each other—we'd been in our late twenties when we met, living the single life in cheap rentals in iffy Manhattan neighborhoods, and the dating pool was growing narrower. Those who hadn't already been snapped up seemed to still be single for a reason.

Her neuroses blended with mine—she liked to clean, and I was a mess; she spent every penny she earned and needed me to keep her on a budget—the usual routines. If she hadn't asked for a divorce, I think we'd still be married. Unhappy, for sure, but carried along by relationship entropy. The way space junk continues to circle the earth long after it's been ejected or blown apart.

Did I regret that old life? The one where I was moving up the corporate ladder, married to a pretty, intelligent woman, with the hope that we'd start a family? I tried not to feel sorry for myself. I had taken those proverbial lemons and made lemonade, and if the brew was a little tart now and then, I just pursed my lips and got on with things.

After our walk, I went back to the computer, outlining a fire safety manual for a warehouse client. When I looked up, it was bedtime, and I went to find Rochester for a quick walk before we settled in. I found him on the dining room floor, with my cell phone in his paws.

"Rochester!" I yelled. "What are you doing? Dogs don't need cell phones!"

He leaned his head down and put his paw over it. "Oh, you think if you can't see me then I can't see you? You're about as smart as one of my students."

That's when I saw that the bottom half of the phone was a mangled mass of metal and plastic. "Rochester! That was my phone!"

I pulled it away from him. "Bad dog! Not yours!" I looked around for a newspaper I could roll up to whack him with, but all my papers were already in the recycling bin. I settled for a couple more "bad dogs" and then surveyed the phone. It was not salvageable. I couldn't even call Rick Stemper to complain because the only place I had his cell number was plugged into my phone.

"What am I going to do with you?" I asked. "Do you know the words 'animal shelter'? That's where you're going if you don't shape up and behave."

He looked at me and cocked his head.

"You're not the sharpest knife in the drawer, are you?"

I found his leash where I'd left it on the dining room table, and it was as if somebody had plugged him into an extension cord. He turned into a manic creature, jumping and skittering around on the tiles like a kangaroo on crack.

"Life is all a big game to you, isn't it?" I said, when I grabbed hold of his collar and clipped the leash on. "Well, the rules are different here, pal."

My god. I was channeling my father. That was one of his favorite mantras, the idea that the world was not fun and games, that one day life was going to give me a big punch in the teeth and he wasn't going to pay for the orthodontia.

When Rochester and I returned from our walk, I tried to coax him into his crate, but he wasn't having any of it. He scampered to the landing halfway up the stairs, where he stopped and watched me. After a quick attempt at dog-proofing, I turned out the lights downstairs and climbed up to the second floor. Rochester was under my feet the whole way, and when we got to the top of the stairs, he took off toward my bedroom. As I followed, I saw him take another flying leap and land on my bed, and he wasn't budging.

"All right," I said, standing by the side of the bed, trying to be stern. "But tomorrow when I leave for work you're going into that crate."

He looked like he would go along with that. I picked up *Jane Eyre* and got into bed, planning to read for a while, but Rochester wanted to crawl all over me and be petted—so my plans changed. "Are you a good boy?" I asked, ruffling his ears. "Is Rochester a good boy?"

He finally had enough reassurance, and retreated back to the end of the bed. He was still there when I turned the lights out.

The Break-In

I'm not sure if it was Rochester's leap from the bed that woke me, sometime after two a.m., or his barking—probably a one-two punch. "Rochester! Shut up!" I said. I jumped out of bed and went looking for him. He was in the office, where my house backed onto Caroline's, barking at the wall.

"Are you crazy?" I asked, grabbing his collar. "You're going to wake up the whole neighborhood."

He wiggled out of my grasp and ran back to the bedroom. When I followed, I saw him jumping into the Roman tub in the master bathroom, and leaning his paws against the window frame. "What's the matter, boy? What do you see?"

I stepped into the tub and stood next to him. From that angle, we could just see a corner of Caroline's bedroom window—and the pinpoint of a flashlight moving around in the darkness inside. "Good boy!" I said, patting his head before I jumped out of the tub and rushed to the phone to call 911.

I reported the burglary in progress, and thought about getting out my dad's 9 millimeter handgun from the bedside table and standing watch at Caroline's front door until the police arrived. Of course, since I'd never mentioned to Santiago Santos that I owned a gun, and it was probably a violation of my parole, I didn't think that was a good idea, especially because I was neither Starsky, nor Hutch. So I returned to the window with Rochester, where we watched and waited. The pinpoint of light was gone, and I started to worry that I had imagined it. Suppose the police showed up and there was no one inside Caroline's house. They'd think I was crazy.

A squad car pulled up five minutes later, red and blue lights flashing. By then I was dressed and went outside to meet them. "You called this in?" asked the female officer, whose badge identified her as P. Reinhardt.

"I saw a light moving around inside there." I pointed up at the master bedroom window. "And my dog—well, it's really her dog—he heard something and started barking."

That wasn't the order things happened, but I was nervous.

"You're sure no one's home?" Officer Reinhardt asked.

As we walked up to the front door, I explained about Caroline. The entrances in River Bend have glass sidelights on either side of the door, and the glass panel next to Caroline's doorknob had been smashed. The door was unlocked.

Reinhardt used a handkerchief from her pocket to open the door. From behind her, I saw that the living room was a shambles—books strewn all over the floor, the sofa cushions slit and stuffing everywhere.

"It wasn't like that this afternoon," I said.

She and her partner went inside, while I waited by the street. She came down a few minutes later. "The upstairs was trashed, too," she said. "There's no one there now."

She called for a crime scene investigation, and Rick Stemper showed up a while later, wearing a pair of jeans and a polo shirt and looking like he'd just rolled out of bed. It was a replay of the previous night—cops everywhere, Rick asking me questions. This time he took my fingerprints, to eliminate them, he said.

My pulse started to race. I'd had my prints taken in California, of course, which meant that when Rick entered them in his system, my record would pop up. I thought about telling Rick about my incarceration and parole—but it wasn't the time.

It had never been the time. All those nights at The Drunken Hessian, the times we ran into each other at The Chocolate Ear or at the grocery, I'd kept from mentioning it. I was lonely, and Rick was my only friend in town, and I thought that he wouldn't want to hang out with me if he knew about my record.

So I kept quiet. I did say, "You know I was there yesterday. I went back again this afternoon."

Rick raised an eyebrow. "Just can't stay away, can you?"

I explained about the crate, and that I'd gone through the house, looking for Rochester's toys. I didn't mention looking through her closet or her books—I didn't think he'd understand. I was glad that I hadn't touched her computer. I could just see Santiago Santos raising his bushy eyebrows as he asked me to explain what I was doing with my neighbor's computer, when the conditions of my parole restricted me to a single laptop with an audit trail.

That alone might be enough to violate my parole and send me back to California as a guest of the state.

While Rick and the male officer performed a complete search of the townhouse, I stood outside with Rochester, making small talk with Officer Reinhardt. "We see this kind of thing now and then," she said. "Somebody dies, and it gets in the paper, and some jerkwad takes that as an open invitation to rip the dead guy off."

It didn't seem like that kind of burglary to me. A jerkwad like she was describing would want to get in, steal whatever was handy, and get out. But I kept my mouth shut.

It was close to four-thirty that morning before I took Rochester back to my own house. "You're a good watch dog," I said, leaning down to stroke his head. "You heard somebody and you warned me. That's a good dog."

As I sat on the floor, stroking his golden fur, I felt all the nervous energy and adrenaline of the last few hours catch up with me, and I yawned. And then I started to think. It was clear this wasn't the kind of obituary-motivated robbery Officer Reinhardt thought it was. After all, the *Courier-Times* hadn't even identified her. Somebody was looking for something in Caroline's house—that's why they had ripped open the pillows and the couch and dumped the contents of the drawers.

Was the burglar the same person who'd killed Caroline? If so, what had he been looking for? Had he found it? What if he hadn't—would he be back?

What if it was Rochester he was looking for? Or what if he thought I had whatever it was—would he come after me next? I couldn't confess these feelings to Rick; it just wasn't a guy thing to do. So I sat and told Rochester instead. I worried, and petted the dog, and the acid feeling in my stomach dissipated a little—but not that much.

The next morning I was on auto-pilot. I took Rochester out for a walk, then sat in the living room with him watching mindless morning TV shows. My mystery fiction class doesn't meet until 12:30 on Tuesday and Thursday, and I use those mornings for grading papers or working on client projects. But I was exhausted, and my brain was still having trouble wrapping around everything that had happened.

At eleven-thirty, I motivated myself to get dressed for work. When I was ready to head out, I stood by Rochester's crate and asked him nicely to go inside.

Surprisingly, he did.

I felt better about leaving him alone, but my brain was still fuzzy from lack of sleep, so I stumbled through my mystery fiction course and hurried back home as soon as I could, stopping at the cell store for a new phone on my way. They were able to move the SIM card from the old phone to the new, so I didn't lose any numbers. I went right back to bed after taking Rochester out for a quick pee, and he joined me up there for a mid-afternoon nap.

When I awoke, I was too restless to stay in the house. It was sunny and crisp outside, and I thought maybe a good long walk would help clear my head. I got Rochester's leash, and he began jumping around the living room floor in a repeat of the previous night's performance. This time, though, I refused to chase him. I sat in a kitchen chair and waited for him to come to me.

"I guess you do want to go for a walk, too, don't you?" I asked when he did. However, as soon as I tried to clip the leash onto his collar, he ducked his head between his paws.

"Is this a game? I try and hook you up and you hide from me? You know, even if you can't see me, I can still see you." I was able to wrestle him enough to get his leash on, and I grabbed a jacket and a couple of plastic bags.

It took a lot longer than usual to walk up to The Chocolate Ear. Rochester believed it was his duty to sniff out every detail of every other animal who had passed by, and he was strong and stubborn when I tried to drag him along. It was a beautiful afternoon, the sun sitting high in a bright blue, cloudless sky, and though the air was chilly there was no breeze and it felt warm out in the sun.

Every bush, every tree trunk, every fire hydrant needed to be investigated. He peed over and over again, making me wonder how much liquid he had stored up in his bladder. "Can Rochester come in?" I asked when we reached the café, sticking my head in the door.

Gail, her grandmother Irene, and Edith were all sitting at a big round table, along with Gail's high school friend Ginny, a stay-at-home mom and part-time real estate agent who also helped out at the café as needed. I remembered that I had meant to call Edith and tell her about Caroline, make sure that her financial troubles had been figured out. But I'd just forgotten.

"Of course," Gail said, jumping up. "But what are you doing with him? I have some pumpkin biscuits in the back just for him."

I told them about Caroline when Gail returned a moment later with a biscuit, and Rochester settled on the floor. Since the *Courier-Times* hadn't identified Caroline the day before, they didn't know what had happened. "I read that a woman was killed by the nature preserve," Irene said. "But I had no idea it was Caroline. The poor, poor girl." She touched her iron-gray hair, which was always shellacked into a big globe around her head.

As we all fretted about Caroline's terrible fate, Gail made me a café mocha with a couple of pumps of raspberry syrup, and brought me a slice of lemon cake to go with it. She wore a man's white shirt with the sleeves rolled up over a pink tank top and jeans. "You need something sweet," she said. "You've been through a lot."

"I just can't believe it," Ginny said, shaking her head. "It's so tragic."

"You don't know the half of it," I said. "Last night, somebody broke into her townhouse. Rochester woke me up barking."

There was a collective gasp around the table, and I described the events of the previous evening. "You must be exhausted, dear," Edith said, reaching over to pat my hand. Her fingers were long and pale, twisted from arthritis, and her hand was cool to the touch.

"What a terrible thing," Ginny said. "Do you think it was someone who knew Caroline? It just seems so random. Any of us could be shot any time." She crossed her arms over her cream-colored sweater.

"And I always thought Stewart's Crossing was so safe," Gail said. She and Ginny had grown up in Levittown, a big suburb on the other side of the railroad tracks from Stewart's Crossing. Burglaries and even the occasional shooting were much more common over there.

"No place is safe," Irene said. "When it's your time, it's your time, and no doubt about it."

"I'm with Gail and Ginny," I said. "Especially after last night. It's spooky just to go outside after dark. If I didn't have to walk Rochester, I'd stay in the house as soon as the sun went down."

"That's what Caroline was doing, walking Rochester," Ginny said.

"Enough," Irene said. "Ginny, you should ask Rick if he knows Caroline's next-of-kin. Maybe you can get the listing on her townhouse."

"Grandma!" Gail said, in a scandalized tone.

"The world goes on," Irene said. "When you get to be my age you'll realize that. It's a terrible thing that poor girl is dead, but somebody's got to sell her house, and it might as well be Ginny."

We talked about Caroline, but none of us had any insight into who might have killed her or why someone had trashed her house. "Stewart's Crossing isn't the same place it was," Edith said, shaking her head. "Every week you read in the newspaper about a house broken into, a car stolen. Last week a boy I taught to play Chopin was stabbed at the junior high by a boy from another class."

"Rick told me that Caroline's murder was the first since the shooting at The Drunken Hessian," I said. "That didn't make me feel any better."

That was another sad story. Johnny Menotto, a guy who'd been a few years ahead of us at Pennsbury High, had come back from the first Gulf War with a lot of problems. He freaked out at loud noises and sudden movements, and imagined persecution all around him. He'd lost his job and his marriage— just like me—only he'd ended up hanging out at The Drunken Hessian, a bar slash tourist trap in the center of town. A plaque outside said that an inn of some kind had been on that spot since the Revolutionary War, and the décor hadn't much changed, except for the introduction of indoor plumbing. The sign depicted one of the Hessian soldiers whom Washington had surprised at Trenton on Christmas day, looking like he'd had quite a few too many.

It was the kind of dive that looked innocent on the outside, sucking in the clueless tourists with quaint charm and delivering flat beer and overcooked burgers served in plastic baskets shaped like Stewart's ferry boat. Johnny had gotten to be a pest, bugging the tourists for change and harassing them about Republican politics. The night bartender, a high school science teacher picking up extra cash because he and his wife had a baby on the way, had asked Johnny to leave a couple of times.

One night Johnny returned an hour after leaving, with a sawed-off shotgun, which he used to blow the poor bartender away. The tragedy had rocked Stewart's Crossing, and my father had relished the chance to tell me all the gory details.

"It's still a terrible world," Edith said. "It makes me glad I never had children."

"I feel just the opposite," Irene said placidly. "It's a terrible world, so I'm glad I had children and grandchildren who can do their part to make it better."

I didn't know how I felt. The door hadn't closed yet on my fatherhood possibilities, though I suspected my ex-wife had been right when she said I was too self-centered for fatherhood. Look at how much just taking care of Rochester had changed my life—and that was only for a few days.

The dog in question rolled over on the floor below me, resting his head on my foot. I chatted with the women for a while longer, and just before I left Gail gave me a half-dozen of the pumpkin biscuits in a plastic bag, all of them shaped like her signature ear. Then Rochester and I made our way back to River Bend—slowly, as usual.

In the newspaper the next morning, there was a brief follow-up article, which identified Caroline and said that the police were still following leads in her murder. There was an obituary, too; she was being shipped to upstate New York, where her parents were buried and her great-aunt lived, but there was going to be a memorial service at a church near her Center City office in two weeks.

All that day, when I tried to sit at the kitchen table to grade papers, Rochester draped himself over my feet. If I sat at the computer, he lay behind me and curled his legs around the chair so that I couldn't move. Throughout the weekend, when I came home after being away—even if I'd just run to the grocery for a single item—it was as if I'd abandoned him and then come back just as he was about to lose all hope.

Sometimes I felt like he was sucking up all the oxygen in the house. It was always all about him—feed him, walk him, pay attention to him. He was worse than Mary had ever been— at least she had her own career, her own clique of girlfriends who believed every mean thing she said about me and who sympathized with her in a way I couldn't seem to. All Rochester had was me.

On Sunday afternoon, after three days of calling at random times, I got hold of Rick Stemper again. "That dog has chewed up my cell phone, a pair of glasses, a stuffed bear, and a pair of socks," I said. "Find some place for him before he chews me out of all my belongings."

"Sorry, nobody seems to know what she wanted to do with him, and nobody I talked to wants him," he said. "You'll just have to take him to the pound."

"Did you find out who killed her yet?"

He sounded distracted, like he was listening to another conversation in the background. "We're still pursuing leads," he said. The background noise disappeared, and Rick was there again. "Hey, would you do me a favor?"

"What?"

"Caroline's mailbox key is on her kitchen table. Could you pick up the mail for the next few days? Just until the great aunt can get her act together?"

"Sure."

I lost him again, I could tell. "Great. Listen, I'm following another case right now, but I will let you know if anything new comes up."

I thanked him and hung up the phone. "I guess we'll never know what happened to your mom," I said to Rochester, who was lying at my feet. "But now, what do I do with you?"

He looked up at me with his brown doggy eyes. His mouth was open and his tongue hung out, and it looked about as close to a smile as a dog can get. Maybe I'm reading into it, but it looked like he was asking if he could stay with me.

I remembered conversations I'd had with the Wicked Witch of the Valley. We'd talked, off and on, about getting a dog, but she worried she'd get stuck doing all the work. "You're just not a caretaker, Steve," she'd said.

"I can take care of you," I said, leaning down to scratch behind Rochester's ears. "Don't you think so, boy?"

In answer, he rolled over onto his back so I could rub his stomach. I got down on the floor next to him. "I know I'm not as self-centered as Mary thought. I can take care of a dog." He squirmed under my touch, and his head lolled to the side, his long tongue rolling out. "I can take care of you. What do you say, boy? You want to stay with me?"

Rochester rolled around to his feet and started to climb on me, licking my face. "I guess that's a yes," I said, laughing.

Romeo

I'd forgotten how much snow fell in Eastern Pennsylvania during the winter, and it was disorienting to navigate familiar roads when they were covered in white. Landmarks disappeared, and cars without snow tires skidded on the ice. That weekend, the snowfall was so heavy that Eastern almost closed down, only deciding to open after Sunday was sunny.

Driving to Eastern on Monday morning, River Road was still dangerous, and I narrowly saved myself from a skid on a patch of black ice. It was with great relief that I pulled into the newly-plowed parking lot, where a group of two dozen students, bundled in down vests and colorful knit caps, waved signs which read "Olive Us Love Olives" and "Bring Back the Olives."

The week before, the administration had announced that in a cost-cutting measure, olives would no longer be available on the salad bar in the dining hall. The saving to the college was estimated at $100,000 a year.

I didn't even eat olives when I was in college, and I marveled that these students were giving up sleep time or study time, cutting classes or jobs, to march around in the parking lot protesting about olives. As I got out of my car, a campus police patrol car pulled up and two cops got out, wielding polyethylene shields and metal batons, as if they were breaking up a demonstration in Watts or South Central rather than Leighville, PA. One of them spoke into a microphone, though the words were garbled and unintelligible.

The group's chant changed to "Down with Pigs," and for a minute I thought it had morphed into some kind of anti-bacon demonstration. Then I realized somebody was channeling the SDS, circa 1969. Since that was even before my time, I hurried on toward Blair Hall, as the two campus cops began banging their batons against their shields, and I heard sirens approaching.

I had been back at Eastern three months by then, but it still seemed like an alien world. I'd be walking along, talking to a student, and look up to realize I had no idea where I was. The bookstore had moved, the student union expanded beyond recognition. The concrete sidewalks were often icy, and the grassy shortcuts full of unsuspecting dips.

In Dog We Trust

I walked to my freshman comp class, which meets in a second-floor room in Blair Hall. Tall, gothic-arched windows along one side let in the light and give students the chance to look outside in case I'm boring them. Fluorescent lights hang on pendants around the room, and a rich wooden wainscoting runs around the perimeter of the room, a legacy of our long history of deep-pocket alumni. The chairs, though, are a relic of the seventies, with a slanted arm attached to one side just at the right angle to dump an unsuspecting student's laptop into his lap.

From outside the classroom, I could hear raised voices, though I couldn't tell what the arguing was about, and as soon as I opened the door the voices stopped. Tension hung in the air, until Menno Zook raised his hand and said, "Are we allowed to bring animals to class?"

Menno had a short beard, and often wore overalls and white t-shirts. Give him a straw hat and a horse and buggy, and he'd be at home in the Amish country.

"He's not an animal, he's a dog," Tasheba Lewis said. Since I wasn't there to teach biology, I didn't think it necessary to correct her.

Tasheba is one of my sharper students, which is like saying there were worse dictators in history than Nero or Attila—weak praise, at best. She has skin the color of cinnamon and straight brown hair, and carries herself with an air of privilege. "This is Romeo," she said, lifting him out of a Burberry traveling bag on the chair next to her.

"One of the great lovers in literature," I said. I decided not to address Menno's question, but instead to shift our emphasis back to something close to English composition. "Romeo, Romeo, wherefore art thou Romeo?" I turned and wrote that phrase on the blackboard. "Notice that there's no comma after the word thou," I said, when I turned back to the class. Romeo the dog sat next to Tasheba, who wore a matching Burberry tennis visor, as if she was planning to head from English class to her next match. Like most of my students, she paid more attention to her attire and her social life than to her class work. "Anybody know why?"

No one seemed to know why there was no comma. "Let me repeat it for you," I said, and I did. "The key is in the word wherefore." I put the chalk down and brushed the dust off my hands. "In Shakespeare's time that word meant 'why.' So Juliet's asking 'Why are you Romeo?' not 'Yo, Romeo, where are you?'"

The class laughed. Take a forty-something white-bread English professor, and drop in a word or two of urban slang. It's a sure laugh-getter, and sometimes it wakes them up.

"Can someone tell me the basic plot of *Romeo and Juliet*?"

Open-ended questions like that are always iffy. Is anyone awake enough to consider it? Did any of them study Shakespeare at the expensive private schools that are Eastern's biggest feeders? Did they recognize the undercurrents of violence that ran through Shakespeare's works were the same ones that passed through our lives—parking lot protests, court cases, jail time and death?

I looked around the room, which had filled up in the last few minutes. By then, I knew all the students by name, though the two slim girls with matching long dark hair who sat next to each other tripped me up. One was Dianne and one was Dionne, and I just marked them both present if at least one was there.

The lovebirds in the back row were Billy Rubin, who wanted to be a doctor, and his girlfriend, Anna Rexick, who wanted to be a nurse, specializing in eating disorders. She was painfully skinny, as if she lived off bird seed and water.

There were three Jeremys, two Melissas, two Jennifers, and two Jakes. Almost all of them looked like generic, interchangeable college students, distinguished only by piercings and hairstyles.

Jeremy Eisenberg raised his hand. "Romeo loves Juliet but their families don't get along so eventually they kill themselves," he suggested. He had a shaggy mop of brown hair, shorn close to the scalp on both sides, a torn Butthole Surfers t-shirt, a studded dog collar around his neck and many earrings, as well as an eyebrow ring and a tongue stud.

"Close enough," I said. "So Romeo has gained this reputation as a great lover." I walked over toward Tasheba, whom I always imagine was named after the Japanese electronics manufacturer. She's the kind of young woman who always has a brand name plastered across her body, whether it's Juicy Couture, Rocawear, or whatever's hottest at the moment. "Tell me, has Romeo been neutered?"

"Uh-huh."

"Ah, irony! The great lover can't consummate his love!" The class laughed. "But who can define irony for me?"

Melissa Macaretti disapproves of any antics in the classroom. She's a bulky young woman with mousy brown hair, wearing kilts and Fair Isle sweaters—the kind with the embroidered yoke that was popular back when I was a student—and she's often frowning. "The use of words to express something different from and often opposite to their literal meaning," she said, and I suspected she had some kind of electronic dictionary stuck away in her purse. But then, she always spoke that way.

"Exactly. So Romeo's name is ironic. He's a lover who can't love. Let's think about the readings in our description unit. Where else have we seen irony?"

There was a general restlessness, as students stared down at their desks, holding their bodies rigid, as if the slightest movement might cause me to call on them. At times like that I felt like my class was full of wild creatures, and at the slightest provocation they could turn on me. Joaquin and Wakeem, athletes who lurked in the back row, always wore T-shirts with aggressive sayings on them, things like "Fuck Authority," and other phrases that were probably the titles of hip-hop songs. Though I was only forty-two, they made me feel as old and frail as a 90-year-old with a walker.

We made it through the rest of the class, though I can't say for sure what else we covered. Part of my brain was still focused on the student demonstration, and another part was obsessing about Caroline Kelly.

Just as I was gathering my papers, Menno raised his hand again, and without waiting for me to call on him, said, "Professor, you never answered my question. Are we allowed to bring animals to class?"

Everyone stopped their hurried packing to look up at me. "I don't know what the college's policy is, but as long as Romeo is quiet, it's OK with me." I waited a beat, then said, "But I'm not grading his papers."

Everyone except Menno laughed, and they all scurried out, like shaggy, pierced rats leaving a sinking classroom. On my way up to the third floor, I overheard a student in the hallway say, in a plaintive voice, "I can't believe he smoked crack. We made a new year's resolution."

The faculty lounge is a sunny room on the top floor of Blair Hall, lit by metal-framed skylights. The department secretary, Candice ("Don't call me Candy") Kane, a Wiccan whose love for the natural world exceeds any tiny bit of affection she might harbor for humans, has a green thumb, and she tends a series of spider plants in hanging baskets. Cabinets full of coffee filters and paper plates hang over a sink, with an adjacent refrigerator. A half-dozen round tables, with straight-backed wooden chairs, complete the room.

I joined Jackie Devere at the cappuccino machine and began preparing myself a café mocha. "I had a new student in my freshman comp class this morning," I said.

"Three months into the term?" she asked. "Let me guess. He had some kind of elaborate excuse why he hasn't come to class. His dog ate his computer?"

"Close. The new student is a dog."

She looked at me. "Now, Steve. I know that you are not trying to tell me that you have some butt-ugly girl student in your class. Because if you are, butt-ugly is a much better term than dog."

"No, a real dog," I said. "In a Burberry carrying case. He even has a matching plaid bow in his hair. I'm not sure what breed he is; one of those little fluffy things."

"Are you sure it's a boy dog?"

I nodded as I pulled the hot water for my tea out of the microwave. "Yup. His name is Romeo." I paused. "And he expressed his opinion of the class with a lifted leg on the way out."

Jackie grew up on the mean streets of Newark before escaping to Rutgers and the world of English literature. At twenty-nine, she's petite and slim-hipped, a mix of street-smart woman and super-educated college professor. If not for her brain, you might even mistake her for a college senior.

"He'll probably end up being one of your smarter students," she said. Jackie was quite a coup for Eastern; our department chair, Lucas Roosevelt, had been plagued by the lack of diversity in his faculty, and no matter how hard he'd tried, it was tough to convince smart, well-educated African-American or Hispanic faculty to come to the Pennsylvania countryside for a second-tier college.

Jackie's family still lived somewhere around Newark, and she thought Eastern was close enough but not too close. She also said she preferred Eastern's emphasis on teaching over research, but I'm sure Lucas opened the department's wallet, too.

We retired to her office once our beverages were complete, a room that might have been considered spacious had it not been lined with overflowing bookshelves, the floor a minefield of piled books. Two gothic-arched windows, similar to the ones in my classroom, framed one wall of Jackie's office, with the original leaded panes. They were poorly sealed, and let a stream of cold air float into the office, which Jackie counteracted with a very illegal space heater under her desk.

I knocked into one of the piles as I followed her in, and a couple of books toppled to the ground. "Occupational hazard of teaching six courses a term," she said. "You don't get much time to organize."

The standard course load for a full-time professor like Jackie was four courses, though Jackie had told me she'd taken on the extra load for the cash.

As an adjunct, I could only teach three courses, or the IRS would think of me as a real employee instead of an independent contractor and demand that the college give me pesky little benefits like life and health insurance, a department secretary to do my photocopying, and lunch on Eastern once a semester. That was a shame; adjunct pay barely covered my mortgage and car payment. If I had a full-time teaching gig, Santiago Santos would stop bugging me about my future plans. But then, if I didn't have a felony conviction, I wouldn't have Santiago around at all. So all in all, my problems were more my fault than Eastern's.

I moved a torn jiffy bag to the trash, spilling nasty gray fluff as I did, and sat across from Jackie. In the background I saw a photo in which she cuddled with her black dog, a mix of German Shepherd and woolly mammoth.

"I'm so glad you've adopted a dog," Jackie said. "Living by yourself is not healthy."

"I decided yesterday that he can stay," I said. "We'll see how it works out. Dogs are so needy. Walk me, feed me, pet me. The great thing about being divorced is that you don't have to cater to anyone else. 'No, honey, that dress doesn't make you look fat. No, honey, I don't mind driving two hours, while you nap in the front seat, so that you can argue with your mother in person.'"

"Cranky, party of one," she said. "Your table is now ready. Seriously, you get selfish living by yourself. It's good to put yourself out there for another creature. Didn't you ever have a pet?"

"Mary Queen of Snots had a cat," I said. "A fluffy Persian that hated me. For ten years that cat hissed at me every time I walked past. What a pity she died just a few months before Mary and I divorced."

"I thought your ex was Jewish. Her name was Mary?"

"Her Hebrew name is Miriam, which means bitter. Need I say more?" I looked at my watch. "Back to the grind," I said. "I have tech writing in five minutes."

"I have the next period free," Jackie said, "If you can call having a stack of essays from African American Lit to grade 'free.'"

"Free at last, free at last," I said. "Thank god almighty, we are free at last."

"Go to class," she said, and waved me out of her office. The nasty gray fluff clung to my pants as I walked away.

Sniffing and Searching

When I sat down to work on Tuesday morning, Rochester came into the office, sniffed around, and then settled at my feet. But every half hour or so, he'd wake up, sit up on his hind legs, and try to stick his face onto the keyboard.

"Rochester, this is getting old," I said, pushing him away with my knee after about the fourth time. "Is there something on the Internet you want?"

I looked at the page on my screen. I'd been at Google, searching for some information for a client, and a light bulb went off over my head. Why didn't I Google Caroline? Maybe there was a clue online that would lead Rick to her killer.

At the time, I didn't even think about Santiago Santos, or wonder if he'd care what I was doing. I put "Caroline Kelly" in quotation marks, so that Google would search for it as a phrase, and brought up over 31,000 hits. Even adding extra key words, such as "Quaker State Bank" and "accountant," didn't get me much in the way of results.

None of the other commercial engines were much help either—Yahoo, MSN, Netscape, Metacrawler—there was just too much out there. I searched by her phone number, her corporate title, even with "golden retriever" as an additional search term. I either got too much, or nothing.

You search for my name online, and even though there are other Steve Levitans out there, you can find me—ghostly reminders of website work I had done in the past, for my job, my legitimate clients. But Caroline Kelly? Nothing.

Rochester woke up to check on my progress, stretching his long legs first and yawning, then sticking his big golden head up by the computer keyboard. "Nothing yet, boy," I said. "But I'm not done, not by a long shot."

The thrill of the search was back. This was what I had loved to do back in Silicon Valley. When Mary and I first moved to California, I was unable to find a job. I adjuncted for a while, then took a temporary gig providing technical support for a software company called Mastodon Systems. After a year, I'd been offered a full-time job doing technical writing. Every time they developed a new program for data entry or job tracking, I wrote the manual. I wrote all their HR policies, and created a book with procedures and responsibilities for each position at the company.

In addition to my writing, I had a specialty in information. I built (or had built for me) tools that I could use to search our massive databases for documents, customer orders, even employee information. I found, with a little tweaking, that these tools could be used not just in-house, but on the big, broad Internet as well.

The big furry monster rolled over, popping the cord that connected my in-home network. "Rochester!" I said. I nudged him with my foot and he rolled away. When I plugged the cord back in, I went through the process of initializing the network, which included viewing all possible connections. Since the townhouses at River Bend share common walls, I can often see my neighbors' networks, and connect to them if I want, as long as they're not password-protected.

While I waited I remembered Santiago Santos, and started to worry about what he would say when he viewed my audit trail. I was supposed to be working on a business plan, not playing amateur sleuth. I remembered seeing Caroline's laptop in her home office. If I used her laptop, and another neighbor's network, there was no way anything could be traced to me.

Looking back now, I see that was the first step in a long process. I knew I was violating my parole, and I knew the consequences could land me in jail. But I had to know what happened to Caroline. For me, and for Rochester.

My problems had begun at Mastodon. If one of our competitors had some interesting information about new products, and they didn't take care to secure it—well, then that was almost the same as public record, wasn't it? I learned how to use back doors into protected sites, and I learned how to sniff out unprotected ports on home computers that I could use to launch my searches.

I began to make some money on the side doing freelance work, finding information. Mary and I had been trying to have a baby, and it was around that time that she discovered she was pregnant. I took on a few questionable jobs to build up our savings. And then, two months later, Mary miscarried.

I tried everything I could think of to make her feel better. When I told her we could try again, she began to sob. When I asked her to consider our faith, that perhaps God had a plan for us, she hit me. The only thing that made her feel better was retail therapy.

We both made good livings, and we had always maintained separate bank accounts and credit cards, with a joint account for household bills. So I didn't realize how much money Mary had been spending until about six months later, when I accidentally opened one of her credit card bills, thinking it was mine.

Between massages, manicures, expensive shoes, designer clothes, and a pocketbook named after a British vocalist, she'd rung up the debt of a small country. I confronted her that night, and after days of arguing we worked out a plan. She agreed to speak to a counselor, and I helped pay off her debt.

Things got better for a while, and then Mary got pregnant again. She did everything the doctor suggested, including quitting her job to stay at home, without stress. It didn't work, though; she miscarried a second time.

This meltdown was worse than the first. Mary was convinced that she could never have children, and she was angry that she'd quit her job only to end up childless. I was scared she was going for another spending spree, so I hacked into the three major credit bureaus and put a flag on her account, trying to keep her from getting any new credit cards.

I thought it was a pretty harmless little hack. I wasn't trying to steal anything, after all, just keep my wife from dragging us down into debt again.

The judge saw it differently, especially when all three credit bureaus filed briefs against me.

Caroline's laptop was buried under a pile of papers in her office. Bringing it back to my house, I plugged it in and connected to one of my neighbors' networks.

My first target was Quaker State Bank. A little investigation showed me just how I could slip past their ineffective security—though before I did anything, I checked that I wasn't being lured into a "honey pot," a system set up to trap hackers who are attracted to a site. We'd had one of those at Mastodon.

It appeared to be part of our network, a gateway that would let you into our customer and employee databases, but instead captured the IP address and other data from any computer that tried to access it. We belonged to a consortium of software companies, and we shared those IP addresses and forwarded them to the police for further investigation.

I copied some files to Caroline's computer from a set of disks that Santiago Santos would not have approved of, and then set my sniffers to work finding an open port on an unsuspecting user's computer that I could use to launch my surveillance of the bank. I ground some beans and brewed myself a cup of coffee while I waited.

Rochester followed me downstairs, guarding the entrance to the kitchen for me. By the time my coffee was ready, I had to step over him to get to the stairs—and he scrambled up and followed me. When I got upstairs, I saw the sniffers had discovered a couple of open ports I could use.

When you go online, you should be protected. There are a lot of guys like me out there in the world.

I took a sip of coffee, burned my tongue, and sat down at Caroline's laptop. A half hour later, I was reviewing QSB's employee records—only for Caroline Kelly, though. I discovered she made $80,000 a year, that she had eight vacation days remaining in the calendar year, and that she had left a life insurance policy in the amount of double her salary to her great-aunt, who lived in Utica, New York.

Her job title was director of corporate accounting, and she'd been promoted three months previously. I followed a hyperlink to a description of her job, which was about as interesting as watching Rochester shed hair all over my sofa. I clicked another hyperlink from there, and took another sip of my cooling coffee.

That new link was much more interesting. It seemed that Caroline's boss had been fired and she had been named to replace him. There was mention of some corporate impropriety—wisely, not spelled out in the document—and a note that the fired employee, whose name was Eric Hemminger, was going to sue the bank.

I opened another window and Googled Eric Hemminger. I got a couple of hits, including one that indicated he had filed a lawsuit in Pennsylvania Commonwealth Court for unfair termination.

I'm not good enough—or dumb enough—to try and hack into any government database. I did some searching through legal means, including the Lexis/Nexis database I have access to through Eastern, but couldn't find anything more about Hemminger's suit.

What if his anger toward Caroline had gone beyond legal means? I didn't know why he'd been fired or if he'd held a grudge. But I bet whoever had taken over Caroline's job would know. I pulled up the bank's website and searched for employees. Caroline's name was still listed.

I picked up my cell and dialed her office number. The phone rang for a while, and then a voice mail system picked up. A woman with a soft Hispanic accent said, "Evelina Curcio," and then the system's mechanical voice continued "is not available now. At the sound of the tone, please leave a message."

I hung up. Back at the bank's website I found that Evelina Curcio was an assistant vice president – the most common, and most meaningless, title at a bank. I wrote her name down and decided to think about how to approach her.

I could tell from her name and accent that she was Hispanic. There had been a report on the news a few weeks before that blacks and Hispanics were uncomfortable talking to the police—even just as witnesses. They were less likely to report crimes committed against them, and they were less apt to provide information than white, non-Hispanics were.

I could tell Rick what I had found—but would Evelina Curcio talk to him? Maybe not. But I could go to the memorial service for Caroline the following week, and strike up a conversation with Evelina. Who knew what she might know?

When I gave up on the bank, I found a website for military brats, a place where you could type in your father's posts and then search for kids you might have known whose parents were posted at the same time and place.

Their information was in an SQL database; I didn't even need to hack to get into it. Caroline had signed up, using "Rochester" as her password, and I was able to generate a complete list of the military bases where her father had served, along with the names of the international schools she had attended in Korea and Germany, as well as the public schools in the Florida panhandle and in North Dakota.

"Your mom got around," I said to Rochester, and he came over to me and nuzzled his head against my knees.

I wasn't sure why I was taking the time and the risk to look into Caroline's life and death. On the one hand, I felt bad that I hadn't gotten to know her better while she was alive. She was my neighbor, and I'd found her attractive. I suppose you might have called her a friend, or at least an acquaintance. Maybe getting to know more about her now would help me feel better about her death.

I needed to focus on my business plan. But the lure of information was so seductive that I kept on surfing and hacking long after I should have stopped. I justified it by saying that I might find something important I could give to Rick.

When I looked at the clock, it was almost time to leave for class. Rochester refused to get into the crate, and I worried about leaving him alone in the house. So I decided to take him to Eastern with me. If Tasheba could bring Romeo to class, what was to prevent me from bringing Rochester?

First, though, I had to convince him to get into the front seat of the BMW. He preferred sitting on the front floor, resting his head on the seat. As I drove I reached over and petted him, and tried to keep the drool from staining my cloth upholstery.

I'd just put him on the leash in the faculty parking lot when I saw Jackie Devere. "Is this the dog?" she asked, leaning down to pet him. Rochester sat on his haunches and submitted to having his neck rubbed.

"Yeah, I thought I'd bring him to class with me today."

"You can't do that, Steve. Haven't you noticed the signs?"

She pointed to one a few feet away from us, at the entrance to the lot. "No animals permitted on the Eastern campus," it read.

I'd never noticed it, because it had never mattered before. "What am I going to do?" I asked. "I have to teach in ten minutes."

"I'll take him up to my office," she said. "You can pick him up when your class is over."

"Thanks." We walked together to Blair Hall, Rochester stopping to sniff and pee. "I never thought about it," I said. "I told you that girl brought her dog to freshman comp."

"There's a difference between a little dog you can stick in a purse and a big moose," she said. "I'd never bring Samson here."

All the way to Blair Hall, I kept looking around for college security, expecting them to come roaring up in a little golf cart and insist that Rochester leave the campus. We made it without incident, though when I handed his leash to Jackie he gave me a look that spoke volumes about abandonment.

I hurried through my presentation on resumes and cover letters and galloped up the stairs to Jackie's office on the third floor. I needn't have worried; Rochester was sprawled between piles of books.

"As long as you're up here, you should take him to the dog park," Jackie said.

"Where's that?"

"Down by the river at the foot of the hill. Just below Birthday House."

"You want to do that, Rochester?" I asked. "You want to go to the dog park?"

He tried to do one of his crazy kangaroo jumps, which was just about impossible in Jackie's crowded office. He knocked over a pile of papers, and when I picked it up I saw one by Menno Zook on the top. "You have Menno, too?" I asked.

"Last term," she said. She reached down to rub Rochester's neck as I hooked his leash. I should have gone right home and worked on my business plan, but I felt like playing a little hooky. If my students could throw together their papers at the last minute, I could delay my business plan for a few more days.

Rather than walk through campus to Birthday Hall, I scrambled Rochester back into the Beemer and drove down to the river.

Tasheba Lewis was lounging just inside the dog park fence watching Romeo sniff the butt of a Doberman Pinscher, who seemed to be enjoying the experience. "Hi, Mr. Levitan," she said as we walked in.

Rochester began trying to hump poor little Romeo. I tugged on his leash and pulled him off. "Rochester! Sit!"

"Oh, I know Rochester," she said. "I thought he belonged to a lady."

"My next-door neighbor," I said. "Did you know her?"

Tasheba picked Romeo up on her lap and sat down on an ornately-scrolled wrought-iron bench. Rochester put his head right in her lap to continue sniffing Romeo's private parts.

"Just here at the park," Tasheba said. "She liked to talk

about skin care."

"Skin care?"

"I use Clinique but she used Kiehl's," she said. "We always compared notes."

I wished Tasheba had paid as much attention to her notes for freshman comp. "You can let him off his leash, you know," she said. "He can't get away."

"But what if he goes crazy on some little dog?" I asked.

"The little dogs can take care of themselves," she said, as Romeo growled at Rochester, tired of the inquisition.

I unhooked Rochester's leash, and he went bounding away from me, toward a pair of whippets. I sat down next to Tasheba and watched Rochester. If only Caroline had said something useful to someone—Tasheba, some other dog owner, Gail at The Chocolate Ear—even me. Then I'd have some place to look for who killed her.

Tasheba and Romeo left, and after a long time spent running around the dog park, sniffing and pawing and trying to mount every other dog, Rochester's battery wore down and he came back to sprawl at my feet.

"Do you know anything about what happened to your mom?" I asked, reaching down to rub behind his ears. "I wish you could tell me if you did."

I thought he was tired out, and I considered leaving him off the leash for the walk back to my car—but I was glad I didn't. Just after we left the dog park I saw three of my freshman comp students—Menno Zook, Melissa Macaretti, and Jeremy Eisenberg, walking together on their way somewhere. I hoped they were going to the library, but more likely they were off to throw Frisbees or buy drugs or burn textbooks on the lawn of Blair Hall.

"Hey, Professor," Melissa said. She wasn't wearing her usual uniform of Fair Isle sweater and plaid kilt; instead she wore black pants and a white blouse under an open parka. I saw the edge of a tattoo peeking out just above her collar.

Menno and Jeremy were dressed like typical college males—jeans that rode down around their hips, baggy t-shirts advertising some hip-hop artist, hooded sweatshirts artfully left open. The only things that distinguished them were Menno's Biblical beard and Jeremy's multiple piercings. He was wearing matching earrings, which looked like pencils stuck through his earlobes rather than behind his ears. They both echoed Melissa's greeting, though with somewhat less enthusiasm.

Rochester went nuts, barking and jumping and straining at his leash. "Sorry," I said. "He's not usually like this."

Menno gave me one of the looks he reserved for Tasheba and Romeo. "He's a pretty dog," Melissa said tentatively.

"Pretty badly behaved at the moment," I said, wrestling him away from them. "Have a nice afternoon," I said over my shoulder, as I dragged Rochester down the lawn toward my car. He didn't settle down until we'd reached the parking lot.

"What's up with you, psycho dog?" I asked. "You get overheated running around out there in the dog park?"

His only response was to climb back into the front well of the Beemer.

Our Lady of Sorrows

Romeo was back with Tasheba on Wednesday, sitting in his Burberry bag, though at some point he'd lost his matching bow. It didn't go with his image. "In honor of Romeo's return, let's talk about doggerel," I said, after the class had settled down. I pulled out our text and found the definition in the index. "Doggerel is defined as 'crudely or irregularly fashioned verse, often of a humorous or burlesque nature.'" I paged forward in the book as I said, "Let's see if we can find some examples."

We read through some Ogden Nash, and Menno Zook perked up when he heard about purple cows. "There's no such thing as a purple cow," he said. It was clear he thought the rest of the class believed that there were, the way they thought milk came from a refrigerated cabinet at the grocery store, not the udders of a big sloppy farm animal. And perhaps some of the city-bred students, like the three Jeremys, Dianne and Dionne, thought so.

"That's right, Menno," I said. "That's where the humorous part comes in." In his denim overalls and plain white shirt, Menno didn't look like he had much of a sense of humor, but I persevered. All he needed was one of those straw hats to look like an Amish farmer. Though Lancaster, a big Amish stronghold, is just a couple of hours west of us, I somehow doubted Eastern did much recruiting there.

"Here's another example, again in honor of Romeo," I said. I turned to the board and wrote two lines there.

Turning back to the class, I said, "Alexander Pope wrote this: 'I am his majesty's dog at Kew; pray tell me sir, whose dog are you?' What can we say about this poem?"

Either Dianne or Dionne said, "It's a couplet."

"That's true. Remember, we said that a two-line stanza is called a couplet. This is a particular type of couplet—an epigram. Two lines that rhyme, and make a clever or humorous statement." I looked around. "Anything else?"

Melissa Macaretti said, "The dog is a metaphor, isn't it?" She was as rigorous in her clothing as Menno, back in her standard uniform of kilt and sweater. Her dun-colored hair hung around her head in shapeless waves, tamed by a white headband.

"Absolutely," I said. "Pope is saying that anyone who can be jerked around by a boss – on a leash, if you will—is a dog, metaphorically speaking." I guessed that made me Santiago Santos's dog, I thought with a jolt, remembering my still unfinished business plan.

"Or a student," Jeremy Eisenberg said, half under his breath, and we shifted into a discussion of simile and metaphor, and the class sped by—at least for me. I can't speak for the students.

The next day I met with the mystery fiction class, which I referred to as my "grocery list." The students included Beri, Honey, Felae, Candy, Dezhanne, and Cinnamon; I told Jackie I got hungry just calling roll.

We were reading a Raymond Chandler story at the time, and we talked a lot about the hard-boiled tone. "He's just so matter-of-fact about people dying," Beri complained. She was a sunny blonde who wore skirts so short they just covered her butt. "I mean, I know people who have died, and I've been bummed out."

"But Chandler doesn't know these people," Dezhanne said. She wore a T-shirt which read, "Change is inevitable, except from vending machines," and I had managed so far in the semester to avoid asking her if she knew she had been named after a mustard. "It's different when someone you know dies."

"And it's different how they die," Felae said. He was from Moldova or Romania or some other gloomy Eastern European place that had been immortalized as a model or street name in River Bend. It had been built when the Soviet bloc was breaking up, so each model was named for a country and each street for a city. My two-bedroom townhouse, with an attached garage, was the Latvia. Caroline's, which had no garage, was the Estonia. I knew there were models for Serbia, Lithuania, and Croatia. The largest was the Montenegro, which I'd heard one of my neighbors call the Mount Negro.

I lived on Sarajevo Court, which ran into Minsk Lane. I thought it was funny that my grandparents and great-grandparents had struggled to escape the real Minsk, only to have me end up driving past street signs that would have read better in the Cyrillic alphabet. It was that old demon, irony, again—like the year I spent sharing a tenement apartment on New York's Lower East Side with my graduate school friend Tor, paying a thousand dollars a month. I discovered, when my parents came for a visit, that my father's family had lived down the block for a few years upon their arrival in the New World. "At least you have a toilet inside," he'd said at the time.

Felae had a mordant view of the murder mystery. "It's one thing to have your grandmother die of a heart attack, and another to have her throat sliced." He was a husky, dark-haired guy, like a Russian spy in some BBC Cold War drama, while the rest of the class would be innocent bystanders killed during a terrorist attack.

Beri, Honey and Dezhanne made groaning noises, and I tried to divert the conversation back to discussing the story's literary merit. Driving to Center City Philadelphia later, though, I kept thinking about what the students had said. If Caroline Kelly had been felled by a massive heart attack, a stroke, even a cancerous tumor, would I have felt as I did?

I had to put aside those thoughts, though, when I got into the city, stuck for blocks behind a family of born-again Christians from Massachusetts driving a Volvo wagon filled with herb tea. I resisted the urge to slam into their bumper to see if Jesus would protect them from fender-benders. I had a feeling he wouldn't.

Our Lady of Perpetual Sorrow was a small, somber building, built of gray stone, with a stained glass window of the Virgin Mary facing the street. I arrived at the church, a block off Rittenhouse Square, just before Caroline's memorial service began. About a dozen people were seated up front, and I slipped into a pew by myself. A middle-aged priest in a black cassock read a few prayers, and then a couple of Caroline's co-workers walked up to the pulpit to speak about her.

The last one was Evelina Curcio, who said that Caroline had been her mentor. "As you all know, when Caroline came to Quaker State Bank I was her secretary," Evelina said. "I was having a tough time finishing up the last courses for my associate's degree, and Caroline was very good to me. So many nights she stayed late to help me with my homework, and she kept telling me, 'You can do it, Evelina. You can do it.'"

Her voice broke, and it took her a moment to regain her composure. She was a stout woman in her late thirties, Caroline's age, with frizzy brown hair. She wore a neat dark suit and sensible black shoes, and spoke with the same gentle accent I'd heard on the voice mail system.

"It's thanks to her that I got my promotion out of the secretarial pool. And as you may already know, I'm graduating with my associate's in May, and I'm going to start on my bachelor's at Temple in the fall." There was some light applause in the audience. "And it's all thanks to Caroline. I know that God has made her one of his special angels."

The priest returned to the pulpit for a few final prayers, and then invited everyone to share some refreshments, sponsored by the bank, in the social hall.

As I was getting up to follow the others out of the sanctuary, I spotted Rick Stemper behind me, and I lagged back to talk to him.

"What brings you down here?" he asked.

"I could ask you the same thing."

"It's my job," he said. "What about you?"

I told him about what I'd learned about Caroline's predecessor, and this time he didn't ask how I'd found out. We walked down a musty hallway, and he said, "I spoke to Evelina Curcio a couple of days ago and she didn't say anything about a previous boss."

"That's why I think she might talk to me," I said. "Nothing personal, Rick, but you're a cop."

"You noticed."

"Let me give it a try, all right?"

He shrugged, but after pulling a bottle of cold water from a tray I walked over to Evelina Curcio and introduced myself. "Your remarks were very moving," I said.

"Thank you. Even though Caroline was my boss, I thought of her as my friend."

"I wish I'd known her better," I said. We talked for a few minutes, and I told her that I had adopted Rochester.

"Oh, Caroline would be so happy," she said. "She loved that dog."

"He's very lovable." I paused. "I just wish I knew more about what could have happened to her," I said. "It haunts me, you know? Seeing her like that, and then living next door to her house, and having her dog—she's always on my mind."

I looked at Evelina. "Do you have any idea who wanted to hurt her?"

She shook her head. "She didn't tell me much about her

background," she said. "Just that she'd moved around a lot. And she was still trying to get settled here, and maybe to find herself a guy."

"What about at work?" I asked. "I understood there was some bad blood about her promotion."

She squirmed a bit, and cast a guilty look around us to see who might be listening. The rest of the bank's employees were talking together in a group, though, and so Evelina lowered her voice and said, "Mr. Hemminger—Caroline's boss. He was the manager of financial planning and analysis, and her title was senior analyst."

"What does that mean?"

"Every company has financial assets," she said. "Cash, securities, real property, and so on. Caroline would study interest rates and make decisions about how to invest the bank's money. Sometimes she would look at decisions Mr. Hemminger made and she wouldn't agree with them. But he wouldn't listen to her."

She looked around again, just to make sure no one was overhearing us. "She got suspicious and started looking into his decisions. She asked me to help her."

"It's obvious she trusted you."

She smiled weakly. "We found what Caroline thought was a suspicious pattern. Mr. Hemminger had been buying corporate bonds from a real estate development company, but they weren't the right grade."

"Grade?" I asked.

"We only bought double-A bonds or better. These were BBB—it just means they weren't as safe as double-A. There was more chance that this real estate company would default on paying the bonds and then the bank would be stuck."

I nodded. "OK. I get it."

"Caroline did some searching, and she discovered that the company was run by Mr. Hemminger's brother-in-law, and they were in some financial trouble. She thought it was unethical for him to be investing in those bonds, and she reported him to the president of the bank."

We were getting somewhere. "I'll bet he didn't like that."

She shook her head. "No, he didn't. He was suspended, and as the security guards were escorting him past Caroline's office he stopped to yell at her."

"You were there?"

She nodded. "He told her that she would be sorry she messed with him." She shivered with the memory.

"Wow. That must have upset her."

"It did. Afterward, she was crying in her office. I had to sit with her and keep telling her that she did the right thing."

"You were a good friend to her."

She smiled. "I owed her so much."

"What happened?" I asked. "To this guy Hemminger?"

"He filed a lawsuit against the bank. The lawyers said Caroline was going to have to testify."

Rick was going to love this, I thought. Here was a motive wrapped up with a red ribbon. "I'll bet that scared her," I said. "Especially after he threatened her."

One of Evelina's coworkers, a man in a navy suit with a red tie, came over to say something to her, and I shook her hand and walked away. The rest of the employees were walking out together, and I ended up leaving with Rick Stemper.

"You drive in or take the train?" he asked.

"Drove. You?"

"Train. You can give me a ride back to the Yardley station."

In the car, creeping up I-95 at rush hour in the commuter lane, I told him what Evelina Curcio had told me. "I'll check it out," he said.

"He could have been the one who shot her."

"Don't go all Miss Marple on me, Steve. I said I'll check it out."

"But I did pretty good, didn't I?" I asked. "I got all that information when you got nothing."

"Information that's probably going to be irrelevant." He looked over at me. "What? You want a gold star for your forehead? An honorary sheriff's badge?"

"I had one of those when I was six."

I thought I had done a good job, and it made me cranky that Rick didn't seem to recognize that. Suppose I'd found the key piece of information that would lead to the crime being solved. I thought I deserved a little commendation.

When we pulled up at the Yardley railroad station, Rick said, "Look, you did get the Curcio woman to talk. And I appreciate that. But don't go getting any ideas. I'm the cop here, and I'm the one who does the detecting. If you find anything out, you bring it to me."

"Message received," I said. That didn't stop me from spraying gravel as I peeled out of the railroad station lot, though.

Ten-Digit Number

I'd been home for an hour when my doorbell rang, and Rochester began barking. As I tramped down the staircase, I could see Ginny Pryor through my sliding glass doors. Then I remembered Irene's suggestion that Ginny get the listing on Caroline's townhouse.

"Hi, Steve," she said. "Rick Stemper told me you have a key to Caroline's house. He hooked me up with her great-aunt and I'm going to list it."

"Sure, come on in."

"I see you decided to keep Rochester." She reached down to rub behind the dog's ears. He jumped up and down like a crazed marionette, only settling once Ginny was sitting at the kitchen table across from me.

"What can I say? I'm a sucker. Nobody else would take him and I couldn't just drop him off at the pound."

"Caroline would be happy," she said. "If I can borrow the key from you, I'll get a copy made. I've got to get a cleaning service in before I can advertise it."

She said she'd take a cup of coffee, and as I started grinding the beans she said something I didn't hear. When I'd finished, I asked her to repeat it.

"Have you heard anything more about what happened?" Rochester had curled his big golden body around her feet, keeping her from getting up.

"Nothing since the night after she was killed." As I poured the grounds into the coffee maker and set it, I reminded her about the break-in at Caroline's, though I didn't mention that I'd been in the house afterward to pick up Caroline's laptop. "I'm afraid you're going to have a lot of cleaning to do."

As I poured the coffees and we drank, we speculated about what was going on, but neither of us had much to offer. I gave her the key, and she said she'd be back after a trip to the locksmith. I spent the next half hour playing with Rochester. I couldn't motivate myself to go back to grading papers after reliving what had happened to Caroline.

Ginny returned and said, "You were right, the house is in terrible shape. There's no way I can get it ready to show without taking everything out. There's just too much damage.

I'm going to arrange with a thrift shop to come and pick up the furniture, but I want to pack up Caroline's personal things for her aunt."

She reached down for Rochester, who placed his big head in her lap. "You know Caroline's model doesn't come with a garage, and I'm going to need a place to store those boxes until her aunt can have them shipped up north."

"Let me guess-- you want to use my garage."

"It would save her aunt some money," she said. "And it wouldn't be for more than a couple of weeks."

I planned to keep my Beemer in the garage during the summer, and to do that I needed to sort through the boxes and other debris left over from my move. "Sure. That'll give me a reason to clean the garage up, and then I can get the car in there once Caroline's boxes go."

"Great. I'll let you know when I get the cleaning service. I'll have them carry the boxes over and stack them for you, so you won't have to do anything. "

"Any afternoon is good for me," I said. "I've been coming home right after my classes finish because I don't want to leave Rochester alone for too long. I can't afford to keep replacing cell phones and eyeglasses."

"You're so good to take care of him." She reached down and scratched his belly, and he sighed with contentment. I was starting to get accustomed to him, though I still didn't think I had room in my life for a dog.

Rochester was settling in to life with me, but there were certain behaviors that the amateur psychologist in me couldn't help but diagnose. Whenever there was a loud noise – a gate banging shut on someone's courtyard, a trash can lid flipping shut, an insistent car horn—Rochester was alert, and sought me out. Even once he'd established I was still alive and breathing, it was hard for him to settle down again.

He didn't like thunder, and as soon as the first crack rang out he scurried for the safety of the dark area under my bed, and I had to get down on all fours, grasp a handful of hair at the back of his neck, and drag him out when the storm passed.

He didn't like fireworks or motorcycles either, and when a delivery van pulled up anywhere in the neighborhood he began to bark. Reasoning with him did no good. "He's three houses down, Rochester," I'd say. "Thank you for warning me but you can go back to sleep now."

Instead he would pace around for a while, all his senses on alert on the off chance that some evil UPS driver would be delivering a package to me. The nerve of those guys in brown.

I didn't know if he'd had any phobias before, but he sure did now. He always had to know where I was in the house, and even if he was asleep on the carpet at the foot of my bed, and I tiptoed downstairs, he woke and followed me.

It was particularly annoying when I was trying to clean up or organize—I'd be moving things between office and bedroom, or trying to make the bed, and there would be this huge golden retriever underfoot. "Settle down, Rochester!" seemed to have no effect. Only when I stayed in to one place in the house—the bed, the kitchen table, the computer—could Rochester do the same.

The next day, the two Puerto Rican women Ginny had hired to clean Caroline's house stacked a dozen boxes in my garage, all labeled by the room where the things had come from. Rochester was very eager to sniff each box and I had to manhandle him back into the house to get ready for his evening walk.

Even after we returned, Rochester was determined to get into those boxes, so I opened the first one he sniffed, just to show him there was nothing there for him.

It was a box of books, and the one on the top was called *Befriending Your Golden Retriever*. I picked it up and flipped through sections on weaning, feeding, and training. Rochester was very interested in what I was doing, and nosed the book as I turned the pages, until I saw a picture that looked so much like him he could have posed for it.

The dog in the photo was the same honey-gold color, with the same squarish head. They both had a couple of curlicues of golden hair mixed into an otherwise straight coat, and the same large, alert brown eyes. The other photos showed that there was a lot of variation within the breed—some goldens were thinner, with narrower faces, and they ranged in color from ivory to deep red. But Rochester was the star, what the book called "the breed standard."

"Hey, boy, that's you," I said, pointing. He sniffed the page.

Caroline had made some notes throughout the book, in

margins, particularly in the section on training, and I'd been able to understand what she meant. But here, she had written a cryptic series of numbers above the picture that looked like Rochester. I wondered if it was a phone number—there were ten characters in the sequence. Could it be a golden retriever owner, or breeder? Maybe whoever it was knew something about Caroline that would help Rick understand what had happened to her. I decided I wanted to show him that I could investigate, too.

I carried the book with me to the office and turned on Caroline's laptop. I was still nervous about doing anything regarding Caroline, however legal, on my own computer, because I worried that Santiago Santos wouldn't approve. I Googled the number—but it turned out to belong to an industrial cleaning service in Terre Haute, Indiana. Oh well, so much for showing Rick. I wasn't done investigating, but that number was a dead end.

By this point, Rochester had given up on sniffing at me, and gone to lie down on the carpet behind my chair—locking me in place, because I couldn't move the chair backwards without running over him.

Since he'd adopted me, I decided I'd have to do what I could to make a good home for him. I went back to Caroline's laptop and started Googling resources about dogs, and goldens in particular. I passed several hours that way, and when Rochester got up and stretched, I was free to back away from the computer—but only to take him outside.

I was getting more and more puppy-whipped.

It was most evident when I was out walking him, and we came upon another neighborhood dog. With Caroline, he'd met and befriended almost every Shih-Tzu, every Newfoundland, and every dog of any size in between. I could barely walk him a few hundred feet without him spying another dog ahead and dragging me down the street behind him like the streamers on a just-married car.

"Are you walking him, or is he walking you?" one of my neighbors asked that evening.

"He's the only one who knows the answer to that, and he's not talking," I said, as Rochester tugged me onward.

At home, he was establishing that he was in charge as well. I learned to secure my small objects, and we had entered a period of truce when I was no longer losing anything valuable to Rochester's ravenous jaws.

Now that I was a dog owner, I saw dogs everywhere I looked. Despite the on-campus signs, Tasheba wasn't the only student at Eastern with a puppy; I saw big black dogs running around the parking lot, a mutt rolling on his back in the grass while his owner read nearby, a girl parading two Dachshunds who were so tiny they looked more like rats than dogs.

At the mall, I saw the head of a teacup Yorkshire Terrier sticking out of a woman's pocketbook, and a pair of white dogs so low and fluffy they looked like walking floor mops.

I was also much more aware of crime news on TV or in the paper. Every time I saw a woman stabbed by a jealous boyfriend, a man whose car had broken down run over on I-95, or a convenience store clerk stabbed in a botched robbery, I remembered Caroline. I couldn't shake the feeling that I should be doing more to find out who killed her, but I didn't know what I could do. I was resisting the temptation to go back on line and try to hack into different databases.

Late Saturday afternoon, Rick Stemper called me. "My date bailed on me tonight," he said. "Like I believe she has contagious gingivitis. Want to meet me for dinner? We were supposed to go to some Chez Shithole in New Hope, but I'd be just as happy with a burger at The Drunken Hessian."

He was at the bar when I arrived, chatting up a busty blonde in a low-cut top. As I was walking in the door, she said something to him, shrugged, and walked away.

"Women," Rick said. "Can't live with them, and can't kill them."

"At least not if you're a police officer. What was up with the blonde?"

"Had to get home and finish grouting her bathroom tiles," he said.

We sat down at a table in the back, and ordered beers and burgers. "I did a little computer searching on Caroline," I said, after the beers had arrived. "Did you know that her boss was fired, and she replaced him?"

"By 'a little computer searching,' what do you mean?" Rick asked.

I shrugged. "You know, Google, search engines, that kind of thing."

Rick fiddled with the handle of his mug for a minute. It was cheap plastic, embossed with the logo of The Drunken Hessian, a redcoat unsteady on his feet. "I know about your trouble in California," he said, after a while.

I felt an immediate adrenaline surge. "Oh," I said.

"You even supposed to have a computer?"

"I am. My parole officer has some tracking software installed so he can make sure I'm not getting into trouble."

I didn't mention that I'd figured a way around it, using Caroline's computer and a neighbor's network. Professional secrets, you know.

"That's good. Because I wouldn't want you to get into trouble because of Caroline. I'll admit, I haven't made the kind of progress I'd like, but I've still got some things to look into, some leads to follow."

The waitress brought our burgers over, and I spilled some beer trying to move the mug out of her way. I couldn't seem to get control of my nerves. After we'd messed with ketchup, napkins, and so on, I asked, "Does it matter to you—my trouble?"

He took a bite of his burger, and said, "Should it?"

I shrugged. "You're a cop. Maybe you're not supposed to hang out with criminals."

He raised his eyebrow at me. "Hanging out with a parolee doesn't bother me, if hanging out with a cop doesn't bother you."

"How'd you know?" I asked. "You look me up in your system or something? The state of California send out a be-on-the-lookout?"

"Santiago and I work out at the same gym," he said. "He tells me about all his clients in Stewart's Crossing, and in return, I keep an eye on them."

"That what this is—keeping an eye on me?"

"You can call it that if you want," he said. "I prefer to think of it as hanging out with an old high school friend."

There was an uncomfortable silence for a minute or so, while both Rick and I sipped our beers and I thought about what to say. He spoke first. "Listen, I am your friend, Steve. If you're running into any problems, I hope you'll talk to me about them."

I took a deep breath. I had to redirect the conversation, because I didn't want to lie to Rick and I didn't want to tell him what I'd been doing, especially now that I knew he worked out with my parole officer. "Santos is on my back about a business plan, and I don't know how to go about it," I said. "He wants me to show him how I'm going to get new clients, but so far, I've only been working for people I already know, former coworkers who've gone on to other jobs."

I played with a packet of sugar. "But will anybody who doesn't know me want to hire me? Do I have to tell them about – you know?"

"What does Santos say?"

"He said I can't lie, but I don't have to volunteer the information, either. But what if they ask one of my references? What if they Google me? There were a couple of articles in local papers about my arrest. The information's out there."

"You could look for guys who got a second chance of their own," Rick said. "They might be sympathetic to your situation."

"Or they could be super-careful, worried that I might bring them fresh trouble."

"Why don't you start out looking for small jobs," Rick said. "Somebody who's going to pay you fifty or a hundred bucks isn't going to waste time Googling you. Then you'll be there if they have bigger jobs."

"That's a great idea. There are a lot of websites out there that advertise little freelance jobs. I could build up my portfolio that way. And Santos would see that I'm making progress."

Though I was glad of the advice, the exchange with Rick left me feeling uncomfortable all weekend. Sunday morning, I took Rochester for a nice long walk, then retired to bed to work my way through the paper and the New York Times crossword. I'd always loved puzzles, and in jail I'd begun satisfying my curiosity by crosswords, word searches, acrostics, and anything else that kept my brain working and my fingers away from the keyboard. Kind of like a nicotine patch for hackers. By noon, though, I had no more excuses to avoid my business plan.

I went online, looking for sample business plans, and found a few. The first question they all asked was where the market was for my product or service. That was easy; I knew a lot of companies had been downsizing, cutting back their staff of technical writers and outsourcing projects on a freelance basis.

I started making a list of websites where freelance work was offered. I found a few jobs I could bid on, and every so often I had to stop working on my plan to put together a proposal. By the time I closed the laptop on Sunday evening to take Rochester for his walk, I felt I'd made some progress. I hoped that Santiago Santos would agree, and that he'd get off my back a bit.

Like a Kid for the Childless

Maybe it was Rochester's influence, but I'd enjoyed Romeo's presence in the classroom. I was a little disappointed when Tasheba was late on Monday morning, arriving without her little dog.

Teaching that morning was like walking through quicksand, or explaining retirement investment to my ex-wife. Slow going, without any promise of results. The high point was when Dionne or Dianne asked what "seersucker" meant.

Jeremy Eisenberg said, "A seersucker is a person who gives blow jobs to clairvoyants," and everyone in the class who understood the words laughed—about half. His tongue stud glinted when he spoke, and a new dumbbell pierced his chin.

Toward the end of the period I wanted to give them a chance to brainstorm ideas for their next paper—"An event that changed my life." All three Jeremys wanted to write about high school graduation; Dionne was going to write about selling Girl Scout cookies, while Dianne wanted to write about her mother's MS diagnosis. Or vice versa.

Billy Rubin, who made no bones about thinking English class would have no meaning for his life as a physician, wanted to write about meeting one of his neighbors, who drove a Porsche, and discovering the man was a doctor. It was the inspiration for Billy's career choice.

Neither of the Melissas had any idea what to write about. Tasheba announced she was going to write about adopting Romeo, whom she found at the Humane Society in Leighville. Menno grumbled, "More animals," so I turned to him.

"What about you?" I asked. "Have you thought about what you'd like to write about?"

"My father stole some cows from one of our neighbors, and when he got caught the community shunned us," he said. "We had to sell the farm and move away. I want to write about that."

"More animals," Tasheba mimicked. In a low voice she said, "He's such a turkey you could stuff him and eat him for Thanksgiving." Dionne and Dianne giggled.

Menno glared at her. Open war seemed to have broken out between them, though I wasn't sure why. The class had started to take sides. Melissa Macaretti was in Menno's camp, while two of the three Jeremys sided with Tasheba (the third was neutral, sort of like Switzerland, if Switzerland's neutrality was based more on lack of interest than on any philosophical basis.)

Before either Tasheba or Menno pulled out any weapons, I dismissed the class. "Email me or call my cell if you have questions," I said, as they were all packing up to leave. Candy Kane had already told me in no uncertain terms that she was not my secretary, and any students who wanted me had to call me directly. "I want three pages, typed, double-spaced, next Monday. And I know all about super-sized fonts and big margins, so don't try and pull any crap."

That wouldn't stop them, but it was always good to get that information on the table. As Tasheba was walking out, I asked her how Romeo was doing.

"I can't bring him to school any more," she said. "That's why I was late. Security was waiting on me outside. They told me someone had complained, and I couldn't bring Romeo to class, even if you didn't mind. So I had to take him back to my house." She sneered. "I bet it was Farmer Boy, with his stupid beard. He doesn't want to mess with me."

I nodded. I didn't want to mess with Tasheba, either.

I met up with Jackie at her office, on my way to the faculty lounge. "I got this idea from this sign I saw the other day," she said, holding up her Polaroid camera. "You know, those 'George Washington slept here' signs. I'm going to take pictures of every student who falls asleep in my class, and post them around the room, with signs like 'Araly Fernandez Slept Here' or 'George Chu Slept Here.'"

We walked into the lounge and set about making our drinks. "Hey, I baked some biscuits for Samson," she said. "And I brought some in for your new dog." She handed me a baggie with a half-dozen cookies shaped like dog bones.

"Thanks. I'm sure he'll appreciate them."

Jackie was on a roll that morning, making catty remarks about the rest of the full-time faculty and about administrators I only knew by name. I could see why other professors sometimes called her "The Blair Witch" behind her back. She may have been petite and under thirty, but her personality was as large as if she'd been teaching for decades.

On my way to the parking lot, in quick succession, I saw students wearing t-shirts which read, "Save the whales. Collect the whole set," "Hard work pays off in the future. Laziness pays off now," and "Half the people you know are below average." Typical for the Eastern student body.

I took my time driving home, with the windows wide open for the first time since late fall. It was pretty cold, but if I went slowly enough the cool breeze was more like the opening of a refrigerator than an Arctic blast.

It had been a rough couple of weeks, between Caroline's death and Rochester's arrival in my life, topped off with the ungrammatical rantings of privileged undergraduates who've been brought up to believe their thoughts matter, even when they ignore all the rules of punctuation. It was nice to snatch a few minutes to myself, rolling down River Road with the Delaware on my left and a series of wooded hills and fallow fields on my right. For long stretches, the Beemer was the only car on the road, and I took joy in the burgeoning nature around me.

It's another world out there along the river. Pine, blue spruce and fir gather in clusters, holding remnants of the frequent winter snows in their branches. You can drive for a mile or two without seeing a house or driveway, past the abandoned quarry and the flat piece of land, now overgrown with weeds and saplings, where there used to be a child-sized railway train my parents took me on.

Years of traveling that road, as a kid, a teenager and a college student, had given me intimate knowledge of its twists and turns. I remembered where the high school late bus had stopped, and which road you took to get to the ruined mansion, called Xanadu, which my buddies and I had explored on a dare in eleventh grade.

A mile or so north of Stewart's Crossing, traffic slowed, and as we crept forward I saw flashing red and blue lights and a Mini Cooper that had run off the road and perched halfway down the slope to the Delaware, butted up against the trunk of a weeping willow.

The road there was narrow, with no shoulder to speak of, and accidents were common. An ambulance appeared from behind me, and the cars in the southbound lane moved over to the right, hugging the stone wall built during the Depression by the WPA. I remembered the last time I'd seen Fire Rescue; they had come to take away Caroline's body. I wondered if Rick had made any progress in finding her killer.

Traffic moved again, and I didn't get to see how fast the EMTs moved, whether the occupant of the Mini Cooper could be saved or not. But when I got home, I made sure to pet Rochester and even let him lick my face.

Responses began coming in to the queries I'd sent out soliciting freelance work, and I was pleased to learn I'd been given two small jobs. Neither paid much, but they added to my client roster, and there was always the hope that if they liked what I did, they'd give me more work. Santos would be pleased. Of course, I had to sandwich that work in between preparing for classes, grading papers, and taking care of Rochester.

As we walked the next morning, I realized that I was getting to know him more every day. He had a bunch of habits which were starting to emerge, the more he got comfortable with me. The one I found most annoying was the way he seemed to like an audience when he pooped.

There was no other way to explain it. We'd walk past six houses in a row—closed up, no cars in the driveway, no lights in the window. Then there'd be one where a woman was unloading groceries from her minivan, or a guy had the hood up on his Mustang, or a kid was playing in the front yard. That's where Rochester would scoot his hind legs up and squat.

Usually I was paying attention and I dragged him onward. I didn't want anybody to complain about me letting my dog poop in their yard, even if I was cleaning it up. Every now and then, though, I'd be thinking about something, or I'd get in conversation with some kid who wanted to pet the dog, and when I'd look down there he'd be, turds popping out of his butt.

By inheriting Rochester, I'd turned into a kid magnet. Before he arrived, I'd never talked to a single child—and yet once I was walking a big, happy golden retriever, every kid on the street was saying hi and asking to pet him.

It's not that I don't like kids. I was a kid once myself. And the students I teach are barely out of childhood. But if you say no, then the kids think you're some kind of meanie. And saying yes means reining Rochester in, getting him to sit so he doesn't overwhelm some three-foot munchkin. It's just a hassle.

Sometimes I long for those quiet, peaceful, dog- and kid-free walks I used to be able to take. And then Rochester will stick his big shaggy head in my face as I'm lying on the sofa, or try to climb over me in the bed like I'm an obstruction in the roadway, and I start to laugh.

I drove up to Eastern, and was there early enough that I stopped by Jackie's office just before my mystery fiction class. "Did Rochester like the biscuits I sent him?" she asked.

"Absolutely. I had to put the rest of them up on top of the refrigerator or he'd have eaten them all at once."

"You can always give him one after you brush his teeth, as a reward," she said. "You have been brushing his teeth, haven't you? You have to brush them every couple of days and clip his toenails."

"Do I look like a dog beautician?" I asked.

"A dog's breakfast? Only in that shirt."

"What's wrong with this shirt?" I was wearing one of my collection of vintage rock T-shirts—a collection I had assembled at thrift shops all around the Bay area, much to the evil ex-wife's dismay. I think I kept the collection going just because it irritated her so much.

"Nothing, if you're on your way to a Stones concert," Jackie said.

I started to strum my air guitar, pursing my lips and strutting.

"Please, not Mick Jagger," she said, holding her fingers up in front of me in the shape of a cross. "At least not before I've had my coffee."

"Seriously, I have to brush his teeth?"

"Or take him to the vet," she said. "That dog is like your child now. It's up to you to take care of him."

That was an interesting thought. Even when Mary and I were recovering from the effects of her first miscarriage, discussing cats and kids, I'd never considered that having a pet could be like a kid for the childless.

But then, I stopped at the pet shop that day on my way home from school to replenish Rochester's food, and got sidetracked by the display of rubber chew and squeaky toys.

I found myself picking up squeaky fire hydrants and plastic chew toys shaped like the Statue of Liberty and the Eiffel Tower. "So cute!" escaped my lips, and I looked around to make sure no one had heard me.

"What kind of dog do you have?" the clerk asked me, as I wheeled my wagon, laded with an industrial-sized bag of dog food, mailbox-shaped treats flavored with pumpkin, liver toothpaste, and a guillotine-like implement for trimming Rochester's toenails.

It took me a minute to answer. Even though I had a cart full of doggie products, I still hadn't connected myself as Rochester's owner. More like I'd been running a bed-and-breakfast for orphaned dogs.

"Golden retriever," I finally said.

"They're so sweet," she said. "Does yours slobber?"

"Like the Delaware," I said. We chatted and laughed as she rang me up. With what I spent, I could have sponsored a couple of African orphans, but I handed over my credit card in good spirits.

Coming home that evening, I noticed a For Sale sign on Caroline's front lawn, another reminder of what had happened to her. Rick had made no real progress in finding her killer, and the case was in danger of going unsolved. It made me sad—but then when I let Rochester out of his crate, he nearly did a somersault in his excitement, and who can stay sad in the face of a greeting like that?

That night, I tried to put into practice the things Jackie had told me I had to do for Rochester—brushing his teeth, trimming his nails and so on. He wasn't into the health aspect of teeth cleaning, nail clipping and brushing. He thought everything I tried was a fun new game. Instead of having his teeth brushed, he wanted to play hide-the-head in the sofa pillows. When I grabbed one paw to examine his nails, he used another to whomp away at whatever body part of mine was closest.

And when I tried to brush him, he attempted to scoot under the kitchen table, reappearing as soon as I pulled the brush away. It was just a barrel of laughs. We spent the evening hanging out—me avoiding grading papers and doing client work, him just hanging out being spoiled.

Rochester was changing my life almost without my conscious action. I found myself rushing through my grading to have more time hanging out with him, hurrying home after I finished teaching instead of lingering, so that I could be sure he got out to pee. Caroline's memory came to me in odd moments—driving past the spot where she had been killed, playing with Rochester, coming home with a raspberry mocha in my hand. She was dead, and I was living her life, in a way. It was a sobering thought.

Quaker State Bank

When my mother died, I discovered that my father had become a few bricks shy of a load, to use one of his own expressions. I told my friends that his brain had fallen and couldn't get up, and I felt that way about some of my students at Eastern, too. Sometimes, they were witty, like the girl who once announced in class, "I always hold on to my ex-boyfriends. Or at least their remains."

On Wednesday after freshman comp, I overheard a guy say to his friend, "Dude, I am so over that word of the day toilet paper of yours."

Then as I was on my way to my car, a stocky guy in a *Napoleon Dynamite* t-shirt, the kind that says 'Vote for Pedro,' said, "I'm writing my history paper on Nelson Mandela."

His buddy was built like a wrestler, short and squat. He asked "The dude who hosts *Deal or No Deal*?"

A third guy walking with them, the preppy type in a polo shirt with the collar turned up, snorted. "No that's Howie Mandel. Nelson Mandela was the butler on *Ozzie and Harriet*."

The wrestler said, "Dude, Ozzie is married to Sharon, not Harriet. Harriet's like one of those dogs that's always crapping around the house."

The 'Vote for Pedro' guy, who probably had never voted in his life, except for "Most Likely to Have the Best Dope at a Party," said, "You guys are so lame. Nelson Mandela is like the George Washington Carver of Africa. We studied him in high school during Black History Month."

I was shaking my head over that when I ran into Edith Passis at the faculty parking lot, and it was such a surprise to see her somewhere other than The Chocolate Ear that I almost didn't recognize her. Though it was early April, it was a cold, bright, blustery day, and Edith was wrapped up in a knee-length wool coat, her white hair covered in a matching tweedy cap. She had black leather gloves on her hands, and big plastic sunglasses over her face. She looked like Greta Garbo on her way to the grocery store.

I remembered that Edith tutored advanced piano students in Eastern's musicology program. "How are you doing?" I asked.

"I'm hoping the winter is behind us. I get so afraid of driving in ice and snow."

"I know how you feel." We chatted for a couple of minutes, and soon enough the topic of Caroline Kelly came up.

"The poor thing," Edith said. "She told me she was getting close to figuring out what was going wrong with my money." She shifted her pocketbook to one arm so she could pull off her leather gloves. The gesture reminded me of my mother, and a wave of memory hit me, missing her and my father as much as I ever had.

"But I never did get the chance to sit down with her and find out," Edith continued. "And I gave her all my paperwork, too."

"Ginny hired a cleaning service to box up all Caroline's stuff, and she's storing it in my garage." I loosened my scarf as I warmed up standing in the sun. "I can take a look through what I've got and see if I can find that paperwork for you."

"Would you, Steve? At least then I can find someone else to help me. Right now I just don't know what to do."

"After all the torment I put you through with three years of piano lessons, it's the least I can do."

She pooh-poohed that notion, telling me I was far from her worst student, but I thought that was the gloss of memory rather than actual truth.

Later that night, I found Rochester sniffing at the door to the garage and whimpering. I guessed he smelled his mom's stuff out there, and wanted to go sniff it some more, so I let him out there, making a mental note that I had promised Edith Passis I'd look for copies of her paperwork.

I sat down to read essays. The first on my pile was Menno Zook's, which began, "My father had been stealing cows from our neighbors for years before anyone caught him."

I'd just gotten hooked by that intriguing beginning when Rochester started barking at the garage door. "Hey, what's with the noise?" I asked. When I opened the garage door he went right to one box, sniffing and pawing at it. "What's the matter, one of your toys in there? Come on, you've got plenty of toys inside."

He wouldn't budge, even when I grabbed onto his collar and tried to drag him across the concrete floor. "Fine, I give up. Let's take the box inside and open it up."

I carried it to the kitchen table and used a pair of scissors to cut through the heavy packing tape. The legend on the outside of the box identified it as coming from Caroline's home office. I started lifting out file folders, books, and office equipment, looking for anything that might qualify as Rochester's toy. I found a leather business card case, with a stack of her business cards inside, and held it up to him. But that wasn't what Rochester was after.

She also had a nice PDA, one of the newer models, and after admiring it I placed it on the table. Rochester went for it, putting his paws up on the table and nosing the PDA around. I held it up for him to sniff, but he just kept pushing it back to me with his nose. "You want me to do something with this?" I asked him.

I was starting to realize why people talked to their pets, even though I had no expectation that the dog would ever answer me back. Maybe it was a childhood spent watching *Mr. Ed* on TV. Or maybe it was just my way of communicating with Rochester—he had his ways, like barking and wagging his tail, and I had my own. Together we might come to some satisfying level of interaction.

In any case, I turned on Caroline's PDA and started playing with it. I checked her calendar; there was nothing suspicious there, no "meet with shady characters while walking dog." She had a few dozen listings in her contacts, including my own.

I resisted the impulse to play one of the games that came with the unit. All that was left was the built-in notepad. There, however, I hit pay dirt. "Where are account statements?" read one entry. Underneath it was "Follow the money," and beneath that a series of ten numbers with the notation, "Who opened account?"

I went over to the bookshelf where I'd placed the golden retriever book and paged through to the picture that resembled Rochester, where she'd scribbled what I thought was a telephone number. The sequence of ten digits in Caroline's PDA matched the set in the margin of the book.

So it was an account number, not a phone number. But did it relate to her murder? Mindful of what Rick had told me, I hurried over to the telephone to call him, but before I reached it, I stopped short. What did I have? A couple of notes in a PDA, and what might be an account number of some kind.

I needed to do some more research before I called Rick. Otherwise I would look like an idiot, and this information, if it was important, might end up only as a few lines scrawled in a case file.

All this time, Rochester was watching me, sitting on his haunches on the floor next to the kitchen table. "What do I do next, boy?" I asked.

He came over to me and nudged the book in my hands. "I guess I have to know for sure if this is an account number and see if I can figure out what it has to do with Caroline. Could it be an account at the bank where she worked?"

He followed me upstairs and lay on the floor behind me as I opened up Caroline's laptop and Googled Quaker State Bank, the bank on Caroline's business cards, and the phrase "account numbers."

It's amazing the stuff you can find online. A link directed me to a guy's blog which dissected the account numbers from prominent banks. I discovered that the account numbers for Caroline's bank were indeed ten numbers long. The first three digits identified the branch, and I figured out that this account had been opened in Easton, the next town of any size upriver from Stewart's Crossing.

The next six digits were sequential numbers that indicated when the account had been opened. It appeared that the account I was looking at had been opened in the previous autumn. The last digit identified the status of the account holder. If it was a zero, the account holder was an individual; if it was a one, the account belonged to a corporation. The number before me ended in a zero.

This was all still a big assumption: that the number in the golden retriever book, which matched the one in Caroline's PDA, was connected to an account at Quaker State Bank. But I'd studied a bit of philosophy and remembered Occam's Razor. Make no more assumptions than necessary. Caroline worked at QSB. QSB accounts had ten numbers which fit certain patterns. A ten-digit number that matched those patterns was found among Caroline's effects, along with her own guess that it represented an account. Therefore, the easiest assumption was that the number indeed identified a QSB account.

I wasn't sure if that would hold up in a court of law, but it was good enough for me. I didn't quite know what to do next, though. How was I going to follow Caroline's instructions to "follow the money?"

Caroline had been on the track of some evidence—and I was sure that finding that evidence had gotten her killed. The shiver that ran down my spine told me I was on to something—but still nothing strong enough to take to the police.

It was time to turn my sniffers loose to find me an unsecured port on some ordinary user's computer, from which I could launch yet another visit to QSB's network. It was late by then, and while I waited for the sniffers to find me a port, I took Rochester out for a bedtime walk. The night sky was covered with fast-moving clouds, but in a velvety black gap, I recognized one constellation: Orion. The three stars hanging from Orion's belt, representing his sword, shone brightly, even when a thin sheen of cloud passed between me and them. I wondered if that was an omen for me. Was Orion's sword the weapon that I could use to bring Caroline's killers to justice—or did it represent danger for me?

Back inside, the sniffers had found me a port on a computer connected to the Internet that I could use without detection, and I logged into QSB's system. "This is why I got in trouble in California," I said to Rochester, who had sprawled on the tile floor at my feet. "I'm good at this." It was a scary feeling, how much fun it was to break in somewhere I wasn't supposed to be. Especially knowing how much trouble I'd be in if I were caught.

But still, I navigated my way to the customer database and typed in the account number, then hit Enter. There was a brief delay while my request was relayed over the Internet to the QSB server, which reached into the bowels of its database to display the result.

Edith Passis.

What? I tried again, just to be sure. After a few seconds, the same result.

Edith Passis.

Caroline hadn't left me a road map to her killer. All she'd left was Edith Passis's account number.

I frowned, and shut the laptop down. Rick was right; I wasn't the detective, he was. I had to leave things in his capable hands.

On the other hand, I could help Edith figure out where all

her money was, so the search hadn't been a total loss.

I shut off the computer and went into the bedroom, and Rochester followed on my heels.

Shell Casing

It poured that night, and Rochester spent most of it huddled under my bed. I lay on the floor next to him for a while, stroking his fur and making sympathetic noises, and I don't know if it helped at all.

When I woke in the morning, it was still raining, but I didn't want Rochester to have any accidents inside, so I dug out my raincoat, found myself an umbrella, and grabbed his leash off the counter.

For once he wasn't underfoot. "Rochester! Walk!" I called.

No Rochester.

"Don't make me come upstairs."

He wasn't listening. What the hell; I sounded just like my own father, and I hadn't listened to him either.

I climbed the stairs to the second floor and found him huddled under my bed, as close to the back wall as he could get.

"Come on, Rochester, let's go for your walk. You like walks."

I could almost hear him saying, "Yeah, but not in the rain."

I crawled under the bed, hampered a bit by the raincoat, which had not been designed for such adventures. I petted Rochester's head and smoothed the fur on his back, talking to him in dulcet tones, and nothing seemed to work. I hooked the leash into his collar, backed out from under the bed, and applied brute force to the situation.

He splayed his paws out, but the carpet was old and worn and he couldn't get much purchase. When I had his whole body out from under the bed, he gave up and followed along with me.

He didn't like the rain. Neither did I, even though I had the benefit of a lined raincoat and an umbrella to protect my head. We walked down Sarajevo Court to Bratislava Circle and then back home, and when he saw my house ahead he lowered his head down and bulled forward, dragging me behind him.

As soon as we got inside the house, he stopped and shook, and water went flying everywhere. "I guess you need a towel," I said, slipping and sliding across the tile floor to get one. I did my best to dry him off, but it wasn't the greatest job, and he retreated back under the bed to shelter himself from me and the storm.

I left around 11:00 for mystery fiction, leaving Rochester under the bed rather than forcing him into his crate. I hurried home right after class to make sure he was OK and that he hadn't destroyed the house while I was gone.

As I drove back into River Bend, I could see that the wind and rain had played havoc with the neighborhood. There was an unfamiliar door mat under the oak tree in my front yard, and the driveway was strewn with leaves and twigs. Puddles of water still littered the roadway.

Since he'd been gypped out of his long morning walk, I took Rochester out for an afternoon stroll. We were drawn back to the place where Caroline's body had been found. Though I tried to restrain him as we neared the area, he was just too strong for me, and pulled me down the street like a dog on a mission.

"I'm not your pull toy. What are you, part Eskimo sled dog?" But nothing would stop him, and he dragged me toward River Road, stopping at the grassy lane that led to the Revolutionary War cemetery, the area where Caroline had been shot.

Rochester sat his furry butt down in the street and wouldn't be budged. "What is it, boy? What do you want?"

He barked once.

"I'm sorry, I don't speak dog." I stared at him. "What?"

He heaved a big sigh, as if I was the dumbest human in the world, and started sniffing the area where Caroline's body had lain. "Come out of there, Rochester," I said, pulling on his leash. "I'm sure you're disturbing a crime scene or something."

But he kept moving farther into the underbrush, dragging me behind him, til he stopped, sat on his haunches and barked once. "What's up, boy? Did you find something that belonged to your mom?"

The rain and wind had cleared out the underbrush, and as I looked ahead I saw something shiny, an empty metal cylinder a little over an inch long; the outside was a copper color. All those years of reading mysteries and watching forensics programs on TV paid off. I recognized I was looking at a bullet casing.

I pulled out my phone and called Rick Stemper. "Did you

ever recover any casings from the gun that shot Caroline?" I asked.

"Good afternoon to you, too. Got your junior detective kit out again?"

"I'm asking because Rochester dragged me down to where Caroline was shot, and there's a casing here."

He heaved a big sigh. "Wait there. I'm on my way."

He brought gloves and an evidence bag, and he agreed there was a pretty good chance that the bullet casing came from the gun that shot Caroline.

I was going to tell him about finding Edith's account number, but I knew he'd frown on my ability to get into Quaker State Bank's systems, and maybe even violate me to Santiago Santos. Since I doubted Edith had shot Caroline, I decided to keep that information to myself.

He walked the area again with me, but the shell casing was the only new piece of evidence he was able to find. "The dog dragged you out here?"

I looked at Rochester, who sat in the middle of the grassy path. "Yup."

"You sure you haven't been out here every day looking for evidence?"

"Get a life, Rick."

"Just checking."

He drove off, and Rochester and I walked home. He rewarded me with a big stinking pile of poop, which I got to scoop up with one of my plastic grocery bags. The joys of dog ownership.

Back home, I had to return to grading, and there was Menno's essay, waiting for me. I read about his father's many crimes, and the way the Amish community had shunned him. Menno, his mother, and his brothers and sisters were all expected to adhere to the shunning—his father couldn't live with them any more, and no one in the community would buy the produce grown on their farm, or sell his father any of the seeds or equipment he needed.

His father had left home and moved to Easton. Menno and his brother Godfrey had chosen to go with him, though their two sisters and youngest brother had remained with their mother on the farm outside Lancaster.

The essay was well-written, with few small errors, and I

found it very powerful. Having to choose your father over your mother, life outside the cloistered environment of the Amish to the life you'd always known—those were big steps for a boy of fourteen.

Without her husband and sons to help on the farm, his mother had been forced to sell the property and move in with her brother's family. The community would not allow her to divorce Menno's father, or to accept any money from him, not even child support. According to Menno's essay, she now worked for an Amish farm store, baking dozens of shoo-fly pies a day.

Menno had left school at twelve, but in Easton he'd been forced by the state to return, and he'd graduated from the public high school and qualified for a diversity scholarship at Eastern.

"If my father wasn't a thief, I'd never have graduated from high school," he concluded. "I would be married by now, and working my own land. But I would still be bound by a useless religion. Now, it is clear to me that what my father really stole was freedom for me, and I am grateful to him for it."

It was a different approach, and I gave him a high grade and then went on to the rest of the papers in my pile. Each of the Jeremys made the same tired points about high school graduation, and Dionne's essay on her mother's MS diagnosis, which should have been moving, was so riddled with grammar and spelling errors that all I could see were the comma splices, the fused sentences and the dangling participles.

Both of the Melissas wrote about boyfriends. Melissa Bintliff met hers at a debate competition, and in the end, she wrote, it was a debate that broke them apart. He was from a Catholic school and wanted to wait until marriage to have sex, while she disagreed. They broke up, and she later discovered that he was gay. "No wonder he didn't want to have sex with me," she concluded.

I refrained from comment on her conclusion, but did mark up the way she began every sentence with I. "Try to vary your sentence structure," I wrote. "I know this is a personal essay, but there are other ways to begin sentences."

Melissa Macaretti met her boyfriend at Eastern, she wrote, and he was unlike any boy she'd ever known in high school.

Yes, I wanted to scrawl in the margin, college romances

are always like that. Get on with it. But I kept my red pen to myself. He was a bad boy, the 21st century equivalent of James Dean or Marlon Brando (the thin, sexy Brando, not the walrus of his later years.) Though she didn't come right out and say they had great sex, she implied that he had "broadened" her "horizons."

God save me from adolescents, I thought, as I graded her essay and moved on to the next.

I kept waiting for the phone to ring—Rick telling me that the shell casing Rochester and I had found was the key that broke open the case—but no one called. Late in the day I called him and suggested we meet up for a drink. He agreed, and around 6:30, after I'd given Rochester his evening walk and fed him, I convinced him to go into his crate and I headed down to The Drunken Hessian.

Rick was already there, sitting in a booth in the back and cradling a bottle of Corona. I got one of my own, then joined him.

"Were you able to find anything out about Caroline's ex-boss?" I asked, after being careful to say hello first.

He nodded. "Dead end. The bank made him a settlement and he dropped the lawsuit at least three weeks before Caroline was shot. He used the settlement money to prop up his brother-in-law's business, and they got a big contract. He told me that he was glad about what Caroline did—otherwise he'd still be stuck at the bank, and his brother-in-law's business would be bankrupt."

"That's a bummer," I said. "He seemed like such a good suspect."

"That's the way it goes."

We ordered a platter of nachos to go with our beers. After the waitress had left, I asked, "Did you get any results from that shell casing?"

"This is not *CSI: Stewart's Crossing*," he grumbled. "We don't get results back from stuff like that before the next commercial break. I have to send that casing to a lab in Philadelphia. And they're backed up at least two or three weeks. It's going out tomorrow morning, so I'll get back to you, say, by July 4th."

"You're not taking this very seriously," I said.

"You don't get it, do you?" Rick asked. "Caroline's murder

is the first one we've had in Stewart's Crossing since Johnny Menotto shot up this place six years ago. I don't have a team to help me. I'm tracking four break-ins, a vandalism at the synagogue on Ferry Road, two cases of domestic abuse and a peeping Tom."

He started playing with a sugar packet. "I want to find out who killed Caroline as much as you do—more, because it's my job." He took a breath, and I could tell he was trying to calm his voice. "Most people are killed by someone they know—a family member, ex-boyfriend, jealous co-worker, that kind of thing. We've ruled all that out in Caroline's case, and I'm stuck. I don't like this feeling but I haven't figured out what else I can do."

"Is there anything I can do to help you?"

He shook his head. "Not without ten months at the police academy and at least three years as a patrolman. Oh, and there's that messy issue of a felony conviction. The police frown on hiring the opposition."

"Come on, Rick. I found out that information about Caroline's ex-boss. I know computers. I can see what else I can find out."

"If you even use the word 'hacker' I'm getting up from this table. Don't forget that I'm an officer of the law and if I find out you're violating your parole I'm bound to report you to Santiago Santos."

Well, then, I wasn't going to tell him about hacking into QSB's system to find out about Edith's account. Looking back now, I wonder why it didn't frighten me more that Rick could rat me out to Santos. I guess the lure of hacking was so strong that I disregarded the signs, the way a smoker might ignore those warnings about nicotine, even as his lungs were filling with cancerous polyps.

We played a couple of rounds of pool and shared the platter of nachos. He started flirting with a girl playing pool with friends, and I took that opportunity to duck out and head home to Rochester.

Rick was stuck in his investigation, and I knew that with the press of other cases, if he didn't get some new information soon, Caroline's murder would drop into the cold case file, and there would never be justice for her. With Rochester underfoot every day, a living reminder of her death, I couldn't let that happen, even if there were going to be consequences.

Edith's Investments

Rochester woke me Friday morning, barking like crazy. When I looked out the bedroom window, I saw Ginny's car pulling into Caroline's driveway. She had a young couple with her.

"You don't like the idea of somebody moving into your old house," I said, sitting next to him and stroking his head. "But it's going to happen."

He lay his head in my lap and sprawled the rest of his body on the carpet next to me. I petted him for a while, until I heard Caroline's gate swing shut and I was sure Ginny and the prospective buyers were inside. Then I stood up, pulled on my sweat pants and an Eastern sweatshirt, and headed downstairs, Rochester right on my heels.

He did his crazy pre-walk dance, but I was getting better at anticipating his moves and got him on the leash.

The weather was warming up, and River Bend was full of mothers, grandmothers and nannies pushing babies in strollers. When had all those kids been born? Like the crocus blossoms, the budding trees and the baby ducks, they all seemed to pop out when spring came.

When we got home, I decided to forego working for my clients or polishing my business plan for a while in order to look for Edith Passis's paperwork among Caroline's belongings. I'd match up the account number I had with the paperwork I found, and I'd create some kind of spreadsheet program she could use to keep better track of her money. That would be one way to honor Caroline's memory—to finish the job she'd started.

Rochester watched me from a position in the doorway between the house and the garage. Working in the chill, my bare arms and legs started to get cold. I picked out five boxes and I dragged each one into the kitchen.

At that point, I was ready to call it quits. I was cold and sweaty and tired, and I hadn't made any real headway. But Edith Passis had put up with my lack of piano progress for three years, so I figured I owed her at least another hour or two.

Plus my supervisor, Rochester, looked like he wasn't ready to let me give up. So I stripped off my t-shirt and used it to wipe the sweat from my forehead, then sat at the kitchen table to go through the first box of paperwork.

Everything was out of order, and it took me a few minutes to remember that someone had trashed Caroline's house the night after her murder, strewing her papers around. I recalled a filing cabinet that had been dumped on the floor, and I groaned. This was going to be worse than grading freshman comp essays.

It wasn't until one o'clock that I found the first piece of paper with Edith's name on it. I took a break for dinner and to walk Rochester, and then went back to work by the light of the hanging lamp over the kitchen table. By the time I gave up at eleven, I'd found a half dozen statements on various accounts. From what I'd seen so far, Edith's late husband had left her quite well-fixed. None of the paperwork I found matched the account at Quaker State Bank.

Saturday morning, I took Rochester for a long walk, circling our way through all the different corners of River Bend. We were on Budapest Lane when we saw a father dragging his five-year-old out to his Land Rover SUV. "Yeah, yeah, life's a disappointment," he said to the boy. "Come back to me when you're forty years old and your life sucks and then we'll talk."

That could have been me, I thought, as Rochester sniffed his way along the street. If one of the babies who had begun life in Mary's womb had come to term, and I was still back in an unhappy marriage in Silicon Valley.

I was into delaying that morning. I took a leisurely bath, then fixed myself croissant French toast with maple syrup. After cleaning up the dishes and tidying the living room, I had no choice but to finish sorting through Caroline's boxes. By the time I was done, I'd found eight statements, which showed me that Edith's financial affairs were a mess. She had a checking and savings account at QSB, brokerage accounts with two different brokers, as well as a 401K account and an IRA, both managed by separate companies, which appeared to have been passed on by Walter, her late husband.

In addition, it appeared that she held some stock certificates herself and had the dividend checks sent to her, rather than going through one of the brokerage accounts. No wonder she was having trouble keeping track of everything.

Using Caroline's laptop once more, I logged on to the website for the company that managed Walter's 401K. I knew Edith didn't have a computer, which made me pretty sure she hadn't yet set up online access to her account, so I did. At every step, though, I had to jump through hoops, often simple things I'd always taken for granted. E-mail address? I didn't want to use mine, because I didn't want anyone to think I was trying to hijack her account, so I had to jump to another site and set up a free email account for her there, then once that was set up come back to the brokerage.

Looking through the papers I had, I was able to piece together enough information—her husband's social security number, her date of birth and so on—to get the account access established. Finally I got to the point where I could see the records of her most recent transactions.

I could have invited her to come over to my house and watch me while I did all this—but it was bad enough that I had Rochester hovering around. I didn't have to explain every last thing I did to him – and I was pretty sure I'd have to do that with Edith.

When I pulled up her account information, I discovered that she had changed her address to a post office box six months before. Her statements and quarterly dividend checks had been mailed to that address since Thanksgiving.

It was strange that she hadn't mentioned it, and even stranger that the post office box was located in Easton. There was no reason for Edith to have set up a box there when there was a post office in Stewart's Crossing.

That reminded me of the Quaker State Bank account in Easton. What if Walter had set the account up before he died, and Edith kept using it?

But the account number indicated the account had been set up in the past year—long after Walter's death. I started to wonder if Edith had business that took her to Easton. I knew she went to Leighville once a week, but Easton was another forty-five minutes north, in the opposite direction from Stewart's Crossing.

Edith paid her bills from the checking account based out of the Stewart's Crossing QSB branch. Maybe that account and the one in Easton served different purposes—one for her personal expenses, perhaps, and another for her piano teaching revenue and expenses? But Edith had stopped giving private lessons, and only taught at Eastern, where I could see her paycheck was automatically deposited into the account at the Stewart's Crossing branch.

It was all too confusing. I went back to the records of the online account, and discovered that her quarterly dividend checks for January and March had been cashed. But they had not been deposited into her checking account. And since these were checks to her, and not checks she had written herself, I couldn't see any more information, such as the endorsement, and I had no idea what had happened to the money.

I was about to call Edith and ask her what she was doing in Easton, when I realized that it might be connected to secrets she didn't want to reveal. What if she was supporting an illegitimate child or grandchild up there? Or doing some charitable work she didn't want publicized? Or could someone else be diverting her mail and her checks?

It was all supposition. In any case, I thought it would be better to see what I could do with each one of her statements before I presented her with anything that might be unpleasant.

I tried to spend some time that afternoon on my client work—what I would have done the day before, if I hadn't gotten so caught up in Edith's missing paperwork. Using my own laptop, I reviewed the work I had to do. It wasn't much; just finish up a set of forms for a client—petty cash reimbursement, vacation requests, and so on. But I was only using half my brain, so I quit after a couple of hours. I just couldn't stop thinking about Caroline.

I'd known people before who had died—both my parents, for starters, and miscellaneous friends, neighbors, in-laws and co-workers. But maybe because I'd seen Caroline's body, or because I'd inherited Rochester, or maybe just because her case was still an unsolved homicide, her death kept haunting me.

But what could I do about it? Rick was stuck, and if he didn't know what to do, with all the resources of the police department, how could I know?

I happened to notice the instructions I'd written for retrieving available employee sick time from an SQL database. Something rang in my head but I wasn't sure what it was. I turned away from the computer, and Rochester was there, wanting attention. "What's up, puppy?" I asked, ruffling the fur around his neck. "I know, you miss your mom."

That was the connection. I'd seen Caroline's name in an SQL database. But where? I turned to Caroline's laptop, leaving Rochester staring at the place where my hands had just been. A couple of keystrokes later, I was back at the site for military brats.

I ran a couple of queries against the database, looking for people who'd been at the same bases with Caroline, and came up with half a dozen hits. Two people lived in New York City, making it likely Caroline had been back in touch with them: a guy named Christian McCutcheon and a woman named Karina Warr.

Was McCutcheon the guy whose SUV had been parked in Caroline's driveway? She'd mentioned a guy in New York to both me and Evelina Curcio. If that was the case, his name and address would be in her PDA.

Sure enough, both McCutcheon and Warr were there, and hunting backwards through her appointments (a very tedious chore made even more tedious by Rochester's insistence on banging into my knees while I was doing it) I found a couple of cryptic references.

Caroline had gone to Utica to spend Christmas with her great-aunt, and she'd stopped in New York City on her way back for dinner on December 30 with Karina, and then a party with Chris. Farther back, 'Chris – visit' spanned a weekend in early November.

I wondered if either of them had been notified about Caroline's death. Rick had called Caroline's great-aunt, but would he know her friends? Was there anything more on her calendar about them?

I keep my calendar in Microsoft Outlook, and Caroline did the same thing. But the calendar was just as empty as her PDA had been. She probably hot-synched the two of them together—I did—so there was no reason why one would be different from the other.

While I had Outlook open I checked Caroline's email. It had been three weeks since she had been shot, and there were over a hundred new messages in her mailbox. Instead of an address connected to her ISP, or internet service provider, Caroline's email was a free one offered by SUNY for alumni. So the address would remain open until someone told the university she had passed away.

Dozens of the messages in her inbox were spam—Nigerians needing help laundering money, stock tips, offers for breast or penis enhancement. When I got rid of all of those, I was still left with fifty messages.

A quick survey showed me that there were a half-dozen that seemed personal. I put them aside, and started going through the rest, one at a time. A lot were digests of online lists, and I tried to identify each list and see if it might be relevant to her death.

In the end, there were two that interested me. One was on golden retrievers, which I signed up for myself. The other was a message board for those military brats, connected to the website and SQL database I'd found.

The rest were banking or finance-related, and after a quick scan I got rid of all those. By then, it was time for dinner and Rochester's evening walk. He was restless, and we ended up leaving River Bend, crossing a bridge over the canal, and walking along the Delaware for a while. It was dark and starry by the time we got home, both of us frozen and tired.

I broiled a steak for myself and fed a few pieces of it to Rochester, washing mine down with a Sam Adams Winter Wheat. Then I spent four hours going through every post and didn't find a single point of interest. It was boring reading the mundane details of people I'd never met. There were requests for information: "Anyone who lived on or near Bad Kreuznach from 1986-1990," for example. There were endless threads about current TV shows, musicians I'd never heard of, and political rants.

Chris McCutcheon wasn't a poster—at least not over the last couple of weeks—but Karina Warr often posted on the social life threads. She seemed to have something to say about every party, concert or singles' night in New York, and the desperation rose off those posts like a foul smell.

When I lived in New York, before I met Mary, I'd been a minor player on that kind of party circuit. There was a network of second-tier college alumni groups—Bates and Bowdoin and Tufts and Oberlin and Eastern, among many others—and there were often singles mixers, sneak previews of art openings and so on. I was an assistant editor on a magazine for meeting planners at the time, and I used to go out after work a couple of times a week, either with college friends, to work-related events, or the very kind of parties Karina Warr attended.

I'd met Mary at one of them. We always disagreed on which event it was; I insisted it was a fund-raiser at the Frick Museum, while she was sure it was a party at South Street Seaport. "I remember the fish guts," she always said.

A nice way to remember our meeting.

She wasn't conventionally beautiful, with frizzy brown hair she was always struggling to tame, wide-set eyes, and a high forehead, and when she laughed, her whole face lit up. She had enough charisma to light the Statue of Liberty's torch.

We'd bonded over books, movies and music. Our tastes were in synch, and for our first date we went to an off-Broadway show a friend had given her tickets to, a spoof of *Cats* called *Dogs*. Her friend played a cocker spaniel, and though he had a good voice, the lyrics, the costumes and the choreography were worse than anything you'd see in a suburban high school production. We'd laughed the whole time, pulling on straight faces to compliment her friend backstage.

Though I'd known lots of smart women at Eastern, Mary combined her intelligence with street smarts and business savvy. She was working in marketing for one of the big banks, and she achieved one success after another. She convinced her bosses to place ads in foreign language newspapers, and soon new accounts were zooming in ethnic enclaves like Jackson Heights and Brighton Beach.

She arranged sponsorships for street festivals, set up career-day visits by bankers, and carried out a dozen other clever ideas. We celebrated every promotion at classy restaurants and with spending sprees at Bergdorf's. When she was offered the job in Silicon Valley, it was a big promotion with a lot more money, the chance to manage all marketing communications for a high tech company, and I saw it as the chance for Mary to continue to blossom. I was happy I could be there to share in her success.

I gave up searching around nine, and sprawled out on the couch to relax after hunching over the computer. Rochester jumped up next to me, then rolled over onto his back and rested his head in my groin, snuffling and waving his front paws.

"OK, I get it," I grumbled. "You don't have to turn on a neon sign." I reached for the TV remote with one hand and started scratching his stomach with the other. As mindless sitcoms unraveled before us, I stroked him, wondering what I had done to fill my nights before he had arrived in my life.

Accidental Detective

On Sunday morning, I walked Rochester and then retreated to bed to read the paper. He complicated matters by insisting on sharing the queen-size with me, and by refusing to stay in one place. Every time I'd get the sections I'd read organized along with the ones I hadn't, he'd move around and mix everything up.

I was relaxing on the sofa around three o'clock when Rochester came over and started butting me in the side with his head. "You want something, boy?" I yawned and stretched. "Come on, I'll take you out for a walk."

The walk didn't do it for him, though. He was still in a playful mood when we got home, and he kept hopping around, trying to get me to play. "I have work to do, Rochester," I said, but he wouldn't stop.

I followed him into the kitchen, where he stopped and sat down next to the kitchen table, sniffing at Caroline's laptop, which I'd left there. I remembered that there were still a few of Caroline's email messages that I hadn't read, and sat down and turned it on. As soon as I did, Rochester was satisfied, and he sprawled around behind my chair.

I'd saved the half-dozen personal emails she had received for last. She wasn't a great correspondent; no one yet had sent worried messages asking why she had been out of touch for weeks.

The last message from Karina Warr was a response to one Caroline had sent about a book she was reading, another in her series of novels centered around romantic heroes. "Wake up and smell the cappuccino, girl," Karina had written. "Guys like that don't exist any more and you're wasting your time hoping one of them is going to ride through your little town and swoop you up in his arms."

The only message from Chris McCutcheon was one asking when Caroline would be in New York next.

How do you respond to your dead neighbor's friends asking about her? Send an email from her account? An email from your own account? A phone call? Hi, you don't know me, but I lived next door to your dead friend.

In the end, I passed the buck to Rick Stemper. I copied the

contact information for both Chris and Karina into an email to Rick from my own account. Before I clicked send, though, I stopped to think.

How could I explain having access to Caroline's email? I didn't want to tell him about her laptop, because I didn't want word to get back to Santiago Santos that I'd been using another computer. I got up to pace around the downstairs, made more complicated by Rochester following me around.

Once again, I'd gotten myself into trouble, trying to do what I thought was right. You'd think that six months in the California penal system might have taught me a lesson—but no. I sat back down at my laptop, at the email to Rick. "I was cleaning up my inbox and saw a message from Caroline," I typed. "I thought maybe she'd used 'Rochester' as her email password, so I gave it a try. Hope it doesn't get me in too much trouble!"

I hoped that would be a convincing explanation, and that instead of focusing on me he'd contact Chris and Karina and see if they knew anything that might shed light on her death.

Feeling guilty, I spent a couple of hours researching potential clients, and then playing with Rochester. After dinner I looked back at Edith's paperwork, and realized that each of the accounts Edith had lost track of had been shifted from her home address to the same post office box in Easton.

I wasn't sure how to move forward, though, once I'd figured all that out. Was Edith the one who'd changed the addresses, and opened the account at the QSB branch in Easton? Or had someone stolen her identity? The more I thought about it, the less it seemed that sweet, elderly Edith was hiding some dark secret in Easton, and the more it seemed that she was the victim of an ongoing fraud.

Edith was going to be upset—and since there was something criminal going on, Rick would get involved. There was a lot more work to be done—Edith was going to have to contact each of these companies, let them know that there was fraud on her account, and then wait while they completed their own internal investigations.

I called her and got no answer. That was a surprise; it was Sunday night, and I knew she didn't like to drive after dark. I was worried enough to call Gail Dukowski and see if she knew anything.

I liked Gail, and I'd always been attracted to pretty blondes with a head for business. "I hope it's not too late to call," I said, when she answered. "I know you get up early to bake."

"No, it's OK," she said. "What's up?"

I wondered if she'd go out with me, if I asked. That wasn't what I'd called for, but the thought jumped unbidden into my mind.

Then I remembered my felony conviction, and focused on the business at hand. "I called Edith's and she didn't answer. Do you know if she went out of town?"

"Yes, she went to see her cousin in Charleston," Gail said. "Just for a few days, though. I think she'll be back Tuesday or Wednesday." She sighed. "She's having her handyman recaulk her tub and shower while she's gone. I wish I had a guy who could do that sort of thing for me."

I laughed. "You'd probably want more than just caulking," I said.

She laughed, too. "Well, yeah. And it wouldn't hurt if he was cute and had a sense of humor."

I had the definite impression that Gail was flirting with me, and so I flirted back. "Modern women," I said. "You want it all."

We carried on like that for a few minutes, and when we hung up I was smiling.

The smile faded once I checked the balance of the fraudulent account. A lot of money was moving around, but the account held a minimal balance. A few weeks before, there had been a $400,000 deposit—one which had remained in the account just long enough for the check to clear.

Poor Edith, I thought. She had been victimized. I wondered if the culprit was the handyman she'd mentioned; but if you were smart enough to cheat an old lady out of $400,000, would you come back to caulk her bathtub? I wouldn't.

On Tuesday afternoon, I stopped by Jackie's office after class to say hello. I saw Menno Zook coming out and remembered that she taught the developmental writing class, and that she'd mentioned him to me at the start of the semester. She'd had him as a student in the fall and liked him, though she knew he was going through a rough patch getting accustomed to college.

"How's Menno doing?" I asked. "Is he complaining about me?"

She shook her head. "No, he thinks your class is fine. I'm just his general sounding board. I can relate to him. He's like me. A fish out of water. We're both far removed from our home environments."

Jackie had grown up in Newark, the oldest of three kids in a single-parent household, and I figured it hadn't been easy for her. Menno's life was dramatically different, growing up on a farm in Amish country. But I could see her point; he was the only Amish kid at Eastern, as far as I knew, and though there were a sprinkling of other black faculty and black students, she had to feel isolated.

"How are things going?" I asked, settling into the chair across from her.

She shrugged. "Swamped, as usual." She pointed at a stack of papers. "That's my afternoon and evening project. Sometimes I wish I could just run them all through a paper shredder and be done with it."

"Give it a try sometime," I said. "See if the students notice the difference."

She laughed. "You are a bad influence on me. And if I let you stay in my office, I'll never get any grading done. Begone with you."

"Have it your way," I said, standing up. "But you could just give them all A's and then you'd have plenty of time to hang with me."

"And when Lucas Roosevelt found out, he'd hang me out to dry," she said. "Remember, I don't have tenure yet. I have to be on my best behavior."

"Ah, the joy of being an adjunct," I said.

"I'm going to throw something at you. Like these biscuits for Rochester."

She tossed me a plastic baggie. This time the biscuits were somewhat darker than the ones she'd sent home before. "Carob," she said. "Dogs can't eat chocolate, you know. It can kill them. But carob is OK."

"Thanks. I'm sure he'll like them."

"You're welcome. Now git."

I got, leaving Jackie to an afternoon of marking up papers. I would have sworn I saw her getting into a black SUV and hot-footing it out of the parking lot as I was walking to my car, but it could have been someone else.

That night, I had just returned from walking Rochester when Rick called. "You gonna be home for a while?" he asked. "I want to run something by you."

I said sure, I'd be home, and about a half hour later he was at my door. Rochester went crazy, jumping up and down in glee, as if I ignored him and he had hopes that this stranger might give him a biscuit or a belly rub.

Rick had just come from work, and as he walked into my house he pulled off his tie and unloosened the collar of his gray-and-beige striped shirt. His short hair was mussed and he looked like he hadn't been getting enough sleep.

We made small talk over a couple of beers, then he got down to what he wanted. "I spoke to those two people you emailed me about," he said. He opened up his notebook and consulted it. "Karina Warr and Christian McCutcheon."

My pulse raced for a minute, but he seemed more interested in them than in how I'd gotten hold of their information. "Uh-huh," I said. "You get anything interesting from them?"

He shook his head. "Neither of them knew anything," he said. "They were all friends when they were teenagers, back when all three of their fathers were stationed at Camp Henry, a military base in Korea."

"And?"

"And I think there's something more. It's just a gut feeling, but one or both of them is hiding something from me."

I looked at him, and my brain raced ahead. "Evelina Curcio," I said.

He nodded. "You got her to talk, when she wouldn't talk to me," he said. "You think you could give it a try with these two?"

My first reaction was to back off. "Evelina Curcio talked to me because I ran into her at the memorial service—I caught her off guard. What's to say either of these two will talk to me?"

He took a sip of his beer. "I don't want to say Caroline's murder hasn't upset me—because it has. I don't see a lot of dead bodies. But you're a civilian. You don't see the stuff a cop sees. So I know Caroline's death has hit you harder than me."

I reached down to stroke Rochester's golden head. "I think maybe you can relate to these guys," Rick said. "Go up to New York. Meet with each one. Play it just the way it is—you knew

Caroline, you lived next door, you feel bad that she's dead. You just want to talk to someone else who knew her." He smiled. "Plus you get to play Nancy Drew."

"How about Frank or Joe Hardy instead?" I asked. "Somehow the whole teenaged girl thing doesn't work for me." We came up with an email message I could send, where I indicated that I hoped it wasn't an intrusion, but I'd been trying to find someone I could talk to about Caroline. I said I'd be in New York that weekend, and would appreciate the chance to sit down and chat.

"I have to get permission from Santiago Santos in order to leave the state," I said. "I'm supposed to give him at least two weeks' notice."

"I'll square it with him," Rick said. I sent the messages, and decided to turn the weekend into a mini-vacation. First, though, I had to find someone to take care of Rochester while I was away. I called Ginny Prior first; I figured she owed me a couple of favors. But her husband Richard (as she always said, 'not the burned-up comedian,') was allergic to dogs. "Annie will do it, though," she said, referring to her neighbor. "She loves dogs, and she always liked Rochester."

I called Annie next, and she agreed I could drop Rochester off on Friday morning. I worried what he'd think; would he imagine that like his mom, I was abandoning him?

Through Eastern, I had access to a small private hotel in midtown that gave discounts to academics, and I was able to get a last-minute reservation for Friday and Saturday nights. I emailed my graduate school roommate, Tor, to let him know I'd be in town, and surfed around to see what the hot shows on Broadway were. By the time I was done with all that, I had an email response from Karina Warr.

"I know exactly what you're going through," she wrote. "Caroline's death has just devastated me." She suggested we meet for brunch on Sunday morning, and I wrote back to agree.

When I clicked "send," my email client downloaded anything new, and there was a message from my newest client, the HR manager I'd been working on the forms for. It was the equivalent of a dear John letter; she was breaking up with me.

Reading between the lines, it was clear she'd heard about my criminal past and wasn't comfortable giving me access to sensitive information. She offered to pay for the work I'd done, if I returned all materials to her within 24 hours.

Damn. I'd enjoyed the technical aspects of putting together the forms, and thought I'd done a good job. I'd been hoping she would have more work for me, that her firm could be the centerpiece of my business plan for Santiago Santos. The worst part was her implication that I had been less than forthcoming to her about my background—which was true. Irrelevant, but true.

I spent another hour cleaning up the project and then emailing everything back to her, promising to delete all files from my hard drive. I tried to be very professional, closing with an offer to consider any other work she might have for me—though I knew the chances of that were slim.

I stayed up late on Wednesday night, Rochester sprawled behind my chair, looking for additional work to replace what I'd lost. I found myself bidding on jobs for as little as $50, just to establish relationships. It was a sucky way to build a business, but it was all I had.

Chris McCutcheon's response to my invitation came through on Thursday evening, and he was a lot less welcoming. He did say he could meet me for coffee on Saturday afternoon, though, and I emailed back to confirm.

I went downstairs for coffee, and Rochester followed me down. While I was in the kitchen waiting for the water to boil, I heard him in the dining room, and my developing instinct told me to check him out.

He had his paws up on the dining room table, and he was pushing at Caroline's laptop with his nose. "You don't need a computer," I said, pulling him to the floor. "Look, Rochester. I have papers to grade and I can't mess around with Caroline's laptop now. If you won't leave it alone I'll put it away."

He stared at me and barked once. "Fine," I said. I carried the laptop up to my bedroom and placed it on the top shelf of the closet. When I came back downstairs, Rochester was dozing by the kitchen table.

While the coffee maker was percolating, I got out the stack of instructions the tech writing class had written and began marking them.

The doorbell rang ten minutes later. Rochester went into his crazy routine, and I peered out through the peephole to see

Santiago Santos on my doorstep.

My pulse raced as I opened the door. "Hey," I said. "An unexpected pleasure." What a close call. If he'd come just a little earlier, he would have spotted Caroline's laptop on the dining room table. The terms of my parole were clear; I was allowed one computer, which had to have the tracking software installed. Just having Caroline's laptop in my house was enough to violate my parole, especially if he impounded it and found the special software I'd installed.

"Rick told me about your trip to New York," Santos said, unbuttoning his jacket with one hand and petting Rochester with the other.

"Yeah, he asked me to do him a favor," I said. "Is it OK with you?"

"I just don't want you to get distracted," he said. "How are you coming with your business plan?"

We sat down in the living room, and Rochester sprawled at my feet. I didn't want to tell Santos about the client who had dropped me, so instead I focused on all the work I was applying for. It was a pretty impressive list—though it was just a list, at present, and I hadn't gotten much response to my latest bids.

"Good job," he said, when I was finished. "I'm going to OK your trip, but I expect to see a strong business plan when we meet up next."

I wanted to argue that I was already showing good faith by helping out the Stewart's Crossing police, but I'd already learned it didn't do any good to argue with a parole officer. So I just agreed that I'd have a killer plan ready, shook his hand one more time, and he left.

Of course, between tracking Edith's finances, grading papers for my three classes, taking care of Rochester, and playing Joe Hardy to Rick's Frank, I wasn't sure what else I could do, but hey, sleep is overrated, right?

Identity Theft

Friday morning, I packed up Rochester's crate, his food and water bowls, his food, and a half dozen toys, along with my stuff for New York. I stuck the crate in the trunk and tied the lid shut with a rope, then loaded Rochester into the front seat.

Annie's house wasn't far from mine, just past Main Street and up the hill, where a couple of suburban developments clustered on what had once been farmland. The houses were big split-levels on large plots of land, and Annie's front yard was littered with a Big Wheel, a couple of headless dolls, and the remains of a plastic fort. She had two dogs, a Shih-Tzu and a terrier mix, but she insisted they would both get along with Rochester.

"And you don't even need to unpack the crate," she said, pointing back to the Beemer. "My boys will keep Rochester in line."

He seemed delighted to have new playmates, and after watching him growl and wrestle with Annie's dogs, I drove to the Trenton train station, where I caught the New Jersey Transit train to New York.

I'd taken that train many times as a teenager. Since then, the fields the train ran past had turned into housing developments, and the stations had become more run-down, but sitting by the window, watching the landscape rush by, I could have been seventeen again.

I remembered that longing I'd had, wanting to get out of my little town. Columbia had been my first choice for college, but Eastern had given me a full scholarship and there was no turning that down. My parents had promised I could go to Columbia for graduate school, and I had.

I'd loved living in the city, right up until the day the moving van came to the apartment Mary and I had shared on the Upper East Side and taken our worldly goods on a cross-country trip. I still remembered that last cab ride to the airport, staring back at the skyline as we crossed into the Bronx and wondering if I'd made a huge mistake.

Of course I had, but it took another eight years for both of us to figure that out. Now, going back to the city was like recapturing a bit of my lost past, and every time I took that train in I felt the same anticipation I had as a teenager.

My hotel room was about the size of the master bathroom in my townhouse at River Bend. There was a two-foot clearance on each side of the queen-sized bed, and the window looked out on an airshaft, but I was back in Manhattan.

I spent the afternoon shopping, cleaning Balducci's out of gourmet stuff I knew I couldn't get in Stewart's Crossing, and then met my old friend Tor for dinner that night.

Tor was a Swedish exchange student in business school when I was in the MA program in English, and we'd lived together for a year in the graduate dormitory, then shared a couple of crummy apartments on the Lower East Side until I met Mary. Tor and I were young and single together in the city, and that's a bond that you always share—remembering drunken adventures in Tribeca, parties that lasted til dawn, getting lost in the Village on the way to some strange theater event Tor's girlfriend had invited us to.

Tor had gotten himself a green card and begun his career in investment banking when we lived together, working eighty-hour weeks, traveling to every little Podunk town that wanted to float a municipal bond. He'd gone through a string of girlfriends until he found one who would put up with his work ethic. Sherry, a former model, now sold high-end real estate and worked as hard as Tor.

The effort had paid off for him; now he was a partner, with a huge co-op apartment on the Upper East Side. He traveled everywhere by town car, and his kids went to expensive private schools in Riverdale. I was lucky he could squeeze in dinner with me, but one of his deals had gone sour the day before and he was at loose ends.

I couldn't help comparing our lives since we had lived together. When Mary and I left New York, Tor and I were on parallel courses, heading for happiness and prosperity. I'd worked just as hard in Silicon Valley as he had on Wall Street, but the dice had rolled his way and not mine.

I didn't mind at all, though, because I knew that if I needed anything Tor could provide, I only had to ask him. I'd considered, when my marriage broke up, asking him for a leg up on a job in Manhattan, but I realized it would be going backwards, trying to reclaim my lost youth—which seemed more and more lost every time I looked in the mirror.

In Dog We Trust

He knew about my trouble in California; he'd even offered to hire an attorney for me if I needed. I worried, as I was on my way to meet him at a fancy steak house in the meat packing district, that things might be awkward between us, based on how my life had fallen apart, but he greeted me outside with a big bear hug. Tor looks like he should be winning an Olympic medal in the giant slalom; he's six-three, blond and blue-eyed, his build gone beefy in middle age.

"Hey, you have been such a stranger," he said. "You come all the way back from California, but down there in Pennsylvania you are almost as far away."

"I'm not the one with the high-powered career. Every time I invite you and Sherry to come down to Bucks County you have too much work to get away."

"Soon. We will make it soon. Now, we eat."

We ordered massive porterhouse steaks, drank imported beer, and talked non-stop for two hours. The restaurant was elegant in an understated way—wooden booths with thick cushions, fake gas lamps and a pressed-tin ceiling. It was filled with people like Tor—prosperous, well-dressed, men whose ties alone cost more than everything I had on my body.

At some point, our conversation passed over Caroline Kelly, and how I'd inherited Rochester from her. "Good for you," Tor said. "You need a dog. Man's best friend. Give you someone to take care of."

"I can barely take care of myself."

"Exactly," Tor said. "That's why you need a dog."

I wasn't sure I agreed with his logic, and I wanted to change the subject. "Hey, you know anything about identity theft?" I asked.

"What you want to know?" Tor wiped his mouth with his napkin and laid it down next to his plate. He sighed. "Good food."

I told him about Edith Passis, that I thought someone had stolen her identity in order to cash checks made out to her.

"So someone has access to her mail," he said. "This person either stole the checks from her mailbox or changed her address so the checks would go elsewhere."

"Sounds right."

"It's classic case of identity theft," he said, dropping his articles as he often did. "Someone uses your personal information without permission to commit fraud or other crimes. This person uses your friend's information to cash checks in her name—steal from her."

"It's hard to imagine," I said.

"Identity theft is fastest-growing crime in this country," Tor said. "Your friend must request credit report right away. These people may have new credit cards in her name, too, and ring up big bills without her knowing."

I shook my head. Edith was in a world of trouble.

When the check came, Tor wouldn't even let me leave the tip. "We come to Pennsylvania, you can treat us," he said. He pulled out his cell phone and speed-dialed a number, requesting a car to meet him at the restaurant. "I can drop you somewhere?"

I shook my head. "I have to walk off this dinner."

He gave me another bear hug before he got into the town car, and I watched it head east for a block or so, until I lost it in the welter of traffic. I crossed over to Fifth Avenue and headed south, enjoying the crisp night, the lit shop windows, the noise and vitality of the city. Soon enough, I would have to go back to Stewart's Crossing, work on my business plan and tell Edith Passis someone was stealing from her. But for a moment, I was a free man in a great city.

When I lived in Manhattan, I was fearless. I took the subway home from friends in Washington Heights at three a.m. I walked through dark corners of the Village, withdrew cash from ATMs on deserted streets. It was the hubris of youth.

That night, though, when I turned a corner onto a dark street near the Hudson, I felt scared. Caroline had been shot to death in just such a deserted place, though she'd had much more reason to feel safe in Stewart's Crossing. Two guys approached me, swaying and talking loudly, and I hunched down into my jacket and quickened my step.

"Hey, buddy, spare a couple of bucks?" one of the guys said, and I didn't hesitate; I took off at a sprint down the street, and didn't stop until I'd reached a brightly-lit avenue. Nobody followed me and nobody shot at me, but I was reminded that the world was a dangerous place.

The next day, I was waiting for Chris McCutcheon at a Starbucks on Broadway in the West 90s when he pulled up on a Colnago CF4 Ferrari carbon-frame bicycle, which I recognized by the signature yellow and black stallion logo on the top tube. I'm no biker; I only knew about the Colnago because Rick Stemper had been raving about it to me. It was one of the best bikes in the world, if not the best, and Rick had said they went for over $8,000.

Chris was wearing black compression shorts and a tight black T-shirt. No helmet; that would have messed up his perfectly uncombed blonde hair. I admit it; he reminded me of all those guys in high school who were faster, stronger or more coordinated than I was, and I disliked him on sight.

I was sitting at a table on the street, shivering in my lightweight windbreaker, as he dismounted and locked his bike to a parking meter. "I don't have much time," he said, coming over to shake my hand, as he was pulling off his black bike gloves. "I'm meeting a friend in half an hour for a ride over to Brooklyn and back."

I didn't know where to start—how to get into such a complicated subject in a matter of minutes—but Chris McCutcheon saved me the trouble when he returned to the table after a minute with a bottle of water. My grande raspberry mocha seemed wasteful and decadent in the face of his asceticism—at least to me. "You wanted to talk about Caroline?" he asked, as he sat down across from me.

I tried to remember if I'd ever noticed him when that black SUV had been parked in Caroline's driveway, but I drew a blank. "I found her body," I finally said, and the words spilled out. "It's just really freaked me out, you know? And I realized that I hardly knew her, but we didn't have any friends in common, we were just neighbors, you know? And there was nobody I could talk to about her, to, I don't know, get to know her a little better."

If only to stop my blathering, Chris McCutcheon jumped in. "We lived on the same base in Korea when we were teenagers," he said. "I was, I think thirteen or fourteen, and she was a year younger."

He unscrewed the top of the water bottle and took a long drink. "She used to tag along behind me. There wasn't much for kids to do on the base, but they'd have movies now and then, and once in a while they'd have some kind of dumb social event—a Korean food tasting, for example." He made a face. "So, I don't know, we just hung out. There weren't a lot of other kids our age."

"What was she like then?" I asked, just to keep him talking.

"A lot skinnier," he said. "Smart. She was always reading. She had this lousy little dog, too, used to follow her everywhere. When it ran away she was bummed."

I could see the beginnings of the Caroline I had known—smart, bookish, loved dogs. "When did you two meet up again?" I asked.

He used the bottom of his t-shirt to wipe a bead of sweat from his forehead. "About five, six years ago," he said. "She was living in the city then, and we ran into each other on the Upper West Side. She was with this other chick we knew in Korea—Karina."

"I'm having brunch with her tomorrow."

"She'll give you all the details, I'm sure." He frowned. "Caroline and I went out a couple of times, but then we just ended up friends." He drank some more water. "Military brats—we don't attach to people real well. Sometimes the only ones we get to know are other people like us."

"You came to visit her in Stewart's Crossing, didn't you?"

He nodded. "Tried to get her to go biking with me. There's some great trails there, down along the river, by the canal. She wasn't interested. Truth is, we didn't have that much in common, besides Korea."

He looked at his watch. "I gotta go," he said. He reached over to shake my hand. "Listen, don't let yourself get too freaked out. People come and go in life."

"Yeah," I said. "Thanks for meeting me."

"Sure." He unlocked the bike and hopped back on, and in a moment he was lost in traffic.

In Dog We Trust

Karina Warr

After I left Chris McCutcheon, I was didn't have anything else to do until my brunch the next day with Karina Warr. I started walking down Broadway, figuring I'd meander back to the hotel.

I'd almost forgotten how many beautiful women there were in New York, too. Living in Stewart's Crossing, most of the women I saw were either harried young mothers, or blue hairs like Edith and Irene. But in the city! I've always been a sucker for a professional woman. A tailored suit, a silk blouse, and stiletto heels draw me in right away. Manhattan was full of women like that, blondes and brunettes and raven-haired beauties shouldering their expensive handbags, talking on their cell phones, clutching their designer coffee cups.

Since it was Saturday, there were plenty of casually-dressed women as well. Mary's favorite weekend look was jeans, a t-shirt and sneakers, and I saw that style was still in fashion on upper Broadway. She liked to pull her blonde hair into a ponytail, then pull it through the back of a ball cap. She'd appropriated my favorite, a soft, faded denim one with the logo of a Fortune 500 company whose meeting I had covered for the magazine where I worked.

We spent our Saturdays running errands. Mary loved to cook, and she was always dragging me down to Chinatown for exotic spices, to Little Italy for handmade sausage, to the Greenmarket in Union Square for fresh produce. I was her beast of burden, tagging along behind her carrying the bags while she picked through bunches of Swiss chard or examined the freshness of salmon fillets. We'd laugh and talk, share apple fritters from a stand in the Greenmarket, and just enjoy each others' company.

Broadway seemed to be conspiring to remind me of Mary and our life together. I passed the store where we'd bought our mattress, the office building where she'd been working when we met, a favorite Italian restaurant. I saw young couples holding hands, as we'd done long ago, before the move to California, the miscarriages and the ugly divorce.

At Columbus Circle I looked into the park and my heart skipped a beat when I saw a woman about Mary's size, a blonde ponytail pulled through a denim ball cap. She walked into the park and I couldn't help it. I followed her.

I knew it wasn't Mary. She'd cut her hair short after we moved to Silicon Valley, and the ball cap was in one of the boxes of stuff she had shipped to Stewart's Crossing while I was in prison. But the past was drawing me back.

The night of our first anniversary, we went to one of the free concerts in the park. Mary had taken the afternoon off, packing a picnic basket at Balducci's, including a chilled bottle of champagne with plastic flutes. I met her right there at Columbus Circle, kissed her in front of the statue of old Chris, and then we walked into the Sheep Meadow, where we staked out a piece of lawn.

"I'll spread the cloth, while you open the champagne," Mary said. While I wrestled with the wire and cork, laid out a colorful Indian throw she'd had since college, anchoring the corners with books and take-out containers.

We fed each other grapes and slathered Brie on Swedish flatbread. "I can't believe we've been married a whole year," she said.

"I can."

She turned on her side to look at me. There was a little bit of Brie on her lip and I picked it off with a napkin. "What's that supposed to mean?" she asked.

"It means we've packed a lot into the last year, and I remember it all."

"Speaking of packing," she said. She reached over and picked a clover from the grass, then discarded it when she realized it had only three lobes instead of four.

"Packing for a vacation?" I asked. We'd gone to France for our honeymoon, spending a week in Paris and then another traveling to the chateaux of the Loire Valley, but we hadn't been away since then.

I was munching on a croissant filled with chicken salad when she said, "Maybe a different kind of trip." She sat up.

I looked up at her. "What kind?"

"I've been offered a promotion," she said. "Manager of public relations and publicity for the west coast region."

She reached over to brush a stray hair from my forehead. "The job is based in Palo Alto. Silicon Valley." The high-tech industry had just begun to boom, and we'd talked a bit before about the possibility of relocating to California. But it had never been more than idle speculation.

"When did this happen?"

"Yesterday. I didn't want to tell you until I had a chance to think about it."

I finished my croissant and picked up the champagne bottle. Both our glasses were empty, and I filled them both.

I'd accepted a long time before that Mary was more ambitious than I was, and that happiness in our life together lay in going along with what she wanted. It wasn't much of a sacrifice. I loved her, and I wanted her to be happy. I thought I would do just about anything to make that happen.

It turns out I did a lot more than agree to move to California to try and make Mary happy. I remember the concert, which finished with "The William Tell Overture," complete with cannons and fireworks. How it felt to lie there under the stars with Mary, my arm around her shoulders, her head nestled into me, the music and the light show celebrating the commitment we had made to each other the year before, the new commitment we were making.

Our life in Silicon Valley was full of fireworks, too, though not the good kind we'd experienced in Central Park. I taught as adjunct for two semesters, making pocket change and complaining about student papers, before I found the gig at Mastodon, and Mary wasn't happy with her new job, either. But we'd made that big move, and we had to make the best of it. Eventually she got a job she liked, and my temp job at Mastodon turned permanent, and we started trying to make babies.

Looking back, it seemed like our lives had been on a trajectory, one that began in Central Park that night, and which ended right back there—only this time I was on my own. I followed the blonde in the ball cap for a little while, thinking, and then realized that I'd lost her when I wasn't paying attention.

I looked around. I was surrounded by trees, dappling the ground around me with sparkles of daylight. I sighed, and started to find my way out of the woods.

The next morning I woke early—but had no dog to walk. Instead, I went down to the hotel's business center and checked my email. There were three responses to my bids for work—all no. Had they discovered my background? Had someone else been just better for the job? What would Santiago Santos say? Why was I wasting my time, and money, spending a weekend in New York when I needed to be back in Stewart's Crossing, job-hunting and watching my pennies?

Back up in my room, I put on my sneakers, my sweat pants and a sweatshirt, and headed out for a brisk walk around Manhattan. I went south on Fifth Avenue all the way to 14th Street, then headed east to the river. The area seemed a lot safer in the daylight, but I still shivered when I remembered the drunken guys I'd run from on Friday night.

As I walked, I was reminded of how expensive it was to live in Manhattan—doorman buildings, high-performance cars on the street, expensive clothes and other merchandise in shop windows. Where did people get the money? What would I do if my plans for a technical writing business fell apart?

My bank balance kept shrinking; the twice-monthly paycheck from Eastern wasn't quite enough to pay my bills, so I continued to dip into the little money my father had left me. What if I got sick? What if Rochester got sick? I'd seen how fast the bills piled up when my mother was hospitalized. What would I do in May, when the Eastern paychecks stopped coming in?

I worried my way back up First Avenue, crossing over to the hotel just in time to take a quick shower and head out to brunch with Karina Warr.

We'd agreed to meet at a little café on the Upper East Side, just around the corner from her apartment. "Fabulous breakfasts," she had emailed. "Their Eggs Benedict are just to die for." It was a charming place, decorated like an Italian country inn, with rough stone walls, tendrils of flowers dangling over the bar, and waiters in white shirts, black pants and spotless white aprons.

There was no single woman in the dining room when I arrived, so I waited on the curb for her. Ten minutes passed, then fifteen, then twenty. I was just starting to worry that I'd been stood up when a cab pulled up and a breathless blonde jumped out.

"Steve?"

"Karina?"

She embraced me in a big hug, kissing my cheek. "I'm just so devastated about Caroline," she said.

She looked anything but devastated. Her wavy blonde hair was carefully styled, and her skin glowed as if she'd just stepped out of a beauty ad. She wore a pink strapless dress with a flouncy skirt, and a black linen jacket over her shoulders. "Sorry I'm late," she said, pulling back. "It was a bear getting a cab."

"I thought you lived in the neighborhood," I said.

"I do. But it's six blocks. Can you imagine six blocks in these shoes?"

I looked down at her feet, and realized she was quite a bit shorter than I'd thought. The strappy black sandals she wore had at least a two-inch heel. "I can't imagine walking from here to the restaurant in those shoes," I said.

"You men," she said, playfully slapping my shoulder. "Come on, I'm ravenous."

I'd known women like Karina Warr when I lived in New York. Hell, I'd married a woman like her. She had Mary's taste in footwear, and I remembered that when we were dating Mary had the same flirtatious tone. Of course, after we married we said little more to each other than, "Can you stop and buy toilet paper on your way home from work?" But that's the way true romance turns out.

Despite her obvious familiarity with the restaurant and each and every waiter, Karina agonized over her menu selection. I'd already decided to go with her recommendation on the Eggs Benedict, but she was worried about her cholesterol, and the French toast was *loaded* with sugar, and pancakes just *laid* in her stomach all day.

She settled on an egg-white omelet with mushrooms and green peppers and just the merest hint of cheese. "I mean it," she said to the waiter. "You tell the chef just to wave the cheese over the top—just to let the aroma float into the omelet."

"Certainly, Signora," the waiter said, in an Italian accent that had detoured through Croatia.

"Signorina," she corrected him as he collected the menus.

"Certainly, Signorina," he said, as he beat a grateful retreat.

"Now, Caroline," Karina said as he left, grasping my hand.

It felt nice, though she was as much of a drama queen, if not more, than Reynaldo the law firm proofreader. "You must just be devastated. I know I am."

I nodded. I realized that I hadn't held hands with a woman for a long time, and I liked it. Some long-dormant part of me started to wake up and take notice of the little blush on Karina's cheeks, the scent of her perfume, the way her foot nestled against my leg.

It didn't take much prompting from me; Karina had a lot to say. "I just adored Caroline when we went to school together," she said. "She was a few years older than I was, and I looked up to her so much." I heard a lot about how life on a military base was just dismal, especially when you moved around every couple of years as your father got transferred. "When you met up with a kindred spirit, like Caroline, you just *treasured* the time."

She shifted in her seat, and her foot rubbed against my ankle. My body started reacting to her, and I had to shift around a little on my chair to adjust myself. For a moment or two as she talked, I got lost in a little fantasy of moving back to the city and dating Karina Warr. What would she be like in bed? Mary and I had clicked sexually from the first time we slept together. Would Karina and I have that same connection?

With difficulty, I brought myself back to the present, figuring out from what Karina was saying that despite everything, she and Caroline had not been close for a while. "When she lived in the city, we were like *sisters*," Karina said. "I mean we went *everywhere* together. But then she moved out to Dismal, PA and we just sort of lost touch."

She finally listened to herself and turned a bit pink. "I'm sorry, you were her *neighbor*," she said. "I never actually *visited* your lovely little town, but I'm sure it wasn't as bad as I expected. Living in New York you do get a little spoiled."

"I lived in the city myself for years," I said. "I can tell you there's a point when you welcome the chance to live someplace quiet and peaceful, without graffiti on the corner, the smell of urine everywhere, and a drunk sleeping on your stoop."

The waiter brought our food, and Caroline poked at her omelet, as if she was going to find a wheel of Jarlsberg lurking under the eggy shell. It seemed to meet with her approval, though, and she sighed happily. "This is the most wonderful restaurant," she said. "They know how to take care of their customers."

"I met up with Chris McCutcheon yesterday," I said, as we ate. "He mentioned he lived in Korea with you and Caroline."

"Oh, *Chris*," she said. She leaned in close to me, and once again the scent of roses washed over me. "Tell me, didn't you think there was something—not quite right—about him?"

"What do you mean?" I figured that to her "not quite right" meant "not interested in her."

"He was the oddest boy in Korea," she said. "Very secretive. He was just enough older than Caroline and I were to be dangerous. He loved to flick his cigarette lighter, and he was always threatening to set our hair on fire."

"That is a little odd."

"Did he happen to mention her little dog?" Karina asked.

"He did say she had a dog."

Again, she leaned in toward me. Damn. If she didn't stop doing that I was going to lose track of the conversation altogether. "And did he say what happened to it?"

I had to think for a minute, remembering our conversation and trying to ignore the stirrings in my groin that worsened every time Karina got close to me. "Did it run away?"

"That's what everyone said." Karina put down her fork. "I don't think so."

"What do you mean?"

"Chris would catch bugs and then twist off their wings," she said. "He used to brag about it. And he didn't like Caroline's dog at all. He was always saying what he'd do to it if it ever came near him."

I thought of Rochester. "But he came to Stewart's Crossing to visit Caroline. He must have been OK with Rochester."

"He must have grown out of it," Karina said. "But don't you think it's strange that he hated that little dog so much, and then one day it just disappeared?"

"Wasn't there any investigation?"

"Caroline's father didn't like the dog. He said she was overreacting. But I'll bet Chris had something to do with it."

The thought gave me the creeps. Chris McCutcheon presented such a confident face to the world—was that all a façade? Had he been responsible for hurting Caroline's dog all those years before?

"So tell me about you," Karina said, reaching out to touch my hand again. "You lived in the city?"

My skin tingled where she touched me, sending those messages to my groin again. Mary and I had stopped having sex when she got pregnant the last time, and there hadn't been anyone since. I realized how much I'd missed that intimacy. Taking care of yourself just doesn't have the same impact.

We talked through the rest of our meal, and through cappuccinos. But the more Karina talked, the more she reminded me of Mary—and that was a turn-off. I had loved Mary once, found her sexy, loved taking her to bed—but things had changed a lot since the days of our Manhattan courtship. By the time Karina and I finished our coffee, all I wanted to do was go back home. Maybe I wasn't quite as ready to start dating as my body hoped.

"Would you like to come over to my place?" she said, after the waiter had taken my credit card away. "It's not far, and we could continue—getting to know each other."

"You're so kind to offer," I said, taking her hand and squeezing it lightly. "But you know, I took in Rochester after Caroline died. I have a friend looking after him for the weekend, but I'm worried about him. I don't want him to think I've abandoned him so soon after Caroline's death."

Karina frowned, but then she smiled, as if she was worried about what the frown lines would do to her perfect complexion. "Well, then, I may just have to come down to what is it—Steven's Crossing—myself."

"Stewart's Crossing," I said. "You'll have to let me know if you do."

She kissed both my cheeks as we stood outside the café, and squeezed my hand. I ignored the pressure in my groin. "Feel free to call me again," she said. "It's so good to talk about the things that upset us."

It had gotten colder outside, a brisk wind whipping down the street from the East River, and I shivered in my windbreaker. Like a dumb college kid, I'd been seduced by the early spring sunshine.

"Thank you," I said. A cab came by, and with a shrill whistle she flagged it down.

I felt a tremendous sense of relief as the cab passed out of sight.

Online Research

I called Rick from the train and arranged to meet him for dinner at The Drunken Hessian. Then I sat back to consider everything I had learned. I had a much better understanding of identity theft after my conversation with Tor, and I knew that I had to collect more information from Edith before I could consider contacting anyone to try and recover some of the money that had been stolen from her.

I didn't know quite as much as I would have liked about Chris McCutcheon, Karina Warr, and what had happened between them and Caroline Kelly in Korea when they were teenagers. I would have to do a lot more research—but I knew that there was something there.

Had Chris hurt Caroline's dog? Had she suspected him? How could she have remained friends with him if she had? I'd only had Rochester living with me for a few weeks, but I knew I would be pretty angry if anyone hurt him.

As the countryside sped past, I was worried that Rochester might have forgotten me, that he'd have settled into life at Annie's as easily as he'd settled in with me. And that bothered me. As soon as the train reached Trenton, I ransomed my car from the station garage and headed back to Annie's house.

I needn't have worried. When Annie opened the front door, all three dogs rushed at me, yipping and barking and jumping around like performing seals.

"Maslow! Lacan! Come here," Annie called, and her dogs rushed up to her, tails wagging. "Can you tell my husband is a therapist?" she asked.

I was left with Rochester, who was so happy to see me that I felt even worse about leaving him. "Were you a good boy?" I asked, ruffling his ears. "Did you play nice with the other doggies?"

"For the first day, he sat around and moped," Annie said. "But Maslow and Lacan convinced him to play. He was just fine in the end."

I had about an hour to play with him at home before I had to leave for The Drunken Hessian to meet Rick. Rochester just seemed happy to be back home, and after a quick walk and a bowl full of doggy chow, he was content to sprawl under the dining room table until I returned.

When I got to the bar, Rick was already there, flirting with a twenty-something brunette in a dancer's leotard, and I had to wait until he'd gotten her phone number for him to come over to the booth and sit down. I recapped what I'd learned about Chris and Karina, though he was most interested in the Colnago, the fancy bike Chris had ridden. "That's the price of a small car," he said.

"He drives an SUV, too," I said. Somewhere in the back of my head, a bell rang. "Hey, I saw a black SUV speeding away after Caroline was shot. It could have been his car."

"Or it could have been one of a thousand others," he said. "You didn't notice the make or model?"

I shook my head. "I wasn't paying attention."

"The story of my life," he said. "Witnesses never pay attention to anything."

"Can you see if Chris McCutcheon has a criminal record?" I asked. "The way Karina was talking he was some kind of budding psychopath in Korea. He might have gotten in trouble since then."

Rick shrugged. "I can try, but I don't know what that will tell us." He took a swig of his beer. "I got the ballistics results on that shell casing you found."

"And?"

"It matches one of the bullets that the coroner pulled out of Caroline Kelly."

"What can you do with that?"

He shrugged. "Not much. However, there was a partial fingerprint on the casing, and that will tie the shooter to the weapon."

"Great! Whose print is it?"

"No match in any of our databases. But if we ever find a suspect, it's a way to connect him or her to the crime."

"Him or her? Can't you even tell if it's a man's or a woman's print?"

"There's no reliable way to distinguish whether a fingerprint belongs to a man or a woman," he said. "A man can have big hands or small hands, and so can a woman."

I wanted to get right to work at researching Chris McCutcheon when I got home, but instead I ended up playing with Rochester and unpacking. I had laundry to do, and I needed some down time to process the weekend, seeing Tor and the way memories of Mary had clung to some places we had been together.

On Monday in freshman comp, I waited until the class had settled down and said, "Let's go around the room and brainstorm on your research paper topics."

Of course none of them had thought about what they wanted to write about, despite the fact that they had less than a week before their rough drafts were due. "OK, who has even the vaguest idea?" I asked.

There was no response from the room until Melissa Macaretti raised her hand. "I'm thinking about a music topic," she said.

"Any kind of music in particular?"

"I really like Pachelbel's Canon in D," she said, surprising me. I bet most of the class had no idea what that sounded like, even if they'd heard it as background music dozens of times.

"That's an interesting topic," I said. "You could research Pachelbel himself, the baroque era—maybe even on the number of different variations there are."

Melissa looked satisfied with herself, and the fact that she had survived that brief inquisition caused a few other students to raise their hands. Wakeem wanted to write about ballistics, while Joaquin was interested in a comparison and contrast paper between the 9 mm and the 357 Magnum. Billy Rubin wanted to write about treating gunshot wounds, and another one of the Melissas wanted to write about being a crime scene tech. One of the Jakes was interested in pathology, and the other in trace evidence.

Jeremy Eisenberg wanted to write about Ecstasy, and either Dionne or Dianne wanted to write about date rape. The other—I had just three more weeks to try and tell them apart—wanted to write about careers in nursing.

"That's a pretty broad topic," I said. "See if you can narrow it down a little. There are so many different kinds of nurses. If you like kids, you could be a pediatric nurse. If you like excitement, you could work in an emergency room. If you don't like dealing with patients, you could work in the operating room, because the patients are always knocked out by the time they get there."

The class laughed. I noticed that the lovebirds, Billy Rubin and Anna Rexick, had split up, with Wakeem and Joaquin now between them instead of to one side. Anna wanted to write about emergency room medicine. She announced to the class that she was no longer interested in nursing; she was going to medical school. "More than fifty percent of entering medical students are female nowadays," she said. She loved the TV program *ER* and wanted to work in an environment like that.

I was relieved when Menno bucked the trend and announced he wanted to write about offshore banking. "It's where you put all your money in a bank in some foreign country so you don't have to pay taxes on it."

Tasheba snickered. "You can't open a bank account with two nickels."

"How about you?" I asked. She was debating between writing about animal shelters or Shih-Tzus; as she reminded us all, Romeo, her Shih-Tzu, had come from a shelter.

"Is Shih-Tzu spelled like shit?" Menno asked, earning a glare from Tasheba. I moved on fast. One of the Jeremys wanted to write about *manga*, a kind of Japanese comics, while another wanted to research computer hackers.

I was tempted to make a smart remark, something like "Be sure to include what happens after you get caught," but my jail time wasn't the class's business. It was a reminder of how the rest of the world viewed what I referred to as my little problem. In my opinion, your garden variety hacker is a lot like me, somebody who breaks into sites just to see if he can do it, for that rush that comes with forbidden behavior.

If they'd been honest, I'll bet everyone in the class could have copped to a range of felonies and misdemeanors. Slipping a highlighter at the bookstore into your backpack without anyone noticing. Driving over the speed limit. Smoking or ingesting a controlled substance. How was hitting computer keys in a particular sequence any worse than those?

Maybe you think I don't regret the things I did that got me sent to jail. Could I have protected Mary some other way? Cut up her credit cards? Forced her to go to counseling? None of those would have worked. Mary was too strong-willed, too much her own person.

Would I do it all again? My conviction and prison term had been the death knell for my marriage. Why would I sacrifice so much for a woman who dumped me and took almost everything

I owned?

Then again, I loved her. I thought it was my job, as the husband, to protect her. I know, it's sexist, and I know Mary was quite able to take care of herself. But we are wired in certain ways. I couldn't seem to tame my curiosity, and I doubt I could have held back when there was something I thought I could do to help Mary through the aftermath of the miscarriage.

I gave the class my cell phone number again. "Since I don't have an office here at Eastern, you can't just drop by and ask me any questions. So feel free to email me or call me, and I'll help you out."

Up in the faculty lounge, I ran into Jackie Devere. "Do you know what kind of license plate frame I saw this morning? 'Jesus Died 4 U.' As if the sacrifice of our Lord was something to instant message about. What is up with that? Were they charging by the letter when that idiot ordered his frame?"

"Conservative Christians are destroying our nation's educational fabric," I said. "News at eleven."

Jackie left for a committee meeting, and Dee Gamay, one of the other adjuncts, came in, grumbling. "People on this campus have no respect for human life," she said.

It sounded like "human laugh." "What happened?" I asked, eager for any diversion.

"This big black SUV nearly ran me over in the parking lot," she complained, dropping a pile of books on the table next to me with a thud.

"Disgruntled student?"

"More like nasty faculty member," she said. "It was that Jackie Devere. I know she doesn't like adjuncts, but that doesn't mean she has to kill us."

I left a little later, and when I got home I pulled Caroline's laptop down from the closet shelf, to log on and snoop around. I thought of what Santos would say if he ever found the computer or discovered what I'd been doing. My natural curiosity, as well as the seductive power of knowledge, pulled me forward.

I started with a basic Google search, just getting to know Chris a little. I discovered that he was a real estate speculator—he bought apartments, houses and commercial property all around the five boroughs, did some fixing up, and resold for a profit. He'd spoken at a conference on Rehabbing the City, and

I read the brief bio he had supplied.

"After a globe-hopping childhood, Christian McCutcheon has made New York City his home," it read. "Educated at NYU, he has bought and sold property from Washington Heights to the Battery, and almost every subway stop in between, as well as ventures in the Bronx, Brooklyn, Queens and Staten Island."

From there I went to NYU. With a little finagling, the kind that both Santiago Santos and Rick Stemper would have disapproved of, I discovered that Chris had attended class there almost twenty years ago, but had not received a degree. Searching property records, I found he had bought his first building, a storefront in the East Village, after he stopped going to class.

How had he come up with the money, I wondered. Had his parents been wealthy? Had they left him money? I kept making notes. There was a clear paper trail of his property acquisitions; every time, he traded up. His latest sale had netted him a profit of over $100,000. I found a post on a Porsche site where he mentioned his black Cayenne. But had that been the SUV I saw speeding away after Caroline had been shot?

And if Chris had shot her—why? Had he been obsessed with her since they were teenagers together? Perhaps she had rejected him. He didn't look like the kind of guy who took no for an answer. If he'd kidnapped and killed her dog in Korea, he was capable of growing into murder.

When Rochester came over to lay his head in my lap, I realized I was letting my imagination get away from me. I didn't like the guy, but that didn't mean that Karina's unsubstantiated belief that Chris had killed Caroline's dog was true. And there was no evidence of any bad feelings between Chris and Caroline.

I opened her email again. The online service she used archived messages back three months, and I searched for any email to or from either Chris or Karina. There was nothing of interest. The messages between Chris and Caroline were simple—friends who were busy but keeping in touch, like the messages Tor and I exchanged.

I was getting frustrated. I'm accustomed to finding what I look for online. But maybe there just wasn't anything there to find.

And if that was the case, then I was no closer to finding out who killed Caroline Kelly.

My phone rang as I was preparing dinner. "Chris McCutcheon has a juvenile record, which is sealed," Rick said, jumping in just the way he didn't like me to do. "And he has two misdemeanor convictions for criminal mischief. The first got him a suspended sentence, the second got him a hundred hours of community service."

"What does that mean, criminal mischief?"

"He damaged someone's property. I'm not sure about New York, but in Pennsylvania, it's a third degree misdemeanor if the damage is between $500 and $1,000. Second degree misdemeanor if it's between $1,000 and $5,000, and third degree felony if the damage is over $5,000."

"Which means what?"

"From the penalties, I'm guessing these were second degree misdemeanors," Rick said. "It could have been anything—a bar fight, a landlord-tenant dispute, getting back at an ex-girlfriend. The fact that there are two convictions a year apart means your guy is a bit of a loose cannon."

"You said real or personal property, right?" He agreed, and I told him about Chris's career as a property redeveloper. "Maybe he goes around and bangs up houses, then tries to buy them at a discount."

"You have a real imagination, you know that, Steve? You ever consider writing fiction?"

"Ha funny ha," I said. "So the guy has a temper. He could have been mad at Caroline Kelly and shot her."

"Try taking that to a judge," Rick said. "Right now I've got nothing, and the chief is pressuring me to shelve this as a lost cause and move on. My case load is piling up. Catch you later."

Walking Rochester a little later, I worried that Caroline's murder would go unsolved if Rick had to move on to other cases. But what could I do about it? My few attempts at finding information hadn't been successful. Even my hacking hadn't turned up much information, just a couple of leads that hadn't panned out.

I resolved to look further into Chris McCutcheon's background. There was something more there—I knew it. And if the answer didn't lie with him, then I would keep scratching and digging until I found out who killed Caroline. I owed that much to her, and to Rochester.

Caroline's Diary

After dinner, I decided to take a thorough look through Caroline's boxes before they were shipped off to upstate New York.

Ginny had donated Caroline's clothes and linens to the Episcopal Thrift Shop on Canal Street in Stewart's Crossing. It was right across the street from Mark Figueroa's antique shop, and I thought it was a good source of merchandise. The rest of the stuff from her bedroom was packed in a set of boxes I hadn't looked through yet, so I started with those.

I carried four boxes into my living room and set them on the floor, then sat down to look through them. Rochester was right on top of me, trying to get into the boxes himself. "What's up, boy?" I asked, stroking his head. "You smell your mom?"

The first box I opened was filled with Caroline's cosmetics, so I could understand Rochester's strong reaction. Perfume, face cream, eye shadow, lip liner—every product women were bamboozled into thinking was necessary in order to snag or keep a husband. I sealed the box back up. I'd had quite enough of Mary's endless cabinet of cosmetics.

The second and third box contained jewelry and heirloom linens—lace shams, embroidered pillow cases, and so on. The last was full of knickknacks, stuffed animals, framed photos, and so on. Toward the bottom, though, I found mementos of Caroline's time in Korea, including her junior and senior yearbooks. Chris McCutcheon was a graduating senior in the first; he'd been voted "Least Likely to Pursue a Military Career" by his classmates. He had been a member of the tae kwon do club, the karate dojo, and the wrestling team. Great background for a potential psychopath. And he was only a year older than she was; that wasn't the impression he had given me.

I flipped through the pages, hoping a clue would jump out at me. Had the seeds of Caroline's death been sown that long ago? If Karina was right, Chris had been a dangerous kid, but the casual shots of him showed a skinny boy with long, stringy hair and a leather jacket—just your standard-issue adolescent rebel. There was no neon sign blinking over his head saying, "Danger, Will Robinson," no robot frantically waving mechanical arms.

Caroline was in the second. She had been on the math team, vice-president of the French Club, and on the Honor Roll all four years of high school. There was one casual shot of Karina Warr; she'd been in the French Club with Caroline. Below the yearbooks I found a couple of photo albums, one full of Polaroids from her teenaged years. I could make out Chris and Karina along with a young Caroline. There was even a picture of the Shih-Tzu Karina thought Chris had kidnapped and killed. There was a lot of other memorabilia—programs from school plays, souvenirs from a class trip to Hong Kong and so on.

At the very bottom of the pile there was a faded, clothbound book with a fold-over snap to hold it closed.

I opened the clasp. The title page read, "DIARY: CAROLINE GRACE KELLY."

Sweet. Her father had probably called her "princess."

I put the diary aside, then packed the boxes back up. Rochester was very interested in the book, sniffing it and butting it with his head. "I'm going to read it, Rochester," I said. "Give me a minute to get organized."

I took the boxes back into the garage, and when I returned to the living room Rochester had the book between his two front paws and was gnawing on one corner. "Not yours!" I said. "Give that back to me!"

I had to tug hard on the book to get it out of his grip. I went upstairs, the dog right on my heels. I lay down on the bed, and he disappeared for a minute—but I knew what he was up to. And sure enough, he was building up speed in the hallway for a jump onto the bed. He came galloping into my room and landed with a huge whoomp on the bed next to me.

"Stay down there," I said, using my right foot to position him. He lay down with his head on his front paws, watching me.

I opened Caroline's diary and started to read. I skimmed a lot; she wasn't Anne Frank, and the prose was about the level of my students' papers. Descriptions were non-existent, as was dialogue and characterization. But hey, she wasn't trying to write the Great American (or Korean, for that matter) Novel; she was just recording the thoughts and feelings of a teenaged girl in unusual circumstances.

The dog was named Kimchee, after the spicy Korean

cabbage dish; her father didn't like either very much. There were a lot of mentions of him, and then one day, in capital letters, KIMCHEE IS GONE! She and her mother had hunted all over the base. They had asked the MPs to keep an eye out. They had put up lost dog posters. There had been no sign of him.

Caroline's father said some Korean on the base had taken Kimchee home for dinner, though there was only enough meat on his bones for an appetizer.

Caroline thought he was cruel, and described at length how she had cried over the dog's disappearance. Karina and another girl had been very supportive, though the boys, led by Chris McCutcheon, had tended to agree with her father.

For some time after Kimchee's disappearance, Chris had mimed gnawing on a bone every time he saw Caroline. She thought he was "a real meanie."

Karina had believed Chris was behind Kimchee's disappearance even then. She had led Caroline on a snooping expedition behind Chris's family quarters, where there was some fresh dirt. That had sealed it for Karina, and she had pressed Caroline to challenge Chris.

Caroline had refused—good sense on her part. If he was guilty, he was damaged, and you didn't want to press someone like that. If he was innocent, she was just going to make life in a small community that much more difficult.

There was one entry, after Chris had left the base for college in the states, that intrigued me. Caroline had written about how devastated Karina had been when Chris left, and how she couldn't seem to stop talking about him. "Does Karina ♡ Chris?" she had written. "Is she jealous of me + Chris?"

What did that mean, I wondered. Caroline hadn't written about Chris as a boyfriend; she hadn't even spun any romantic fantasies about him. They were friends, it seemed; he was a bit like a big brother to her, especially when it came to teasing her. Their fathers were friends, so the two were often thrown together.

But once Chris left Korea for NYU, there was no more than a fleeting reference to him—a postcard he had sent home of the Statue of Liberty as a torch singer. "Had to explain to Karina what a torch singer was," Caroline noted. "Even then she didn't get the joke."

After Caroline graduated from high school, her father had been posted to Germany. Caroline had gone to Utica to spend the summer with her great-aunt, then on to SUNY. The diary's entries stopped after a couple of months in college. There was no indication of whether she'd been in touch with Chris once she returned to the States. I knew only that the three of them had reconnected when they were all living in Manhattan.

I closed the book and looked down at Rochester, who had turned on his side, his legs splayed out. He snored lightly, and his chest rose and fell with each breath.

Had the diary provided me with anything I didn't already know? At least I had Caroline's viewpoint on what had happened to Kimchee, not just Karina's. All the suspicion was still on Karina's part.

I looked at the materials stacked next to me on the bed. Caroline's great aunt wouldn't have any use for them, but Karina or Chris might. I left Rochester sleeping on the bed and went into the office, where I emailed Karina to let her know what I had and ask if she wanted any of it.

I'd just finished sending the message when my cell phone rang. "Hi, Professor Levitan, it's Melissa Macaretti. Sorry, but I'm at my boyfriend's place, and he doesn't have internet, or I'd have emailed you. Can I use information I got from talking to one of my professors in my paper?"

"Sure," I said. "You reference it like a personal interview."

"Which is how?"

"OK. Who was the professor?"

"Professor Richard Livorno, in the music department."

I knew him. He'd been around when I was in school. His cousin, Francis "Chickie" Livorno, was a minor Mafioso who'd been indicted my junior year, and there had been rumors running wild around campus that his cousin Richie was connected, too. The school paper had a field day, learning that Livorno was the Italian name for a city called Leghorn in English, which was also a breed of chicken—hence Chickie's name.

The paper had christened Professor Livorno as "Strings," because in addition to teaching he played the violin, and for a few years afterward had always referred to him as Professor Richard "Strings" Livorno, in the style of Mafia figures.

I explained to Melissa how to quote him, using a signal

phrase, and had to resist saying, "According to Professor Richard 'Strings' Livorno." Then we went over how to cite the interview in her Works Cited list. By the time we were done I wanted to ask her, "Do you want me to write the paper for you, too?"

I took Rochester out for a quick walk around eleven, and then out of habit, I glanced at my date book for the next day, and realized, with a sudden drop in my stomach, that Santiago Santos was due to come by for a follow up visit the next afternoon.

I'd just wasted the entire evening looking through Caroline's diary, when I should have been working on my business plan. I was sunk. Sure, I had been looking for new clients, even picking up a couple of small jobs, but I still didn't have a clear idea of what I was going to do for money once the Eastern paychecks stopped coming in. Santiago Santos wasn't going to like that.

I had trouble sleeping, thoughts of Santos and a possible return to prison in California rolling through my brain. I got up around two AM and tried to work at the computer, but it was no good.

I woke up around seven, not feeling refreshed at all, and let Rochester drag me around the neighborhood as I continued to stress over the visit from Santos. When I got back home, the phone was ringing—never a good sign so early in the morning.

"Steve, it's Santiago Santos," he said. "I'm sorry, but I'm not going to be able to get out to your place this afternoon. I've got an emergency with another client."

"That's OK," I said, trying to keep the relief from my voice. "I understand."

"I know it's irregular, but do you think I could come by Sunday afternoon? Say two o'clock? My calendar is pretty jammed."

"Sure, Sunday's fine," I said.

The day looked a lot sunnier. I gave Rochester a biscuit, which he appreciated, and sat down to breakfast myself. When I checked my email after breakfast, there was a message from Karina Warr, saying that she was going to try and get down to Stewart's Crossing on Saturday afternoon. Would I be around to show her the personal stuff Caroline had left behind? I emailed back to her and said yes. I offered to send her directions, but I didn't get a response.

It struck me that I didn't know much about Karina beyond her connections to Caroline and Chris. What did she do for a living, for example?

I knew I was supposed to work on my business plan—but I had a reprieve of a couple of days, so I indulged my curiosity instead of doing what I should. Gee, isn't that how I got in trouble in the first place?

Opening Caroline's laptop once more, I Googled Karina and was surprised at how many hits I got. Many of them were useless; she attended an awful lot of parties that got written up in online gossip columns. However, I did find out that she was in charge of location scouting for a chain of fast food sushi restaurants called Wok 'n' Roll.

To me, fast food sushi was an oxymoron; good sushi was prepared by a trained chef, not thrown together by a high school kid in a paper cap. It was served according to long-standing Japanese traditions, not slung onto paper plates and handed across a counter by a teenager with an attitude.

Karina Warr sure had attitude, though. I'd seen it demonstrated at brunch, and I saw it online, too. She'd rubbed a couple of people the wrong way, and they'd taken to the Internet to voice their complaints. A man named Surinder Darthy accused her of underhanded negotiations, concealing her affiliation with Wok 'n' Roll as she negotiated for a lease on his storefront in Washington Heights. He thought she was a real witch.

C.S. Verdad owned a shopping center in Manhattan Beach that was in danger of default. If Karina had signed the lease for a Wok 'n' Roll outlet there as she had promised, he would have been able to use that commitment to hold off his lenders; instead, she had delayed until the deadline had passed, and then negotiated a deal with the creditors who had taken over the plaza.

Karina had agreed to serve on the board of an organization called Kids in Danger, whose sole purpose seemed to be preventing gay men and lesbians from adopting children. Karina had also promised that Wok 'n' Roll would cater their fundraiser. A woman named Mary Cone, who claimed to be the president of this idiotic organization, accused Karina of defaulting on her obligations.

There were more—articles in neighborhood flyers, posts to discussion boards, but they were all in the same vein. Karina was a sneaky, unscrupulous bitch who would just as soon rip you off as look at you.

Reminded me a lot of my ex-wife.

But had she expanded her repertoire to include murder? I found a picture taken at an event called "Shooting for a Cure," a breast-cancer fundraiser held at a private gun club in Manhattan, which showed Karina in plastic glasses and protective ear muffs, aiming a handgun at a target. So she could shoot.

Was that Chris McCutcheon behind her, steadying her hand? It was impossible to tell for sure, but he was the right height and it could have been him.

The photo implied that both Chris and Karina knew how to shoot, and I knew both had access to Chris's black SUV. Karina might have been jealous over Caroline's friendship with Chris. Based on what Karina said of his youth, and his criminal record, Chris might be some kind of psychopath. But I had nothing more than that. I knew what a defense attorney would claim on *LA Law* or *Boston Legal*—circumstantial evidence. Rick would need a lot more to arrest either one of them.

I still had some time before I had to go up to Eastern for my mystery fiction class, so I loaded Rochester into the Beemer and drove up to The Chocolate Ear. As usual, Gail had a couple of biscuits for Rochester, and it was warm enough that the two of us could sit out at one of her curbside tables to enjoy our respective treats.

I was reading an essay that analyzed the dialogue in Rita Mae Brown's talking cat mysteries when Rick Stemper pulled up in front of the café in his white pickup. He nodded hello, then came out a few minutes later and sat with me. Rochester was all over him. "Hey, boy, down," he said. "I don't have any treats."

Rochester didn't believe him. "All right, I have one," Rick said. "Courtesy of your Aunt Gail."

He gave Rochester the biscuit, and the dog flopped down at his feet, chewing noisily. "Yeah, you guys keep giving the dog treats and then he turns into a big fat monster," I said.

"Get over it. What's new?"

I told him I had found Caroline's teenaged diary.

"You think that has any bearing on her murder?"

I shrugged. "Karina Warr thought Chris McCutcheon killed Caroline's dog in Korea," I said. "I wanted to see if Caroline believed that."

"And did she?"

"She didn't say so in the diary. But maybe Karina had an ulterior motive for suggesting it." I told him about Caroline's suspicion that Karina had a crush on Chris.

"I'm waiting for this to matter somehow," Rick said.

"Suppose Chris and Caroline have been getting together, and Karina's jealous," I said. "I know Chris has been down for the weekend, because I saw his SUV in Caroline's driveway. If Karina wants Chris for herself, she could have killed Caroline to get her out of the way."

He sipped his coffee. "It's a motive. But how could I prove it?"

I saw the way Rick was holding his coffee cup, thumb on one side, the four fingers wrapped around, and something registered. "Fingerprints," I said. "If I got you Karina's fingerprints, you could compare them to the print you found on the shell casing, right?"

"How are you going to get her prints? You going up to New York again?"

"No, but she's coming to Stewart's Crossing on Saturday." I told him about the email, that she wanted to see Caroline's mementoes of Korea.

"Offer her a drink," Rick said. "Then leave the glass wherever she puts it down, and call me after she leaves. I'll come over and pick it up."

"Why don't you just come over?" I asked. "We don't have to tell them you're a cop; you're just a friend of mine who stopped by."

He nodded. "That would preserve the chain of custody," he said. "If I witness her use the glass and then I take direct possession of it."

I told him what I'd learned in my online research about her. "Just because she's a bitch doesn't make her a murderer," he said. "God knows if bitchiness was a crime, both our ex-wives would be behind bars for life."

"That's something I can toast to," I said, raising my cappuccino.

He drained the last of his coffee and reached down to scratch behind Rochester's ears. "You take care of this pup," he said to me. "He's a good boy."

I watched his truck merge into the busy Main Street traffic. Rick was a good cop, and I wanted him to keep his job. Maybe Karina would have some answers for us. If she didn't, I feared we might never find out who killed Caroline.

Edith's Money

That afternoon, since I wasn't going to get a visit from Santiago Santos, I decided it was time to tell Edith Passis what I thought was going on. Before I did, though, I did some quick research on the three main credit bureaus and how Edith could request her credit reports.

I called Edith to make sure she'd be home, gave Rochester a biscuit, and then set off. It was a gorgeous spring afternoon, the kind that make me wonder why I would live anywhere other than southeastern Pennsylvania. The sky was a cloudless, crisp blue the color of Tiffany boxes. Every tree seemed to be coming into leaf, a burgeoning sonata of green. The flowerbeds under the Victorian street lights on Main Street were sprouting tulips and daffodils.

An interconnected series of three lakes were the centerpiece to Lake Shores, the suburban neighborhood on the south side of town where I'd grown up. My parents' house was on Center Lake, and I couldn't resist making a quick pass by it.

It was an unassuming ranch in a neighborhood of similar houses. The back yard sloped down to the lake, and I remembered summer days spent with my arms twined above my head, my legs locked, rolling down the broad green lawn. We had a little sandy beach and a concrete post where my father tied up an aluminum rowboat. I'd had a swing set and a ranger tower back there as a kid, and when I'd outgrown them my parents had planted apple, pear, peach and cherry trees.

My father had sold the place when he moved to River Bend, and the new owners had ripped out all the overgrown landscaping, even the fruit trees from the back yard. Gone was the dogwood tree my mother planted the year my grandmother died, and the low boxwood hedge outside my bedroom.

The windows were all new, and instead of white, the house had been painted a pale terra cotta. The scrawny weeping cherry at one corner of the front yard was gone, replaced by a pair of maple saplings. The lawn glowed a verdant green, and daffodils peeked out of a bed in front of the living room windows.

Life moved on, I thought. Mine hadn't been an idyllic childhood, and I had been glad to see the back of that house when my parents drove me up the river to Leighville for my Eastern College orientation. Even so, there were kids like Caroline, Karina and Chris who hadn't had the solid, rooted childhood I had, and envied it, just as I envied their chance to live in exotic locations and see the world.

Despite the changes in my parents' house, and in many neighbors', Edith Passis's looked just as it had when I was a kid going there for piano lessons. It was a one-story Cape Cod, freshly painted white, with a red roof. The bushes were trimmed, the grass edged next to the driveway.

The upright piano was in the same place in the front room, gleaming with a coat of furniture polish. "Edith, this is a trip back in time," I said, after she'd hugged me, taken my windbreaker, and led me to the dining room table, where her financial paperwork rested in haphazard piles. "Your house looks just the way I remember it."

"I have a great handyman," she said. "I have to admit, things started falling apart after Walter died. I just didn't know what to do or how to do anything." She smiled. "Walter did everything for me. He used to say, 'Edith, you just concentrate on your music and leave everything else to me.'"

We sat down across from each other. "But just when I was lost, my angel from heaven showed up, and he cleaned my gutters, trimmed the hedges, repaired my leaky kitchen sink—I just don't know what I'd have done without him."

"It's good you found him," I said. My parents' friends were running into the same kinds of problems—old men who couldn't do what they'd once done, old women who'd never had to do anything for themselves. Mary's mother had never even learned to drive, and when Mary's father died she'd had to move into an assisted living facility.

"I wish I had the same good luck with all this paperwork," Edith said. "Walter, bless his heart, left me very well off, but lately, I feel like I've just lost control."

"Let's see if we can get you organized," I said, holding off the bad news until I got a better sense of what we were up against.

We sat down at the table, and the scent of lemon Pledge rising off the wood was enough to remind me of how her piano had always smelled. We spent the next two hours just sorting paperwork into piles. There were brokerage statements on three different accounts, a checking account, and a savings account. Each one sent her monthly statements, and some of the envelopes hadn't even been opened.

She had an old ledger Walter had maintained, which listed corporate bonds, municipal bonds, and a bunch of what appeared to be loans to individuals. "Edith, you own a bus?" I asked, when I pulled out one piece of paper and read it.

"A bus? What on earth would I do with a bus?" she asked.

"According to this, you own a twelve-passenger bus that's leased to Royal Limousines. They've been paying you annual payments for the last six years, and this year the ownership of the bus transfers to them."

"I had no idea," she said.

That was Edith's refrain no matter what I asked. There were some corporate bonds that should have come due in the past year, but she had no record of receiving them. There was a $50,000 certificate of deposit in Walter's records, but the last statement she had was six months old.

It was just a nightmare. I've never pretended to be a financial genius, but when Mary and I had money, we invested in a couple of stocks and CDs, paid our mortgage on time and so on.

By the time we had the piles sorted, Edith was getting more and more upset. "Could I have a cup of coffee?" I asked, just to give her something to do.

"Of course! How silly of me. Here you are working so hard and I haven't even offered you anything to drink. And I made cupcakes specially for you."

She bustled off to the kitchen, returning a little later with some watery supermarket brand coffee and a tray of orange-frosted cupcakes. She calmed down a bit, but I could tell she was watching me and worrying over what I was finding.

Finally I said, "Edith, I'm not going to be able to finish this afternoon. Can I take the rest of these papers back to my house?"

She looked quite grateful, and found an empty box in her garage that we could use, along with a dusty, unopened package of file folders. I put her to work labeling the folders and filling them with the appropriate papers as I began putting each pile into chronological order, opening the unopened envelopes and throwing away all the advertising circulars that came with them.

Before I left, I sat down in the living room with her. "Someone has been taking advantage of you," I said. "You're missing a lot of documentation, and I found this account at Quaker State Bank in your name that you say you never set up. It's likely somebody is trying steal your identity."

I had to stop and explain identity theft, and Edith got more and more concerned. "I've heard about it on the news," she said, and her voice warbled a little. "This lady lost her house."

"You aren't going to lose your house," I said, trying to smile. "I'm going to go through all this paperwork, and then we're going to talk to Rick Stemper. But first, I want you to get copies of your credit reports."

"I don't know how to do that," she said. She looked like she was ready to cry.

"I wrote it all up," I said, handing her the instructions on who to call and what to ask for. "You do this, and I'll look over all your paperwork, and we'll talk."

I hated leaving Edith so upset, but I didn't know what else I could do. I'd already spent much more time at her house than I'd anticipated, and I knew Rochester would be eager for his dinner and walk. I just didn't know how I could make things any better for Edith.

On impulse, I drove through the center of town and made a quick stop at The Chocolate Ear. Irene Meineke, Gail's grandmother, was still there. I explained to her what had been happening to Edith, and she agreed to go right over to Edith's and sit with her for a while.

I felt better as I headed home, though I had that big box of Edith's paperwork next to me on the passenger seat of the Beemer, and I knew it would take me hours more to get it sorted. When I walked into the courtyard of the townhouse, I could see Rochester through the sliding glass doors. He was on alert—head high, tail erect, looking just like the picture in the golden retriever book. When he realized it was me, the whole effect was spoiled and he went into his mad kangaroo routine.

That night, I neglected my clients and the business plan for Santiago Santos, and ignored the papers I had to grade. I was about halfway done with Edith's paperwork by the time I took a break at eleven to walk Rochester, and I didn't get to sleep until after two. But everything was organized.

The next morning I put a piece of brisket in the crock pot and invited Edith to dinner. For good measure, I invited Rick, Gail and Irene, too, and Gail didn't have to twist my arm to get me to let her bring dessert.

That morning, students in the tech writing class began making their presentations, so I had nothing to prepare, just the pleasure of sitting and listening. Of course, there wasn't much pleasure in their choice of topics – you could call it *25 Ways to Die*. Colon cancer, cervical cancer, skin cancer. Diabetes, multiple sclerosis, drug overdoses, eating disorders and brain tumors. I thought I might have to go on anti-depressants just to sit through their presentations.

I collected the rough drafts of research papers from the freshman comp class, ignoring the simmering tension between Menno and Tasheba. I promised to read them all over the weekend and return them on Monday with advice and suggestions, so they could submit the final drafts the last day of class. Of course, five of the twenty-five students either weren't in class or hadn't brought their rough drafts.

I sat in the faculty lounge with Dee Gamay and a couple of other adjuncts after class, all of us bent over stacks of papers, red marking pens in hand. Her cell phone rang while we were grading, and she answered, "Dee Gamay." She listened for a minute, then said, "I don't speak Spanish. Speak English, god dammit," and then slammed the phone shut.

"I tell you," she said, and her accent made it sound like she was saying, 'I tail you.' "I get these calls every now and then—people just start in talking in Spanish, like I'm supposed to understand what they're saying."

"Do you speak Spanish at all?" I asked.

She shook her head. "Not a word. And I'm not about to start learning."

"I learned a little, living in California," I said, sipping my tea. "And I know that *digame* means 'speak to me.' So even though you think you're saying your name, some Spanish person is going to think you're saying 'talk to me' in Spanish."

"I never heard of such a thing," she said, as if she didn't believe me.

"Check with the Spanish department if you want," I said, as I went back to work. Most students had improved enough that I could get over the basics of grammar and punctuation and focus on content. Menno's paper was one of the better ones. Though I didn't have much interest in offshore banking, the paper was well-organized, with a solid thesis statement, topic sentences for the paragraphs, and correct punctuation.

I'd just given him an A for the paper when something caused me to look back and pay closer attention. He'd mentioned that the Cayman Islands were one of the prime locations for offshore banking, and something clicked. I remembered that a great deal of Edith's money had been transferred to accounts in the Caymans. Was that a coincidence, or was it significant? I wasn't quite sure.

I got through half a dozen papers after Menno's before I had to give up. Cruelly, the weather had warmed up, and spring had sprung in Bucks County. I put the windows down in the Beemer for the drive back down the river and enjoyed the only time I'd be out in the sun for the next few days.

I spent an hour whipping the house into shape for company, baking potatoes in the oven and tossing a salad. The guests started arriving at five, and by quarter past everyone was enjoying a quick sangria I'd tossed together and making appreciative noises about the scent rising from the crock pot.

I held off talking about Edith's problems until we were relaxing over decaf cappuccino and slices of Gail's chocolate raspberry torte, which was worth all the work I'd gone through on Edith's behalf. I could definitely fall in love with a woman who baked like that. I missed Mary's cooking more than I was willing to admit, even though she'd stopped preparing most of her special dishes after the first miscarriage.

"With your permission, Edith, I'd like to share what I've found about your problems with Rick, Gail and Irene," I said. I knew Irene could provide moral support for Edith, and Rick could help us figure out her legal recourse. Gail, of course, had brought the cake.

"I just feel so terrible," Edith said. "Walter would be so disappointed in me."

Irene reached over and squeezed her hand. In broad strokes, I sketched out what I thought was happening. "Somebody got into Edith's mail," I began.

Homes in Lake Shores had mailboxes at the street, so anyone could walk or drive by, open the mailbox door, and pull out anything they wanted if they knew Edith's schedule—the day she taught at Eastern, for example, or the way she could be found at The Chocolate Ear nearly every afternoon.

"The thief did a couple of things," I continued. "Some of her brokerage and bank statements haven't been coming in, because the delivery address was changed. There are checks Edith should have received from those accounts and she hasn't. Those appear to have been cashed by the person who set up the account at Quaker State Bank in Easton and who changed the addresses on her accounts."

I saw Rick pull out a pad and start to take notes. Gail and Irene looked concerned, and Edith just looked miserable.

"Walter left Edith a number of investments," I went on. "Some stocks, some municipal bonds, some certificates of deposit." I looked at Edith. "Now, I don't want to speak badly of Walter, but I have to say he didn't make it easy for you to keep up with things, Edith. There are so many different accounts, and loans he made to people, mortgages on property and so on—there's no way he could have expected you to keep track of it all."

Edith's lip was quivering. Irene said, "Now, Steve, remember, Walter didn't plan for his death. He had a heart attack."

Edith said, "Steve's right, Irene. Walter used to spend hours looking after things, and he should have known I didn't have the head for numbers he had."

Somehow, a change had come over Edith. Her chin had stopped quivering, and she didn't look ready to burst into tears any more.

I looked over at Rick. "What do you suggest we do next?"

He turned to Edith. "First of all, you have to contact every one of the places where you have accounts, everyone Walter loaned money to, every IRA and 401K and what have you, and make sure that they know someone has been messing with your accounts, and that all communication has to come to your address."

"I'll help you with that, Edith," Irene said. "Tomorrow morning, I'll come over to your house before I go to the café, and we'll start calling people."

"I have the folders in the living room," I said. "Everything is organized by account. You may have to look up a few phone numbers, but you'll have the account numbers and the names of the companies."

"Good," Rick said. "Now, you say there's an account at Quaker State Bank that Edith didn't know about?"

I nodded.

"Then I think she ought to go over to the branch where the account was set up and talk to the manager. You want him to put a fraud alert out and monitor any activity in that account. Maybe even some of the money that was stolen from Edith is still in the account, and he can freeze it. It'll take you a long time to get the money back, but at least it's a start."

"When do you teach at Eastern, Edith?" I asked.

"Tomorrow morning."

"I teach until 1:45. The bank branch is in Easton, so why don't we meet up at the music department and I'll drive you up there?"

Edith smiled. "You all are being so good to me."

Rick promised to file a police report for Edith the next day, and he said he'd get her the information on filing a fraud report with the FDIC. Irene had already helped her call for copies of her credit reports the day before.

"We're making a lot of progress, Edith," I said. "You'll see, we'll get this all sorted out."

I wished I felt as confident as I tried to sound.

"Now it's up to Rick to get poor Caroline's murder sorted," Irene said. "Did you all see the *Boat-Gazette*?"

The *Boat-Gazette* was Stewart's Crossing's weekly newspaper—a few pages of grocery ads, church service listings, and the occasional article on a local retailer. Irene pulled the paper out of her big canvas pocketbook and flourished it. "Is Stewart's Crossing safe?" the front-page headline blared.

"It's all taken out of context," Rick said.

"Can I see?" I asked, and Irene gave me the paper. Rick was busy explaining while I scanned through the article, which mentioned the "crime wave" that had hit our little town—the burglaries, the acts of vandalism, Caroline's murder.

"I think it was a mistake for the chief to decline to comment," Rick said. "It gives them a chance to blow everything out of proportion."

"I'm worried about the vandalism," Gail said. "It says there's a gang called the SC Boyz who have been damaging local businesses."

"I saw something down by the river that read 'Black Power,' Irene said. "It made me very nervous."

"Who here went to Pennsbury High?" Rick asked, raising his hand, though he already knew the answer. Gail and I raised our hands too. "And what are our school colors?"

"Orange and black," Gail and I said together.

"Kids have been writing 'black power' slogans as long as I can remember," Rick said. "Along with 'orange rules' and a bunch of other variations."

"There's still the murder," Edith said. "People are saying it just isn't safe to walk around Stewart's Crossing after dark any more. They're bringing up the shooting at The Drunken Hessian again."

"Now, you know that's silly, Edith," Rick said. "Two murders in ten years is not a crime wave."

"But people are talking," Gail said. "I hear it at the Chocolate Ear every day since this article came out. Are you any closer to finding out who killed Caroline?"

"I wish I could say we were. But the trail is cold and until we get a break, I don't know what else I can do."

After everyone left, I graded research papers for a couple of hours, then sat with Rochester on the living room sofa, stroking his silky golden head. "There has to be something I can do to help," I said to him. "The question is what."

Easton

The next day, Thursday, the mystery fiction class handed in their final papers. I was carrying the stack out of Blair Hall when I heard two girls talking.

"What's with the whole list thing?" the first girl asked. Frizzy-haired and chunky, she looked like the stereotypical best friend on some eighties sitcom.

"It's like a hobby," her friend said. She was the pretty one, wearing a form-fitting tank top in black with silver spangles, and white slacks. She looked like she was ready for a night on the town, not a lecture in economics or history. "I keep lists of the guys I've slept with, looking for patterns. I've got a Matthew, a Mark, a Luke and a John, and when I was on vacation in Florida I even slept with a Jesus, though he pronounced it Hay, Zeus."

"You are nuts, girl," the best friend said.

"Now I'm working on the rest of the apostles." The pretty girl, whose brown hair was cut and styled like some MTV goddess, started counting on her fingers. "Peter, Andrew, two James, John, Philip, Thomas, and Matthew were pretty easy. I even lucked out and met a British guy at a club in New York whose name was Simon. But I'm lost when it comes to Thaddeus, Matthias and Judas. You know how hard it is to find a guy named Judas? It's not exactly the most popular name in the Bible."

"You could always stretch the point and find a lesbian named Judy," the best friend said. "Or maybe a drag queen with a Judy Garland fixation."

I had to turn left for the music department, so I missed what the first girl had to say in response. I was heading toward Granger Hall, one of the newer buildings on campus. Harley Granger had made a fortune in the pharmaceutical business, and had donated a couple of million bucks for a building for visual and performing arts, provided the building would be shaped like a pill bottle.

It was round, six stories, with tall glass windows that wrapped around three-quarters of the building. The roof was white, with a white cornice and an extra tab so that a giant could flip it off if he chose. The soaring lobby provided a gallery space, and the current exhibit focused on the landscape of the Delaware Valley. Pretty river scenes alternated with stark lithographs of trees in winter. The art studios were on the second and third floor, and the music department was on the floors above.

When I exited the elevator on four, I was surprised to see Melissa Macaretti sitting at the reception desk. "Hi, professor," she said.

"Your work-study job?" I remembered we'd discussed music topics for her research paper.

"Uh-huh. How can I help you?"

"I'm looking for Mrs. Passis," I said, and she directed me down the hall to a wedge-shaped room where a violin quartet was practicing something baroque. Behind them, through the tall windows, I could see down to the Delaware, where a small power boat was creating a v-shaped wake behind it. Edith sat in the back of the room, a happy expression on her face. Her smile darkened a bit when she saw me and remembered what we were going to do.

When the concerto finished, we walked out to where Melissa sat. "Goodbye, dear," Edith said to her. "You be sure to say hello to your young man for me."

Melissa said she would. As we waited for the elevator, Edith said, "I hate the idea of going up to confront this bank manager, but I know it has to be done."

"It won't be so bad," I said. "Remember, they're the ones at fault, not you."

Though there was still a chill in the air, the drive up the River Road to Easton was very pleasant, and we chatted about spring and the exhibit in Granger Hall.

Easton is an old stone city which grew up around the intersection of the Lehigh and Delaware Rivers. The canal that passes through Stewart's Crossing on its way to Bristol begins up at Easton, where it connects to a similar canal along the Lehigh. As in New Hope, you could take a mule-drawn boat down the canal, or you could walk along Lafayette Hill, around the Lafayette campus—or you could just pass through town on I-78 on your way to or from more important places.

The stately granite building had First Valley Bank and Trust etched in the stone lintel over the front door. Inside, the two-story lobby showed its age as well as the attempt to update to modern banking practices. The tellers stood behind a marble counter with decorative wrought-iron grilles that slid down when the station was closed, and four desks clustered in one corner of the cavernous space.

The cheery, bright-colored signs advertising credit cards, free checking accounts and other services looked small and out of scale with the rest of the room. A series of stanchions and a black rubberized rope slung through them kept the customers in line while they waited. There was a long line, even though there were three tellers working, and a half dozen people sat on orange vinyl chairs waiting for one of the loan officers.

"Is this the only bank in town?" Edith asked.

"Sure looks like it," I said. We walked over to the reception desk, and a young African-American woman in a blue suit with a bright green scarf asked if she could help us. We asked for the manager, and I explained that we thought fraud was being committed on Edith's account.

"Just a moment, please," she said, and she got up and walked over to an young-looking guy in a white shirt and a tie the same shade of green as her scarf. After a whispered conversation, she brought him back to meet us.

His bright red hair didn't help in the overall impression he made, which was of a junior high school debater. "I'm Alvin Jesper, the branch manager," he said. "How can I help you?"

He reached out to shake our hands as we introduced ourselves, and then he stood there, holding his arms close to his chest, his wrists folded down like the paws of a kangaroo.

I explained again about the fraud. "Are you an attorney?" he asked me.

I shook my head. "Just a friend, trying to help Edith out."

We followed him to his desk, where I laid out the details I had—that we believed an account had been established in Edith's name, and that someone was using it to steal from her.

"How do you know this isn't another customer with the same name?"

I explained that the social security number on the account was Edith's, and that I had been able to establish online access to the account using that number. "I was able to answer all the questions using Edith's personal information," I said. "Date of birth, mother's maiden name, and so on."

"I'm not sure that was legitimate," he said. "You created online access to someone else's account."

"To an account in Edith's name, with her permission," I said. The last thing I needed was to get in trouble with Santiago Santos over unauthorized internet use.

I showed him a printout I'd made of the transactions on the account. "Here's the first of the fraudulent transactions. Someone changed the address on Edith's brokerage account, so that her statements and dividend checks are being mailed to a post office box here in Easton. I can match the checks that were issued over the last four months to deposits into the account here."

He scanned the paper. "It could all be coincidence." He shrugged. "Let me see what we have on the account." He turned to his computer and began typing.

He made humming noises as he scanned the screens, then stood. "Let me check some records." He walked through a door to the vault.

"This isn't going well," Edith said. "I was sure the manager would be much more cooperative."

"He looks like he's on a high school internship," I said. "I doubt he's been working here more than five minutes."

I said some more encouraging things to Edith while we waited. Alvin returned from the vault, carrying a couple of pieces of paper. He sat back down and pushed the first over to me. "This is a copy of the driver's license and social security card that was used when the account was established."

The picture was gray and fuzzy, of a much younger woman than Edith. She produced her own driver's license and social security card, and the numbers on both matched what had been submitted. "We had no way of knowing that the person who presented us with this documentation was not the real Edith Passis," Alvin said.

He seemed a lot more cooperative once he had come back from the vault—maybe because he realized how much trouble the bank could be in. "I shouldn't show you this, but you seem like such nice people," he said.

Yeah. He probably thought the fake Edith Passis was pretty nice, too.

He pushed another piece of paper across to me. This was a copy of the account application, using all of Edith's information, though the preferred address was a post office box in Easton, and the secondary address was in Easton as well.

The other information that didn't match was the phone number on the account. Looking over my shoulder, Edith spotted the discrepancy and pointed it out.

"We don't verify phone numbers," Alvin said.

"I'm going to verify it," Edith said, pulling out her cell phone.

"Wait, Edith," I said. "Let Rick do that."

I turned back to Alvin. "Detective Rick Stemper, from the Stewart's Crossing Police. He's investigating the fraud on Edith's behalf." I held the two pieces of paper in my hand. "Can we get a copy of these for him?"

"You can keep those," Alvin said. "I'm going to have to open an internal security investigation." He looked like he might cry.

Kids. They wear their emotions so close to the surface.

"Do you have this detective's phone number?" he asked.

I pulled out my cell phone and retrieved Rick's work and cell numbers. Alvin turned back to his computer and typed for a while. "I'm putting a freeze on the account, so that any transactions will have to be approved by a manager," he said, when he turned back to us. "We see this kind of abuse too often. A lot of older people just don't keep track of their finances very well."

Considering how young he was, I'll bet he counted anyone over thirty in that category.

"Thank you very much for your help," I said. We all stood up and shook hands, like adults, and I'll bet Alvin Jesper was very glad when we walked out the big glass doors.

"I can't thank you enough for coming up here with me," Edith said, as we walked back to the Beemer. "I never could have done this myself."

It was late afternoon by then, and shadows stretched across Northampton Street. "I'm happy to help, Edith," I said. I was a little disappointed; though we'd set some wheels in motion, it wasn't like I'd done much to help. "I'm sure the post office won't tell us who is registered to the P.O. box," I said. "Rick can get it, though."

I thought for a minute. "Why don't we drive past that street address on our way home? We won't stop or go inside, but we can tell Rick what we see."

I didn't know much about Easton, but I figured out that the numbered streets began at the Delaware and ran west. We were looking for an address on North 24th Street, which seemed like a pretty straightforward proposition, since Northampton Street was the dividing line between north and south. I pulled out of the parking space and headed west.

There was no North 24th Street. There was a South 24th, but it dead-ended into a park on the north side of Northampton Street. "They used a false address," Edith said.

"I'm not surprised. If the bank manager had been old enough to have a driver's license he might have recognized it was a fake."

"Steve, that young man was very nice." We argued, in a genial way, over the bank manager's youth, and within about forty-five minutes we made it back down the river to Leighville. I dropped Edith at her car, and then made a quick stop at the English department to fax the paperwork Edith and I had picked up to Rick Stemper.

Thinking of Rick made me think of Caroline. What hadn't we seen? Was there a clue in front of us that we weren't noticing? Part of the thrill of hacking came from thinking outside the box, from looking at a problem and coming up with a creative approach. Why couldn't I do that with this problem?

The question I kept coming back to was motive. Why would someone kill Caroline Kelly? All the usual avenues had led us nowhere—family, friends, coworkers. As I pulled into my driveway, I looked once again at Caroline's house.

The break-in. We hadn't thought about that. I had to assume that her death and the break-in were connected. From the damage done, it was clear that whoever broke in was looking for something. They'd torn through her office, dumping out the contents of her filing cabinet. Was it paperwork they were after?

Again, I wondered if her death had something to do with her job. Suppose she'd found evidence of corporate malfeasance—money laundering, stock fraud, something like that. That evidence would be on paper, and if she had the only copies then the crime might go undetected.

How could I look for what the burglar wanted, when I didn't know what it was, or if the burglar had found it? While I was walking Rochester, I called Rick from my cell phone and asked if anything unusual had happened at Caroline's office.

"What do you mean, unusual?" he asked.

"What do you think the burglar was looking for at Caroline's house?" I asked. "Maybe they looked for it at her office, too."

"Evelina Curcio got her office," Rick said. "I asked her if she noticed anything missing or anything unusual, and she said no."

I juggled the phone as I bent over to grab Rochester's poop with a plastic bag, and almost dropped it right into the steaming pile. Rochester seemed to find that very funny.

"Did you pick up fingerprints at Caroline's house?" I asked Rick.

"Didn't match anything in the database. It's possible that the burglary is unrelated to her murder. We've seen cases where somebody breaks into a dead person's house, or breaks in during the funeral."

"But an ordinary burglar wouldn't tear the house up," I said.

"You know about burglary?" Rick asked, and my heart skipped a couple of beats, wondering if he was making some oblique reference to my unfortunate incarceration. Before I could think of a response, he said, "Gotta go," and disconnected.

Later that night, I tried Googling the phone number the fake Edith had used when she set up the account. No luck. I had a feeling it was a cell phone, but it might just have been unlisted. I sat staring at the computer when Rochester came into the office and rolled over on his back, waving his legs in the air like a dying beetle. "I guess you want me to rub your belly, don't you?" I asked.

I got down on the floor next to him and obliged, rubbing my face against the soft, downy hairs of his stomach. "Who's a good boy?" I asked. "Rochester? Is Rochester a good boy?"

We rolled around for while, him trying to scramble on top of me, me scrambling out from under him. They say that a few minutes each day of petting your dog can raise your serotonin levels; I think rolling around on the floor with him works just as well.

In Dog We Trust

The next morning I went over to The Chocolate Ear so that I could focus on grading my mystery fiction papers without a big golden dog nuzzling me. Rick was at the counter as I walked in, holding an extra-large coffee and talking on his cell phone. "Hold this for me, will you?" he asked, thrusting the coffee at me.

As soon as his hand was free, he pulled a notebook from his pocket, and cradling the phone against his ear, started to write. "Uh-huh. Yeah. Nobody noticed? I thought you had a flag on the account." He listened. "Even new employees should know the rules," he said. "You have surveillance tapes I could look at?"

I raised my eyebrows at him, and he shook his head. "What? How can the recorder be broken, Alvin?" His body tensed even further, and his mouth set in a grim line. "Well, thanks for nothing. You'd better get the recorder fixed pronto, before anybody else finds out."

He snapped the phone closed. "Somebody closed out the fake Edith's bank account at the QSB in Easton this morning," he said. "But the bank was busy when the customer came in, and the employee who closed the account was new and didn't realize what the flag meant. And on top of it all, the digital recorder that collects the information from the cameras is broken, so they don't even have a visual on who closed the account."

He shook his head. "And people wonder why crimes don't get solved."

He took his coffee back from me and stalked out of the café. I forced myself to sit down and start grading papers, though my attention kept straying back to Edith, and then from her to Caroline. Those were just two of the unsolved crimes that were dogging Rick, and I knew there were many more. The chances of finding Caroline's killer seemed to get smaller every day.

By Friday afternoon I'd finished grading all the mystery fiction papers, and I had no choice but to face my business problems. By searching jobs posted online, I'd gotten two new clients, but the loss of the client who I figured had discovered my background left me with a net gain of one. One job was quick, but the other client was paying me just $200 to revise a

200-page manual, which left me with a net hourly wage equivalent to working in a sneaker factory in Southeast Asia.

But it was a client. I hadn't spent much time on the project yet, because of all the time I'd spent researching Caroline's friends and Edith's money problems. I spent some more time online that evening, bidding on jobs and sending out resumes.

When I took Rochester out for his walk around eleven, he made a point of peeing on the "For Sale" sign on Caroline's lawn. As usual, he tried to get me to take him up the driveway and into the house, and as usual I manhandled him on down the street.

It was a cool, clear evening, a scattering of stars strewn across the dark sky. As I've done since I was a kid, I wished on the first one I saw. It was a habit I'd lost, living in New York and then the suburban maze of Silicon Valley where Mary and I had bought the house we thought we'd live in with our children. Since coming home, though, I'd started again.

Sometimes I wished for simple things: I wanted to get through all the papers I had to grade quickly, or for a cold to clear up fast. Sometimes I wished for things for other people— I'd been wishing for a quick resolution to Edith's troubles, and when the roof of The Chocolate Ear had been damaged in a storm, I wished that the insurance money Gail received would be enough to fix it. When money was tight, I wished for a lucrative new client, or an unexpected check, and sometimes those wishes came true. When I was feeling melancholy I wished for something to happen, something good, something that would shake up my life.

I guess the old adage is true—be careful what you wish for, or you just might get it. I tugged on Rochester's leash as we passed Caroline's house again, and took my adopted child inside.

The Visit

I didn't know what time Karina was going to show up, which was annoying, but I worked on that big manual, and I'd made a lot of progress when the guardhouse called to say I had a visitor.

It was Rick Stemper—but a few minutes later, the guard called again. "There's a Chris here to see you."

Chris. Who was Chris? "For me? Levitan?"

"That's what he says." He was off the phone for a minute. "Chris McCutcheon, he says."

"Oh," I said. He must have driven Karina Warr down from the city. "Sure, send them in."

Rick was at my door a minute later, and Rochester went into his big happy dance. Rick had parked down at the guest parking, to leave the other side of the driveway free for Karina, and was pleased when I told him that Chris had driven her.

We hung around the front door, waiting, and I had the chance to look at Rick in his off-duty mode. From his posture and his military-short brown hair, you'd peg him as a cop, and the touches of grey at his sideburns gave away his age, though he was in better shape than he had been in high school. He was wearing khakis, deck shoes and a dark green polo shirt. If I'd made a couple of different wardrobe choices that morning, we'd have looked a lot alike, but instead I was wearing jeans and a T-shirt from a Meat Loaf concert years before. I wondered if Rick had a gun hidden somewhere on his person, or maybe a knife stuck into the side of his shoe.

Oh, wait, I'm in TV mode again, I thought.

A few minutes later, a black SUV pulled into my driveway. At the sound of the car doors opening, Rochester started barking, and when I opened the front door he went ballistic, barking and snarling and struggling to get out of my grasp.

Karina and Chris hung back as I manhandled Rochester into a sitting position. Chris wore jeans, a fitted T-shirt, aviator sunglasses, and finely tooled leather boots. Karina, on the other hand, was dressed for cocktails at a chic SoHo bar—low-cut white blouse, red leather miniskirt, matching red high-heeled shoes. She had a brown leather jacket over her shoulders. Despite myself I thought she looked hot.

I introduced Rick as a friend who'd dropped by. By then, Rochester had stopped barking, but he was growling and showing teeth. "Why don't I take the dog for a walk," Rick suggested. "Has he got a leash?"

"On the kitchen counter," I said.

"He always used to like me," Chris said.

"I'm so sorry. I've never seen him like this."

"I knew there was a reason why I didn't like dogs," Karina said.

Rick returned with Rochester's leash, and it took both of us to get him hooked up. Then, pulling the leash tight so that Rochester's collar was almost up to his ears, Rick walked him out.

Once the way was clear, Karina and I touched cheeks, and Chris and I shook hands. I offered them both lemonade, and brought it out in big plastic tumblers—red for me, blue for Chris, green for Karina. We sat on the sofa and chatted about their trip. "No trouble finding the place?" I asked. "Oh, that's right, you've been to Caroline's before."

I turned to Karina. "But this is your first time in Stewart's Crossing, isn't it?"

"I'm allergic to the suburbs," she said, sounding only half kidding.

"Let me get the stuff that Caroline left behind," I said. I'd tidied up as much as I could, vacuuming Rochester's golden hair, dusting the bookshelves and even mopping the white tile floor on the lower level. Karina made suitable noises about how *sweet* the house was—how much *space!* Chris sat on the leather sofa as if the day was about Karina and he was just along for the ride.

I brought the box out, and we spread the contents on my coffee table.

"I remember this play!" Karina exclaimed, pulling a program for a high school production of *West Side Story* off the top of the pile. "You were Tony."

To me, Chris said, "There weren't a lot of boys in our school that year."

"You were fabulous!" Karina said, pushing him lightly in the side. "You know you were." She began to sing, "Tonight, tonight..."

Chris said, "Musical theater is not your strength, Karina,"

and she shut up.

They went through the yearbooks, the programs, and the other paperwork. Karina took a couple of things, but Chris didn't want anything. "I just came down to drive Karina," he said. "Unlike her, I like getting out in the country."

"The *country* is different," Karina said. "You know I love to go biking with you in Westchester."

I found it hard to imagine Karina on a bicycle—but if she liked Chris McCutcheon enough, I could see her pretending until she had a ring on her finger.

"It's nice that Chris brought you down here," I said to her. "You guys will probably get to spend a lot of time together, now that Caroline's out of the picture."

"What do you mean?"

"You wanted Chris for yourself, didn't you? Ever since Korea, you've wanted to be the center of attention—but Caroline was always around. Convenient for you that she's gone, now, isn't it?"

"What a *terrible* thing to say!" Karina said. She stood up. "And I thought you were so nice, taking care of her dog after she was shot."

"It's touching that you care about Rochester. But then, you're not the one who hates dogs, are you? Isn't that you, Chris?"

"What do you mean?"

"Come on, Karina and I both know what you did to Caroline's dog when you were a teenager."

"What the fuck?" He stood up, too.

"That's ancient history," Karina said. "I can't believe you brought that up."

"You still have those violent tendencies, Chris?" I asked, still reclining on the sofa. "Like maybe you got mad at Caroline about something and shot her?"

"We should go," Chris said. Dragging Karina along, he stalked to the front door, then outside, not even saying goodbye.

When I followed them out, I saw Rick down the block, lying on someone's lawn with his hand looped through Rochester's collar. As soon as Chris and Karina drove away, he let the dog go, and Rochester came galloping down the street to me.

"Hey, boy, what was up with that behavior?" I asked, as he

jumped on me, placing his front paws on my waist.

"Do you remember what kind of car you saw leaving after Caroline was shot?" Rick asked.

We walked into the house. "I just remember it was a black SUV."

"And what was Chris driving?"

"You think Rochester recognized the car?"

"At least the type of car," he said. "I don't think he got the license plate number that night. At least he didn't tell me."

"Which is why he barked at Chris, even though he's been here before and Rochester liked him."

"That's what I think." He emptied the lemonade from the blue and green tumblers, then put each one in a separate evidence bag. "The crime lab's backed up at the moment," he said. "But I should get prints back within a week."

Rick started for my front door, but stopped when I said, "I might have stirred the pot a little this afternoon."

He turned around. "What do you mean?"

"Well, I might have pointed out that both Karina and Chris had motives for killing Caroline."

"You didn't." He shook his head. "Who died and appointed you detective?"

"Caroline Kelly."

"That's low, Steve. I'm working this case, you know I am. There just isn't a lot to go on."

"I know. That's why I'm trying to stir things up."

"You are not the cop here, Steve. You've got to let me handle things."

"You needed my help to get their fingerprints."

He blew a big breath out. "Yeah, and I can see it was a mistake. Listen to me. You are NOT to do anything else without checking with me first."

"Yes, Dad."

"You know, that attitude was cool when we were seventeen. It's lame and childish at forty-two."

And with that he stalked out the front door. Rochester came tumbling down the stairs, sliding across the tile floor to me. "I don't know, boy, people just keep leaving without saying goodbye. Nobody seems to have any manners these days."

I knew Rick was right; I spent my life among teenagers and their snarky attitude was rubbing off on me. And I shouldn't have provoked Chris and Karina the way I did, but I was frustrated with the lack of progress. The detectives on *NYPD Blue* would have goaded one of them into a confession before the commercial break. But as Rick had pointed out, I was no cop.

Rick's reprimand reminded me that if I didn't get a business plan together by my appointment with Santiago Santos the next afternoon, I'd be getting bad feedback from him, too. So I sat down with the sample business plans I'd downloaded a few weeks before and tried to come up with one of my own.

I'd already put some of the material together—demand for my services, my qualifications and so on. I'd also created a list of all my personal contacts, including friends, relatives and former co-workers, who might be able to point me toward some work.

I went back through my email and generated a log of all the jobs I'd applied for, along with the responses I'd received. There wasn't much good news there.

Maybe my plan was flawed. Suppose there wasn't the demand I expected, or potential clients were scared off by my felony conviction? Would you trust your sensitive computer materials to a convicted hacker, after all?

What else could I do? I'd spent the last twenty years working around words and computers, and I didn't know anything else. I didn't even know how to work the computerized cash register at The Chocolate Ear, though I supposed I could learn. Would Gail hire me? Would any responsible business owner trust a felon with access to money?

I started to feel worse and worse. Rochester must have known what was going on, because he came over and laid his big golden head in my lap. I gave up worrying and sat on the floor to play with him.

After reading the paper Sunday morning, I spent a couple of hours finishing up that big manual. I decided that the only thing I could do was talk over my problems with Santos; at least he'd feel that I was trying, even if I didn't have much of a plan ready to show him.

He couldn't send me back to prison before the semester was over, right?

Jobs for Felons

Caroline's laptop was stored on the top shelf of my closet by the time Santiago Santos arrived on Sunday afternoon. But possession of an illicit computer was going to be nothing if he couldn't help me put together a business plan.

He checked the audit trail on my laptop, then pushed it aside. "Sorry we have to do this today," he said. "Let's see if we can make it quick and painless. How's your business going?"

"I wish I had better news," I said. "I just can't seem to get things going." I went on to confess the fears that I had, that perhaps the whole freelance business was a bad idea, that I worried no one would hire me. "I've been trying," I said. "But I'm just not getting enough work."

I showed him the business plan in its rough state, worrying that he'd get angry, threaten to send me back to California. But instead he said, "This isn't bad, Steve. You've just got to have faith in yourself."

"It's just that I don't know what else I can do. I don't have a backup plan."

"Well, let's work on that," he said. "What else can you do besides writing and teaching?"

I shrugged. "I haven't done anything else for twenty years."

"Have you looked into the Work Opportunity Tax Credit?" he asked. "Private employers get a tax credit if they hire individuals from eight different groups—and one of those is ex-felons." He opened up his briefcase. "I think I have a list somewhere in here of jobs you could look into."

I was excited. I figured his list would show some things I hadn't considered, some companies that would be willing to hire me. But when I looked it over, my heart dropped. "Laundry worker? Receiving clerk? Meat cutter?" I asked, looking up at him. "Is this all I can do?"

"It's a drop in status from college professor," Santos said. "But these jobs pay money. Not much, I grant you." He looked around. "There aren't any meat cutters living in River Bend, I'll bet. What about a union apprenticeship? You ever work construction? There's a lot of money there."

"My father always said I didn't know which end of the

screwdriver you hammer the nails with," I said. "I can't even paint a wall without making a mess."

He tapped the list with his finger. "Take a good look, Steve. You may find something there you can do." He reached into his briefcase and pulled out another list. "These are some social service agencies in the area who work with ex-cons. Job training, that kind of thing. Don't be embarrassed about going there; you won't be the only guy with a college degree."

I took the paper from him and glanced at it. I remembered shopping at Goodwill stores for vintage clothing when I was in college. I'd never thought I'd end up one of their clients.

"I think I lost a job because they found out about my record," I said. "I was thinking maybe I could sue them to get the job back. I read somewhere on line that you can sue an employer if they discriminate against you based on your record."

Santos sighed. "Discrimination based on criminal history is illegal in Pennsylvania, as long as the job isn't related to your offense. But you're in a strange situation. It would be hard for you to find a white-collar job that doesn't require some use of computers, internet, that sort of thing. And you have a record for hacking into private data. Any employer could be concerned that if they gave you a log on to their network, you might wander into some files you weren't supposed to see. You'd have a hard time convincing a judge that discrimination wasn't relevant."

I felt deflated. There just didn't seem to be any good alternatives.

"Consider a lawsuit your last resort," Santos said. "Do you want to work for somebody when you have to sue to get the job?" He looked at his watch. "I've got to get going," he said. "I'm meeting my girlfriend at the nature preserve around the corner from here."

Mention of the preserve flashed a memory of finding Caroline's body next to it. I don't know what my face said to Santos, but he hurried to continue. "My girlfriend and I, we've started bird watching. You know, something to do together." He had a sheepish grin on his face. "She's a tour guide at Independence Hall, and she started noticing all the birds around, so she bought a book. Now she's got me hooked. You know they post alerts on the Internet, migrating birds?"

He laughed. "Guess I don't have to tell you what's out there online," he said, standing up. "Anyway, keep your chin up. You're going to find something. Just keep plugging away."

I thanked him for the advice, though I didn't feel better after our meeting. He hadn't threatened to send me back to California, which was a good thing, but I didn't see myself in a hairnet slicing beef at the Genuardi's either. He was right, you didn't see many blue-collar workers in River Bend. Most of my neighbors' cars cost more than a receiving clerk or forklift operator made in a year.

I couldn't think about dating until I had my economic house in order. I could just imagine hanging out with Rick on a Saturday night at The Drunken Hessian, picking up women. A hardware store clerk with a felony conviction wasn't going to score the kind of women I was attracted to.

That evening, after I'd walked and fed Rochester and watched mindless TV to take my mind off my troubles, my cell phone started beeping its low battery alert. When I picked it up to plug it in, I noticed Melissa Macaretti's phone number in my call log from Monday night. I was about to delete it, but there was something familiar about that number, something dancing on the edge of my conscious brain.

I was holding the phone open when I saw the photocopies of the paperwork used to open the fake account for Edith at the bank in Easton. At first I thought the number on the paperwork was just similar to Melissa's cell—but it was the same.

I remembered seeing Melissa at her work-study job, at Eastern's music department. She knew Edith. I peered at the grainy driver's license photo on the page; it could be Melissa, with a different hair style and different makeup. Or it could be someone else.

I plugged the phone into the charger and called Rick, worried that he'd yell at me again. But hey, I wasn't snooping in Caroline's murder, just making a connection that might solve Edith's problems. Before he could launch into any arguments, I explained what I had found. "Give me the girl's name," he said. I spelled it for him. "You have an address other than that PO box?"

"I might be able to get it," I said. "Let me call you back."

I logged into Eastern's mainframe and pulled up my class roster. As I'd remembered, each student's name was a hyperlink, opening a new window with social security number, date of birth, and address, among other things. I called Rick back and read him the information. "She lives in the freshman dorm called Birthday Hall. So it's reasonable that she would have a post office box."

"I'll run her through the system tomorrow and see what comes up," he said. "In the meantime, remember what I said. No detective work on your own."

"I was out of line yesterday," I said. "You were right. I shouldn't have said anything to Chris or Karina."

"And don't say anything to this girl, either," he said. "You don't want to spook her. If she's still got any of Edith's money on her, we want to catch her with it. If you let her know we're on to her, she's likely to hide it or spend it, and that's no good for Edith."

I sighed. "I understand. I won't say anything to her."

A Walk Along the River

On Monday, the tech writing class continued giving their presentations. I was curious to see what Layton Zee was going to do, since he'd never handed in a research paper. He was scheduled to give his presentation that day, and not surprisingly, he wasn't prepared.

He was wearing a t-shirt that read, "On the other hand, you have different fingers," and beltless jeans that threatened to slip off his hips.

"Come out into the hallway with me," I said.

He followed me. "You haven't handed any papers in this semester, Lay," I said. "Did you think I would pass you just based on your attendance?"

He shrugged. "I did the in-class work."

"Not enough. Right now, something like eighty-five percent of your grade is an F. You don't have to make a presentation—at this point it doesn't matter. You don't even have to come back for the rest of the semester."

"Can't you cut me a break, Prof?" he asked. "I mean, showing up every day's got to count for something."

"Yeah, ten percent of your grade. It's all spelled out on the syllabus, Lay."

"You're an asshole, you know that?" he said. He stood up straight, as if that would give him some kind of height advantage on me, but I'm just over six feet so we were pretty much at eye level.

"You want to call me names? Call me whatever you want—in front of the academic dean, so it'll go on your record."

"I can't believe this shit," he said. For a minute it looked like he wanted to hit me, but then he turned away, heading down the hallway muttering.

I'd heard about students who got violent from other professors, but this was the first time I'd experienced it myself. While the class pretty boy, Ira K. Lindo (who went by the nickname I.K.) was giving his presentation, I wrote down everything I could remember of the conversation.

I went from there to freshman comp, where I returned the rough drafts of their research papers. We went over MLA style citations again, and I repeated, for what was probably the fiftieth time, "If you use someone else's exact words, you MUST use quotation marks, and you MUST identify who said those words, and why I should trust them. To do anything else is theft."

I caught myself. I didn't mean to be sending any coded messages to Melissa Macaretti. "I mean plagiarism, which is a kind of theft, after all."

Jeremy Eisenberg didn't get the whole citing your sources thing, and so I went over it again. And then again. By the time the hour and a quarter had passed, I thought maybe I'd gotten it through their heads. But only the final drafts would prove if I had.

I resisted saying anything to Melissa about Edith's stolen identity. I was pretty shaken from my encounter with Lay Zee, and Rick was right; I wasn't the cop. It was up to him to see if he could catch her with Edith's money. I'd already done what I could for Edith; I had driven her to Easton and set the wheels in motion for her with the bank and with Rick.

After class I went up to the English department and used one of the computers in the adjunct area to type my confrontation with Lay Zee into an email to Lucas Roosevelt. I'd just finished when Jackie came by on her way to make copies.

"You won't believe what happened to me today," I said.

"If it involves a smart, well-behaved student, then I probably won't," she said. "Otherwise I'd believe anything, especially at this point in the semester."

I told her about Lay Zee, and how he'd threatened me. "It makes me a little nervous to go out to my car," I admitted. "I mean, suppose he wanted to run me over?"

"Our students may be slow and lazy, but I doubt they're homicidal," Jackie said. She knocked on wood. "Though you never know."

"It's not homicide, but you won't believe what I figured out while I was helping my old piano teacher."

"Helping her how? Tuning her instrument?" She waggled an imaginary cigar, á la Groucho Marx.

I ignored the humor. "She's an adjunct in the music department, and one of my students has a work-study job there. The student stole my friend's identity and started intercepting her mail and moving money out of her bank accounts. I'm still trying to figure out how it all comes together."

"In little old Stewart's Crossing? Where nothing ever happens except the stop light changes from green to red and back again?"

"Even there."

I knew that Jackie knew Menno, so I didn't mention any names, but she was still suitably horrified. "I know some of our students behave badly, but it's hard to believe they'd stoop to something like that," she said.

"I'm still pretty shaken up," I said. "I think I need to go home and take Rochester for a long walk, just to calm down."

"You live in Stewart's Crossing, don't you?" she asked. "River Road is so pretty over there."

"It is. Maybe I'll take Rochester down there."

On my way out to the parking lot, keeping an eye out for Lay Zee, I called Edith to let her know about Melissa, but there was no answer. I called The Chocolate Ear and found that Edith wasn't there, but Irene said she came by almost every afternoon.

"I'm on my way there," I said. "If she shows up, tell her to wait for me."

I found Edith sitting at one of the white wrought-iron tables in the corner of the café, right under a poster for a French chocolate bar, drinking tea. "But she's such a sweet girl," she said, when I told her about the matching phone numbers.

I shrugged. "Appearances can be deceiving. You know that, Edith." I sipped my raspberry mocha, watching her.

"Poor Menno," she said.

"Menno?"

"Her boyfriend, Menno. He'll be just shocked to know what she's done."

"Menno. You mean Menno Zook?"

"You know him?"

"He's in my freshman comp class, along with Melissa. I didn't know they were going out. They never sit together."

"Oh, yes, they've been dating since the fall," Edith said. "Melissa's the one who recommended Menno to be my handyman."

The revelation hit Edith the same time it hit me; I could see it play across her face. "You don't think..." she began.

"Did Menno ever come to your house when you weren't

home?"

She nodded. "At Thanksgiving, I had him paint my bedroom while I went to visit my cousin. When I went to Charleston he came over to recaulk my tub."

"I think the first one of your statements was missing from December," I said.

Edith began to cry. "I was such a silly old woman."

I took her hand and squeezed. "Don't say that, Edith. You trusted a nice girl and her boyfriend. Anyone would have."

Irene saw Edith crying and came over to see what was wrong. I explained what we'd figured out. "At least now you know who's behind all this," Irene said, in her no-nonsense way. "You'll see, Rick will get it all wrapped up for you. Probably get most of your money back, too."

"Just in case you see or hear from Melissa or Menno, don't let either of them know that we've been talking," I said. "And if Menno wants to come over and work on something for you, make an excuse to keep him away for now."

Edith nodded, and then thanked me again for my help. I left Edith and Irene at the café and drove back to River Bend. As usual, Rochester was delighted to see me. I decided to take Jackie's advice and go out with him for a good, long walk. But it was a little far to the River Road, so I hooked up his leash and we headed to the canal. Except for the kitschy mule-barge rides up in New Hope, there's no longer any commerce on the canal, though way back when, before there were highways, those old barges used to transport coal from the mines upriver down to the deep water port at Bristol.

The canal was abloom with wildflowers, and the towpath was roofed with fiddlehead ferns and spotted with daisies, black-eyed Susans and the tiny pansies we called Johnny Jump-ups. Fish splashed in showy leaps, and cattails grew in the marshy shores. The smell of wildflowers mingled with the aroma of stagnant canal water. Rochester surprised a pair of nesting birds, and despite the presence of the town just a few hundred yards away, the area was quiet and peaceful.

I'd often come down to the canal as a kid. My parents' house was on the other side of Stewart's Crossing, in one of the first suburban developments to take over the farmlands that once blanketed Bucks County. I'd ride my bike into town, stopping at the five and dime for candy, buying my mother a single carnation at the florist, browsing for greeting cards at the drugstore in the shopping center in the heart of town. I loved the gingerbread Victorians with their peaked roofs and front porches, and the old stone houses that dated back to the Revolutionary War.

My grandparents would tell me stories of escaping from the Czar's army, of wriggling on their bellies across battlefields, and then I'd go downtown and feel secure, like no one could ever chase me away from my home in Stewart's Crossing. Maybe that's why I came back.

I let Rochester off the leash and he ran back and forth along the towpath, sniffing the new flowers, chasing butterflies, and making his mark on trees and stones. When we came to one of the locks, I sat on a bench and thought about Edith.

Had Melissa and Menno been able to prey on her because she was old and alone? She had no children or grandchildren to help her manage her money, to fix her leaky faucet or clean the leaves out of her gutter. Needing help from others had made her vulnerable.

Would I end up that way? I was forty-two, divorced and childless. I might marry again, but I doubted at this stage in life I would ever be a new father. Perhaps there would be step-children involved—but what if I never married? Or had no one to look after me when I got old? I was an only child, like Caroline Kelly. If I died, who would survive me? I had a few cousins, a few friends.

Who would take care of Rochester if anything happened to me? I couldn't trust to chance, the way Caroline had. I had seen death up close.

I was so engrossed in my own morbid speculations that I hardly noticed dusk falling. It had gotten cold, too. And where was Rochester? One minute he'd been lying at my feet, and then he'd gone off to explore again.

"Rochester! Here boy!" I stood up, rubbing my hands to restore their circulation, and called the dog again. I heard a woof! in the fields that ran to the river, and I started making my way through the new green growth, calling his name.

I caught up with him almost at the River Road. "Bad dog," I said, grabbing his collar. "You come when Daddy calls."

He jumped up and I knocked him down. "Come on, we've got to get home."

We started walking up River Road toward Ferry Street, which would take us back over the canal toward River Bend. It was pitch dark by then, and only the river side of the road had a shoulder, so we walked up that way, cars coming up fast behind us and then zooming ahead into the night.

I never saw the car that hit me. I heard it, felt its headlights getting closer, but when I looked back I saw it on the roadbed. Rochester was nosing ahead of me, and I must have let go of his leash when I was launched into the air, sailing through the underbrush toward the fast-moving Delaware, just a few feet away.

Recovery

Rick told me I was very lucky. A woman returning home from her shift at the exotic ice cream store in New Hope saw me go flying, and saw the car that hit me keep going. She pulled over and dialed 911.

She caught Rochester to keep him from running in the road. With a flashlight and his help, she found me lying in the underbrush at the water's edge, though she didn't touch me, just waited for the ambulance to arrive. The parallels between her finding me, and my finding Caroline, were spooky, and I was grateful my story hadn't ended the way Caroline's had.

I hadn't been carrying any ID, but Rick heard the description of a Caucasian male and a wild Golden Retriever on the police radio, and he drove out to investigate.

I had a concussion, and a couple of fractured ribs, but other than that I got away pretty lucky. They kept me knocked out for about twenty-four hours, but on Tuesday evening Rick was at my bedside ready to ask me some questions, and though my head hurt like crazy I managed to sit up.

"Where's Rochester?" I asked.

"Annie Abogato has him," Rick said. "Don't worry about Rochester. What happened to you?"

All I remembered was walking Rochester by the canal, night falling, and then walking back along the River Road. "That's a dangerous stretch," Rick said. "People go way too fast. Accidents happen all the time."

"What if it wasn't an accident?" I asked.

Rick looked up at me from the chair next to the bed. "Somebody got a grudge against you?"

"You got a pen and a piece of paper?" I asked. "Make a list."

Tops on the list was Layton Zee. "You told the kid he was failing?" Rick asked.

"And he got violent. Started cursing, and I thought he was going to hit me."

While Rick wrote the information down, I looked around. Hospital rooms had gotten nicer since the last time I was in one, with Mary. It was painted a soothing light green, with a lot of complicated electronics around, including a computer on the table next to the bed. Rick was sitting in an upholstered recliner, and two nice local landscapes hung on the wall. It still smelled like a hospital, though.

"I didn't say anything to Melissa Macaretti in class," I said, when he'd finished writing. "But she saw me taking Edith to the bank on Thursday, and maybe she or her boyfriend wanted to keep me away from Edith."

I explained about Melissa's work-study job. "So that's how she's connected to Edith," he said. "You neglected to mention that when we talked on Sunday."

"And how she got her boyfriend a job as Edith's handyman." I told Rick what I remembered from Menno's essay on his father and how he'd been shunned by the Amish community. "I got the sense his father's a pretty bad guy," I said. "I wouldn't be surprised if Menno's been learning from him."

Rick took more notes. "Throw in Chris McCutcheon and Karina Warr," I added. "Maybe what I said to one or both of them on Saturday hit home."

"Now you see why I told you that you shouldn't have said anything?"

My head hurt. Being proved wrong can do that to you. So can getting knocked on your ass by a car. "Yes, and I told you that you were right. Are we over that yet?"

"No, we're not. Not if one of them was driving the car yesterday."

"Yesterday?" I struggled to sit farther up in the bed. It just made my head pound harder. "So today is Tuesday?"

"All day."

"Jesus. I've got a class to teach at 12:30."

"Missed it," Rick said. "It's what, six now? Six p.m., that is."

"Shit."

"Don't worry. I called over to the college this morning and let them know you were laid up. The secretary's getting you substitutes for the rest of the week."

"But this is the last week of school. I have so much to do."

He shrugged. "Talk to the doctor."

He got up and started to pace around the room. "I don't need all this shit, " he said. "I've got unsolved cases all over town. The chief has been coming down hard on my ass since

173

that article in the *Boat-Gazette*."

"But he must know what it's like when you don't have any clues. Can't he cut you some slack?"

"If I can't solve this case, somebody's got to take the fall," Rick said. "You see the article in the *Courier-Times*?" I shook my head. The *Courier-Times* was a daily paper out of Levittown, much bigger than the *Boat-Gazette*. "Not as stupid, but it made the same points. Now the mayor's picked up the baton. I had to spend an hour in her office this morning explaining everything I've done."

After Rick left, I tried to turn on my side, and the pain was so great that it brought tears to my eyes. I remembered once hearing a student at Eastern talk about the different names the Native Americans had for the moon at different times of the year. "There's the harvest moon and the hunter's moon," she said. "And the handkerchief moon. That's the one you cry in front of."

I could cry to the moon about getting run over, but it wasn't going to do any good. The best thing I could do was go home and be with my dog. If he licked my face, I knew I'd feel better.

The doctor agreed that I could leave the next morning, and Rick recruited Edith to pick me up at the hospital, run me home for a change of clothes, and then take me up to Eastern. I sat through the remaining presentations in the tech writing class; fortunately, Layton Zee did not show up.

Then, after a brief break, I met with the freshman comp class and accepted the final drafts of their research papers. I announced that I would be grading them over the final exam week, and that they'd be available for pick-up in the English department when I was finished.

Dianne or Dionne (I still couldn't tell them apart, and it hardly mattered any more) exclaimed over how bad I looked. "What happened?" she asked.

"I had a little accident," I said. "Nothing serious, though. I guarantee you it looks a lot worse than it feels."

That wasn't true; I felt pretty crappy. But I wanted to see if Melissa or Menno had any reaction. Either they were both very cool customers, or neither of them had been behind the wheel of the car that ran me off the road. Melissa wished me well as she walked out of the room, and Menno told me he hoped I had a good summer.

Edith was waiting for me in the faculty lounge, and she drove me over to Annie Abogato's house. The yard was just as cluttered with toys as it had been before, though the Big Wheel had been replaced with a pair of tricycles.

I was just as glad to see Rochester as he was to see me. As soon as Annie opened the front door, he came bounding out, skidding to a stop just as he got to the open door of Edith's car. He tried to jump in with me, putting his front paws on my lap and licking my face.

I petted his head and back. "I know, puppy, I'm glad to see you, too," I said. "Don't you worry, I'm not leaving you."

Annie came to stand by the car. "You look like shit, Steve," she said.

"But you look lovely," I said. "That housecoat brings out the blue in your eyes."

She laughed, and opened the back door of Edith's sedan. "Go on, get in back, you big moose," she said. "I had to feed him Maslow's chow," she said. "I hope it doesn't upset his digestion."

"Thank you," I said. "You're a sweetheart."

"Rochester's always welcome here."

Edith insisted on fussing over me and Rochester back at the house, making sure that he had food and water, that I had hot tea and something to eat for dinner. "We'll be fine, Edith," I said.

"I feel so terrible, Steve. What if you were run over because of me?"

"If I was, then you're in just as much danger," I said. "I don't like the idea of you going home alone, Edith. After all, they know where you live."

She sat down at my kitchen table. "I hadn't thought of that."

"Can you go stay with Irene for a few days?" I asked. "Just in case."

"I hate to be a burden to anyone. Maybe I should go to visit my cousin."

"You don't want to leave town. Suppose the police need to talk to you." I picked up the phone. "Go on, call Irene."

Irene was at the café, and from what I heard of the conversation she said it would be no problem for Edith to come and stay. When Edith hung up, she said, "Irene's going to meet me at my house so I can pick up a few things, and then we're going to her place in Cornwell's Heights. I'm just worried about leaving you alone."

"Rick's going to come over this evening to check on me," I said. "He said he'd take Rochester for his evening walk, too."

I convinced Edith to leave, and struggled upstairs to bed. Rochester took another of his flying leaps and joined me there, and we were both asleep when the guard at the gate rang to announce that Rick was there.

The visit was a quick one; he was on his way home after a long day. "There is one thing I'm going to need from you," he said. I'd come downstairs, and we were sitting at the kitchen table. "I need you and Edith to sit down with me and go over how much money she's missing."

I nodded, and yawned. "Can we do it over the weekend?"

"You'll be up to it by then?"

"I will." I yawned again. "Hey. Did you get the fingerprint results back on Chris McCutcheon and Karina Warr?"

"Yup. No match to the partial we found on the shell casing."

"Which doesn't mean that one of them didn't shoot Caroline," I said. "It just means someone else loaded the gun, right?"

"You've been watching too much TV," he said. "But yes, you're right." Rochester came over to lay his head on Rick's lap.

"What am I, chopped liver?" I asked the big dog. "You traitor."

"He knows who's going to walk him," Rick said. "Leash on the counter?"

"Yup." I yawned again. "Man, getting run over takes it out of you."

"I wouldn't know," he said. "Come on, Rochester."

I struggled to stay awake until Rick returned with Rochester, who came bounding in the house and rushed toward me, as if to make sure I'd survived the few minutes he was away.

"I'll call Edith and get her over here on Saturday," Rick said.

"She's staying at Irene's."

"I'm the detective," he said. "I know everything."

"Yeah, that's what your ex-wife said," I said, yawning once again.

"Go back to bed, jerkoff," he said.

I walked him to the front door. "Yeah, your ex-wife probably said that, too."

Chris Returns

I managed to get Rochester fed and walked Thursday morning, though I did have to go back to bed for a nap. I drove to Eastern, and climbed the stairs in Blair Hall with effort. My ribs still ached and a headache still hung around the back of my brain. But I handed back the papers to my mystery fiction class, then stopped by Jackie's office to say goodbye.

"What happened to you?" she asked. "You look all beat up. It wasn't that student you told me about, was it?"

I shrugged, and my ribs reminded me that I shouldn't. I told her about getting run over. "I doubt it was Lay Zee. I don't think he could get up the energy."

"I'd report it to Lucas, though. Are you going to be here this summer?"

"Lucas He doesn't need me. Which is fine; I need to work on a plan for developing my tech writing business." I didn't mention that my parole officer would ship me back to prison in California if I didn't.

"You know Menno Zook, don't you?" I asked.

"Sure. He's an oddball, isn't he?"

"Maybe more than that." I told her how I suspected that Menno and Melissa had been involved with Edith's identity theft. "I'd just be careful around them both, if I were you," I said. "And you might want to check your credit report, just in case they got hold of any of your information."

"Wow. Thanks. I'll do that."

I left her office a few minutes later, and felt sad leaving Eastern that Thursday; I knew I'd have to go back up to hand in my grades and leave the graded papers at the English department, but it was the last time I'd be teaching for a while, and I'd enjoyed the work. I hoped that Lucas Roosevelt would hire me as an adjunct again in the fall, but you never knew with that sort of job; if enrollment was down and he needed fewer instructors, I was low on the totem pole. I had a feeling that the administration didn't know about my felony conviction. If they did, I might not be welcome back there. And if my tech writing business didn't take off, I'd have to take a full-time job somewhere, and I wouldn't have the time to spare for teaching.

When I got home from Eastern, I had to take a nap. When

I woke, I was feeling almost myself again; the headache was gone, and my ribs only ached when I breathed. I went downstairs to make myself some tea, and while I was waiting for the water to boil, I saw Rochester put his front paws up on my dining room table. "Rochester! No! Bad dog!" I said.

He dropped his paws back to the floor, scattering the pile of Caroline's mail that his paws had landed on. "You are not a good dog," I said, leaning over to pick up the scattered mail. My eyes landed on Caroline's cell phone bill.

I suppose I shouldn't have opened her mail. But I just couldn't resist. I know, it's the story of me and the computer all over again. But thus far, curiosity hadn't killed this cat, just incarcerated him.

The last call Caroline made had been on the day she died, to what I thought was probably her office voice mail. I took the bill upstairs with my tea and sat down with her laptop, Rochester curled around the back of my chair as if he was keeping me there until I found something useful.

I went back, day by day, Googling every number and trying to identify it. I was pretty successful, except for a handful of numbers, which were probably the cell phones of friends or colleagues. I saw that she'd called Karina Warr's cell a couple of times, and Chris McCutcheon's home number.

Nothing else jumped out at me. I copied the three numbers I'd been unable to trace and then put the bill back in the envelope. Too many dead ends; it was getting frustrating.

Just then the phone rang. "Listen, I need to talk to you," a man's voice said.

I knew the voice was familiar, but I just couldn't place it. Layton Zee? Some other student? "Who is this?"

"Chris McCutcheon."

"Oh. Chris."

I flashed on Chris and Karina arriving the previous Saturday in Chris's big black SUV, and the way Rochester had gone nuts. Had Chris run me off the road on Monday night?

"I want to come down and talk to you," he said. "Finish up what we were talking about on Saturday. Without Karina in the way."

"I don't think you have to say anything to me. Tell it to the police."

"I want to talk. Can I drive down tomorrow? I need to get this resolved."

This kind of thing always happens towards the end of the episode—the killer comes after the detective. Only I would make sure that Rick Stemper was around to protect me. "OK," I said. "You know where I live. When can you get here?"

"I'll be there at one." He hung up.

I called Rick. "I told you to stop messing around in this case," he said.

"And I told him to talk to the police. He said he had to talk to me."

"What time is he showing up?"

I told him. "I'll be there." I thanked Rick and hung up. I felt pretty smug about pulling Rick in as my witness and backup. Despite the fact that his prints didn't match the one on the shell casing, Chris McCutcheon was still high on my list of suspects and I was worried what he might do—especially since I was still feeling crappy after the hit-and-run accident.

Rick was at my house the next morning, Friday, at 7:30, wearing a t-shirt, shorts and running shoes. "I came to borrow your dog," he said. Rochester went into spasms of joy upon seeing Rick, jumping up and down and doing the deranged kangaroo routine he'd once saved for me.

The two of them took off, and about forty-five minutes later they were back. Sweat was streaming off Rick's face and soaking his t-shirt; his short brown hair was plastered to his head. Rochester was panting, his long tongue lolling out of his mouth like the red carpet at some fancy event. He went straight for his water bowl, and after slurping up the contents, spilling half of it on the floor, he flopped on the tile with a happy grin on his face.

"You're coming back at one, right?" I asked.

Rick shook his head.

"No? But I don't want to meet with Chris McCutcheon alone." I felt my voice getting higher by at least an octave.

"Good. Maybe I'm knocking some sense into your head after all. I'm not coming back at one because I'm not leaving. I've got clean clothes in the car. I'm going to take a shower and hang out until McCutcheon arrives. He may be planning to show up earlier to sabotage you."

"Wow. Good thinking."

"That's why I'm the detective."

While Rick showered and dressed, I made chocolate chip pancakes for us and gave Rochester his chow. Then Rick settled down with my laptop and his cell phone at the dining room table. I didn't tell him that I had Caroline's laptop upstairs; it wasn't the kind of thing I wanted him to mention to Santiago Santos.

I went upstairs and started going through the list Santos had given me, looking for anything I could do. I didn't have the mechanical aptitude for construction, and I had the feeling I'd probably slice my hand off if I tried to become a meat cutter. I called the social service agencies on the list and got the dates for workshops and training sessions, enduring a humiliating litany of questions. No, I didn't have substance abuse problems. No, I was not a registered sexual offender. I did not need debt counseling or a psychological evaluation. I just needed a job.

Just before one, the guard called to announce Chris McCutcheon. I told him to have Chris park in the guest parking lot—I wanted to see if Rochester would go nuts again if he didn't see the car.

"You going to hide somewhere?" I asked Rick.

He gave me a look. "No. I'm going to sit right here."

Chris was surprised to see Rick, who was wearing a tan polo shirt with the Stewart's Crossing Police emblem embroidered on the breast. But he was happy enough to see Rochester, who did his gleeful visitor dance for Chris—unlike the mad, wild beast he had become the previous Saturday. Maybe it was the car, after all.

"I wanted to clear some stuff up with you," Chris said, as the three of us sat in the living room. Since we didn't need his fingerprints any more I didn't bother to offer him anything to drink.

"Like what?" Rick asked.

"Like what happened to Caroline's dog, for starters." He looked down at his knees, then back up at us. "I'd only had my license for like a week," he said. "And it wasn't even my fault. I wasn't speeding, just driving along this road that ran along the perimeter of the base. And I felt the wheel bounce, like I'd run over something."

"Let me guess," I said. "Caroline's dog?"

He nodded. "He must have gotten out of the house and run away. There was a lot of underbrush out there; I didn't even see him."

"Why didn't you tell anybody?" I asked.

"My father was a real hard-ass. He'd have taken the keys away from me for a year. And for something that wasn't even my fault. 'We all have to accept responsibility for our actions, Christian,' he used to say. I wanted to ask him if he took responsibility for moving us around every two years."

"What about Caroline?" Rick asked. "Didn't you want to at least tell her?"

"She had this huge crush on me," Chris said. "I knew it, and I was kind of flattered. If she'd found out, she'd have hated me."

"And you never told her, even after all these years?"

"I wanted to. You know, just to clear the air? But then we hooked up for a while, and I didn't want to mess that up. Especially after she moved down here and got Rochester, I knew that she would hate me and never want to talk to me again."

"And why tell us now?" Rick asked.

"I've got this deal about to go through," he said. "In Brooklyn. I'm buying this old warehouse, going to convert it to condos. I need city approval for the deal, and if you guys keep nosing around, asking questions, they might get cold feet. I've leveraged everything I own on this deal—if it goes south I'm in receivership."

"Talk to me about malicious mischief," Rick said.

Chris looked at him. "Those charges were so bogus," he said. "The first building I bought? It was this little one-story in Washington Heights. Some Dominican dude who it turns out was just fucking with me."

"So you fucked with him?"

Chris frowned. "No, man. I was naïve—it was my first deal. The guy told me he'd signed the papers and sent them to his attorney. So I thought the building was as good as mine, and I went in there to start rehabbing. I cleared out all the trash and started knocking down walls. Dude comes in, goes ballistic on me."

"And?" I asked.

"He didn't want to sell. He was just trying to hold up his tenant for higher rent. When he saw I'd started tearing the place apart, he called the cops. I paid to have everything fixed, and the judge gave me a suspended sentence."

"And the second time?" Rick asked.

"Another asshole. I was buying this fourplex in Jackson Heights, in Queens. One of the units was vacant, and somebody broke in, to use it as a shooting gallery."

He looked at us to make sure we knew what he was talking about. I'm sure Rick did, but I had no idea why someone would try and set up a gun range in an abandoned apartment. "For drugs," he said. "That's what they call them. These abandoned buildings where the junkies hang out."

He leaned back on the sofa. "There wasn't a shred of evidence to connect me, but somehow the asshole got in that I had a prior, so the judge thought I was just trying to knock the price down. He gave me a hundred hours of community service. I could have fought it, but it was easier just to go along."

"What did you have to do?" I asked. Rick shot me an angry glance, but I was curious.

"I worked with Habitat for Humanity," he said. "Fixing up properties in Bedford Stuyvesant. It was pretty cool. I still help them out when I can."

I looked over at Rick, and he shrugged. I knew the fingerprints didn't connect Chris to the shell casing, and Karina's theory that his psychopathic behavior had begun with killing Caroline's puppy was beginning to look flimsier than Jeremy Eisenberg's research paper on Ecstasy, which had represented it as a happy kind of drug, what pot was to the sixties.

"You ever let Karina borrow your car?" Rick asked.

Chris frowned. "She drives like shit. But yeah, I let her sometimes. She works for this fast food place; she's the one goes out to look at new locations, and sometimes it's too far for a cab and there's no other way out there but to drive. But I try to have excuses whenever I can."

"She borrow your car back in March?" Rick asked.

Chris thought about it for a minute, and then recognition dawned in his eyes. "You mean, like when Caroline—no way, man. Karina can't shoot a gun for shit. I know—I've been to the range with her. Plus, Caroline was like her friend, almost her only female friend. She'd never have shot her."

"Not even over you?" I asked.

"Especially not over me," he said. "I admit, I've been bouncing back and forth between them. Never at the same time, you know. But I'd break up with one of them and then see the other, and we'd hook up for a while. Then break up again."

"And which were you hooked up with when Caroline was killed?" Rick asked.

"Neither," Chris said. He started counting off on his fingers. "Last year, New Year's, Caroline stopped by my place on her way home from her aunt's. I hooked up with Karina once, a few weeks later, but then I met this girl on Valentine's Day and the two of us were going hot and heavy for like, months."

"So Karina had no motive to kill Caroline based on your relationship with her?" Rick asked.

He shook his head, then pulled his Palm Pilot out of his pocket. "When was Caroline killed?"

I told him the date and time. He plugged it into his calendar. "I was in Connecticut that week," he said. "I can prove it, if I need to. Guys I met with and so on. That day, I had a dinner in Westport. There's no way I could have driven down here, shot her, and gotten back to Connecticut for dinner." He closed the PDA. "And I had the car with me, the whole time. So Karina couldn't have borrowed it."

"She could have rented," I said.

"But she wouldn't have done it," Chris insisted. "I mean, I know she's a bitch. But her and me—and Caroline—we have this bond, you know? Had, I guess, when it comes to Caroline. The whole military brat thing, Korea. You know."

"We spent our whole childhoods here in Stewart's Crossing," I said. "Rick and me both. But I'll take your word for it."

Chris left a little while later. "Do you believe him?" I asked Rick.

"In general, yes. Unless he's a hell of a good liar. I took this course a while ago, on how to read body language. He wasn't doing any of the things liars do. His whole body language was open, like he had nothing to hide."

"What he said did make sense," I admitted. "But doesn't that knock out your two main suspects?"

Rick grimaced. "If they weren't guilty, it's good to get them knocked out," he said. "Lets me focus elsewhere."

As Rick was getting ready to leave, I mentioned that I had pulled Caroline's cell phone bill from her mailbox. I remembered how Rochester had knocked it off the table, and wondered if he'd done it deliberately.

A couple of times, it had seemed like he was pointing me toward clues. He'd alerted me to the break-in at Caroline's, he'd found the shell casing and Caroline's PDA, and he'd sniffed out the box that had all Caroline's Korea souvenirs. Was there something in the cell phone bill he wanted me to see?

Rick asked for the bill, and I went upstairs to get it. While I was there, I picked up the list I'd made of who the numbers belonged to, as well as the unknown ones. Something was familiar about one of them, and I closed my eyes, trying to place it. Like my own cellular number, it began with a prefix I knew was unique to my carrier. But there was something more than that; where had I seen it before?

I grabbed my cell phone and opened it to the call log. Melissa's was a match for one of the unidentified numbers on Caroline's bill. For a minute I was confused—hadn't I already figured something out about Melissa's number? Then I noticed Edith's Quaker State Bank paperwork—and made the final connection.

Melissa had used her cell number when she opened the account at Quaker State Bank. Caroline must have discovered that, and called her.

Wow. That was a revelation. I carried the paperwork downstairs and showed it to Rick. "I need to write this down," he said, pulling his pad out. "All right, so we know Caroline promised to help Edith sometime in March. And then we have a call that Caroline made to the phone number on the account."

"They've got to be connected," I said. "Caroline's death and the fraud on Edith's account."

"But how?"

"Caroline started looking into Edith's account. She called Melissa and confronted her. Four days later, Caroline was killed."

"Why wait the four days?"

I shrugged. "They had to figure out who she was and where she lived, and then they had to track her for a day or so to figure out how to kill her."

He nodded. "But why kill her? All Caroline had was a phone number."

"But she worked for the bank, and she had the power to shut down the account," I said.

While he made some notes, I went upstairs to the bathroom, and on my way back I noticed the student papers I had collected from the freshman comp class. Gingerly, I picked up the pile and carried it downstairs.

He'd put his pad and phone away and was ready to leave. "Can you pull fingerprints from paper? Even if lots of people may have touched the same paper?"

"I can try. What's up?"

"I might have fingerprints from Melissa and Menno." I pointed at the papers. "You could match them to that print you pulled off the shell casing. And then you can arrest both of them, and get Edith's money back, and get the chief off your back. That'll be a story for the *Boat-Gazette*."

"Don't get ahead of yourself," Rick said, but I could see he was pleased.

If all my problems could be solved so easily, I thought, as he packed up to go. Maybe I could get a job with the Stewart's Crossing police department-- but they probably didn't hire convicted felons. Oh well, another career option down the drain. I'd have to get back to work on my tech writing business plan—and fast.

Show Me The Money

Late Saturday morning, Rick arrived, followed quickly by Edith and Irene, and we sat down to focus on how much of Edith's money was missing. "OK, in a nutshell, Walter did some good things for Edith, and some bad things," I said. I looked over at Edith. "Sorry, but it's the truth."

"You say what you have to, Steve," she said.

"First of all, every place that Walter did business with allows account holders to set up online access. Whoever has been stealing Edith's money didn't do that, but I did." I held up a sheaf of papers. "These are printouts of the activity on Edith's accounts."

I held up a different set of papers. "I was able to do the same thing with the account at Quaker State Bank, so we have a paper trail of how the money left Edith's accounts and went into, and out of, the account at QSB."

"You can just do that?" Irene asked.

"Well, I had all of Edith's information," I said. "These online accounts are secure—but only so far. If you have someone's social security number, account number, date of birth and so on, you can set up the account, and establish your own password. If the thief had done this already, I wouldn't have been able to get in without knowing her password. And then I'd have had to get in touch with the institution. But because no one had set the online access up already, I was able to do it pretty easily."

I handed Rick the paperwork from QSB. "What we don't know is where the money went once it passed through the account at Quaker State Bank in Easton." I looked at Edith. "Right now, all I can see from the online access is that 'a check was issued' or 'a transfer was made.' I can't see who the checks were made payable to or where the transfers went."

"I'll put together a subpoena for the records," Rick said. "It may take a few days, but then the bank will be able to tell us that information." He looked at Edith. "If they handed money out in cash, it's as good as gone, frankly. But if they transferred money to some other account, at another bank, for example, and we can find that account, then there's a good chance we can get some money back for you."

"All right," I said. "Let's get started. The good news is that Walter left Edith a lot of money. The bad news is that he left it in a dozen different investments, making it hard for her to keep track of it all."

"For instance?" Rick asked.

"OK. You have an IRA, don't you?"

He nodded. "So did Walter. As you probably know, once you turn sixty-nine and a half, you can take money out of the account without penalty. As a matter of fact, you have to start taking money out then."

Everyone looked like they were following along.

"As of the last paper statement I have, December 31, Edith had $95,000 in an IRA Walter left her with an investment group called Trust Options, out of New York. Some time after that, someone contacted Trust Options and changed the address on the account to the same post office box used on the paperwork for Quaker State Bank."

I pulled out the printout I'd made. "On March 1, Trust Options issued a cashier's check, payable to Edith Passis, in the amount of $90,000, leaving the account open with the minimum balance of $5,000."

I passed a pile of papers over to Rick. "These are the records of the fraudulent account at the QSB branch in Easton. Can you follow as I point stuff out?"

He nodded, and started looking at the first page. After a minute of evaluation, he said, "A $90,000 deposit was made into the account on March 5."

"And withdrawn when?" I asked.

He frowned. "It's not so clear. There are so many different deposits, in different amounts, and then withdrawals in different amounts. The bottom line is that the money is no longer in the account."

Irene gasped. "Oh, dear," she said. "Edith, you poor thing."

"Unfortunately, there's more," I said. "Walter had a $10,000 CD with Countryside Bank and Trust in Doylestown, which matured on February 15. The account was closed at that time, and the money transferred to the account at QSB."

Rick looked at his paperwork. "Yup, I see the transfer." He looked up at Edith. "I don't need to keep saying this every time—there's only about a thousand dollars in this account at the moment. So everything Steve says went in also went out."

Irene got up and walked to my kitchen, returning a moment later with a box of Kleenex. She handed a tissue to Edith, who had begun to cry.

"This is not your fault, Edith," I said. "And we're going to make it right. Aren't we, Rick?"

"We're going to do our best."

"I hate to keep pounding away, but Rick needs to know exactly what has gone missing," I said. "Walter had a stock account with a discount brokerage called Cheap Trades. Again, some time in February, someone changed the address to that post office box in Easton, and the dividend checks Edith had been receiving monthly were diverted to that address." I ran through a series of amounts, and Rick verified that the dividends had all gone into the QSB account.

There were a couple of other small accounts like that, and we got through them quickly. "Now, this is our final account, but it's a big ticket item," I said. "Edith, did Walter ever mention someone to you named Nancy Fancy?"

"Is she a friend of Turkey Lurkey and Henny Penny?" Rick asked.

"Hey, you're supposed to be the professional here," I said. "Edith?"

She pursed her lips and thought for a minute. Finally her eyes brightened. "I know! We used to have a cleaning lady named Nancy Rodriguez, and she married a man named Jim Fancy. I guess that makes her Nancy Fancy."

"Well, Nancy borrowed $400,000 from Walter six years ago," I said.

"Oh, my. That's a lot of money."

"You'd be surprised," I said. "It barely buys you one of those big split-level houses in Annie Abogato's neighborhood. Apparently, from some notes Walter left, Jim had some bad credit, and even though he had a good job, it was hard for them to get a mortgage. Walter loaned them the money to buy a house, with a balloon payment after six years."

I could see from the look in Edith's eyes it had already been a long afternoon, and she wasn't following everything. "When the bank gives you a mortgage, generally you pay principal and interest every month for a set period of time—say thirty years—and at the end of the term you've paid off the loan. With a balloon payment, you pay interest only, for a period of time. And then you pay off the principal in one big payment."

"Who would take out a loan like that?" Irene asked.

"I'm guessing that after six years, Jim Fancy's credit was in good shape again, and he and Nancy could jointly qualify for a conventional mortgage. It looks like that happened, and they paid off the balloon note at the beginning of April."

Rick looked at his paperwork. "Yup. The deposit went through."

"What did they do with all that money?" Irene marveled. "Walter invested it all over town—but did they do the same thing? Or do you think they just spent it?"

"I just don't know, Irene," I said. "They were college kids, and kids spend money without even thinking about it. Electronic gadgets, CDs, maybe even drugs. But Rick and I did figure something out yesterday."

"What?" Irene asked.

I pulled out a calendar. "Edith asked Caroline for help figuring out her financial problems in March. Since Caroline worked for Quaker State Bank, we think she did some investigating that led her to Melissa and the cell phone number she used when she set up the account. On the Friday before she was killed, Caroline called that number."

Edith and Irene both gasped. "Melissa must have known that the $400,000 mortgage was coming due on April 1, so she had to keep Edith in the dark until after that happened."

Gently, Rick said, "We think Caroline was killed to prevent Edith from finding out what was going on until after that mortgage check came through."

That was the last straw for Edith. She began crying openly. "That poor girl," she said. "I had no idea. I should have gone directly to the police. This is all my fault. If I wasn't such a silly old woman, Caroline would still be alive."

"This is not your fault, Edith," Rick said. "You didn't even know a crime had been committed when you talked to Caroline, and if you'd come to me instead of her, I would have told you I couldn't do anything—that you should just get yourself a good accountant."

He frowned. "You're just as much a victim here as Caroline was. And I guarantee you, we will find out who did this to you and make them pay."

I told Irene about how Edith knew my student, Melissa, through her work-study job at the music department, and how Melissa had recommended her boyfriend, Menno, as Edith's handyman.

"I'm glad I never asked him to do anything for me," Irene said tartly. "Although if he was here now I'd certainly give him what for."

"Any luck on tracing Melissa or Menno?" I asked Rick.

He shook his head. "Yesterday afternoon, I had deputies go to the dorm at Eastern, Birthday Hall. Her roommate hasn't seen her since Thursday morning, though she hasn't moved her stuff. I called her parents in Massachusetts, and they haven't heard from her."

"You think she's on the run?"

"I don't know. The street address that the college has on file for Menno Zook is the same one that was used on the application to start the fake account in Edith's name—and as you and Edith discovered, that address doesn't exist. His father has a record, so I tracked him through his parole officer. He says Menno doesn't live with him, and he hasn't seen him in a couple of weeks."

"Well, I saw both him and Melissa in class on Wednesday."

"They may have gone to ground out in the Amish country," Rick said. "The father, Floyd, told me his ex-wife's name is Sarah, but you know the Amish and technology. There's no phone listed under her name, and he says she had to sell the farm and move and he doesn't know her new address."

"Yeah, he was shunned," I said. I explained what I had read in Menno's paper. "So it's not surprising that he doesn't know where his ex-wife is."

"Zook is like Jones to the Amish," Rick said. "There's dozens of them. And Zook's her married name; her maiden name is Yoder, which is just as common, and she could be staying with her family. I've got a detective out in Lancaster who knows the Amish checking around, but that could take some time."

He frowned. "I even went into the property appraiser's database to see if Melissa Macaretti or Menno Zook had bought property in their own name, or in their parents' name. No luck."

"They're both a lot smarter than I gave them credit for," I said. "When I was in college I had no idea about money—CDs and IRAs and bank accounts. My parents gave me an allowance, and I had a work-study job. If I ever had more than fifty bucks to my name I'd be surprised."

Irene shepherded Edith out a little later. "Well, that was a pretty lousy experience," I said, once they were gone.

"Had to be done," Rick said. "She has to understand the whole problem before she can start to solve it."

"That doesn't make it feel any better."

"You up to walking the dog? Or you want me to do it?"

"How about we divide the labors. You walk the dog, I'll order a pizza."

He called, "Rochester!" and the traitorous dog went right to him.

In Dog We Trust

Back at Eastern

I spent the rest of Saturday, and most of Sunday, grading papers. By Monday, I had finished and was ready to return them to Eastern. It was the kind of day that made me love living in Bucks County: the sun was shining, all the trees were in bloom, and the flowerbeds in River Bend were a riot of bright colors.

Our townhouses are built in pods of sixteen—for example, eight facing Minsk Lane and eight backed up against them, facing Sarajevo Court. Wherever there's a space between pods, the original developer landscaped a walkway between streets. Where Minsk Lane curves, there's an extra-large empty lot, big enough just for a single townhouse, which the developer left empty.

It seems every dog in the neighborhood feels obliged to leave a deposit, and many of my neighbors don't pick up there, since it's not in someone else's yard. Thus, the place is like a minefield, and I don't let Rochester go in, for fear he'll drag me through something that will be hell to get off my shoes.

That morning, though, I let him walk in, sniffing out an interesting trail. Tiny white butterflies danced in the field, like a symbol of resurrection – I'd survived being run off the road, and I had my dog with me. All was right in the world.

I discovered buttercups pushing through the grass, which reminded me of my childhood, when we'd hold those flowers up under our chins to determine if we were "sweet" or not. The more pollen that rubbed off, the sweeter we were.

If I held one under Rochester's chin, I knew the pollen would coat his muzzle, because he was such a sweet dog. I decided to take him with me to Leighville and let him loose in the dog park. He deserved a good run, and I hadn't been the best walking partner for the last few days; my ribs ached and I still slept a lot.

Rochester found he was most comfortable with his back paws on the passenger seat, his front paws on the door ledge, and his big golden head stuck out the window, his fur flying behind him like a thousand small prayer flags. The slopes along River Road were sprinkled with wildflowers and it was clear spring had arrived.

I always preferred to drive the River Road between Stewart's Crossing and Leighville, rather than taking the inland road, which ran through the centers of Washington's Crossing and New Hope. River Road hugged the Delaware's banks and threaded its way under maples and sycamores, past broken-down stone walls, fallow fields, and renovated barns that served as vacation homes for wealthy New Yorkers. The fields were already green, the trees in leaf. Sunlight glinted off the river, and fish jumped in the shallows.

I parked in the faculty lot, hooked Rochester on his leash, and took him upstairs to meet Candy Kane, who'd warmed up to me once I'd started talking about my new dog. And yes, I knew I wasn't supposed to call her Candy, but I couldn't resist. Kind of like my problem with computer information. In case security stopped me, I figured they would be more forgiving now that school was out.

I handed in my grades for the term, as well as a stack of graded papers for students who would never come back to pick them up. Rick had taken away Menno's and Melissa's papers for fingerprint analysis, but I didn't tell Candy.

"This place is like a ghost town," I said.

Usually, when I walk down the hallway toward Candy's post at the center of the third floor of Blair Hall, a half-dozen faculty members have their doors open. There are students milling around waiting to speak to Lucas Roosevelt, or coming and going from faculty consultations. The part-time tutors hold court at the big round tables outside Candy's office, which has a pass-through window where students can hand in late registration cards to be stamped, drop off messages for professors, and interact with the staff without being able to intimidate them.

That Tuesday, there wasn't a single faculty door open, except Jackie's, and there were no students anywhere in sight.

"Today's the last day of finals," Candy said. "Most of the students have already left for the summer. And the faculty? They were out of here last week, except for the few who give final exams rather than final papers."

Rochester lay down in front of the faculty mailboxes, and Candy petted his head. "The whole campus is emptying out," she said. "I drove in this morning up that little street that runs by Birthday House. Deserted. It was creepy."

In Dog We Trust

"We're going down that way when we leave here," I said. "I want Rochester to run around in the dog park for a while."

"Just be careful," Candy said. "You know how the crime rate goes up in Leighville when the college empties out."

Leighville is a small town, but it revolves around college students. When they leave for Christmas break or for the summer, whole blocks empty out, and there are apartments ripe for burglary. Those who stick around find themselves walking empty streets at night, vulnerable for mugging, and incidents of vandalism go sky high. The problems of the big city have come down to the small towns—at least Leighville.

Candy and I chatted for a while as Rochester dozed. Her student assistant, a senior, had decided to skip graduation and had left the day before, moving to New York for a fresh start. It reminded me of my own move to the city, and I wondered how many more fresh starts I had left in me, as I said goodbye to Candy and walked down the hall to Jackie's office. I liked living in Stewart's Crossing and didn't want to move again, at least not for a long time. Yet I needed to earn a living, and as I'd already discovered, there weren't that many jobs for ex-felons.

I was forty-two, and still stuck, at least to a degree, in my mid-life crisis. I'd given up my home, career and friendships in Silicon Valley to return to Pennsylvania, and though I'd been able to reconnect with a few old friends, like Rick and Edith, and make a few new ones, like Gail Dukowski and Mark Figueroa, I hadn't settled into the same level of comfort I'd had in California.

Rochester sensed what I was feeling and jumped up on me, putting his paws on my waist and struggling to lick my face, which he couldn't quite reach. I stopped to stroke his head as we reached Jackie's office.

She was sitting behind her desk, with three piles of student papers in front of her. "Hey, Steve," she said, looking up. "You brought Rochester with you!"

She came out from behind her desk, and squatted down to pet Rochester's head. "Hey, boy. Have you been enjoying your biscuits?"

"He loves them. I've been using them as rewards."

"Has he been a good boy?" She stood up, and returned to her chair. I sat across from her, and Rochester sprawled on the floor, halfway between us.

"He's turning into a detective." I explained how he'd been finding clues to Caroline's killer. "So of course, each clue he uncovers earns him a biscuit."

"Really? What kind of clues?"

I mentioned a couple of the things Rochester had done—finding the shell casing, alerting me to the intruder at Caroline's house, nosing out her PDA, and so on. "Are you sure you ought to be messing around with this, Steve? I mean, it could be dangerous for you."

"I've got to help my friend Rick—if this case doesn't get solved, it looks bad for him, and the police chief might have to make him take a fall to save his own skin. And besides that, it's almost like I feel guilty for still being alive, and playing with her dog, when she's dead."

"We're all guilty of stuff like that. Remember, a clear conscience is the sign of a bad memory." She leaned down to pet Rochester. "What a smart boy you are. You deserve a reward for all your detecting." She reached behind her and pulled a biscuit out of a drawer, which she handed to Rochester. He accepted it greedily, and sat on the floor chewing.

"This is a real reward day for him. From here, we're heading to the dog park."

"I wish I could take Samson out," she said. "But I've got all these papers to finish marking up and I have to have my grades in the mainframe in two days."

"Didn't get much done over the weekend?"

"Well, yes, and no. I had to deal with a couple of students in trouble, and that took a lot of time. Plus, with six courses, there's just so much to do."

"We'll leave you to it, then." I stood up, and kissed her cheek. "If I don't see you, have a great summer."

"You too."

With Rochester on his extendable leash, we walked down the hill toward the river, passing Birthday House, which did look spookily vacant. Instead of windows wide open, curtains flapping in the breeze, competing strains of rap and hip-hop blasting out into the air, there was a single student loading plastic trash bags overflowing with clothes into a station wagon with Connecticut plates.

The dog park was empty, and I might have found it creepy

if it was later in the day and darker. But instead, I just opened the gate, let Rochester off his leash, and tried to get him to fetch by tossing a cloth Frisbee someone had left.

He chased it to the end of the park, grabbed it, and settled down to chew on it. "Rochester!" I called. "Here, boy. Come here!"

But he wasn't interested. I had to walk all the way down to where he lay. I looked around. The grass looked pretty clean. So I lay down next to him, stroking his back as I watched the clouds scud by overhead.

Maybe it was nearly getting killed by the hit-and-run driver, but I was feeling reflective and sentimental about my childhood. From the buttercups that morning to the lush grass under me, I was regressing. My dad had been obsessive about our yard all the time I was growing up, watering and fertilizing and filling in dead spots with new sod. I remembered our back yard, the way it sloped down toward the lake, and how I'd lie there and stare up at planes passing overhead, dreaming of places I'd go and flights I'd take.

I spent a while woolgathering in the dog park. It was so quiet and peaceful I think I dropped off. Rochester lay next to me, gnawing on the Frisbee, until he heard the scraping of the gate opening, and took off down the field. I yawned and sat up, looking to see who he might be playing with. But there was no one there; I must not have closed the gate properly, and it had blown open in the breeze.

"Rochester! Come back here!" I called, but he was out the open gate before I could even get up and start to chase him.

He took off, running around the fence toward the wooded area, and the River Road beyond it.

"No! Rochester! Come back!" It was like I was calling some other dog, for all the attention he paid me.

I started running after him, but I was middle-aged and out of shape. By the time I reached the gate to the dog park, he'd disappeared into the woods.

My heart seized. Mary had always complained about my ability to lose myself in my work, shut her out. "You never listen, Steve. You're a lousy husband. It's a good thing we don't have kids because you'd be a rotten father, too."

Maybe she had been right; her miscarriages had been a sign from God that we would not be good parents. Once in a fit of depression and anger, she'd told me I couldn't be trusted to take care of a dog. Now Rochester was going to run into the street and get hit by a car, and it would be on me—the way the breakup of our marriage had been laid at my feet, though I knew it hadn't been my fault alone.

I could feel tears begin to well up in my eyes as I ran around the dog park and toward the woods. Then I heard Rochester begin to bark.

He didn't make much noise, but already I recognized that deep, throaty bark. "Rochester!" I called. I hoped he hadn't found some animal in the woods. There were bobcat, lynx, raccoons and possums in the countryside. What if one of them clawed him? What if he was hurt?

My heart pounding, I stumbled to the edge of the woods, then followed the sound of his barking. "What is it, boy? What have you found?"

And then I stopped short, because I saw him, standing by the body of a young man, probably an Eastern student. Just beyond the man lay a young woman of the same age.

The woods had been a popular trysting spot in the spring when I was a student, particularly for freshmen living in Birthday Hall. The rooms were all doubles; if you didn't have a cooperative roommate, there weren't many places on campus you could go with your sweetheart. And sometimes couples who didn't want to be seen together would meet out there as well—two guys, for example.

I stepped closer. There was something familiar about the bodies. The boy was face down, wearing dark pants and a white shirt. From the side, I could just see the edge of his black beard.

But it was the girl who I recognized first. She was lying so that I could see part of her face, but before I even saw it, I noticed the plaid skirt. There was only one girl at Eastern who dressed that way—Melissa Macaretti.

And if I was right, the boy next to her was Menno Zook.

In Dog We Trust

Tony Rinaldi

I stood there for a moment. I'd seen dead bodies before, most recently Caroline. Sometimes I think I spent a good part of my childhood at funerals. My father's father was one of twelve children, and my father had dozens of aunts, uncles and distant cousins. I was an only child, and so my parents dragged me along with them as we traveled to funerals up and down the Eastern Seaboard.

But there's a difference between seeing a dead person in a coffin, cleaned up, made up, and looking peaceful, and seeing a dead body at your feet—someone you'd known well. Seeing Caroline's body had been a big shock.

And now, Menno Zook and Melissa Macaretti. I hadn't known them more than casually; they'd been students, and I knew how they looked, how they wrote, and something of how they thought. But we'd never shared a pizza and beer, never sat around talking.

I could tell from the condition of their clothing that they'd both been dead for some time. Menno's white shirt had been soaked, and had stuck to his torso when it dried. There were leaves and twigs in his and Melissa's hair, and dried blood pooled around Melissa's head.

My first instinct was to call Rick Stemper. I knew that Leighville wasn't his jurisdiction, but he would know what I should do.

I prayed that he'd be answering his cell phone, and he was. "I found Melissa Macaretti and Menno Zook," I said.

"You did? Where?"

"At Eastern. Actually, Rochester found them." I explained, in too much nervous detail, about taking him to the dog park, about how it had been so empty, how he'd managed to get out the gate when it had swung open in the wind.

"Hold on," Rick finally said, interrupting me. "Are you saying they're dead?"

"It looks like it."

"Jesus. Did you call 911?"

"Not yet. I thought I'd call you first and you would tell me what to do."

"Are you an idiot? Didn't we got through this once before?

You always call 911 first. I know a detective in Leighville—Tony Rinaldi. I'm going to call him. And then I'm going to get my ass up there, too. Now hang up the phone and call 911."

"OK," I said.

"Steve? Are you listening to me? Hang up and call 911."

"OK." I did just what he said. In what was becoming all too familiar an experience, I called the emergency operator and announced that I had found two dead bodies. I explained in excruciating detail where I was; it sounded like the operator had never heard of Eastern College or River Road, no less the dog park or the wooded area nearby.

I was getting frustrated. I wanted to say, "Have you ever heard of Yahoo Maps? Get a grip." But I didn't seem to have the energy to do that, so I just kept explaining about driving up River Road and turning on the lane that led up to the campus, past the dog park.

I was standing at the entrance to the dog park, Rochester at my feet, still on the phone with the 911 operator, when a dark blue sedan with a blue flashing light on the top pulled up. A tall, dark-haired guy in his late forties got out, pulled the light off the roof and tossed it on the front seat of the car. Then he came over to me.

"Professor Levitan?" he asked, sticking out his hand. "I'm Detective Sergeant Rinaldi."

I hung up on the 911 operator. If she couldn't get the cops there based on what I'd told her, then at least this Rinaldi guy could.

We shook hands, and Rochester and I led him over to the edge of the woods as I explained what had happened. "They're in there," I said. "If you don't mind, I'd rather not go back in."

"Sure. Just stay out here, OK?"

He reached down to pet Rochester before he left. "You're a good boy," he said. For some reason it took me a minute to realize he wasn't talking about me.

He came back a couple of minutes later, talking on his radio. Once again he walked me through how Rochester and I had discovered the bodies, and as I did, I heard the sirens approaching. Soon there was a crime scene team there, a woman from the Coroner's office and a couple of techs of her own, and a number of cops in black and white squad cars which blocked off access to the area.

I was getting tired, just standing there with Rochester, waiting for someone to talk to me again. He was antsy; I guess he remembered the last time we'd seen all those cops and flashing lights, and the memories weren't good ones. Finally Rick Stemper showed up.

He waved hello to me but went over to Detective Rinaldi. They talked for a while. It was starting to get dark, and I knew Rochester would be hungry and want to go home. I was pretty eager to get away myself.

After a long time, both Rick Stemper and Tony Rinaldi came over to me. "Rick tells me you have quite a talent for finding dead bodies," Rinaldi said.

"I wouldn't exactly call it a talent," I said. "More like a misfortune."

Behind him, I saw the Coroner's techs carrying a body out of the woods on a stretcher. I didn't know if it was Menno or Melissa, and I didn't want to know.

"The deceased were both your students?"

I nodded. "In my freshman composition class."

"And you think one or both of them might have tried to run you off the road the other day?"

"I thought it might have been one of my students," I said, remembering my confrontation with Lay Zee. "I wasn't thinking of Melissa or Menno." I turned to Rick. "You think it was them?"

"If we believe that they killed Caroline, then there's a good chance they tried to kill you," he said.

"I'd like you to come down to the station so we can talk about all this," Rinaldi said. "Bring me up to speed, so to speak."

"I'm exhausted. And Rochester needs his dinner. Can we do it tomorrow?"

"Really need you to come in this evening," Rinaldi said. "While all these details are fresh in your brain. We've got a K-9 works out of our station—I'm sure we've got some chow down there for your dog."

I looked over at Rick, but his face was a blank. "All right," I said. "My car's up at the faculty parking lot."

"Why don't you and your dog ride along with me," Rinaldi said. "I'll see that you get back to your car when we're finished."

It didn't look like I had much of a choice. I ushered

Rochester into the back seat of Rinaldi's blue sedan and then got in beside him. "You can ride up front," Rinaldi said.

"I'll stay back here with Rochester, if you don't mind," I said.

It wasn't my first trip to the Leighville Police Station. My freshman year at Eastern, I'd lived in Birthday Hall, the dorm right up the road from the dog park, though at the time there had been no park there; woods had stretched all the way from the edge of Birthday's manicured lawn down to the river.

In an attempt to improve the fitness level of the average student, the college had constructed an outdoor fitness course around the perimeter of the lawn. Wooden sleepers were laid out to simulate certain exercises—step-ups, pull-ups, and so on. The idea was to start at the first station and work your way around the square, ending up back at the front door of Birthday House where you'd begun.

One spring night just before final exams, I was playing a drinking game in the student lounge with a bunch of my buddies. Yes, we were all under twenty-one, the legal drinking age in Pennsylvania at the time, but ever since I was about sixteen I'd looked old enough to shop at the State Store, the state-run liquor outlet in Leighville, without being carded.

I don't remember the TV program we'd been watching in the lounge, but every time one of the characters did or said something, you had to chug your beer. They did it or said it often enough that by midnight we were all in our cups.

It was a clear warm night, with the illumination of a full moon. One of the guys had the brilliant idea that we should race around the fitness course—naked.

Hey, it seemed like a good idea at the time.

There were about a dozen of us. We stripped down in the lobby and left our clothes in a big, sloppy pile, then took off outside.

I think we were about halfway through when the cops arrived. I guess we'd woken up some of the nerds in the dorm who thought sleep was important for success at final exams.

A couple of the guys got away, but they pulled in at least nine or ten of us. The cops wouldn't let us go in the dorm to retrieve our clothes, so we were jammed into the back seats of squad cars, an uncomfortable position among a bunch of naked, drunk teenagers.

"Hey, get your hands off me, you mo," I remember my buddy Nick howling.

I was the guy in the middle. "Your ass is touching my ass," I said. "Both of you. Scoot over toward the door."

I don't remember the name of the third guy, but I remember him saying, "Daddy, he's touching me," to the cop.

"Simmer down back there," the cop said.

By the time we got back to the station a couple of the guys had thrown up, and we were all sobering up fast. But when Nick kicked off the trend to give fake names, we all followed suit. My name, if I recall, was Joe Mamma.

They threw us all in a holding cell, and the guys who stunk of vomit had to stay over in the corner. The rest of us tried to maintain a proper distance between us, tried to avoid sizing up each others' equipment. But there wasn't much else to look at, and the whole experience was probably in danger of disintegrating into a circle jerk when one of the cops threw a pile of clothes into the room and we fell on them like wolves on fresh kill.

They never did get our names, but they let us loose at first light to make our way back to campus on foot. After that, I made a point of steering clear of any interaction with the Leighville Police Department.

That is, until I arrived at the back door of the station in Tony Rinaldi's sedan.

The department's located on the first floor of the town hall, on College Avenue in the center of town. It's a three-story brick building with a memorial to Leighville soldiers killed in various wars in a little grassy patch out front.

The offices of the mayor, the town council, the tax assessor and so on were upstairs. The left half used to belong to the fire department, with the right for the police, but some time when I was in California the town fathers built a state-of-the-art fire station a few blocks away and renovated the police department. I didn't remember much of the building from that first visit, but I could tell that the town had put some bucks into the new station.

The desk sergeant took Rochester away to get him some dinner, and I followed Rinaldi down a carpeted hallway to an interrogation room. "Where's Rick?" I asked as we walked in. "Is he going to come in here, too?"

"Detective Stemper's putting together his own statement," Rinaldi said. "You just tell me your side of the story."

"Am I under arrest?"

"Just want to talk to you about what happened," Rinaldi said.

"Should I have an attorney?"

"It's your right to have an attorney present whenever you want," he said.

"Aren't you going to read me my rights?"

He looked like he was getting frustrated, but he took a minute to settle himself. "As I've said, you're not under arrest. Therefore, I don't have to read you your rights."

I thought for a minute. Rinaldi seemed like a nice guy, and he came recommended by Rick—but still. "I'd like to call my attorney, please," I said.

He nodded. "Sure. You need a phone?"

"I can use my cell."

I didn't have an attorney, per se. A guy named Hunter Thirkell had drafted my father's will, and he'd been helpful to me in getting things settled when the state of California wouldn't let me come to Stewart's Crossing in person. I'd gone to see him when I returned to town, just to say hello, and in the course of getting to know him I'd discovered that he'd been a prosecutor in juvenile court in New York when he was fresh out of law school. "My job was to put kids behind bars," he had said.

Since then, he'd moved to the country, where he'd built up a general practice. Since he was the only attorney I knew in Bucks County, I called him.

Rinaldi offered coffee but I figured police coffee would be pretty lousy and asked for tea instead, and he went to get it.

"You haven't been arrested, and you haven't been charged?" Hunter asked, when I explained the situation to him.

"That's what the detective said."

"You made a good choice to call me. Don't say anything til I get there."

When Rinaldi returned with my tea, I told him that my attorney was on his way. He nodded. "All right. I'm going to do some research and the desk sergeant will let me know when your attorney gets here."

He left me alone in the room with my tea. It was probably

overreacting to call Hunter when Rinaldi just wanted to ask me some questions about Melissa and Menno, but I'd been spooked by Rick's conjecture that one or both of them had run me off the road the week before.

I wondered where Rochester was. Had the desk sergeant found some dinner for him? Would somebody walk him? My mind wandered back to the day Caroline had been shot. The experience had traumatized Rochester—the sound of the bullets, the smell of the discharged firearms, the speeding black SUV. Would this experience upset him further? Would we never be able to come back to the dog park without being haunted by bad memories?

And if Menno and Melissa had killed Caroline Kelly, then who had killed them?

Neil S. Plakcy

Interrogation

My mind was still rambling when Hunter showed up. He's a genial blond guy, a couple years younger than Rick and I, and about fifty pounds heavier than he should be. At just over six feet, he was an imposing figure, whether in his suit and tie or in casual clothes, as he was that night-- an extra-large navy polo shirt, khakis and deck shoes. "How're they treating you?" he asked when he came in and shook my hand.

"Fine. I just want to get this over with."

Tony Rinaldi came in then, and after the introductions we sat down. After getting my permission, he turned on a tape recorder, and established his name and rank, my name and Hunter's, and the date, time and location of the conversation. "I'd like you to start way back at the beginning," he said. "Tell me about your neighbor—Caroline Kelly?"

"I only knew her at all because of her dog," I said. "Rochester. The golden retriever. She used to walk him every morning and every night, and I'd be out walking myself around the same time. We would stop and chat now and then."

Rinaldi had light-green eyes, which were arresting in combination with his brush-cut dark hair. They gave him a look of intensity that I was sure suspects found unsettling. "So your relationship was cordial?"

I nodded.

"You liked her dog?"

"He was OK. I wasn't much of a dog person."

"Yet you took over ownership of the dog after she was shot."

"There was no one else. He was going to the pound if I didn't take him in."

"But at the pound, he might have found a family, right? He's what, a purebred golden retriever?"

"As far as I know."

"Those go for what, close to a thousand dollars, right?"

"Are you suggesting I killed Caroline so that I could get her dog? Because that's ridiculous."

Hunter reached over and touched my sleeve. "Let's not jump to any conclusions, Steve," he said. "Detective, is this all necessary? I don't see how it relates to the two bodies

206

Professor Levitan found this afternoon."

"It's just curious, is all," Rinaldi said. "Your neighbor was shot, a woman you hardly knew, and yet you seemed to have a lot of motivation to keep your hand in all the details of the case."

I looked at Hunter, who nodded. "I wouldn't call it motivation," I said. "Curiosity. And Rochester has a knack for finding useful information."

Rinaldi's eyebrows raised. "The dog?"

"It's probably all coincidence. But he led me to the shell casing and to the information on Caroline's friends."

"Which didn't pan out," Rinaldi said.

"That's true. But I still felt obligated to report it to Rick Stemper."

He gave me a look which I interpreted to mean I had been keeping Rick busy with useless diversions, and I was very glad that Hunter was there.

We were sitting at a blond wooden table, in hard, straight-backed chairs in a matching wood. There were two posters on the wall, both advertising scenic Bucks County. One was a photo of rafters running the rapids upriver on a summer day, a mix of men and women in orange life jackets gripping paddles.

The second was a shot of Pennsbury Manor, William Penn's home. We'd gone there on school field trips, learned about life in Colonial times from ladies in white aprons, walked through the herb garden and tried to avoid the smell and noise of the nearby landfill. That part didn't show in the poster.

They were clearly handling a better class of criminals in Leighville these days than they had when I was a college student. "I know you went over all this with Detective Stemper in Stewart's Crossing, but it would be very helpful if you could run through exactly what happened on the evening that Ms. Kelly was shot." Sensing an objection about to arise from Hunter, Rinaldi looked at him and said, "Since the homicides may be related, it would be helpful for me to get the story direct from a witness, rather than just reading through Detective Stemper's notes."

I looked at Hunter, and he quirked an eyebrow, as if it was up to me. I decided to plunge in. "It was just after dusk," I said. "I heard three shots, in quick succession, but at the time I didn't realize they were gunshots. You always hear people banging, doors slamming, that kind of thing. It wasn't until I saw Rochester come running toward me that I thought something was wrong."

He looked at his notes. "You mentioned something about a black car," he said.

I nodded. "Right after I heard the shots, this black SUV came barreling past me. Again, I didn't think much of it, at first. It's a long run from the gatehouse of River Bend to River Road, and people often drive down it pretty fast."

I picked up the Styrofoam cup of tea, which had cooled down, and noticed my hand was shaking a little. I took a sip of the tea, which needed sugar—or flavor of some kind. I put the cup back down on the table before I could spill any of it.

"You and Detective Stemper are old friends, isn't that right?" Rinaldi asked. The tone of his voice was just this side of grating—very determined, edgy. As if he wasn't going to stop asking questions until he had the answers he wanted.

"We knew each other in high school," I said. "We ran into each other a few months ago and got friendly."

"So your friendship with him gave you an inside track on the investigation."

Hunter said, "Detective?"

"Just trying to establish some facts, Counselor." Rinaldi looked back to me. He was wearing a long-sleeve oxford cloth button-down shirt in light blue and a navy rep tie with some kind of small emblem on it. He'd unbuttoned the top button of his shirt, and the tie hung a little bit crooked.

"Let's get to what happened this afternoon," he said. "What made you drive Ms. Kelly's dog all the way up to Leighville for exercise?"

I noticed the way he kept referring to Rochester as Caroline's dog, as if the whole series of murders and thefts revolved around ownership of an excitable golden retriever, but I didn't say anything. I explained about dropping my grades and graded papers off at the college. "I thought I'd take Rochester with me and he could run at the dog park."

I was turning into just the kind of goofy dog owner I'd always made fun of. If I'd left Rochester at home, he'd have slept all day, and I'd be home with him instead of stuck at the police station in Leighville.

"Tell me about the accident," Rinaldi said.

I sighed. This was turning into a huge deal, and I just didn't have the energy. My ribs were aching, and all I wanted to do was go home and sleep for hours. But I described walking with Rochester along the canal, how he'd run off, and I'd tracked him down by the River Road.

"You don't seem to have much control over the dog," Rinaldi said. "He got away from you this afternoon, didn't he?"

"That was different," I said.

"Sorry, I interrupted you," Rinaldi said. "You tracked the dog down on River Road."

"I got his leash on him and we were walking home, sticking to the right side of the street, where there's a shoulder. The next thing I knew, I was waking up in the hospital." I shrugged. "You'll have to get the rest of the details from Detective Stemper."

"I will. You recovering all right?"

"A couple of cracked ribs and a bear of a headache," I said. "As a matter of fact, I'm getting pretty worn out. Will we be finished here soon?"

"Shortly. Anything else I can get for you? More tea?"

"I'll manage. What else do you need to know?"

"So you've been laid up at home for the last few days? Recuperating?"

"Uh-huh. And grading papers. That's why I had to go up to Eastern today, remember? To hand in my grades and drop off papers for students to pick up."

"And then?"

Once again, as I'd done at the scene, I walked Rinaldi through Rochester's escape from the dog park and run into the woods, the barking, and the way I'd followed him in and discovered the bodies. "You didn't disturb anything?"

I shook my head. "I don't think Rochester did either. When I got there, he was standing about six feet away, staring at the bodies and barking. I don't think he got any closer than that."

"If you would, please, walk me through what you did since you were released from the hospital after the hit and run—that was Wednesday?"

Hunter interrupted. "What's your purpose here, Detective? Are you suggesting that Professor Levitan needs an alibi for the time the murders were committed?"

"Until the coroner establishes the time of death for the

victims I'm not suggesting anything like that, counselor. However, it would make my life easier if I already had the information at hand that let me eliminate Professor Levitan as a suspect."

"I'd advise you to hold off on answering that, Steve," Hunter said. "You're upset, your mind might not be working too clearly right now, and that's such a vague question I'd worry you might get some details wrong that might make Detective Rinaldi's life more difficult rather than easier."

Rinaldi shrugged. "We can go on," he said. "I have just one more question for you, Professor. Do you own a nine-millimeter gun?"

The problem was I did, and I wasn't supposed to.

The Gun

Hunter jumped in before I had the chance to say anything. "I think we're well beyond 'helping you get some background,' and into the kind of questions you'd be asking of a suspect," he said. "If you're going to charge my client, you should do so. Otherwise, I think it's time for us to go."

"If I have any more questions, I'll be back in touch." Rinaldi clicked off the tape recorder and stood up, then took the machine and left the room.

I started to speak, but Hunter put his finger to his lips. "We'll talk outside."

We stopped at the front desk, where Rochester was lying watchfully at the feet of the sergeant, a heavy-set Polish guy in his mid-sixties. When the dog saw me come down the hall, he jumped up and nearly strangled himself trying to come down the hall to me. "Yes, here I am," I said, as the sergeant followed him down the hall and handed me the leash.

I reached down and rubbed behind Rochester's ears as I thanked the sergeant for taking care of him. "Sweet dog," the sergeant said. "I've got Labs myself."

"Yes, he's a sweetheart, aren't you, Rochester?" I asked.

We walked outside, and Rochester made a beeline for a boxwood hedge next to the war memorial, where he let loose a long stream of urine. "Thanks for coming out tonight, Hunter," I said. "I appreciate it."

"No problem. I don't get this kind of call very often any more. Helps me keep my hand in, you know."

We were standing there watching Rochester when Rick Stemper exited the front door of the station. "I need to talk to you," he said.

"Not you, too," I said. I turned to Hunter. "You still on the clock?"

"Sure."

"You don't need an attorney," Rick said. "I'm not asking questions. I'm telling you. This is why I told you to lay off the Nancy Drew routine a long time ago. Because you just get yourself in more and more trouble."

"Joe Hardy," I said. "Not Nancy Drew."

"Are you suggesting my client is under investigation?"

Hunter asked.

"Cut the crap, Hunter. This is not Brooklyn Juvie. I know that Steve didn't shoot those students, though he had the motive and the opportunity."

I looked at Rick. Though we'd been out of touch while I was in New York and California, I'd known him longer than anybody in town other than Edith Passis. If I was going to trust anybody, it had to be him. I took a deep breath. "I'll cooperate."

"Good." Rick looked at his watch. "It's seven-thirty. Gail closes in an hour and a half. You want to meet me down there?"

I looked at Hunter. "I can do this on my own. Thanks." We shook hands.

"Give me a ride to my car?" I asked Rick, as Hunter walked away. "It's up at the college."

As Rick drove, I considered my options. Suppose Rinaldi got a search warrant for my house? It wasn't out of consideration. I was an ex-felon, after all, and I had connections to three murder victims. "Do you have to tell Rinaldi everything I tell you?" I asked.

We stopped at a traffic light and Rick looked over at me. I saw the side of his face outlined in red. "What have you done, Steve?"

My heart started to race, but I knew I had to go through with it. "Rinaldi asked me if I had a gun."

The light turned green, but Rick didn't move. "You're an ex-con on parole, Steve," he said, his voice tight. "You can't have a gun in your possession."

The car behind us beeped, and Rick rolled down his window and motioned the car past, turning on his flashers at the same time.

"You know I inherited my dad's house," I said. "It took me a while to go through all the stuff he left. I didn't find the gun until a couple of months after I moved in, in the back of the night table next to the bed."

"Have you touched it?"

"It's in a leather case. I opened it up and looked at it. It was a little dry, so I oiled it."

"But you've never shot it?"

"Nope."

The light had gone through a full cycle, and was green

again. Rick turned off his flashers and started to move again, but he didn't say anything until we'd pulled up at my car, all alone in the lot next to the dog park.

"I want you to go home, drop the dog off, and get the gun," he said. "Bring it to The Chocolate Ear with you. I'll take it from there."

"It's my dad's gun," I said.

"You made a decision a few years ago, Steve. You knew it was illegal to break into computer databases, and you did it anyway. The moment you did that, you left the ordinary world, the place where you had a whole lot of rights and privileges. Listen to me carefully. You are a felon. You are an ex-con. You don't get to keep a gun, even if it belonged to your dad. Even if it was some kind of heirloom that's been in your family since your great-great-grandfather shot some Cossack with it."

I remembered Mary, in a hospital bed after her second miscarriage. The way she had cried, and I had tried to comfort her, knowing that as soon as she was able to she'd be charging her credit cards to the limit again, moving us to the edge of bankruptcy. I couldn't make her feel better, but I could protect her from the consequences of her actions.

That's when I took that step, when I left the ordinary world. I went home that night and hacked into all three of the major credit bureaus, putting a flag on Mary's account that indicated possible fraud, shutting off her access to credit.

Would I do it again? Damn, I didn't know. Could there have been a different solution? We'd tried counseling after the first miscarriage, and it hadn't helped. The only thing that had made her feel better at all was becoming pregnant again a few months later.

How many times could we have kept on trying?

"I understand," I said.

"Look, I'll talk to Rinaldi for you. And when this is over, I'll get him to turn the gun over to me, and I'll hold it until you get your rights back."

"I appreciate it," I said. I took a deep breath. Should I tell him about Caroline's laptop, and the hacking software I had installed on it? Or had I exhausted all his patience by then?

Rochester made the decision for me, jumping up and sticking his head between us. "Guess the pup wants you to get moving," Rick said. "See you at the Chocolate Ear."

The time for confessions was over. I got the dog and set out for home.

I dropped Rochester off, got the gun from the night stand, and pulled up at The Chocolate Ear about thirty minutes later. The glass display cases were nearly empty, most of the delicious smells gone. Rick and Gail were the only ones in the place. She was busy at the espresso machine, and he sat in the front window of the café, at a white metal table for two. I laid the leather case containing my father's 9 millimeter Glock on the table in front of him, then sat down. "It's unloaded."

He opened the case and ejected the cartridge, just to be sure, holding the pistol aimed down at the floor as he did so.

"I'm going to work this with Tony," Rick said, leaning forward in his straight-backed white wrought-iron chair. The room, which had always seemed homey when it was filled with customers, now was creepy and desolate. The lighting was too bright, and the French pop music that Gail always played in the background had been shut off. "Because there's such a clear connection to Caroline's homicide. Now, I don't want you to do ANYTHING on your own, but I do need your brain power working with me."

I nodded. "There's someone else involved," I said. "Someone we haven't considered yet."

"Exactly."

"Someone who killed Melissa and Menno." I shivered, and hoped Gail would hurry up with the hot coffee. "You know, once we figured out that the people behind Edith's identity theft were college kids, I was surprised. Did you know that much about investments were you were their age?"

He shook his head. "Hell, I didn't know half of what you were talking about when you went over Edith's investments with her. I've got the state pension plan and a couple of grand in an IRA. That's it."

"So now it's clear that someone who knew more about money was pulling the strings," I said.

Gail brought out a cappuccino for Rick and a raspberry mocha for me, both in oversized white china coffee cups. A moment later, she was back with chicken salad sandwiches on croissants for us, and a couple of pumpkin-flavored biscuits for Rochester. There was something running around in my head about money and students. Finally it came to me. "Menno's research paper," I said.

Rick was on a different track, though. "Yeah, we matched a fingerprint from the paper to the shell casing," he said. "Now that we have the actual fingers, we can verify that the prints both belong to him. I have a feeling his prints will match the ones from the burglary at Caroline's house, too."

"Good. But that wasn't what I was thinking. Menno's paper was on offshore banking. Usually if a student picks a topic like that it's because he or she wants to be an accountant or major in economics or something. Menno must have been looking into ways to hide the money they were stealing from Edith."

"Even with that, I still think somebody was directing them both." Rick took a deep drink of his coffee. "You have any suggestions?"

"Menno's dad, for starters," I said. "We already know he's a crook."

"He stole a couple of cows," Rick said. "Hardly qualifies him to know about sophisticated financial stuff." He frowned. "Amish don't even use banks, do they?"

"Doesn't he have any record beyond the cattle theft?" I asked.

Rick shrugged. "Some petty crime. He associates with some known low-lifes."

"Low-lifes who could get Menno a gun and Melissa a fake license?"

"Yeah, I guess so." He pulled out a pad and started making notes. "Tony's going to start nosing around at the college for anyone who knew either of them," he said when he finished writing.

"Good luck. It's the end of the term, remember? Students are gone, faculty on vacation—he won't have much success."

"You know any other students they hung out with?"

I closed my eyes and thought. I knew Menno had fought with Tasheba Lewis, but I didn't remember any students in the class he particularly had bonded with. Hell, I hadn't even known he and Melissa were dating. They had sat on opposite sides of the room and hadn't betrayed any boyfriend-girlfriend behavior.

Then an image jumped into my head. I had seen them once, together, on campus. I squeezed my eyes shut and tried to remember. I had been walking Rochester, I remembered. And Jeremy Eisenberg had been with them.

I blew a big breath out. "I know one kid Rinaldi can talk to." I gave him Jeremy's name. "I'm sure he can get Jeremy's home address from registration."

"How about any other faculty?"

I told him that Melissa had worked in the music department. "I know she was close to Strings Livorno," I said.

Of course then I had to stop and explain the whole 'Strings' business to Rick, who had been at Penn State at the time rather than at Eastern.

"You're saying this professor had Mafia connections?"

"If you want to call it that," I said. "And Menno took a course last semester with one of my colleagues, Jackie Devere. I remember seeing him in her office once or twice. Maybe she knows something."

Rick took a bunch of notes and we ate our sandwiches and drank our coffee. He and I walked outside together as Gail shut down the lights and locked the door.

I realized that I still hadn't told Rick about Caroline's laptop, and wondered if that information would come back to haunt me in the future.

Ballistics

I spent most of Wednesday catching up on emails, following a couple of the leads Santiago Santos had given me, and trying desperately to find some new business. My next paycheck from Eastern would be my last, and without that regular infusion of cash I'd be back to dipping into my savings.

Around noon, an email came in from Dee Gamay, the adjunct at Eastern who didn't speak Spanish. She had accepted a full-time job as a writer for a medical equipment company, and needed someone to take over a couple of freelance jobs for her. I called her immediately and agreed. The biggest client was a local hospital, where she worked for the risk manager, editing and polishing manuals and forms. I didn't have much health care experience, but I knew I could learn fast.

"Thanks, Dee, I appreciate it," I said.

"Don't thank me yet," she said. "He writes like a third grader and gets angry when you try and improve his grammar." Even over the phone her accent came through as heavy as soup, with 'writes' sounding like 'rats.'

"I've taught at Eastern," I said. "I can handle third-graders."

She laughed, and when she hung up I called the risk manager and introduced myself. "I've got an inspection coming up next week and changes to make to three manuals and a ton of forms," he said. "How fast can you get on this?"

"If you buy, I fly," I said. "Send me what you need and I'll get right on it."

A few minutes later, an email arrived from him, with a huge document attached that took forever to download. When I opened it, I discovered that it was full of red markups—every page had multiple comments and changes, often referring to other sections of the document that needed to be moved, clarified or rewritten.

It was a much bigger project than the risk manager had led me to believe, not least because as Dee had said, he wrote like a third-grader. I could barely understand the changes he wanted, and sometimes they were contradictory. It was full of made up words, too, like 'cardio-preliminary' when it was clear he meant 'cardiopulmonary' and 'dignosticate' which could either be diagnose or diagnosis.

I could see it was going to be a major pain, but the money was good and with my papers graded and my Eastern responsibilities complete, I had nothing else to do but work on it and take care of Rochester.

The work was mind-numbingly boring, reviewing policies and procedures for all kinds of medical procedures I knew nothing about. But I focused on correcting the grammar, making notes and coming up with questions. A lot of the forms were for patient consent to procedures, and I figured that if I didn't understand what was being said the patients wouldn't either.

Inside, though, I was delighted. From the way the risk manager talked, he had a constant stream of work, keeping up with new regulations and new equipment, and the money we'd agreed on would be enough to replace most of my Eastern paycheck.

The phone rang around five o'clock, and I snapped out of my concentration. As I reached for it, I realized my back was stiff and my shoulders needed flexing.

"Can you be at Gail's café at six?" Rick asked. "Tony Rinaldi wants to talk to both of us."

"That's certainly better than the interrogation room at the Leighville Station," I said, but Rick had already hung up.

I didn't like the idea of putting aside this new work so soon after I'd gotten it, but I figured I could get back to work after our meeting. I hurried Rochester through his evening walk, tugging him past any number of interesting smells in the interest of getting liquid and solid results. As soon as I scooped the poop, we were on our way back home, and shortly afterward I was out the door.

It was a beautiful spring evening, and we'd switched out of Daylight Savings Time so the sun was positioned just over the horizon, bathing the canal in a warm, golden light. Wildflowers had sprung up everywhere, and I passed half a dozen joggers on Ferry Road.

I got to The Chocolate Ear just at six, and found Tony Rinaldi already there, sipping a cappuccino and talking on his cell phone. He'd shucked the tie I saw sticking out of his sports jacket, but he still looked professional and focused. By the time I had a coffee of my own, he was finished with his call.

"You'll be happy to know that I got the ballistics results," he said. "You're in the clear."

"What does that mean, exactly?" I asked.

Rick wasn't there yet, so we had a couple of minutes to kill, and I guess the guy decided to humor me.

"When a bullet is shot through the barrel of a gun, it gets marks on it," he said. "Initially, all guns of the same model from the same manufacturer will produce similar marks. But the older a gun gets, and the more bullets that travel through its barrel, the more distinctive the marks become."

"OK," I said.

"The gun that was used in these three homicides is a few years old, and it's been shot a number of times, so it has had time to develop a particular 'signature.' In addition, Glocks leave a distinctive image on the cartridge case."

He took a sip of his cappuccino. "Once a bullet strikes a target, the impact deforms it," he continued. "But in contrast to bullets, cartridge cases do not strike a target and thus are not deformed by impact. Therefore, case imaging is much better than bullet imaging at linking two cases."

"Rochester found a shell case at the place where Caroline was shot," I said. "Did you find any cases around Melissa or Menno?"

He nodded. "The male victim was shot elsewhere and his body was brought to the site, but we found two casings from shells fired at the second victim. I sent all three casings to Doylestown for further analysis."

Doylestown is the county seat. I knew from Rick that the Bucks County Sheriff's Office had access to more sophisticated equipment than the individual municipalities.

"The examiner there did a manual microscopic evaluation, and she determined that all three bullets were fired from the same gun," he said. "Over the last decade the Bureau of Alcohol, Tobacco, Firearms and Explosives has built a database of case markings, and the ballistics expert in Doylestown ran our cases through it. They are a close match to cases recovered from a home invasion case in Hamilton Township."

Hamilton was a nice suburb on the north side of Trenton. Rick came in then, nodded at both of us, and walked up to the counter where he ordered his own coffee from Gail, who was clearly trying not to listen too closely to what Tony Rinaldi was telling me. He looked like he'd had a long day; the tail of his white shirt had come out of his khakis, and one pant leg was stuck into his desert boot.

"The examiner warned me that it's all a subjective judgment," Tony continued, "and we can only be sure the same weapon was used if we find the weapon. But it does seem to let you off the hook. The signature on your gun is very different— much cleaner." He paused. "Rick's already told you I can't give the gun back to you, hasn't he?"

I nodded. "I understand."

"What?" Rick asked, coming to sit down between us.

Tony ran quickly through the ballistics results with him, then said, "Did I tell you we found the girl's cell phone in her pocket?"

Rick shook his head. "Anything interesting there?"

"Last call was a text message, from the male victim, asking her to meet him in the woods."

"But he was killed somewhere else," Rick said.

Tony nodded. "At this point we're assuming the killer used the boy's phone to text the girl and draw her out to the woods."

"When I was a student, people used to meet up out there for all kinds of reasons," I said. "Sex, drugs."

"And rock and roll?" Rick asked.

"Maybe. If they did have an accomplice, they might have used the woods as a convenient meeting spot. Melissa lived in Birthday House, practically next door. So she probably wouldn't have questioned a meeting there." I looked at Tony. "I don't suppose she called Strings Livorno at all?"

He shook his head. "The only calls are either to her parents, her roommate, or the male victim."

"Did you find Menno's phone?"

He shook his head. "If the killer used it to text the girl it's probably gone."

"But you have his phone number, right? So you can get his cell phone records? Maybe the killer called or texted him first, to get him to wherever he was killed."

"Already on it, pal. I am an experienced detective."

"Yeah, sorry. Dealing with Rick so much I feel I need to ask all the questions." I looked over at him and smirked. He mouthed "asshole" back at me.

I asked, "So if you're on top of everything, why are we

meeting here?"

A harried young mom came in, trailing a crying kid of about five or six. We sat there, listening to the French reggae coming through the speakers, while she negotiated with the kid over chocolate chip cookies.

As she walked out the door, the kid munching on a cookie that I was sure was going to spoil his dinner, Tony said, "You pointed me toward Jeremy Eisenberg. Apparently the boy thinks highly of you."

"That's nice to hear." But I could have figured that out from my course evaluation forms, I wanted to add. I didn't need to hear it from a homicide detective.

"I had several calls back and forth to New York today," Tony continued. "The boy's father is some big shot Wall Street executive, and his mother's the nervous type. They're very concerned about the effect on Jeremy's psyche of being interviewed by a police officer."

He clearly thought that Jeremy's parents were coddling him, but that's life for most of the students at Eastern. "So I asked them if having one of Jeremy's professors along would make it easier for him, and they agreed." He looked at me. "I've got to stay close to the station because I'm waiting for the coroner's report, and for a few other feelers I put out to come through. I need you and Rick to go up to New York and speak to Jeremy, see if he has anything to add."

I nodded. "Sure. When?"

"Tomorrow?"

Shit. I had all that work to do for my new client, work I had promised I would finish very fast. I looked over at Rick. He shrugged. "OK." And before I could say anything he said, "Don't worry, I'll call Santos and let him know."

I thought about asking if the trip could wait a few days, until after I'd made a good impression on this new client, but I already knew the answer I'd get. I figured I'd have to work late that night to make up for the time I'd be losing the next day.

"We have any idea what this guy might be able to provide?" Rick asked Tony.

"I saw him with Menno and Melissa once, outside of class," I said. "If he was friendly with them, maybe they gave him some hint about what was going on."

There was something rolling around in my head, and while

Rick and Tony traded some additional information I tried to focus on it. "Wall Street," I finally said.

They both looked at me. "If Jeremy's father works on Wall Street, he probably knows some stuff about money," I said. "Making him a good guy for Melissa and Menno to ask for advice."

In Dog We Trust

Jeremy

I nearly pulled an all-nighter working on the hospital's manual, not getting to sleep until nearly four. My alarm went off at six-thirty, and I had Rochester fed and walked by the time Rick picked me up and we drove to the Levittown train station to catch the New York-bound train. It was the first time I'd been that way since returning to Bucks County, and I realized again how lucky I'd been to grow up in Stewart's Crossing, rather than in the terrible uniformity of Levittown. A huge planned community built in the 50s to provide cheap housing for returning vets, it sat on the other side of the railroad tracks.

When I was growing up in Stewart's Crossing, I had lots of friends who lived in the forty-one developments which made up Levittown, from Appletree Hollow to Yellowood. Each street in each development began with the same letter—so you knew, for example, that Quaint, Quail & Quiet were all streets in Quincy Hollow. But there were two B's – Birch Valley and Blue Ridge, 2 G's—Goldenridge and Greenbrook, and three D's – Dogwood Hollow, Deep Dale East and Deep Dale West. If someone lived on Crown, Conifer or Candle, you didn't know if they were in Cobalt Ridge or Crabtree Hollow, which kind of defeated the whole naming plan, as far as I was concerned.

It was a Thursday, and the Levittown station was filled with commuters. If I closed my eyes and wished hard I could pretend Rick and I were just two friends heading into the city for the day, not on our way to interrogate some terrified college kid about the murders of two of his friends.

We bought our tickets, then descended to the track level. I saw one of my neighbors at River Bend and nodded hello. I'm not a nosy guy, but I'd have to say I was observant. I knew that the man in the corner house had a male friend who slept over sometimes, that the people two houses down had a sick child who was in and out of the hospital, that Mona Tsouris, the elderly lady across the street, was visited during the summer for months on end by her sister Dinah.

I recognized by sight or license plate the cars of maids, in-laws and poker buddies. Just from walking regularly, I knew most of my neighbors by face, and many by name. I added the fact that this neighbor was a commuter to the store of what I knew about him—that he drove a pickup truck, but wore a suit to work, that he had two adopted Chinese daughters.

There was always so much you could learn about a person if you were observant. Yet my powers had failed when it came to Melissa and Menno; I'd had them in class for a whole semester and never suspected what they were up to.

The train arrived, and Rick and I shuffled together with the crowd, eventually boarding the train and finding a pair of seats facing forward.

"You know anything about this kid?" Rick asked, as the train sped north.

"Nothing much," I said. "I can tell from the address that his parents have bucks, but we already knew Daddy works on Wall Street. He's reasonably smart, though I'm sure he could work a lot harder—but then, so could most of my students. He wrote about very ordinary stuff—high school graduation, ecstasy."

Rick's eyebrows raised. "Ecstasy?"

"Lots of kids write about it," I said. "Usually they're trying to figure out whether it's good or bad, and their research generally tells them it's bad. I doubt we're going to discover he's a dealer."

"But you think he was friendly with the two kids?"

I shrugged. "It's college, you know? You're friendly with all kinds of people, because they live in your dorm, or they take classes with you, or they just happen to study in the carrel in the library next to yours. Hopefully, one or both of them told him something that will make this trip worthwhile."

I had brought my laptop with me, and I worked on the risk management manual while Rick made notes on a PDA. The train filled up, and by the time we got to Newark there were men standing in the aisles and it was too noisy to concentrate. I looked around and wondered if I would ever be part of that rat race again, commuting into the city from the suburbs, with a wife and kids. It was what we'd both been planning when Mary and I got married, but God obviously had other plans in mind for us.

We took a cab from Penn Station to the East Sixties, just off First Avenue, where the Eisenbergs lived. We introduced ourselves to the doorman, who called upstairs for Mrs. Eisenberg's approval.

In Dog We Trust

When she came to the door, we discovered that she was quite a bit younger than expected, very pretty, with a French accent. When she introduced herself, she added that she was Jeremy's stepmother. "His mother died when Jeremy was twelve," she said. "Breast cancer. I married his father three years ago."

"He generally a good kid?" Rick asked as she led us through a foyer bigger than my downstairs, into a huge living room filled with the kind of fancy French furniture I'm always afraid of breaking.

"He's never been in trouble before." She looked worried.

"He's not in trouble now, ma'am," Rick said. "We just need to ask him some questions about friends of his at Eastern." He looked around as we sat on heavily gilded sofa. "Will Mr. Eisenberg be joining us?"

"He's at work," she said. "Jeremy! Can you come out here, please?"

A moment later Jeremy came shambling out from some distant part of the apartment. His khakis seemed in danger of slipping off his narrow hips, and his T-shirt, which advertised Town and Country Surf Shop, hung loosely on his bony frame. I noticed Rick take in the eyebrow piercing, the dumbbell through the chin, and the multiple balls and hoops stuck through his ears. When Jeremy reached out to shake hands, his t-shirt rode up, and I could see his navel had been pierced as well. Basically, he looked just like he did at Eastern, except that he was barefoot. "Hey, professor," he said.

I introduced Rick.

"Can I offer you anything to drink? Water, iced tea, lemonade?" Mrs. Eisenberg asked.

Rick and I both asked for lemonade, and Mrs. Eisenberg called a white-uniformed maid and ordered for all four of us.

Jeremy flopped down across from us on another gilded couch, and I was worried for a minute that it would collapse under him. Mrs. Eisenberg sat catty-cornered to us in a French Provincial-style armchair. I looked at Rick, and he nodded.

"I have some bad news, Jeremy," I said. "Two of the students from our freshman comp class have been killed, and I'm helping Detective Stemper here figure out what happened."

"Melissa and Menno," he said.

"You heard?"

He nodded. "Tasheba emailed me. She's friends with this girl Rawanda, who was Melissa's roommate."

I looked over at Rick and he frowned at me. I didn't quite know what that meant, but I guessed I was supposed to keep Jeremy focused. "Were you friendly with Melissa and Menno outside of class?" I asked.

He shrugged. "Sort of."

We waited. Finally Jeremy said, "I had kind of a crush on Melissa for a while, until it was pretty clear I wasn't wild enough for her."

"What do you mean, wild enough?" Rick asked.

"You seen her Face Book page?"

Rick looked confused. "It's a social networking website," I said. "Like MySpace, only you have to have a college or university email address to sign up. Supposedly keeps the creeps out." To Jeremy I said, "Can you show us?"

"Sure." He pulled himself up off the sofa and disappeared into the bowels of the apartment. The maid entered as he left, handing around crystal tumblers filled with pale yellow lemonade.

"I'm so glad you were able to come up here," Mrs. Eisenberg said to me, taking a glass from the maid. "I'm sure it's a great comfort to Jeremy."

"Dealing with death is difficult for all of us," I said. "I'm sure it's tough on Jeremy being away from school with all this happening."

"He's been on the phone, talking and texting and instant messaging, nearly non-stop," she said. "I'm sure it's just been devastating for him."

While we waited for Jeremy to return with his laptop, Rick and I sipped our lemonade, and I took a surreptitious look around the apartment, which bore the unmistakable imprint of a high-end decorator. Everything went together too well to have been assembled casually. I wondered if the place had always looked that way, or if it represented the taste of the second Mrs. Eisenberg.

The walls were painted a pale blue, and the accent pillows on the gilded sofas were navy. The paintings on the walls had probably been acquired at high-end auctions, and even the few family photos on the end table were framed in silver.

It had probably been tough for Jeremy, losing his mom so

young, and I would have bet anything that his dad didn't sacrifice too much time at the office to hang out with his son. Did growing up in such fancy surroundings make up for it? Probably not. The rich kids I'd gone to school with at Eastern had taken their backgrounds for granted, assuming that everybody went to St. Bart's for Christmas or skiing in Aspen over spring break.

When he returned with his laptop, Jeremy looked anything but devastated. As a matter of fact, he looked sort of gleeful. Oh well, if a girl turned me down in favor of a guy who ended up getting her killed, I'd probably feel pretty vindicated, too.

He logged on to the website and pulled up Melissa's profile.

She certainly showed a different side of her personality than the one I saw in freshman comp. In most of the pictures she'd posted she was barely clothed, and she had several tattoos on strategic body parts. They weren't the standard butterflies and roses you often see on teenaged girls, either.

She had a devil head, complete with horns, on her right shoulder. A unicorn's head, with spiraling horn, was positioned suggestively on her left thigh, and she had a barbed wire rope tattooed around her right ankle. Her favorite saying was "Born to be wild," and in her personal statement she'd written, "I like the contrast between the face I present to the world and my true self, which I keep hidden and only reveal to those I trust."

I remembered Melissa's habitual uniform of Fair Isle sweaters and plaid kilts. What were the other students hiding under their outward costumes? Did a boy like Jeremy, with his gangsta-style t-shirts and low-waist pants, cover up a soul that longed for the days of prep school and squash tournaments? Did our football players secretly long to be poets? And did the preppies in their button-down shirts yearn to play the drums at smoky jazz clubs? I already knew that Menno's simple, Amish-style exterior had concealed his inner thief.

"Did Menno have a page here, too?" I asked.

Jeremy shook his head. "He thought it was all stupid."

"Did you hang out with him at all?"

He shrugged. "Some. He was working on this independent study project, and he was always asking me for help."

"What kind of project?" I asked. "Not in English?"

"Nope, in economics. I'd told him my dad was a Wall Street big shot and he thought that made me one, too."

"What do you mean?"

"He was always asking me stuff. What's an IRA? How do you cash out a certificate of deposit? Can you set up a Swiss bank account without going to Switzerland? That kind of stuff."

I looked over at Rick. Probably every time Menno found another of Edith's assets, he came to Jeremy to ask what it was and what he needed to do about it. "He ever ask for your help with anything?" I asked casually, hoping to hear about how Menno had set up an offshore account somewhere.

"Nah. It was always just asking me what stuff was. Weird stuff, like balloon mortgages. I wouldn't even know what they were, but my dad insists on talking about work at dinner."

"A balloon mortgage?"

"Yeah. It's where you pay off the whole loan at the end of the term, instead of in monthly payments." I remembered that was exactly the type of loan Edith's husband Walter had given Jim and Nancy Fancy.

Jeremy looked interested, for the first time. "You think that was why he got killed? Some kind of mortgage scam?"

"We're looking at lots of different angles," Rick said.

Suddenly Jeremy was full of information. "I thought it was strange, this goofy Amish kid who suddenly wants to know all about high finance," he said. "Man, I should have suspected something." The more he talked, the more he remembered about Menno's questions. "At one point I asked him why he wasn't asking his professor all this stuff—or at least asking where to look the stuff up."

"And what did he say?" I asked.

"That it was more like a research project for the professor," he said. "You know, come to think of it, that's weird. If it was an econ professor, wouldn't the professor have known all that stuff already?"

"You never know what some professors know," I said.

It seemed like we'd learned all we could from Jeremy, and we were just getting ready to go, when he said, "Hey, I remember something else."

"What's that?" Rick asked.

"We were watching this TV program in the lounge at Birthday House one day, like way back in the fall, I think."

"You and Menno?"

"And Melissa, and a bunch of other kids. You know, it was

late and there wasn't anything else on, and nobody wanted to get up and change the channel anyway."

"What kind of program?" I asked.

"One of those news programs, you know? *60 Minutes* or some shit. They did this whole investigation into identity theft. I just remember it because Melissa was really into it—to her, it was like putting on a disguise, like the way she wore those dorky clothes over her tattoos, like nobody should know who was underneath."

"You ever talk about it with her afterward?" Rick asked.

Jeremy shook his head. "I only just remembered it now, because I've been, like, racking my brain for anything I ever did or said with her or Menno."

Rick and I stood up, and Mrs. Eisenberg followed. She glared at Jeremy, and he stood up, too. "Thank you very much for your time," Rick said, to both Jeremy and his mother. "It's been very helpful to us to get more of a sense of whose these two students were."

"You can email me if you have any more questions," Jeremy said. "Yorker_dude@hotmail.com."

"Great. Thanks," I said.

"Hey, Professor, what are you teaching in the fall? I totally want to sign up for you again."

"Not sure," I said. "Check the registration system toward the end of the summer."

We were in the elevator going down when Rick said, in a fake Valley Girl accent, "I totally want to sign up for you again, Professor. You're the bomb."

"What can I say? I have an impact on impressionable young minds."

Fortunately the elevator opened and I was spared Rick's response.

Suspects

While we waited at Penn Station for our train back to Trenton, Rick called Tony Rinaldi to tell him what we'd learned, and I paced around the waiting room, worrying about all the work I had to do.

It was clear that I'd be pulling another all-nighter, if I had any hope of getting the work finished on time. Forget about early delivery, which I'd been hoping for; I'd thought it would be a good way to impress the new client. Now I just wanted to keep the account.

Pacing wasn't doing me any good, so I picked up a copy of the *Village Voice*. I was scanning the classifieds when one of the ads jumped out at me:

"You: girl in black raincoat, DVD of *Mr. and Mrs. Smith* at Blockbuster on 47th Street. Me: blue polo shirt and jeans. We both agreed Brad Pitt is hot. You probably thought I'm gay, but I'm not. Call me."

A woman across from me was on her cell phone. "I want the wedding without the husband," she said. "I want to wear the dress and have a party all about me."

If only I'd been able to convince Mary to do the same thing, how my life would have been different.

"Our train is still a half hour away," Rick said when he'd finished his call. "You want to grab some fast food?" When we'd gotten our trays and picked a table that was almost clean, he said, "I think we're closing in. But I need to know more about all these players. Do you think you could do some of your online magic?"

I was surprised that Rick would ask me to do something that was so opposed to the conditions of my parole, and the surprise must have been evident on my face.

"Nothing illegal," he said. "And I'll square anything you need with Santos. I just don't have the time, or the computer savvy, to do what you can do."

I knew that if I told Rick I didn't have the time, that I had to focus on my new client, he'd back off. But I'd been pushing to be involved in the case for so long I couldn't back out. I'd just have to fit everything in. "What do you need?"

"Right now we have at least three people who could be

pulling the strings here. We know all three have some connection to the kids—Menno's father, the music professor Melissa's close to, the professor in your department who knows Menno. It could be someone else we know nothing about—but right now we need to focus on these three. Which one of them has the motive here—which one needs money, or has some criminal background?"

"I can put some research together for you."

"Only legal," he repeated. "No hacking. Nothing I can't tell Santos about."

"Strictly legal," I said, though in my mind I was crossing my fingers behind my back. Whoever killed Menno and Melissa hadn't been confined by legality, and though Rick had to be there was no reason I had to be, too. I had Caroline's laptop and the neighbor's network, and as long as I was careful there was no way I was going to get caught again.

Oops. There was that hubris. I'd thought I wouldn't get caught when I hacked into the credit bureau databases to adjust Mary's credit rating. I was a master, of course. There was no way anybody would catch me.

See where that attitude got me? Why didn't I seem able to learn from my mistakes? I spent the train ride working on my client manual, trying not to think about the hacking I had ahead of me, but my fingers itched every time the bad grammar in the manual stopped me and my brain immediately switched tracks.

It was early afternoon when I got home, and I walked Rochester and petted him and told him what a good boy he was. I was tired, and the bumpy train ride to and from New York had made my ribs ache. I got into bed, propped my head behind a couple of pillows, and put Caroline's laptop on a cushioned board in front of me. I turned on my own laptop and left it in sleep mode next to me in case I needed it.

I didn't think Menno had been doing an independent study project for some economics professor, but I wanted to be sure. I logged onto Eastern's website and did a quick search. I remembered that there were rules about independent study projects, and buried deep in the bowels of the site I found that you had to be at least a junior before you'd be allowed to undertake such a project. I switched to my own laptop and shot off a quick email to Rick and Tony, copying the relevant portions of the document.

Back on Caroline's computer, I started looking for information, beginning with "Strings" Livorno, Melissa's favorite music professor. I was able to substantiate my memory of the incident involving his cousin, but the professor himself never came up in any criminal connection. Just lots of scholarly articles on the Baroque era in music. Strings had been pretty busy writing and publishing; did he also have a sideline in procuring guns and fake IDs for students?

I looked up his picture on the Eastern website. He looked as I remembered, though a lot older. A thin face, with a pointy chin, accentuated by a neatly-trimmed goatee. The earring in his left ear was a more recent addition, but he looked more like an elderly academic than a Mafia kingpin—or even accessory.

Strings was close to retirement. He probably knew all about IRAs and 401Ks and retirement accounts. He could have counseled Melissa and Menno on exactly what to do with all the money they pulled out of Edith's various accounts.

I checked the Bucks County property records and found that he owned a small home in Leighville. A little more snooping discovered that he hadn't exactly planned well for his retirement; he'd be getting a college pension that was barely enough to buy canned tuna fish, and he still owed nearly $50,000 on his mortgage. He had a checking account at Quaker State Bank with a few grand in it, and a pair of $10,000 CDs at the same bank.

A professor looking at retirement without the assets to support himself. An Italian guy (and I knew from growing up around Italians how much they valued family) with Mafia connections. If Melissa mentioned her boyfriend's part-time job, and Edith's sloppy record-keeping, could he have been directing the two of them?

I emailed Rick about Strings Livorno from my laptop. Then I moved on to Floyd Zook. After digging through a lot of irrelevant results, I found his name on a blog by Rebecca Stoltzfus, an Amish woman who had been shunned, as Floyd had been. She was developing a network of other Amish who had been shunned.

I did a quick search on Rebecca and discovered that she lived in Lumberville, just inland, and on a whim I called to ask if she knew Floyd Zook personally.

"Why are you asking?"

I explained that I taught his son at Eastern, and after reading Menno's paper, I was interested in the practice of shunning. "Is there anything you can tell me about Floyd and his family?"

"I don't know you," she said. "You're just a voice on the telephone."

"I live in Stewart's Crossing," I said. "I'm not far from you. Could I come over, and we'd talk face to face?"

"I don't want to get Floyd in trouble."

"I'm not a cop or anything."

"But you're an English," she said. "You wouldn't understand." She hung up.

Growing up in Pennsylvania, I knew a little about the Amish, including the fact that they called non-Amish people "the English." But I didn't know enough, and I wanted to know more. I sat there staring at the slide show of pictures on Rebecca's website, and one popped up showing her and a beautiful golden retriever.

I looked over at Rochester. "What do you think, boy? You think maybe you can get this woman to talk to me?"

It was just after four. I could make it up to Lumberville in a half hour or so, and if Rebecca wouldn't talk to me, at least Rochester would get a nice ride.

Rebecca Stoltzfus lived in a single-story farmhouse just outside Lumberville. She had a barn and a couple of acres of what looked like corn and wheat. When I pulled up in her driveway, a female golden retriever came running up to the car, which made Rochester very happy.

"You're the English I spoke to on the phone, aren't you?" She stood in the doorway, watching as Rochester bounded out of the car toward the female, who rolled over on her back so that my dog could sniff her private parts.

Rebecca stepped down into the driveway. She was wearing a cotton print blouse, blue jeans and sneakers, with her graying hair pulled back into a bun. "He's a pretty boy," she said, grudgingly.

"His name is Rochester."

"She's Bethesda." We watched the dogs romp together for a moment, and finally Rebecca said, "I don't know what I can tell you. But you'd might as well sit down, as long as you came all this way."

We sat at a picnic table next to the house as the dogs ran and played in the yard. "I'm not comfortable talking about Amish practices with English," she said. "You people think we're all religious fanatics, dressing funny and driving buggies."

"I'd like to understand more," I said. "But some of your practices, like shunning, seem pretty harsh, very old-fashioned."

"We believe in adult baptism, as you might know," she said, her hands clasped on the table before her. "You voluntarily commit yourself to a life of obedience to God and the church. Belonging is important and shunning is meant to be redemptive. It is not an attempt to harm or ruin the individual and in most cases it does bring that member back into the fellowship again."

"Though not in Floyd's case," I said. "Menno wrote a paper about the effect of the shunning on him and his brothers and sisters, and I was very moved by it."

"Though they agree on the big points, each Amish community has its own practices. The group Floyd and his family belonged to is notorious for very strict shunning. Normally, the worst that happens is that Floyd wouldn't be able to eat with his family, for example. But a few generations ago, this sect had some problems, and they tightened up."

She sighed, and looked over toward where the dogs were playing. "Floyd was forbidden from having contact with his family. He couldn't see his kids, give his wife money, or help out with the chores around the farm." She shrugged. "I'm lucky. Though I left my community, I can still see my daughters, and my grandchildren. It's not the same as living among them, but that's a sacrifice I had to make."

I didn't see how anything that tore apart a family could be a good practice, but I wasn't about to start judging. I had my own issues, after all. "What can you tell me about what Floyd did to merit shunning? I understood he stole some cows from one of his neighbors?"

"I don't know," Rebecca said, pursing her lips. "I don't believe in gossip, so I have never investigated exactly what happened to Floyd. I am more concerned with helping those who have been shunned make the transition to the English world." Rochester and Bethesda came running toward us, and he tried to jump up into Rebecca's lap. She pushed him down, but she smiled, and then Bethesda took off toward a field planted with new corn, with Rochester in hot pursuit.

"What I do know is that when Floyd was shunned, his oldest sons were thirteen and fourteen, and he took them with him when he moved to Easton," she said. "The two daughters and the youngest son, who was only six, stayed with their mother. Elizabeth had to sell the farm and move in with her brother's family. Today she and the children work at a farm store her brother owns."

"Can Menno do anything to help?" I asked. "Can he send his mother money?"

Rebecca shook her head. "By choosing to side with his father, he and his brother were shunned, too. They can't visit their mother or their brother and sisters; they can't send money, they can't associate with anyone in the Amish community. Again, I need to remind you that's just his particular group; it's not the case with all the Amish."

What a choice, I thought. If my parents had had problems like Menno's, which side would I have taken? Divorce alone is painful for a kid; to lose the rest of your family, your home, your community—your whole life—must have been incredibly difficult. I could see why Menno had an attitude.

"I'm worried that Menno might have gotten himself involved in violent acts," I said. "What do you think about that possibility?"

Rebecca looked uncomfortable. Had I pushed her too far? Despite Floyd's record, did she sympathize with him to some degree, based on her own shunning?

"The Amish are committed to a lifestyle of peace and non-violence," she said. She stood up. "Now, if you'll excuse me, I have some chores to finish. Bethesda!"

The female golden came running, Rochester right on her heels. I had to grab him by the collar and drag him back to the car. "Thank you for your help," I said, as I manhandled the dog into the front seat.

I didn't know what else I could say. That I hoped she would find comfort in the English world? Instead, I just watched as she and the golden walked away from us, through the new fields.

By the time we got home, it was already past dinner time. I

fed Rochester and gave him a short walk, then returned to bed with the two laptops. I should have been working on the risk manager's manual and forms, but I wanted to finish what I'd started that afternoon, looking into Floyd Zook's background.

I found property records online which indicated Floyd had deeded his ownership of the farm to an attorney in Lancaster for a dollar. The attorney transferred the ownership to Elizabeth the next day, for the same sum. I figured that transaction kept Elizabeth from dealing directly with Floyd.

A year later, Elizabeth had sold the farm, at what seemed like a low price, to Noah and Rachel Yoder. Since Yoder was Elizabeth's maiden name, perhaps she had been bailed out of debt by a relative. Or someone in the community had taken advantage of her misfortune and secured some additional acreage.

All of that was interesting, but all it did was verify what Menno had written in his essay. I wasn't about to try hacking into any government databases to find out about Floyd's criminal history; I took it for granted that Rick had the information correct. But I did find a couple of "police blotter" entries in various newspapers, in which I noted that Floyd had a number of criminal accomplices. I wrote all their names down and emailed them to Rick.

It was clear to me that through his father, Menno had the connections to buy a gun or have a fake license made up for Melissa. But what if he hadn't gone to his father? Where else could he have gone?

I had to face the idea that my friend Jackie might be the puppet master as easily as Floyd or Strings. I didn't want to delve into Jackie's personal life; she was my friend. But she was as much a suspect as Floyd or Strings, so I had to.

It was nearly eleven by then, and Rochester came out from under my bed and put his front paws on the bed. "OK, time for your last walk of the day," I said. I folded up both laptops and tried to get out of bed.

Tried, because it was damned hard. My back ached, and pain shot through my ribs when I bent my torso at all. But I managed to drag my carcass out of the bed, corral Rochester so I could get his leash on, and then take him for a short walk around the neighborhood. The exercise seemed to do me some good, too. But when we got back, I took a couple of pain pills and got back into bed, and the next thing I knew it was Friday morning.

Jackie

The night's sleep did wonders for my pain, and I was feeling like a new man when I walked Rochester around River Bend. Well, maybe not new; marked down, perhaps, but not quite tossed into the trash yet.

After breakfast, I emailed my client the questions I had about the parts of the manual I'd already edited. I figured that would keep him busy for a while, and maybe the stalling tactic could buy me a few extra days.

With that out of the way, I drove up to Eastern, knowing that it was the final day of the spring term and that Candy would be swamped taking in last-minute grades while at the same time preparing for the summer session. The college closed down for a week between terms, so it was the last day to get anything accomplished before the vacation.

When I arrived at the English department at Blair Hall, Candy was on the phone, and there were two students waiting for her at the window. "Can I look something up in the files?" I asked, and she nodded.

The file cabinet which held folders on each faculty member was behind her desk, so that the tall cabinet itself blocked me from her view. I opened the drawer to Jackie Devere's file, which was pretty thin, because she'd just finished her first year. While Candy talked to someone in the registration department about a problem with a course for the summer session, I photocopied everything in the folder.

My heart was racing. If Candy got off the phone and came around from behind her desk to chat with me, she'd see I wasn't copying from my own file, but Jackie's, and she'd want to know why. I didn't know what I'd tell her—that Jackie was a suspect in three murders, including two of my students?

That wasn't a conversation I wanted to have. It wasn't fair to Jackie to put her under a cloud of suspicion without more evidence. And I didn't even know what I could find in her folder, but I wanted to read it and I didn't think I could give it the right level of attention while I was worrying that Candy might finish her conversation at any minute.

Candy was still on hold with registration by the time I finished the copying and returned the folder. I waved my goodbye to her and walked out, carrying a sheaf of papers I'd copied.

In the car on the way back to Leighville, I called Rick. "You want to meet up later and go over that stuff I've been emailing you? I'm working on Jackie Devere when I get home."

"The Drunken Hessian," he said. "Six-thirty."

"You're buying," I said, and hung up.

I didn't look at the photocopies from Jackie's file until I was at home. And even then, I took Rochester out for a walk around the block, then made myself a quick lunch.

There was a return email from my client. He was impressed with the progress I'd made, but he'd answered every one of my questions, so my stalling tactic had failed. I knew I'd have to spend all day Saturday and Sunday pounding his crappy prose into shape.

With that out of the way, I had no choice but to pick up Jackie's folder. Her academic record wasn't quite as stellar as I'd expected. She was a smart, sassy girl, and I assumed there was significant brain power behind her pretty face. In high school, she'd been a star. She had graduated from an academic magnet school, where she had been the lead on the debate team, a champion chess player, and a regular fixture on the dean's list.

But her college-level academic record wasn't stellar. She'd left Rutgers with a C plus average, and I discovered that though she had completed all her course work, again with just over a C average, she had not finished her dissertation.

There was a note from her advisor at UMass, that her topic had been approved, and her outline had been returned to her twice for revision. There was a limit of six years to complete all the work toward a PhD, and he had every expectation that Ms. Devere would complete the dissertation before her time expired. It wasn't clear what would happen if she didn't finish in time; would they make her take extra courses? Boot her out of the program?

That meant there was a time pressure on Jackie. And when you're young, time equals money—if you spend all your time teaching, to earn money, as I knew Jackie did, that left very little time for research or writing. Full-time faculty at Eastern taught four courses a term, and Jackie was teaching the allowable additional two courses, for extra money.

You could get an additional stipend for advising independent study students, and I saw from the department records that Jackie had four of those. She was also the advisor for the African-American Students Club—at yet another stipend.

Where did she get the stamina? She was almost fourteen years younger than I was, and when I was twenty-eight I had a lot more energy. But to manage six courses, all those other requirements, and write a dissertation? If she'd had more money, she could have had more time for her own academic pursuits.

Not to mention the pressure to publish. At Eastern, tenure-track faculty had six years to prove themselves, through a combination of writing and research (well, they were supposed to be good teachers, too, but that was lowest on the list.) During the sixth year, they went up before the tenure committee.

At that time, they had to present the fruits of their labors at Eastern. I knew from other faculty that you had to have at least published one book, preferably from a well-known academic press. You needed a curriculum vitae full of articles published in journals, as well as evidence of serious research that advanced your discipline.

Most faculty depended on publishing their dissertations, and then on expanding and continuing that research. Every year Jackie spent working on her thesis was a year she couldn't spend on writing articles for publication. That had to add pressure to her life.

The same database I'd hacked into to learn about Strings Livorno told me a bit about Jackie. As a first-year faculty member without a PhD, she wasn't making much money. She didn't have an account at Quaker State Bank, and I didn't want to waste time trying to hack into every bank in the region to find her records.

She had a hefty student loan burden. PhDs don't come cheap these days, and the low level of her academic work had meant she didn't earn merit scholarships. She owed over a hundred grand in loans—which was going to take her years to pay off at a college professor's salary.

I'd always assumed she came from a poor family. Why hadn't she gotten more of a free ride?

The more I investigated, the more I was able to move

Jackie from one compartment in my brain to another—from friend and colleague to murder suspect. It was the only way; I had to think of her like Floyd Zook or Strings Livorno.

I'd assumed Jackie had grown up in the get-toe, as she called it, but in her Rutgers record I found her mother's address in Union, a middle-class suburb of Newark. Further research (and the judicious use of private databases) indicated that her mother, Cynthia Hastings, was a registered nurse, and had been married twice, to Freddick Devere, who was born in Newark, and to Otis Roberts, who was from Grand Cayman. Both marriages ended in divorce. Jackie had two brothers, Cyrus Devere and Jamahl Roberts. Jackie was 28, Cyrus 26, and Jamahl 22.

Cynthia still lived in the house on Alice Terrace and worked at a big regional hospital. She had a mortgage of about $20,000 on a house that was worth close to ten times that. Her hospital salary was a matter of public record once I figured what her employment level was. She made a little over $70,000 a year—more than twice what Jackie made. With her kids grown, she was enjoying financial security.

If Cynthia had significant assets, then Jackie would have been excluded from any need-based scholarships. Without academic excellence, all she could count on were a few grants aimed at increasing the presence of minority students in graduate programs. $100,000 was a tough burden, especially on a college salary. Cynthia was in a position to help out, but who knew what other expenses she had?

Jamahl was a DJ and rapper operating as Jam Boy Jay; he was available for private parties at $150 an hour. He had a fancy website, with downloadable MP3 clips of his original music, and video clips of him in action at some smoky club. He specialized in gangsta rap, filled with strong language and a chauvinistic attitude toward women. I wondered if he got into fights with his feminist sister.

Cynthia had been a single mom, and I guessed she had worked long shifts to pay for that house in Union and put food on the table. As the oldest, Jackie had to baby-sit her brothers, help out with cleaning and cooking.

It wasn't what I'd call the get-toe, but it wasn't a bed of roses either.

I couldn't find much on Cyrus Devere. He didn't have a

fancy website like his half-brother. He had not graduated from high school or attended college. Googling him brought up no results.

I don't like being stumped. I searched every local newspaper in north Jersey, looking for references to Cyrus. I found just one—in a police blotter in Weehawken, just across the Hudson from New York City. He had been picked up for possession of a controlled substance.

That gave me an idea. There's a Federal Inmate Locator online; you type in the first and last name and you can find out where the inmate is incarcerated. Time was running short; it was after five by that time, and I had to get Rochester walked and fed in order to meet Rick at the Drunken Hessian.

I typed in Cyrus Devere and waited. After churning through its database search, the site returned one result: Cyrus Devere was in a medium-security federal correctional institution in Fairton, NJ. A quick jump to Yahoo Maps showed Fairton was in south-east Jersey, due west of Atlantic City and just east of Delaware Bay.

It wasn't a part of the state I'd visited; there wasn't much down there, as far as I knew, but cranberry bogs and empty land. Great place for a prison.

I did a quick printout, and then closed Caroline's laptop and put it back in my closet. I was sitting on the floor playing with Rochester, getting him ready for his walk, when my doorbell rang.

Looking out the peephole, I saw Santiago Santos. "Hey," I said, opening the door. "Did I forget a meeting?"

"Last time I was here we talked about getting together in another month," he said. "But I've been talking to Rick Stemper about you, and I didn't want to wait that long to catch up with you. I thought I'd check in and see how things are going."

"Sure. Come on in." I was nervous, but I knew I'd been careful, using Caroline's laptop and not my own. "Let me just get my computer."

When I came back downstairs with the laptop, he was sitting at the kitchen table petting Rochester. "Coffee?" I asked. I looked at the clock. I was due to meet Rick in a few minutes, though I knew he'd understand if I was stuck with Santos.

"I'm good." While he opened the computer and checked the logs, I paced around the kitchen. I knew he'd see all the job boards I'd been surfing, all the local company websites I'd checked out, and all the work I'd been putting into the risk manager's manual. Even if I still didn't have my business plan together, I'd been trying. That ought to buy me some more time.

He looked up. "I see you've been looking for work, and I can see the hours you've put into this new client," he said. "What I don't see is the stuff you've been doing for Rick."

My mouth went dry. "What do you mean?"

"Rick told me he's been asking you to do some computer research for him. I can't say I approve of it, because that's how you got into trouble in California, but I'm only a parole officer. I can't argue with a cop." He pushed the laptop toward me. "So show me what you've been doing."

I knew from the look on his face that I'd been busted. Not only had Rick told him I'd been keeping a gun, he knew that I'd been doing unauthorized surfing. But I couldn't show him Caroline's laptop. That would be a major violation, especially once he confiscated it and had his tech experts find the hacking software I'd installed. I'd have a one-way ticket back to California. I doubted they'd let me take Rochester to prison with me. And if I was in jail, there'd be nothing I could do to help Rick figure out who was behind all the murders.

"I've been doing that research up at Eastern," I said, making up the story as I went. "I knew you wouldn't approve, so I've been using the computers in the library up there. They have this deep-freeze software that resets the computer every time you turn it off so there's no way anyone can trace where you've been. I know it's a violation, but Rick asked me to do it. He told me he'd square it with you."

He shook his head, and his dark eyes glared at me. "I could violate you right now," he said. "I've ot enough ammunition. You just don't seem to get it, do you, Steve? You're not an ordinary citizen any more. You're on parole. You can't just do what you please, even if your friend asks you nice."

I swallowed hard. "What are you going to do?"

He stood up, pushing back the chair. "I don't know. I'm going to kick this one up to my supervisor, see what she says. If it were up to me, I'd end this right now. You've been wasting your time chasing around with your buddy instead of working on your business plan. You had a gun, a clear violation. Now I find out you're using other computers, when I've always made it clear to you that's against the rules." He shook his head again, and walked to the front door.

"I'll be in touch," he said. "In the meantime, I hope you think long and hard about what you've been doing, and what the consequences can be."

Connections

Rick wasn't at The Drunken Hessian when I arrived, and I'd finished my first beer and started my second by the time he showed. I kept replaying Santiago Santos's final words, trying to find a way things could work out. I wasn't having any luck. And when I got my mind off Santos, it strayed to Jackie Devere, and the feeling that I had betrayed her friendship.

"Sorry," Rick said, slipping into the booth across from me. I'd picked one up by the front, far removed from the noise of the bar and the pool tables, so we could talk. "MVA on River Road, with a fatality. Had to wait for the Coroner's Office to arrive before I could get away."

"Anyone we knew?"

Between Rick and me, we knew a hell of a lot of people in Bucks County. Every kid we went to school with, their parents, brothers, sisters, aunts, uncles and cousins; every teacher we had; every store owner we knew; our neighbors and our casual acquaintances. When you added my students and Rick's professional contacts—cops, attorneys, crooks—the net got even wider.

Rick shrugged. "Teenager on a souped-up Kawasaki motorcycle. Born in Haiti, grew up in Trenton. Name of Arsene Philippe."

"Doesn't ring a bell." The waitress came over, and we ordered platters of baby back ribs. Rick ordered a Heineken, but I was good with the beer I had left.

"What have you got for me?" Rick asked.

I wanted to tell him about the surprise visit from Santiago Santos, but I knew Santos would talk to him about it. And there wasn't anything Rick could do at this point. He'd asked me to do the research, after all. He hadn't told me that I had to use my own computer, that Santos would be checking up on me.

There was nothing to do but keep moving forward and hope it would all work out in the end. I'd printed out everything I had emailed to Rick, and I laid the pages on the table, starting with Floyd Zook. "Names to run through your databases," I said, showing him the list of Floyd's criminal acquaintances. "General background on Floyd and the rest of the family."

He scanned through the pages. "OK. Next?"

"Melissa's music professor, Strings Livorno. Ready to retire, looks short of cash." I pushed those papers across to him.

"OK." He stopped when he saw the printouts of Livorno's bank account. "Where'd you get this?"

I looked at him. "You want to know?"

He shook his head. "Nope." He read through the pages more carefully, then got up and walked to the bar.

My pulse started racing. What was he going to do? After my conversation with Santiago Santos, I needed Rick on my side.

He returned a minute later with a pack of matches. He tore the printout of Strings Livorno's bank accounts into small pieces and dropped them into the flat, glass ashtray on the table. He lit a match and dropped it onto the papers, which flared up. Fortunately, the Drunken Hessian is the kind of place that doesn't mind the occasional pyromania from its customers.

"So Livorno must know about retirement accounts," Rick said as we watched the papers burn. "He has motive, too."

I nodded, then took a long drink from my beer. I wasn't sure how far Rick could go for me, but the dying embers in the ashtray demonstrated more than anything he could say that he was in my corner.

That was good, because I was about to burn one of the few friends I'd made since moving back to Stewart's Crossing. Jackie Devere and I had bonded, and I'd been looking forward to continuing our friendship after I stopped teaching at Eastern. Now, I wasn't sure. Suppose she was innocent? How could I go on being her friend after I'd dipped into her confidential background?

Jackie had a financial motive, and contact with Menno Zook. But I couldn't believe that she could be behind the killing of three people.

I took a deep breath. The wheels had been put in motion and I couldn't stop them. "All right, last one. I have to tell you, she's my friend. Jackie Devere."

I explained how we'd hung out together. "She's a good person. I feel bad sneaking around collecting this stuff on her."

"If she's innocent, no harm, no foul," Rick said. "If she's guilty, she needs to be caught."

"Yeah. Right." I pushed the pages I had over to him—the

copies from her file at Eastern, the printouts from various websites—in her case, all legal. "You need to look up her brother, Cyrus. He's in a federal prison in South Jersey."

"You sense a family resemblance?"

"I don't know. Maybe Jackie hasn't spoken to him in years." I took another drink. "I had a surprise visit from Santos this evening, just before I left the house."

Rick raised his eyebrows. "You show him those printouts you showed me?"

I shook my head. "But he wanted to see the audit trail for the research."

"Yeah. Isn't that part of your deal?"

"I haven't been doing this research on my computer."

The waitress brought our ribs, and Rick put away all the paperwork. When she'd left, he said, "Do you want to go back to prison, Steve?"

"No."

"Then stop doing stupid shit." He picked up a rib and waved it at me. "You're a smart guy. I've known that since chemistry class." I'd hung out in that class with Rick and a girl from Lake Shores, and though I'm no science geek I had carried both of them along with me. "But it's like you don't think the rules apply to you. They do. And the sooner you realize that, the better."

He chomped down on the rib, still staring me down. I blinked first.

"When I was in prison, I tried so hard to believe that it wasn't happening to me. That I wasn't the kind of guy who ends up in a place like that. And I was determined that it wasn't going to change who I was." I sighed. "I have to face the fact that it did change things. That I'm not—you know—entitled any more."

"We were lucky, growing up here," Rick said. "Stable family lives, two-parent households, good schools. It's not until you get out into the world that you realize how rare that stuff is these days."

"Look at Caroline Kelly and her friends," I said. "They had to move around every couple of years. Chris McCutcheon said it affected the way that they related to other people."

Some of the tension in my shoulders eased, as Rick and I went on to talk about other stuff—Gail and The Chocolate Ear,

Rochester's behavior, a girl Rick had met the week before and was going out with again on Saturday night. I guess we were both trying to pretend we were just a pair of friends out for dinner, not a cop and an ex-felon who just couldn't seem to stop getting into trouble.

The next morning I read part of the paper at breakfast and left the rest on the kitchen table to look at over lunch. I had spent so much time helping Edith with her paperwork, and Rick with his internet research, that I'd been neglecting work that made me money. I had to spend some serious time on the risk manager's work, even though it was Saturday. If I wasn't going to have teaching income during the summer, and perhaps not ever again, I had to make sure I kept this guy as a client.

I spent the morning reading, editing, and reorganizing. I was just getting ready to take a break when I heard Rochester making a ruckus downstairs. He wasn't barking, but he was making a lot of noise, what sounded like digging. When I came down the stairs, I saw him on the kitchen tile with a piece of newspaper under his paws. He was scratching at it with his claws, trying to rip the paper apart.

"Hey, stop that!" I said. I hurried down the stairs and grabbed the paper away from him. The page was crumpled and there was a big tear in the center. "Bad dog! We don't tear up the newspaper."

I looked at him. "What's the matter? Didn't like something you read?" As I was putting the paper back together I noticed an article about the traffic accident Rick had investigated the day before, right where Rochester had been scratching.

"A motorcycle crash yesterday on River Road in Stewart's Crossing claimed the life of Arsene Philippe, a 19-year-old Trenton resident who lost control of his Kawasaki on a section of the road that has seen numerous accidents. Crossing mayor Neil Down called upon the state to consider widening the road and expanding the shoulders, though environmental activists have long opposed such a move."

"Yeah, yeah," I said. "Save the birds, kill the people." I wondered if it was the same section of River Road where I'd been hit.

The article continued, "Philippe emigrated to the United States from Haiti as a child and attended Trenton public schools. He had recently been released from the federal correctional facility in Fairton, NJ, where he served eighteen months on federal weapons charges. When asked if Philippe's criminal record might be connected to the fatal accident, Stewart's Crossing police detective Richard Stemper declined to comment."

Something in that article rang a bell. "Did you want me to read that, Rochester?" I asked.

In answer, he lowered his head to the floor and arched his back in a long stretch. "I guess you want to go out, don't you?"

He started jumping up and down when I pulled his leash off the counter, and we went out for a quick walk. When I got back, I fixed myself lunch and finished reading the paper.

It wasn't until I'd climbed the stairs to the office again and gone back to the risk manager's manual that it hit me. "Fairton," I said out loud.

I dialed Rick's cell phone and as soon as he answered I repeated myself. "Fairton. Your victim yesterday was incarcerated there."

"Who is this?"

"It's Steve. Somebody else was in Fairton, too."

"Lots of people," he said. "It's a pretty big facility."

"Yeah, but one in particular. Cyrus Devere."

"Why is that name familiar?"

"Because he's Jackie Devere's brother," I said. "Jackie, my colleague at Eastern. Jackie, who knew Menno Zook." My mind was racing ahead. "Arsene Philippe was in on weapons charges, right?"

"Yup."

"So if Jackie needed a gun and she asked her brother Cyrus for help, he could have referred her to Arsene Philippe."

"Assuming he knew Arsene Philippe."

"There is no such thing as coincidence," I said. "You have some way to figure out if Cyrus and Arsene knew each other?"

"You know it's Saturday, right? Some people have the day off on Saturday."

I felt bad for about half a second. "You're not some people. You're a dedicated investigator. I'll bet you're at the station now, aren't you?" In the background I heard some kind of intercom going, doors opening and closing.

"Hey, who's the detective here? I'll check to see if there's a connection between these two. I'll talk to you later."

He hung up, and I went back to work. Around five, Rochester came after me, wanting to play, and I stood up and stretched. My ribs still ached a little from the accident, but I was a lot luckier than Arsene Philippe.

As Rochester and I were walking back, the lyrics to a Cat Stevens song began drifting through my brain. "Another Saturday night and I ain't got nobody," I sang. Rochester looked up at me, as if to remind me that he wasn't just chopped liver.

"No offense, boy, but you're just a dog," I said, reaching down to pet his head. "And a boy dog, to boot."

Letting us into the house, I wondered if there was a woman out there who would consider taking me on. I wasn't bad-looking, I was smart and I could be charming. I was also an ex-felon on parole, though, with a diminishing bank balance and shaky future prospects.

I'd met a few single women since my return to Stewart's Crossing. Caroline Kelly, Gail Dukowski, Jackie Devere, and Dee Gamay, among them. It wasn't the availability of women, though, that was the problem. It was me.

Mary had me served with divorce papers while I was in prison, a month after my dad died, and I refused to think about how my life was falling apart while I was locked up. I signed the papers, corresponded with the attorney handling my dad's estate, but I never let the idea sink in until I was ready to be released and I realized I had nowhere to go but Stewart's Crossing.

I'd shut down, and forced myself to focus on simple things, like getting a job, making meals, keeping up the house. That was why I hadn't dealt with my father's gun—I knew I wasn't supposed to have it, but it was easier to ignore the issue than figure out what to do.

Caroline's death, and Rochester's adoption, had shaken things up. I knew I had to make some changes. I was hoping that once I had put the investigation behind me, I'd be able to continue to move forward. And maybe one of these days there would be a woman to share those Saturday nights with me and my dog.

Occam's Razor

I didn't leave the house on Sunday except to walk the dog. The more I worked on the risk manager's manual, the more I found I had to do. I didn't even have time to slip out to The Chocolate Ear. Gail would probably forget who I was by the time I made it back there, given how much I had to do. And that it made it even less likely that she'd agree to go out on a date with me.

Rick didn't call back until Monday morning, when I was trying to figure out how to make a consent form for the use of gadolinium read like something other than medical jargon. "I got the info on Arsene Philippe. I'm heading up to Leighville to go over the information with Tony. Can you come along? I want you to tell him how you figured out the connection."

I'd have agreed to walk there on my hands rather than work on that consent form, so I said yes, and Rick picked me up a few minutes later.

"Tony knows about your record," Rick said, as he turned from Ferry Street onto the River Road to head up to Leighville. "But he doesn't know about your run-in with Santos, or the papers I burned at The Drunken Hessian on Friday."

"Thanks."

"It's not about you," he said. "I want this case solved, and your problems are just a distraction. I want to keep Tony focused."

"Gee, I wish I could consider my problems just a distraction."

"A couple of years from now, this will all be a distant memory," Rick said. "When you look back you'll be surprised you ever stressed about it."

"That's assuming that I'm not back in prison by then," I said.

Rick gave me a sharp glance. "You're not doing anything else you shouldn't be, are you?"

"No, Dad." I turned to look out the window.

We were both quiet for a while, as the spring landscape unfolded around us. Blue jays swooped in the pine trees by the roadside, and tiny daisies were popping up in the grassy verge. "I have a buddy in AA," Rick said, when we'd crossed through

New Hope, the Delaware swirling beside us in fast eddies. "He has a sponsor he calls whenever he feels like he's in trouble."

I looked over at him. "I'm not an alcoholic," I said.

"But I know you must get tempted," he said. "I want you to know you can call me, like my buddy calls his sponsor. I'm no computer geek, but I know what it's like to want to do something you shouldn't."

"You? Mister straight arrow?"

"Just because I'm a cop doesn't mean I'm not human. I've done some things I'm not proud of. The point is, I know what temptation's like. You ever feel like you're going down the wrong path, I want you to call me. I promise I won't judge you or anything."

I remembered Rick setting the printout from Strings Livorno's bank account on fire at The Drunken Hessian, and I felt sort of warm and fuzzy inside. "Thanks," I said. "I appreciate it."

He pulled into the parking lot behind the Leighville police station a few minutes later, and we met Tony in an interview room. "You have another lead?" he asked Rick.

Rick nodded. "It started with Steve." To me, he said, " You want to tell Tony what you found?"

"It was really Rochester," I said.

"The dog?" Tony asked.

"Just tell him, Steve. Leave the dog out of it."

I frowned at him. "There was an article in the paper on Saturday about the victim in a motorcycle accident Friday on River Road. The article mentioned that the guy had been in a federal correctional facility in Fairton, New Jersey."

"And?" Tony asked.

Rick jumped in. "I got confirmation this morning from Fairton that my victim, Arsene Philippe, was on the same cell block with a guy named Cyrus Devere. Cyrus is the brother of Jackie Devere."

"Jackie is a professor in the English department at Eastern," I added. "Menno Zook took a developmental writing class with her in the fall, and I know he kept in touch with her."

Tony Rinaldi finished his cappuccino and I could see the wheels whirring around in his head. "You think this MVA is related to our crimes?"

"There's no such thing as coincidence," I said.

"Yeah, there is," Rick said. "But sometimes you just have to look at what's in front of you."

"Occam's Razor," I said.

Tony looked at me, and Rick sighed. "Remember, the guy's a professor."

"If it looks like a duck, walks like a duck and quacks like a duck, it's a duck," I said. "Occam's Razor in a nutshell."

He nodded. "*The Name of the Rose.*"

This time Rick looked baffled. "It was a book," I said. "A medieval murder mystery. The hero solved the case by applying Occam's Razor to his deductions."

"Also a movie," Tony said. "I'm a Sean Connery buff. Have everything available on DVD."

"OK, enough diversion," Rick said. "Back to the problem at hand. It's possible that Jackie Devere either met Arsene Philippe when she visited Cyrus at Fairton, or that she asked Cyrus for a gun and he pointed her toward Arsene."

"All conjecture," Rick said. "But IF she got the gun from Philippe, and then she wanted to cover her tracks, she could have run him off the road."

Tony opened up a note pad and wrote some things down, asking for dates, the spelling of names, and so on. Probably to prove he was just as good a detective, Rick took some notes himself. While they challenged each other on whose note pad was bigger, I got a hollow feeling in my stomach. "So it's likely that the accident that killed him was related to everything else."

"And it's likely that your pal Jackie is at the center of it all," Rick said. "What do you say, Tony? I think we should both head up to Eastern to look for her."

"The school's on break this week," I said. "Spring term finished on Friday, and summer term doesn't start til next Monday."

"You feel up to a drive?" Tony asked Rick. "You go to Fairton, talk to Cyrus, and I'll look around for Jackie Devere. Leighville's my turf, after all. I'll see if it looks like her car was in an accident with a motorcycle last week."

They agreed to their division of duties, and I Rick dropped me off back at home on his way to Fairton. I left the investigating to the professionals and went back to the gadolinium consent form. I was sick of radiology procedures, privacy policies and health care regulations, but I wanted to be able to put dog food on the table for Rochester, even if all I could afford was to share it with him, so I kept working. I was so busy I didn't even go out for the mail until I was walking Rochester after dinner.

There was a lumpy package in the box addressed to him. "Hey, boy, you've got mail," I said, imitating the voice from AOL. Back at the house we opened it up.

"Haven't seen you in a while," the note read. "Hope you like these biscuits."

"Isn't that nice," I said. "Your Aunt Gail sent you some biscuits." I sniffed them. They didn't smell like pumpkin. "She must be trying a new recipe."

I gave him one biscuit and left the rest, in their plastic bag, on the kitchen counter. I went back to the big manual, and I was caught up in work until eleven, when I realized it was late and my back and ribs had started to ache again.

"Rochester," I called. "Hey, boy, want to go for a walk before bed?"

I found him sprawled out in the middle of the kitchen floor. The empty plastic bad that had contained the biscuits was near his head, and he'd thrown up twice. "You ate all those biscuits!" I said. "Bad dog! No wonder you threw up."

His body was twitching, and his nose was warm. "Are you OK, boy? Do you need to go to the vet?"

I didn't know what to do. The only other dog owner I knew well enough to call for advice was Jackie Devere, and I figured she had her own problems, especially if Tony Rinaldi had caught up with her.

I cleaned up the vomit and wiped Rochester's mouth with a wet towel. Then I started pacing around, talking to myself as I argued the pros and cons of taking him to the vet's emergency service. Would they think I was stupid and overprotective if he just had an upset stomach? What could they give a dog for overeating, anyway? Some kind of puppy Pepto?

I picked up the plastic bag, which still had one corner of a biscuit left in it, and was about to throw it away when the aroma of chocolate wafted out of it. Chocolate? I didn't know much about doggie digestion, but I knew they weren't supposed to eat chocolate. How come I hadn't noticed that smell before? Didn't Gail know dogs couldn't eat chocolate? I thought she knew everything there was to know about the stuff.

Then I caught my breath. What if Gail hadn't sent the biscuits at all? There was one other person who made biscuits for Rochester—Jackie Devere. I flashed back to the last time I'd seen Jackie, at Eastern, with Rochester. I'd bragged to her about how he'd helped me find clues to Caroline's murder.

A murder she might have committed, or at least ordered.

It was as if I'd signed the dog's death warrant.

I searched through the trash for the envelope that had brought Rochester the biscuits. There was no return address on it, and the postmark read "Southeastern Pennsylvania," which was not helpful. I left it on the counter, and found Rochester's leash. "Come on, boy, we're going to the vet," I said.

He didn't get up, he just banged his head against the floor a couple of times and wagged his tail.

"Come on, Rochester, get up," I said, tugging on the leash. But though he tried to get up, he couldn't move enough. I ran to the front door, opened it, and dashed out to the Beemer. I didn't have the keys. I ran back inside, found them, then ran back outside. I realized I wasn't wearing shoes. I ran back inside, and Rochester thumped his head on the floor again and wagged his tail. "All right, boy, I'm going to make you all better, I promise," I said. The words caught in my throat and I thought I might cry.

Upstairs, I threw on my shoes, grabbed a jacket, and a blanket to put over Rochester. I hurried back downstairs, dropped what I was carrying, and bent over to pick up the dog.

"Oof," I said. "Dog, you're going on a diet." He must have weighed eighty pounds. Bending from the knees, I lifted and stood, then staggered out the front door to the BMW in the driveway. I nearly dropped him twice, but at last I was able to deposit him in the front seat.

A minute later I was back with the blanket. Then I had to grab my cell phone. At the last minute I grabbed the plastic bag containing the broken corner of the last biscuit, then I locked the house.

Rochester's head rested in my lap, and he couldn't stop panting. I backed down the driveway and sped out of River Bend as fast as I could, taking the twisty curves well over the residential speed limit.

The veterinary hospital was near Newtown, and I had to speed up Ferry Road, away from the Delaware, bypassing downtown. All those years of taking the late bus kicked in; I knew how to get there through the back roads, avoiding traffic lights and places where a bored cop might be hanging out looking for speeders.

"It's all right, boy, Daddy's going to make you better," I said, petting his head as I zoomed one-handed around the narrow country roads. The cold air rushed at my face and stung my eyes into tears.

At least I think that's why I was crying.

The Vet

I made it to the vet's in record time. Leaving Rochester in the car, I ran up to the door and rang the emergency bell. Then I rushed back to Rochester and lifted him once again. I was stumbling up to the door when it opened, and a young woman in light green scrubs looked out.

"Let me help you," she said. She propped the door and hurried toward me. With her help, I carried Rochester inside. "I'm going to need his weight," she said, steering us into the hallway, where there was a big scale built into the floor.

We knelt down and placed him on the scale, then stood up. He looked up at me with his big brown eyes and I knew I would do anything to make him better.

"I think he ate chocolate," I said. "A lot."

"He's a big boy," she said. "Seventy-two pounds. That's good—there's more body weight to help disperse the chocolate. How much do you think he ate?"

"Someone sent him biscuits." I pulled the plastic bag from my pocket. "I think maybe they were made with chocolate."

"That's terrible. Who would do such a thing?"

She knelt down and stroked his head on the scale. "Don't you worry, boy, we're going to make you better."

She stood. "Let's get him into a room, and I'll let the doctor know you're here."

With effort, bending at the knees, we got Rochester up off the scale, carried him into an examining room, and laid him on a Formica-topped table. The tech took my name and his and then hurried off to find the doctor.

Poor Rochester. I hadn't been able to protect him. When I'd been run off the road, if Rick hadn't come by and gotten him, he might have been killed. And now, I'd given him poisoned biscuits, and left the bag where he could eat all of them.

The room was small, dominated by the examining table in the middle. On one wall, a set of cabinets was mounted over a sink. The walls were covered with posters—the anatomy of a cat, the reasons why dogs needed dental care, a huge ad for heartworm treatment. Rochester lay on the table, heaving and twitching, and I petted his head over and over again and murmured to him.

I couldn't help it; I started to cry. For Rochester; I loved him and I felt I had let him down by not taking care of him. But it was more than just that. I was crying for all my losses-- my parents, my marriage, my unborn children—everything I'd cared about and hadn't been able to hold onto.

I remembered the day when Mary had her second miscarriage. We were at the hospital, in one of those curtained units of the emergency room, and she would not let me hold her hand.

The first time Mary discovered she was pregnant, we'd told everyone we knew as soon as the home pregnancy test turned color. We'd shared the news of the miscarriage, too, accepting the awkward sympathy of friends and family.

No one knew about Mary's spending spree but me, and no one seemed to notice that the miscarriage had bothered me, too. I was the dad, after all. I'd been looking forward to the baby, too, and I admit I'd been hoping that the little bundle of joy would repair some of the cracks that were already appearing in our marriage.

The second pregnancy was our secret. Only Mary's OB-GYN and her staff knew. Mary quit her job to reduce her stress level, and she spent most of the day in bed, watching soap operas, eating Ben & Jerry's, and crying.

The doctor said it was the hormones, but I think Mary already knew the baby would not come to term, and she was crying for her loss.

That night, while Mary slept, I went on line and hacked into the three major credit bureaus. It was a matter of a few minutes to find her record and place a flag on it indicating that there was a possible fraud, that the cards in her name should not be honored.

Hacking had become such second nature to me that I didn't give a second thought to my actions. For the next week, I focused on taking care of Mary, shutting out my own pain and loss. It wasn't until two weeks later, when a sheriff appeared at the door of our house with a warrant for my arrest, that I thought again of that hack.

I didn't want Mary to know what I had done. I let her believe that I'd been doing work for a client, a guy in Hong Kong who'd hired me for the occasional bit of computer skullduggery. She was angry at me, of course, but we both believed that it was unlikely that a white-collar crime like mine would result in any serious penalties.

My attorney, though, was less sure. "They're looking for a scapegoat," he told me, after I'd been bailed out, and we'd met to discuss strategy. "You did a dumb thing, Steve. If you'd hacked into an ordinary company, they'd let things slide, because they wouldn't want anyone to know that their systems were vulnerable. But the credit bureaus have their own investigative branches, and they don't want anybody else to think they can get away with what you did."

"What does that mean for me?" I asked. I'd dressed up in a rare suit and tie, trying to make a good impression on this attorney, whose brother had gone to graduate school with Tor.

"It means they want you to go to jail."

My jaw dropped open and I couldn't speak for a minute. "What do you mean?"

He recited the relevant statutes for my crime, and the possible penalties. "But I didn't even steal anything," I protested. "All I did was put a flag on my wife's account."

"Doesn't matter. The crime was the hack, not what you did once you were inside."

Things just got worse from there. Within a few weeks, we'd accepted a plea deal that prevented me from going to trial, where I could have been sentenced to up to ten years for each hack—a total of thirty in all. In that context, a year behind bars sounded pretty good.

Within the first month of my unfortunate incarceration, Mary had served me with divorce papers. By the end of the fourth month, my father had suffered a stroke in his sleep. His body had been discovered by a neighbor two days later, when she noticed he hadn't brought in his daily paper.

Mary had found a new job within a few weeks after the miscarriage. She put the house on the market, accepted an offer, and bought herself a new condo in San Jose. She took everything she wanted from the house, and had the rest boxed up and shipped to my dad's townhouse in Stewart's Crossing.

She took half the money from our joint accounts; the rest was eaten up by the costs of my defense. There was just enough left over to pay a storage yard to hold the Beemer until I was released.

I had just received the final divorce papers before my

release, and I asked Mary if we could meet one last time, when I'd sign everything for her. We met for lunch at a café near her office.

As usual, Mary was on a schedule. She didn't even open the menu, but ordered as soon as she sat down. "Chicken salad, no lettuce, light on the mayo, and can you have the chef slice some grapes into it?" she said. "Diet coke, ice on the side. Thank you."

She handed the waiter the menu and stared at me. "Bacon double cheeseburger, medium rare, cheese fries, and a chocolate shake," I said.

"You're killing yourself with food like that," Mary said.

"And you care because…"

She frowned. "Do you have the papers?"

"Yes, Mary. I thought we could do all that after lunch—you know, over coffee and dessert."

"I'd rather do it now."

I sighed and remembered my father's admonition. Well, this was one bed I'd never lie in again. I handed Mary a manila envelope with the relevant paperwork in it. "For what it's worth, I'm sorry," I said.

Her face softened for a moment, and I remembered the lively girl I'd fallen in love with, ten years before. "I am, too," she said. Then she took the envelope from me and slid it into her purse.

Sitting there on a hard metal chair, next to Rochester on the examining table, I hoped Mary was happy. The miscarriages were a cross between biology and destiny; we shouldn't have brought children into that crappy marriage, and the universe was letting us know that.

I had let myself get swept up in the prop wash of the power boat that was Mary Bronstein Levitan. I had buried myself in my work, letting the ones and zeros of computer code take me away from any possibility that we could make that marriage work.

I kept on crying, for those two miscarried children, and for Rochester, who was the child I'd adopted to replace them, without knowing that's what I was doing.

Somewhere in there the tech came back and took Rochester's vital signs and a sample of his blood. I hardly noticed.

I was almost cried out by the time the doctor came in. "I'm Doctor Lee," she said, reaching out to shake my hand. She was a slim Asian woman in her mid-thirties, in a white doctor's coat with her name stitched over the left breast. She looked tired, but she smiled when she looked at the dog.

I introduced myself. "And this is Rochester."

"Hi, boy," she said, petting his head. "Not feeling too good?"

He thumped his tail against the counter top a couple of times.

She gave him a complete physical, listening to his heart, feeling his stomach, looking at his eyes with a pen light. "What time did he eat the biscuits?"

"I gave him one after we came back from our walk," I said. "And that was just after dark. Say six o'clock?"

"And the rest of them?"

"Hard to say. I was upstairs working when he got up on the counter and dragged the bag down. But it was within a half hour of that."

She rubbed Rochester's head. "He's thrown up a couple of times?"

I nodded.

"That's good. There are two things we do when a dog eats something like chocolate, that's poisonous for him. First, we want him to vomit, to get as much of the chocolate as possible out of his system."

"OK."

"Then we give him activated charcoal diluted in water. The charcoal binds to the poison and keeps it from being absorbed. I'll send Tracy in with a slurry of charcoal, and Rochester will have to drink it all. Then I'd like to keep him overnight, just to monitor his symptoms."

"Whatever you think is best." She left, and the tech came back a few minutes later. Between us, we got all the charcoal into Rochester. By the time we were finished, he was able to sit up, and he jumped down to the floor without any help from either of us.

Tracy produced a short fabric leash from one of the drawers, and hooked it to Rochester's collar. I got down on the floor next to him. "You be a good boy," I said, leaning my head against his fur. "They're going to make you all better, and I'll come back for you tomorrow."

"You can settle up with the receptionist tomorrow when you pick him up," Tracy said, as she opened the door. "And we have your phone number, so we'll call you if anything comes up."

Rochester moved slowly, limping a little, as Tracy led him out of the room.

In Dog We Trust

A Walk in the Park

I didn't sleep much that night, and as soon as the sun was up, I drove to the park at Washington's Crossing. I didn't want to stick around River Bend, because I didn't want to have to tell the other dog owners where Rochester was, but I needed to walk and think.

I started to organize the facts as I paced under the old oaks and maples that had seen Washington's men gather for their Christmas day attack on the Hessians at Trenton. I covered big sections of the park, pausing at the statue of Washington and his men in their Durham boat, and by the time I returned to the parking lot, I thought I knew how everything had played out.

From the car, I called Rick on my cell and arranged to meet him at the station. From the vet's office, I learned that Rochester had passed the night well, and was waiting for me to get him. After a quick shower, I dressed and started on my errands.

First was a raspberry mocha at The Chocolate Ear, and a shoulder to cry on. For once, I had no papers to grade, and no prospect of any in the immediate future. I still treated the coffee drink as a reward.

Edith Passis was there, in conversation with Irene Meineke. "The bank has identified three accounts in the Cayman Islands where most of my money was transferred," Edith said. "It's a long process, but with those accounts frozen, there's a chance I can get a lot of the money back."

"I'm glad, Edith."

"And I've decided I'm not teaching any more. My arthritis is too bad, and I just don't like that long drive up to Leighville."

The fact that a pair of students had betrayed her trust added to that, I thought, but I didn't say anything.

Gail came out from behind the counter to bring me my raspberry mocha and a little chocolate tart. "How's Rochester?" she asked. "I haven't seen you in here for a while. I've got a biscuit just waiting for him."

I told the three of them what had happened the night before. They were all horrified. Gail reached out for my hand. "I hope you know I'd never send him chocolate biscuits."

"I know." It was nice to hold her hand for that moment, but I couldn't stick around. The Stewart's Crossing police station was nowhere near as elaborate as the one in Leighville. It was a squat, one-story building from the 1970s built in the poorer neighborhood of town, at the corner of Canal Street and Quarry Road, at the edge of downtown. Quarry Road was one of the main east-west streets in town, running from the river's edge, over the canal on a two-lane bridge, across Main Street and up the hill toward Newtown and Lumberville. Cops could get almost anywhere in town within minutes.

Rick was sitting at a scuffed wooden desk in a big bullpen area; there were three other desks around him shared by other detectives, behind the gated front area where the sergeant sat. I handed him the envelope the biscuits had come in and the plastic bag containing the last uneaten piece, and sat down across from him. "What do you want me to do with these?" he asked, holding up the envelope.

"I want you to prosecute Jackie for trying to poison my dog," I said. "I'm going to tell you why. Edith told me that in October, her gutters got clogged with autumn leaves, and she complained to Melissa, the work-study student in the music department. Melissa gave Edith Menno's name, because he always needed money."

"Hold on," Rick said. "You mind if I tape record this?"

"Not at all." He pulled a tiny digital recorder from his desk and led me into an interview room at the back of the station. He turned the machine on, recited his name and mine, and then asked me to start again.

"Menno made himself an indispensable handyman to Edith, who was accustomed to her late husband, Walter, doing everything for her," I said. "Sometime after that, Menno, Melissa and Jeremy Eisenberg watched a TV program on identity theft in the lounge at Birthday House. Menno, who had seen how disorganized Edith was with her financial paperwork, saw her as a prime target."

"How do you think they got a copy of Edith's social security card, and a driver's license in Edith's name with Melissa's picture and signature?"

"Teenagers have been coming up with fake ID for decades. Remember when we were their age, and our licenses were printed on paper? When I was seventeen I cut numbers from my Cinderella license and pasted them over the numbers on my permanent license so that my birthday was moved back three years, and I could buy liquor at the State Store in Leighville."

Rick reached over and shut off the tape recorder. "Don't tell me those things," he said. He rewound the recorder a minute or so, and we started over again.

"Menno moved to Easton with his father after they were shunned by the Amish community in Lancaster, so he probably knew the Quaker State Bank branch on Northampton Street was so busy that no one would have time to check Melissa's fake ID. Maybe he even knew the teenaged manager didn't have enough experience to recognize fraud."

I was pleased that Rick seemed to agree with everything I said, so I went on. "Around that time, Menno started removing checks from Edith's mailbox and giving them to Melissa to endorse and deposit into the fraudulent account at Quaker State Bank. Then they redirected Edith's account paperwork to the post office box in Easton so that she wouldn't notice she wasn't receiving her checks."

"Pretty sharp for a couple of kids," Rick said.

"You're right. The person who was behind it all must have been directing them to some degree. Menno knew Jeremy Eisenberg's father worked on Wall Street, and he began asking Jeremy questions about cashing in Edith's CD, and about opening an account in Switzerland or the Cayman Islands."

"I don't think Jeremy was the one behind them, though," Rick said. "Like, no way he could be that smart, dude."

I laughed. "Maybe that was when they involved Jackie Devere, when there was so much money building up in the fake account that they didn't know what to do with it. Even smart, sneaky teenagers have limited horizons, after all. What did they know about hundreds of thousands of dollars? Jackie's stepfather was from Grand Cayman, which meant she might have known something about the islands."

I took a breath. "Or maybe they didn't involve Jackie until Caroline Kelly called Melissa's cell phone and said she was from Quaker State Bank, and that she was investigating the account under Edith's name at the Easton Branch."

"Tony Rinaldi went to the house Jackie was renting in Leighville yesterday. She's gone. He got the landlord to let him in, and it's clear she's flown the coop. Then he called her mother's house. Her mother says she hasn't seen her for a couple of weeks or talked to her for the last couple of days. I called up to Union and got a detective to go around and talk to the neighbors, and they said she was there over the weekend but she's gone now. She left the dog with her mother."

"I've got an APB out on her vehicle, and I've got a guy seeing her brother at Fairton later today, trying to connect her to Arsene Philippe."

"It must have been Jackie's black SUV I saw speeding away after Caroline was shot. I don't if she pulled the trigger herself, or if she drove Menno there, or just gave him the gun and the keys to the car."

"She's still responsible," Rick said.

"Once Caroline was dead, they probably thought they were clear," I said. "But then I entered the picture. I discovered Caroline's body, saw the speeding SUV, and adopted Rochester. I began helping Edith figure out her finances, at the same time as I was helping Rick look for Caroline's killer. It took me too long to realize that the two investigations were connected; if I'd known sooner, perhaps Melissa and Menno might still be alive."

Rick reached out and squeezed my shoulder. "You can't worry about that stuff," he said.

"The key was Melissa's cell number—which she used when she opened the fraudulent account at Quaker State Bank, and which had showed up on Caroline's phone bill. If Melissa had never called me for advice on her research paper, it would have taken us even longer to make the connection."

"Why do you think Jackie killed Melissa and Menno?" Rick asked.

"They must have gotten scared after Edith and I started the investigation at Quaker State Bank. Even though Edith's money had been moved out of the account, they must have been frightened of discovery. And Jackie knew that if they were arrested, they'd point to her."

"That's if we assume she's the person responsible," Rick said. "Assuming she got them the gun, and shared in the proceeds of the theft."

"If she got arrested, her academic career would be derailed, and she'd go to jail. I'll be seeing Cyrus behind bars was a powerful motive to stay out of prison." I shuddered. "If I'd known what prison was going to be like, I would sure have been more careful about what I did."

"So she killed the two of them, thinking that there were no clues that would link her to them, or to the thefts from Edith."

I nodded. "Just to be sure, she tried to run me off the road when I was walking with Rochester, and she smashed Arsene's motorcycle along the same road, removing the only other person who could link her to the Glock."

The one thing I couldn't understand was why Jackie had sent the chocolate biscuits to Rochester. What had the dog ever done to hurt her? But then that, too, fell into place. "The last time I saw Jackie, I told her all about Rochester's role in digging up clues to solve Caroline's murder. To finish things off, she sent him the biscuits."

"When we catch her, she's going down for murder, fraud, theft—a lot more than just trying to poison a dog."

"My dog."

There must have been something in my eyes, or my tone of voice, but Rick took the materials on his desk and put them into separate evidence bags. "I'll get an analysis of the dog biscuit," he said. "You never know, the way attorneys are these days, and judges, and juries, we need every piece of evidence we can get."

"Thanks. I appreciate it."

I was just about to leave when my cell phone rang, playing the first few bars of the Baha Men singing "Who Let the Dogs Out."

Rick frowned, but when I flipped open the phone I saw from the caller ID that it was Jackie. I held up a hand to Rick and said, "Hey, Jackie, what's up?"

He leaned in close so he could hear her side of the conversation.

"Samson's driving me nuts," she said. "All he wants to do is play, and I've got to get him worn out so I can work on my thesis. Do you feel like bringing Rochester up to the dog park for a play date?"

Rick was nodding his head. "Sure," I said. "My schedule's pretty open today. What works for you?"

We settled on noon and I hung up. "What do you think she wants with me?"

"Maybe she's checking to see if you got the biscuits," he said.

"When Tony called her mother's house, what did he say?"

"He said he was investigating the death of a student she had been close to, and wanted to ask her some questions."

I drummed my fingers on the desktop. "So maybe she doesn't know for sure that you suspect her," I said. "I told her that I was helping you find out who killed Caroline. Maybe she thinks I know something about the investigation."

We arranged to meet up with Tony Rinaldi at the Leighville station at ten, and Rick asked, "Where's the dog now?"

"He's at the vet. I'm on my way to pick him up."

"Bring him with you." When I started to protest, he said, "We don't want to spook her. If you show up without the dog she'll know something's up."

"But she won't have her dog," I said. "Samson's at her mother's."

"This woman sent your dog poisoned biscuits. Do you want her to go to jail?"

"You know I do."

"Then get the dog and bring him with you."

I hesitated. It was one thing to put myself in danger. Assuming Jackie had killed Melissa and Menno, she might have it in for me, too. And I knew she held a grudge against my big, sweet golden retriever. How could I drag him into trouble?

And how could I risk my own life, knowing that he depended on me?

"Rick, I'm not sure," I started.

"I need your help," he said. "We've got to trick this woman into showing her face so we can arrest her. Don't worry, I'll be right there. Just like with Chris and Karina, OK? You don't have anything to worry about."

Easy for him to say. But I knew how important it was to catch Jackie, and make her pay for everything she had done. So I left the police station and went to get my dog.

In Dog We Trust

Secrets Come Out

When the tech brought Rochester out to me in the lobby, he was back to his old self, jumping as soon as he saw me. I got down to my knees and buried my head in his soft, golden fur. "Did you miss me, boy? You all better now?"

His enthusiasm was all the proof I needed.

I rolled the windows down as we drove up to Leighville. Rochester stuck his head out, enjoying the breeze, and I could almost pretend we were just out for a fun drive in the country. Then we got to the police station and I had to face the fact that I was about to put myself, and my dog, in danger.

The same desk sergeant was on duty. "Hi, boy," he said, ruffling Rochester's ears. "How've you been?"

My traitorous dog looked up at him with adoring eyes, and the sergeant agreed to take care of him until we were ready to leave.

Tony had assembled a bunch of cops, in uniform and plain clothes, in the station classroom, and he briefed everyone on the details of the case. He'd mobilized the county task force, including state cops, local departments, and county sheriff's deputies.

With military precision, he laid out who was going to be stationed where, and how he expected the meeting to play out. There would be cops in the woods, a couple of young guys in plain clothes on the lawn of Birthday House, and more in vehicles in the dog park lot.

"Professor Levitan is going to get to the park in advance of his rendezvous time, and be playing with his dog in the enclosed area. As soon as the suspect pulls up and gets out of her SUV, we move in."

The gravity with which the cops approached the situation calmed me down a little, but I was still nervous as I drove from the station to the dog park, and Rochester seemed to sense it and want to make me feel better. He lay his head on my lap so that I could stroke his golden fur with my right hand.

He recognized the dog park as we pulled into the parking lot, and he was scrambling around, positioned to exit as soon as I opened the door, when my cell phone rang. Checking the display, I saw it was Jackie.

"I'm waiting at the house for a plumber," she said. "I can't leave right now. Can you bring Rochester over here? The boys can play in the yard."

I didn't know what she was trying, but I couldn't let her get away. "Sure. Give me your address again." I grabbed the pen and pad I keep in the glove compartment, but Rochester started trying to climb over me. "Rochester, down!" To Jackie I said, "He's excited."

"I'm sure he'll have fun." She gave me her address and I wrote it down.

"Be there in a few," I said.

As soon as I hung up I called Rick and told him what had happened. "So you can just go over there and arrest her, right?" I asked. "My part is done."

"She called you from her cell, right?"

"Yup."

"So she could be anywhere. This could be a trap to flush us out. We need a visual, Steve."

"You want me to go to her house?" I felt my voice squeak.

"Drive slowly. I'll get Tony to get the troops mustered."

He hung up and I looked at Rochester. His tongue hung open and he looked so happy. Jackie had tried to kill him; I owed it to him, as well as to Caroline, and Menno and Melissa, to see that she went to jail.

I cruised through the Eastern campus. Spring was bursting out all over—trees in full bloom, manicured beds bursting with pink, red, white and purple flowers, rolling green lawns. The campus was deserted, just a couple of staff members moving between the buildings. I remembered a summer I'd spent working on campus, how peaceful it had been.

Eastern was such a beautiful place, dedicated to higher pursuits. A murderer didn't belong there. I looked around to see if there were cops following me, but I couldn't see any. I figured they were all getting into position around Jackie's house.

At the top of the hill I turned onto Main Street. When I was four or five blocks from Jackie's I pulled over and stopped the car, then called Rick's cell phone.

"We have a visual on the house," he said. "There's no car in the driveway. I think she's faking us out."

"What do you want me to do?"

"Sit tight. See if she calls you."

As I snapped the phone shut, I heard Jackie's voice. "You sold me out, Steve. That wasn't a smart move."

Rochester turned at the sound of her voice, and scrambled to his paws on my lap so he could look over me. I turned, too, and saw Jackie standing beside me, a gun aimed straight at my head. "Jackie," I said, and my voice squeaked again.

"You had to go messing around," she said. "Things just got out of hand, but I was covering my tracks. Nobody would have ever connected me to the money if you hadn't stuck your nose in."

I looked around, hoping that the police were somewhere in the area. A few hundred yards behind me I saw Jackie's black SUV parked alongside the road.

"I hate to have to do this, but I can't let you give evidence against me." She aimed the pistol and released the safety.

A series of shots rang out, and my body shuddered. I grabbed onto Rochester and started to cry.

Then I realized I was all right.

I opened my eyes, and there were half a dozen cops converging from all sides. Jackie lay on the ground, the gun a few inches from her hand.

My cell phone started to ring and I recognized Rick's number. I answered, but I was too shaken to say hello. "You OK, buddy?" he asked. I looked up and saw him running towards my car, holding his phone to his ear.

"We're OK," I said. "Both of us. We're OK." I hugged Rochester, and he licked my face.

My troubles weren't over, though. The next day, I drove up to Doylestown for my meeting with Santiago Santos and his supervisor, an African-American woman named Jameelia Cain.

Santos met me at the front counter and led me back to Ms. Cain's office, a barren room without a single piece of personal memorabilia, just copies of various rules and regulations posted on the wall in simple metal frames.

"You don't seem to understand how serious your situation is," she began, after we'd been introduced and Santos and I had sat down across from her on hard metal chairs.

"I do," I said. "I've been working hard, trying to set up my business. I don't want to go back to prison."

"Did Mr. Santos go over the rules and regulations of your parole when he began working with you?"

Santos sat there, not saying anything.

"Yes."

"So you knew that as a convicted felon, you were not allowed to possess a firearm?"

"It wasn't mine," I said. "It was my father's. I didn't even find it in the house until a couple of months after I came back to Pennsylvania."

She glared at me. "Do you know what you should have done at that point?"

I noticed that my hands were shaking. "Yes. I should have reported it to Mr. Santos."

"And why didn't you?"

I shrugged. "I didn't think about it."

"I could overlook the weapons violation," she said. "You were not a violent offender, and it's not like you went out and purchased the gun. But your violation of the agreement regarding your computer use is much more serious."

"I understand," I said. "When Detective Stemper asked me to do that computer research for him, I should have used my own computer, so that Mr. Santos could have seen the results."

"In my opinion, Detective Stemper showed a lack of common sense in asking for your help in the first place," she said. "It would be like sending an alcoholic to a bar, or a junkie out to buy nickel bags."

"The police do that all the time," Santos said, and I was surprised that he spoke up. "Without the use of confidential informants they'd crack a lot fewer cases. And Mr. Levitan's assistance did help solve four murders."

She trained an evil eye on him, but he didn't back down. She turned to me instead. "The law gives a parole officer a lot of latitude in dealing with offenders. I'll be honest with you, Mr. Levitan. It would be hard for me to send you back to prison in California for the violations you've committed. However, I have little confidence that you are ready to function in the civilian population without supervision."

I shifted on the hard chair.

"It is my decision that you remain under the supervision of the parole board, and Mr. Santos, for an additional year. I wish

I could make the penalty more severe, but Mr. Santos has argued on your behalf, as has Detective Stemper."

"Thank you," I said. My whole body seemed to shake with a combination of relief and the loss of adrenaline. I could barely stand up, and I was afraid I'd fall over as Santos and I walked back to the outer office.

"I'll see you in a month," he said. "Be prepared to go over your business plan."

"I will be. Thanks. I appreciate that you stood up for me."

"Jameelia's a good woman," he said. "We all want what's best for you, Steve."

"You ever see those birds you were looking for the last time you were at my house?" I asked.

"Oh, yeah. A couple of really rare ones, actually, migrating through. Another day and we'd have missed them."

We talked about birds and the park for a few minutes, and then I headed back to Stewart's Crossing, where my dog waited for me.

Caroline's house was sold, and a young couple moved in. When I saw them a few days later, holding hands, I remembered moving into our house in Silicon Valley with Mary. For the first time, the memory didn't hurt.

Gail introduced Edith to a stockbroker in town who helped her consolidate her accounts so she'd have less to keep track of, and I gave her a spreadsheet she could use each month to check off that she'd received the money she was expecting. She filled out endless forms for various banks and government agencies, and waited for everything to come together so she could get her money back.

In Caroline's memory, I reread *Jane Eyre*, recognizing that like Rochester, I had a secret. His was a crazy wife hiding in the attic, and mine was the fact that I'd been convicted of a felony. His wife had died in the fire, freeing him to pursue a romance with Jane. Had Jackie's capture done the same for me?

I was at The Chocolate Ear one Saturday morning, picking up a couple of croissants, when Gail and I got into conversation about a new movie that was opening, an adaptation of a Bronte novel. It was a chick flick, but my connection to the fictional Rochester, as well as the canine one, made me interested.

"You want to see it together?" I asked. "Maybe tonight?"

"That would be great," she said. She looked at me. "You

want to get some dinner beforehand?"

"I'd like that," I said.

"Great. It's a date."

That it was. My first since the divorce.

We had burgers at The Drunken Hessian before the movie. It wasn't the most romantic location in town, but I thought I'd better start slowly. After we gave the waitress our orders, I asked Gail, "So I understand from Ginny you were a hotshot pastry chef in New York. What brought you back to Stewart's Crossing?"

"My mother got sick," she said. "And my boyfriend wasn't very supportive, and I was getting worn down from the grind in the city. I quit my job and came back here to take care of her, and after she got better I decided to stay."

She sipped her beer. "How about you?"

I took a deep breath. "I didn't have much choice," I said. "My ex-wife divorced me while I was in prison, and my father died and left me the townhouse. She sold our house and shipped all my stuff here. So I followed."

Her eyebrows raised, but she didn't bolt, and I told her the whole story. Our food arrived and we kept talking, and in the darkness of the movie theater she took my hand and squeezed it. All in all, a pretty successful return to the dating pool.

A couple of weeks after the shooting, Rick came over on a Saturday afternoon. We sat out in the courtyard of my townhouse, drinking beer, with Rochester lying in the shade near us. Jackie was still in the hospital, recovering from her wounds. "She isn't saying a word," Rick said. "But there's damage to her front bumper consistent with hitting Arsene Philippe's motorcycle. We're going to build the case by the book on this one, and we're going to get her."

She denied everything, from masterminding the students' thefts to running me off the River Road, but Rick was accumulating evidence against her. When I tried to remind him of all that Rochester had done to help solve the mystery, he was polite but noncommittal. "It's not something I can take to a judge."

It was high summer by then, and a warm breeze blew through the courtyard. A couple of clouds drifted overhead, and the only noise was the low rumble of air conditioning compressors running all over River Bend. In the distance someone's gate slammed shut, and Rochester looked up. "I'm thinking of taking the dog and heading for someplace cool for a while—maybe the shore, maybe the mountains," I said to Rick.

Then I looked over at Rochester. "You like that idea, boy?" I asked. "Ready to retire from your career as a doggie detective and head for the hills?"

Hearing his name, Rochester looked up at me and wagged his tail, though I couldn't tell if he agreed, or if he was just glad I was paying attention to him.

And as for me, I was just glad to have him around.

***

Rochester and Steve continue their adventures in *The Kingdom of Dog*, now available in print and e-book form!

Made in the USA
San Bernardino, CA
11 October 2017